KISS THE SKY

Also by Farai Chideya

The Color of Our Future

Don't Believe the Hype: Fighting Cultural Misinformation
About African-Americans

Trust: Reaching the 100 Million Missing Voters

KISS THE SKY

A NOVEL

Farai Chideya

ATRIA BOOKS

New York London Toronto Sydney

ATRIA BOOKS

A Division of Simon & Schuster, Inc.
1230 Avenue of the Americas
New York, New York 10020

First Atria Books hardcover edition May 2009

ATRIA BOOKS and colophon are trademarks of Simon & Schuster, Inc.

For information bout special discounts for bulk purchases, please contact Simon &
Schuster Special Sales at 1-866-506-1949 or business@simonandschuster.com.

The Simon & Schuster Speakers Bureau can bring authors to your live event.
For more information or to book an event, contact the Simon & Schuster Speakers
Bureau at 1-866-248-3049 or visit our website at www.simonspeakers.com.

Designed by Suet Chong

Manufactured in the United States of America

10 9 8 7 6 5 4 3 2 1

Library of Congress Cataloging-in-Publication Data
Chideya, Farai.
  Kiss the sky : a novel / by Farai Chideya. -- 1st Atria Books
hardcover ed.
      p. cm.
  ISBN: 978-1-4165-8601-2 (ebook)
  1. African American college graduates—Fiction. 2. African American
television personalities—Fiction. 3. Women rock musicians—Fiction.
I. Title.

  PS3603.H5455K57 2009
  813'.6—dc22

                                 2009008158

ISBN-13: 978-1-4165-8594-7
ISBN-10:   1-4165-8594-X

To Sekai—My Favorite Sister

I.

I don't believe in the devil anymore. But if I did, he would look a lot like Ari Malcolm Klein. My ex has eyes the same amber color as his skin, with flecks of red-gold in the iris, as if you could see the flames licking behind them.

Ari walked into our dressing room with just minutes to spare. This was our first gig in three years, for God's sake. Seventies punk rock, CBGB style, flowed into the dressing room from the club outside. He flicked on a red-fringed lamp and leaned against a battered gunmetal school desk serving as the makeup table. I'd been worried about him, but he looked fine . . . not just as in "Everything's fine," but "Damn, ain't he fine." Still had his near-feminine leonine grace, an economy of movement, and a way of looking you in the eyes until you dropped your gaze.

He did that to me right now, and when I lowered my eyes, I saw he was holding a small glassine Baggie casually between his index and middle fingers. He lifted it a bit, winked at me. "You want some?" he said. He was naked to the waist, a slight discoloration on his arm where a tattoo of my name had once been, with the suspenders of his pants hanging down his legs.

I felt like cussing him out. He couldn't be bothered to say *hi* or *hello* or *we're gonna tear this muthafucka up*. Just, *You want some?* I took a deep breath and played it icy. "No," I said, perching on the edge of a couch that looked like it had been slept on. "The only thing I'm on is Effexor." A little depressive's humor. "I don't get high anymore."

"Oh, you don't," he said, tapping a neat free-form line on the back of his hand. Then he held one nostril and—quickquick—it was gone. "Well, it's here," he said, rubbing his sinuses. "If you want it."

"I don't," I said. For one, I didn't even know what it was, not that that used to stop me. But whatever Ari was taking was always trouble, for him and for me. And I didn't need trouble right now. All I needed was to get this shit right. Just have one killer show, help our friend out, and see what manifested from there.

The last time I was onstage was more than a year ago, just a three-song-solo set at a showcase in Crown Heights. Red, my best girl from college, had put me up to it. Tonight was different, though. Davide, who'd become our drummer after Red left the band, was riddled with cancer. And had no health insurance. And had a girlfriend and two kids. So a bunch of us banded together to get him a little money to pay his bills, and maybe even save a bit for his little girls, if we raised enough.

A month ago, I would have said that the chance of me and Ari playing together was about as remote as the pope announcing he'd gotten married. But Red, who was here now fussing with my wardrobe, guilted us until we agreed to join the three-band bill. Red and the other organizers had wangled a deal where they took both the door and the drink profits from the Orchid—a very good deal.

The Orchid was where the music critics went when they wanted to see what was next. And after college, when I was doing real music criticism, not just being the face for some two-bit video show, this used to be my spot. I was one of the loud ones, you know, who would start talking shit about a weak band while they were still onstage, just to see if they could take the heat. Sometimes they crumbled, and sometimes it made them stronger. I felt like I had earned that power, the right to make or break a band before their album had even hit the streets.

Now, it was my turn to take the heat. And the decision to cross those few feet from the rows of couches and tables, from the safety of the darkness to the glare of the spotlight, seemed more foolish by the second.

We got the five-minute shout from the sound guy, a man with a long white ZZ Top beard. Ari bit his hangnails and I wanted to take his calloused fingertips into my mouth and smooth his eyebrows, just the way I used to.

Red had always been as petite as a pixie, with nappy apricot-colored hair and a delicate face. She tucked my hair into a chignon and asked me if my shirt was too tight. She'd made the shirt herself, in the back

of the little boutique she owned on Nostrand Avenue. And somehow
in the week between the fitting and the show I'd gained just enough
weight to make it seem more like a corset than a blouse.

"Baby, I asked if the shirt was too tight."

"No, Red. It's great." I had to breathe shallowly to keep the seams
from ripping, but man, did it look good on me, bloodred raw silk that
hugged my rib cage and blossomed like an overripe rose around the
cleavage.

Someone came behind me and kissed me on the cheek, his chest
brushing my back. I turned around and tilted my head up so I could
properly see his face. He had flawless rich brown skin and his eyes were
tight, almond-shaped, like a Benin mask. He tipped his head to me and
then bent to give Red a hug. "You remember Leo," she said.

Did I ever. After Red had introduced us at a record release party I
had spent two days wrapped in schoolgirl fantasies: me in his arms, his
arms around me, some heavy imaginary petting. No dream sex . . . yet.

We'd met for dinner once since then. Leo told me all about his
management company, his hip-hop clients, how he was trying to bring
some integrity back to the rap game. And he'd told me I should jump
back in the flow, albeit as a solo act.

"You look good, baby," Leo said. He kissed me on both cheeks and
turned toward Ari. I suspected the two of them were too similar under
the skin to like each other. Leo was dark; Ari light. Leo had his hair in
minitwists; Ari's was cropped. Leo was dressed in a crisp black suit. Ari, as
usual, was punk-rocking it out. But underneath the skin, both Leo and Ari
believed they were crusaders in a world of hypocrisy, and that no one could
tell them how to live. That was what attracted me to each of them, and
what made them insufferable solo and just plain dangerous together.

I tried some fast talking about the wardrobe to distract Leo, but he
put his arm around me and turned his body and mine so we faced Ari
as a unit.

"You might want to get dressed," Leo said softly.

"I'm dressed," Ari said.

"Like that?" Leo said.

"Like this." Ari sported shiny black shoes, tuxedo pants, suspenders, and, of course, the bare chest.

"This isn't some high school talent show." Then Leo focused his eyes on the Baggie, lying on the old desk. He picked it up, drew it close. I'd always had eagle eyes. Even from a couple feet away, I could see the powder's yellowish tinge and the fine grain.

"Do the world a favor," Leo said, tossing the bag back on a table. "Keep this shit out of my girl's life."

I'd been focused on avoiding a fight, but I got distracted by the words . . . *my girl*. I liked his possessiveness, presumptuous though it was. I liked the fact that we hadn't even gone on a date and he was claiming me. No one had in a very long time.

"It's okay," I said to Leo. "Ari's just . . . Ari."

"And you are a queen," he said.

The sound guy shouted, "Get the fuck onstage." He was never one for niceties.

Ari picked up his guitar. Slowly.

I turned to Leo. "It really means a lot to me that you came out. And, as far as Ari's . . . stuff . . . is concerned, I'm not tempted."

"You shouldn't be worried about being tempted," Leo said. "You should get serious about making music your career again. That's the reason I'm here, baby, to see what you got. And you," Leo said, turning to Ari, "should really get the fuck dressed."

"Last time I checked, I wasn't your punk-ass bitch," Ari said. His words slurred slightly, so slightly that no one besides me would probably notice. Ari was looking me in the eyes as he said it. And then he turned, parted the velvet curtains, and walked out on the stage.

"Thank fucking *God*," the sound guy said. "*About . . . fucking . . . time.*"

Red fiddled with my shirt again. "Honey, if it's too tight, you can't breathe. You can't breathe, you can't sing. Quick, let's get you out of this."

"Just let it go. I've gotta go," I said, pushing her hands away.

"That's right," Leo said. "She better get onstage."

"Leo, I know you mean well, but you better get out of my kitchen,"

Red said. And he did, if reluctantly. That was Red, a no-shit-taking Creole girl who could make men twice her size hop to.

"I'm not trying to stress you out, baby girl," Red said. "But we should probably get you out of this. I've got a couple more things in my bag that will make you look out of sight."

"It's all good," I told Red. It wasn't, actually. I was short of breath, and my palms were sweating. Part wardrobe malfunction, part panic attack. Damn. If I could have given this all up, I would have, a long time ago. But music was my heartbeat, my oxygen, my bridge to the world. My demon, too. Oh, Jesus. Showtime.

I'd forgotten what it was like to take the first step out of the shadows, to squint past the lights and listen for the first applause. It came quickly, harder and harder, like rain changing to hailstorms. The corners of my eyes began to ache; my nose tickled; and I clenched my eyes to keep the tears from forming.

"It's been . . . ," I said lifting the mic from its cradle. I stopped, looked at Ari—who wasn't looking at me—and took a deep breath. "It's been a long time, been a long time, been a long lonely lonely lonely lonely time." I managed a laugh and heard echoes in the crowd. "Thanks for coming. Thanks. And, Davide," I said, one of those stupid tears running down my cheek. "Thanks for bringing us together again."

Davide nodded and gave a cheery wave. He'd dyed his hair a shocking platinum and donned a natty retro suit, like the guys from the Style Council. He stood at the back, by the bar, sipping a cocktail through a straw. His lower face was shattered, his mouth wizened. He'd managed to chain-smoke even when he was drumming. His doctor found the tumor a year ago. Since then a stream of surgeons had taken out one side of his jaw and half of his tongue.

I tried to take a deep breath, got halfway there before the fabric of my shirt cut into me. I took a couple of quick shallow hits of the stale club air. "You ready?" I asked Ari, off mic. He nodded yes. And then, just to prove he hadn't forgotten, he twisted two fingers together—*for luck*—and put them over his heart—*for love.*

"This one," I said into the microphone, "is about the day I stopped believing in God."

Ari was already playing. Softly. Flamenco-style whispers and thumps. And I knew if I said, "You ready?" again, he would just look at me and keep playing, and I would want to jump the three feet between us and pick up that fucking guitar and smash its beautiful body over his head.

But instead, I started singing. And just as I'd hoped, just the way it was years ago, when I fell forward into the first note, he was right there with me.

> *Grandma told me God lived in each bead on the rosary*
> *That's when I believed in things that I couldn't see*

This one singer told me that when she went onstage, it was like being an animal. She could hear bits of conversations amid the babble of the crowd, every note from her band became distinct. Smells got sharper . . . her eyesight more focused. Those moments, she told me, were the best times of her life.

I was just the opposite. You see, I get invisible, lose myself. First, I fly like a ghost. This doesn't make any sense, but I see myself from the back of the room, peering through the crowd. When I start to pull away from myself, I can even feel my body, my sense of touch going numb. I used to be afraid of going ghost. But over the years I came to crave it, that moment when I leave my own body behind.

I remember the first time I soloed in the church choir, I got stage fright so bad that the music director had to drag me from my seat beside Mama to the microphone. I remember the long walk between the pews, and the ceiling lights shining down on the altar, and the reassuring smiles from the grown-ups in the adult choir. Right then I learned to do what I did now, fly in my mind to a corner of the room. Back then I saw a little girl in a pink knit dress—made by Mama of course—and white tights with matching pink shoes. Tonight, I saw a woman with a microphone, her shirt the color of a candy apple left to rot, her shoulders hunched high as a kickboxer's. I also saw the audience, their faces falling slowly into the softness of reverie. When I left myself, I wasn't the singer but the song, sound waves traveling through the air . . . no, *swimming* through the air, sinuous as mermaids.

Ari and I did a brisk march through our songbook of nineties alternative-rock hits and misses. It was good to see people still laughing at our old jokes. This brother with long locks standing against the bar couldn't stop cracking up when we sang our song "Shadow," a Devo-esque duet with a rap chorus:

> *We're the babies of the movement*
> *And we raised our fists in pride.*
> *Took a last sip of red Kool-Aid*
> *And said, "Mom, can we go outside?"*
> *[Me] Shit, it's hard to be so righteous when all your fucking*
>   *fans are white.*
> *[Ari] Maybe we should say we're "white-chus"?*
> *[Me] Aw naw, baby, that ain't right.*

Now, the funny thing was, most of the white folks in the audience—and make no mistake, the audience was mainly white—didn't even laugh. The number of black folks who'd come to see a Negro alt-rock duet could fit in one subway car with room to spare. We had to make peace with that. Or laugh at ourselves. Or laugh at them. Or all of the above.

Things were going so well with the crowd that I started to relax back into my body. I don't even know how I was managing to sing, my chest was so tight from that shirt and I was pushing out the lyrics, really selling them, but the breath wasn't coming fast enough for me to keep up. We started singing the song that our fans knew best, a piece we'd penned when we were nineteen, wearing combat boots and baggy black dusters with matching lipstick. (Yeah, Ari, too.) I tugged at my shirt, the kind of things I'd never wear back then, so girly and tight. This song still gave me shivers because it was so stupid and childish; dramatic, extravagant and lovely. Yes, it was lovely, too.

> *Confess*
>   *Confess*
>   *Confess*
>   *Confess*

And I remembered when I wrote the lines on a page I'd ripped from *Seventeen* magazine, on the wide white skirt of Whitney Houston's dress, making up-and-down arrows over the words because I couldn't read music but I could hear it in my head.

> *You are hateful*
> > *You are human*
> > > *You are divine*
> > > > *You are alone*

Back in school, Ari would sit there as I sang from my scribbles. Then I'd watch him write it down as real notes on paper with lines for the scale, and make it solid and real.

But now, onstage, his voice, dark and raspy, joined mine.

> *Confess*
> > *Confess*
> > > *Confess*
> > > > *Confess*

And every time he asked me why I didn't learn to read music, I told him it was too hard. I told him my piano teacher hated me and had traumatized me for life. I told him I was too busy studying for my chem midterm.

> *You are hateful*
> > *You are human*
> > > *You are mine*
> > > > *And mine alone*

What I didn't tell him was, why should I learn when he was there to hear me sing, to interpret my words, to make sure the music matched the lyrics? Back then, Ari was the only audience I wanted. I'd always felt that both of us shared an emptiness, a hole in our hearts. And music could fill that. We could fill it together.

I gathered my breath for the final note, the one I made last as long as I could stand. But the lighting in the room was dim and getting worse. The image in front of me began to pixelate, like grainy TV with a bad antenna, and suddenly I was . . .

Back in the dressing room, lying on the ratty couch. I put my hand over my eyes to shade them from the bare bulb's glare.

"Gone. Bam, hit the floor. You were completely out," said Ari. He was lighting a cigarette right under the dressing room's NO SMOKING sign. Someone, probably Red, had taken off my blouse and dressed me in a T-shirt. Through the velvet curtain that cordoned off the dressing room, I could hear people in the club talking, that kind of furious buzz when something has gone really right or wrong. "Way," Ari said, taking a deep drag of his smoke, "to end a show."

"Where's Red and Leo?"

"Red's outside, saying bye to Davide. She's gotta leave in a couple to meet the babysitter."

"And Leo?"

"That's what I want to know," Ari said. "And Leo?"

"And Leo *what*?" I said, sitting up. It felt good to breathe deeply again.

"*Precisely.*" Ari never moved a muscle on his body, except to lift up his cigarette, but his eyes were narrowed for the inquisition.

"Jeez, he's just a guy," I said. "I met him at this party that Red invited me to. He wants to manage me. But I'm not sure I want to do it." At least not, I thought, without you.

"Great," Ari said. "So this Leo guy went to the bar to get you, I don't know what, a stiff drink. Gin gimlet, if I remember right."

"Not so much anymore," I said. When Leo sat me down over dinner and given me this big spiel about managing my career, I'd laughed at first. And then he started wearing me down with that pimp-style rap. How I was more beautiful than I thought. How more people had followed my career than I even knew of. How they were waiting for me to come back and do something meaningful. It was time for me to speak to the younger generation (one, I wryly noticed, I was clearly no longer a part of). "You could be such a vixen," Leo said. "But there's something . . . I can't put my finger on it. Besides the weight."

I was about thirty pounds heavier than I'd been when we first started performing. I'd like to think the weight went to my hips and ass, but Leo clearly hadn't been impressed. Nor was I with his candor. I almost walked away. But that night, Leo'd kept up that tongue massage, a verbal patter that was two parts ego boost and one part lecture. I started to believe him. All the things I'd been meaning to do, but couldn't, suddenly seemed possible.

"You okay?" Ari said, bringing me back to the present.

"Yeah. It was good . . . us . . . again. Ow!" As I twisted in my seat, I could feel bruises rising from where I'd hit the floor. "Are you good?"

Ari nodded. Then he took out the Baggie again and did a little bump.

My stomach tightened. I asked him what he was using and he just shrugged. Later, much later, he told me it was heroin mixed with meth. "If you get the mix just right," he told me, "you feel just like you're straight." He'd always gone for what sped him up or slowed him down; I took the psychedelics. And we used to joke that it was a mixed marriage because of that. When we could joke.

But that night, when I asked about the drugs, Ari just tucked the bag back in his trouser pocket and said, "Wouldn't you like to know?" And of course I would; of course, me who'd try anything once, or twice, or too many times, like trying to sing a duet with the Devil.

I decided to go out and find Davide. The club had cleared out a bit, but there was still a throng of people by the bar, ordering drinks, talking smack, and shaking hands with the man of the evening.

Leo was in the middle of a conversation with the brother with the locks. He handed me a glass of water and started to pull me into the conversation.

"No, no, keep talking. I'll be back. I'm going to see Davide."

Davide held a pen in his hand, a reporter's notebook, and a Sharpie. His girlfriend had long blunt-cut hair dyed a metallic red. She held him around the waist with one arm while their kids tugged on her free hand. She took them off for a walk outside.

Davide always loved holding court. Tonight, every time someone asked him a question, he'd write down a short answer and hold it up for them to see. But I didn't ask a question before he started scribbling.

I thought I was s'posed to be the sick one here.

"I always was an attention hog," I said. And he always was a fashion plate, partial to jackets with gently padded shoulders and pencil-thin ties. I hugged him, and he was skeletal. The construction of his suit hid that well.

You and Ari?

"Always in limbo."

In the past he would have given me a sardonic smile. This time one corner of his mouth tightened. His lower face was grotesque. I tried my best only to look at the top half, which I'm sure he noticed, but was too polite to say anything about.

And then he wrote about what I'd been thinking all night: what is it like to die?

It feels strange.

He kept writing.

Powerful. Like an orgasm. La petite mort. *Except the real thing. Good-bye and hello at once.*

My other college girlfriend, Mimi, came up with her useless mooch of a husband, Nestor. Mimi had a pale oval face framed with dark curls. She'd always looked like an old painting from a museum, and I was frustrated I couldn't remember what era. The four of us were just one big clusterfuck of connections. Nestor and Davide had been in this band called Black. Mimi met Nestor and fell in love at first sight. Mimi and Nestor got married. Nestor got on the wife-with-a-trust-fund gravy train. He quit Black and the band broke up.

Meanwhile, Ari, Red, and I had been performing as a trio—she on drums, Ari on guitar/vocals, and me on main vocals. And then Ari's love of the junk got too strong, and Red wanted to settle down. So she dropped out, Davide dropped in. Until Ari started being too wasted to even make our gigs, and we called it quits.

"You're looking good for a dead man," Nestor said loudly, drunk, and probably on coke, too.

Mimi and I looked appalled. But Davide had a strong love for gallows humor. He just raised his drink in a salute.

Ari walked up and joined our circle. I could tell he was flying. He didn't bother to talk to the rest of us, but whispered in Davide's ear rapid-fire, and Davide would nod and occasionally attempt to give his puckered hole a smile. I suddenly felt sick to my stomach.

"I'm going to take off," I said to D. The words felt incomplete. I hugged him again, putting my head on his chest and squeezing him as tightly as I dared.

He pulled out his pad.

You must again. You must try again.

Leo walked up and shook Davide's hand.

"Nice party, man," Leo said. "Good stuff." He turned to me. "I heard you say you're rolling. Look, I can drop you off on the way home."

"I'll walk you home," Ari said, coming between us, his speed up like a 33-RPM record played on 45.

"What's your problem?" asked Leo.

"You."

"Stop being childish," I said to Ari, keeping my voice low.

Leo heard and said, "Listen to the woman."

Ari started to reply; Mimi interrupted; and Nestor stood there like an idiot. Leo raised his voice higher and pointed over my head at Ari. Ari practically shoved me away to yell back at Leo.

I could have done a lot of things. I chose to walk away.

"I'll see you later," I said to Davide. I didn't know if that was true.

Leo and Ari chased me to the door and I gave them both a look of absolute disgust. It must have worked because they stopped at some invisible line, glowering at each other. I walked alone down the stairs onto the street.

Thursdays in the East Village were tighter than Saturday nights in other big cities. Pedestrians and cars did a dangerous break dance through lights red and green. It must have rained while we were in the club, because the black streets had that greasy wet sheen that made the traffic lights reflect gloriously from the ground. The cafés and falafel and pizza joints were packed. So were the sidewalks.

As I walked, I thought about the last time Ari and I had been good together. It was five years ago in Ibiza. He had a couple of DJ gigs, not at the big clubs but at a small café on one of the gay beaches. It was one of the most magnificent playgrounds I've ever been to. I mean really, if I were a gay European male, I would have been in heaven. All that meticulously kept-up flesh . . . I mean, there were men there who actually looked good in Speedos.

Ari had his DJ gear set up under a thatched roof, no walls blocking his view of the beach. He'd play what the boys wanted, trance and Latin house and those European dance tracks where the singers sounded like they were on helium. And I loved my gay boys, don't get me wrong. Back home in New York, I was an honorary drag queen. I'd hang out at The Building or La Palace de Beaute, dressed in the same sixties vintage as Deee-Lite's Lady Miss Kier. Mimi and I would sip strong, fruity cocktails, and dance around with girls who are boys, who like boys to be girls.

But here, I wasn't a member of the club. It was all about Ari. He had on creased pants and striped suspenders but no shoes or shirt. I hated the way the men looked at him, because Ari, always the equal-opportunity gawker, looked back. And because Ari looked back, they spoke to him, coming up in ones or twos, leaning in to whisper. Then he'd smile and point at me.

I was lying bare-breasted on the sand next to Mimi. She had the body of a Brazilian samba dancer and wore nothing but a thong. I had on something like the bottom half of a fifties bathing suit, with a flounce of skirt to cover my jiggly bits. I love nothing more than sunbathing on a nude beach where I am as invisible as a grain of sand, but this was different. I felt like I probably irritated the guys. First of all, I wasn't beach-babe eye candy, like Mimi; and I was definitely blocking the DJ hookup. The boys'd look at me and shake their heads as if to say, *Now I've seen everything.* Some thought Ari was joking when he said we were married and tried to get his attention again.

I was about to tell Mimi this was a wrap and we should head back into the hotel, where her husband, Nestor, was resting up from a long night of E-fueled partying. And then Ari took the mic.

"This is for Sophie Maria Clare Lee, named for the goddess of wisdom and the patron saint of television. A beautiful woman. My wife."

And I remember looking at him, and him smiling at me, and the sun shining as if all the saints and the pagan gods whose statues lined the bottom of the oceans had willed it, and all was right with the world.

Sometimes the past and the present slid before me at once, and it was all I could do to strain back into one world. I willed myself back to the moment as I walked down St. Mark's, from Cooper Square to Second Avenue, then made a left. In just that stretch, I saw the grimy teen punks begging for beer money in front of shuttered boutiques; the stretch of cheap restaurants on St. Marks; and then the tonier restaurants along Second Avenue. And then I was home: 156 Second Avenue, above the decades-old Second Avenue Deli. Every single place I'd ever lived in New York was above a restaurant . . . some kind of cosmic joke. I made it a rule to *never* eat at the restaurants you lived above. After seeing (and smelling) the garbage go out in the morning, there were some things you just didn't need to experience.

I used my silver key to open the two sets of doors leading into the building. It smelled overwhelmingly of lemon antiseptic, which meant the grumpy old couple who took care of the place had just done their weekly wash of the cracked floor tile. I used the tiny little key to check my mailbox. Found bills, bills, bills, and one invite to an art opening. Then I walked up the wide stairs to the second floor and used my gold key to go inside my rent-stabilized two-bedroom.

I'd lived here long enough that I didn't have to turn on the lights at night. It was probably decadent for me to have the apartment all to myself. By New York standards, it was supremely well-suited for a share. Two bedrooms, one bath, eat-in kitchen, wood floors, deep closets. Red and I had lived here together for a while when she was between girlfriends.

Went into the front bedroom, the one I had laid out as a study/ guest room, and looked out on the corner of Tenth and Second. Heard the shrieks of partyers and the constant honking of cars. For some reason tonight the cacophony was comforting. I lay down in my clothes on the guest bed and went to sleep.

▷ 5 The Main Ingredient, "Everybody Plays the Fool"

On Monday I was pissed even before my eyes opened. Alarm went off. I hit Snooze, nearly knocking over the picture of me and my girls I kept by my bedside.

The image was already a decade old. Back then we thought we looked grown and sophisticated; today I saw the same photo and thought we all looked like babies. Mimi had gotten married in Mendocino the summer after we'd graduated. Red and I were bridesmaids. The photographer posed us near a hunk of black rock hurled up by an ancient volcanic sneeze. Red had a flame-colored buzz cut back then, so new wave. Mimi, thick ringlets and ruffled black wedding dress, was already pregnant.

I loved the way we were back in college: like sisters, or maybe like a girl gang whose only mission was fun. But they'd gone on to have real lives, real loves, real kids. I was alone, the sounds of the morning commute already filling the space. It was, emphatically, not fun.

One of the worst parts of living alone: no one to make you coffee. I went into the kitchen and poured the beans I kept in the freezer into the small electric grinder. The clack and growl drove me crazy, but I loved the fresh taste. Once I had the coffee brewing I went to get my paper. Leaned out the front door so no one could see I was only wearing a T-shirt—if anyone was there—and grabbed the stack of rags I subscribed to.

The *Wall Street Journal*—fabulous news and features, crazy editorial pages.

The *New York Times*, because it demanded its due.

And finally, my favorite, the *New York Post*. It read like a cereal box, but boy, did it have great gossip.

Turned to the music page. There was this old queen who wrote under the name The Caped Invader. I hadn't seen him at the show. Maybe he'd dressed up in one of his wigs or moustaches, à la Ruth Reichl for her restaurant reviews, because he'd devoted his entire column to us.

An illustration showed a man's hand tugging his ear—the old "sounds like" gesture from charades. I read on.

> There's nothing sadder than a velvet rope with nobody standing by it. But that wasn't a problem for Sky—the naughty nineties threesome reunited as a twosome for Tuesday's benefit show at the Orchid. Of course the tickets were gone before they officially went on sale, but that didn't stop fluttery fans and scenesters alike from showing up to crash the 150 person venue.

> Producer/promoter Leo Masters appears to be hot on Sky to hit the comeback trail. That charming man shook the hand of everyone in the audience (even mine, though he had no idea who he was really speaking to—hah!). According to my sources, he kicked off his evening with a rip-roaring war of words with axman Ari. Rumor has it that Masters wants Sky solo. For her sake let's hope she pops back on the scene as Sky the band, not Sky the pudgy, self-indulgent minor television personality.

> But back to the music.

> The good news: they've still got it. The soul-punk–new wave soundclash of the old Sky has given way to a leaner acoustic sound. Their timing was impeccable. Old standards like "Confess" were just delicious, and the two songs I haven't heard before ("Victory" and "Needless") intriguing, if underdeveloped. Even their tedious protest tunes like "Slavery and War" got a pop makeover that took the

edge off. I downright laughed (for the first time out of many listens) at "Shadow." Let's face it: we're all getting old. A little research tells me these former wunderkinds are 31. Maybe they've turned their personal tragedy into comedy. God bless 'em.

One leetle gripe. Sky's voice was, as usual, divine, but derivative. I personally hear a pinch of Alison Moyet, a soupçon of Grace Jones, and series of trills that might have been an homage to our beloved downtown diva Afro-Diety . . . who happened to be my guest (in disguise, natch). Afro-Diety was none too amused by the similarities, but I reminded her that imitation was the sincerest form of flattery.

Sky's Victorian-style faint at the end was oh too goth perfect. (Depending on who you ask, the cause was stage fright; imbibing; or that tight-but-sexy shirt she was wearing.) Eh, it was a great show, and my alter-ego actually managed to get a phone number. (Now, dare I call? As myself? Hmmmm.) Meanwhile, anyone who has Sky's ear should tell her to stop singing under the influence. We want more of her, more of Ari, and less of everyone else whose albums she's ever listened to.

Signed,
Your faithful friend,
The Caped Invader

I couldn't decide if this was damning with faint praise, or praising with the faintest of damnation. After all, who doesn't steal a few riffs from other singers? At least he didn't say we sucked. Thank God.

I flipped to the next page. That's where I saw it. A picture of Leo with his arm tight around Kristal, the hip-hop starlet du jour, leaning in for a kiss.

At times like this most people's minds go blank. Mine does not. I have an overactive ego that chatters to me all day, sometimes as unintelligible as a monkey on a tree, other times as clear as a priest's homily. *Cinderella*, it said, *it's time to find another prince.*

Now, it was at Kristal's album-listening party that Red introduced me to Leo. He'd only spent a moment with me before someone cornered him to talk business. Then Red had been dragged off by someone looking for her to do costume alterations. So I had to walk the gauntlet alone. The triplex loft had as many bars as floors, all of them crowded with journalists angling for a drink. The space smelled like spilled champagne and blunt smoke. Women in spray-on outfits strutted for men who touched them like they already owned that ass.

"Ain't this some shit," I'd said under my breath. And then Leo was there, looking me up and down like I was a candy cane and he was a tot on Christmas morning.

"Yes, ain't it," he'd said. He had the smooth good looks of certain movie stars, men like Blair Underwood and Denzel Washington. I've never trusted men like that. They're too beautiful, too sought after. And just then Kristal came up, trailed by a string of photographers, kissed Leo casually on the lips, and moved on toward the rooftop lap pool. While she posed for photos with her feet dangling in the water, Leo worked to open me like a puzzle box, teasing and cajoling me until we set our first dinner date.

And it was just that, right? Dinner. Or was it a *date?* Leo told me straight up that Kristal was a client. It was just good for her image, and his, if they *looked* like something was going on. Why was I sweating it? I wasn't his girlfriend. I hadn't even kissed him yet.

But I was sweating it, wasn't I? Fuck. I could say he'd been leading me on, but that would mean I was as gullible as a girl of twelve. (Actually, I was.) So from now on with me and Leo, things had to be straight-up business.

Why did that thought depress me so?

I didn't really understand men. Honestly. I blame it on going to an all girls' high school. Wasn't fast enough to get a boy from the neighborhood, sweet enough to get one from the coed school next door, or interested in dating one of the girls from the basketball team. (Not that they were interested in me, either.) So every night I went to bed dreaming about Prince Charming—usually some mash-up of stars, like Emilio Estevez and LL Cool J.

And obviously, I hadn't grown that much emotionally . . . not even through a marriage and a divorce.

My friends tend to be psychic about my mental states, so I wasn't surprised when the phone rang. It was Red.

"Yo."

"You see . . ."

"Page Six, yeah," Red said. She had the same addiction to the morning gossip pages as me. "I know you were sweating him."

"For what? He's not my boyfriend."

"I just feel bad that I hooked y'all up." A broad Southern *y'all*. "It was s'posed to be strictly business, but I get the sense you're catching feelings."

"Maybe," I said.

"Now you're mad. At him, at me, I don't know . . ."

"I'm not mad, I'm angry. People with tertiary syphilis are mad. But," deep sigh, "I don't even have a reason to be angry. You made a business introduction. . . ."

"And you told me he was on you like Super Glue." Red must have turned her head from the receiver for a sec, because I heard her telling her girlfriend Lin to make sure the baby wasn't dressed too warmly. "Scout's honor—did you give it up to him and not even tell me?"

"No!"

"Just asking. Okay, I'll check in later," she said.

I hung up. Shit, as usual, I was going to be late for work.

I was sound-tracking my way to work, floating on a cushion of music from my Discman, creating my own music video out of my commute.

The train was crowded. The train was always crowded. I'd angled to get a seat but was beaten to it by a crafty old lady who weaved between the slow-moving secretaries and investment bankers. The best seats were on the edge of the row, by the door. Then by one of the rails in the middle. Then anyplace you could plant your ass. The best place to stand was by the door, so you could lean. Then by a pole. And finally, nowhere near a pole, just sandwiched between other swaying commuters, like me.

One man had a starburst of pale scar tissue across his windpipe. Someone in the corner had pulled a hood far down across his face to more effectively sleep. Several women did the high-heel wobble as the train cut quick around the curves. Name tattoos adorned short-sleeved arms, some the name tag of the wearer, others marked with birth and death dates. One was fresh. *Worrell. 1972–2000.*

I should do that for all the men who left me. Kevin, 1993–1995. Liam, 1997–1998. And now Leo, true-life player and imaginary boyfriend, 2000–2000. And then I thought: nobody gives a fuck. And nobody gives a fuck about Worrell. Except this one woman with his name on her arm, which is more than I could say anyone cared about me.

After I'd left the band I found a gig as a music critic for this little rag with offices on Fifth Street and Avenue A. It paid as much as McDonald's, but it took my mind off the divorce. They threw great parties, right in the office, the kind where drag queens mixed with the lit crowd and a few adventurous bankers. We were having our usual Christmas debauchery—a sad little tree and substances galore—when this beet-red man walked up and asked me his name. Not my name: *his*. He was that far gone. And I'll never forget that my boss at the magazine leaned over my shoulder and whispered, "That's Fat Red Rich. But you can just call him Richard."

Richard bragged about launching this new cable outfit called The Video Channel. After a couple of cocktails, he put his hand on my leg and started hinting that I should come in for a job interview, after I went out for dinner with him, that is. I was totally blotto those days, floating on a cloud of cocktails from five PM to five AM. Can't remember much about our dates. I'm pretty sure I let him stick his hand up my skirt all the way to Virginia at a bar once, but I know I didn't sleep with him.

He gave me a host job anyway. And moved on to younger women. He was forty, but anyone over twenty-five was out of his range.

And The Video Channel . . . well, in the five years I'd been there, the company had been bought and sold over and over, absorbed like one of those characters on *Star Trek* captured by the Borg. We'd gained millions of viewers, and you could say we'd lost our soul along the way. Okay, that would be an exaggeration. I'm not sure we ever had a soul to begin with, but we did have a lot of naughty, silly, music-fandom fun. (I'm remembering one specific Madonna album-release party, and how

I ended up in a grope in the handicapped bathroom with our intern.) Now that TV-C was big business, the stakes were higher and the vibe was a lot less freewheeling.

Of course I didn't tell anyone at work about the show at the Orchid. But the first thing the receptionist said as I walked through the frosted glass doors into the waiting room full of music video projections was, "Hey! Heard you slammed it at your show!" She waved a copy of the paper at me, like a good-luck charm.

So much for keeping things under wraps.

I went and checked in with our writers. The scripts were running late as usual. Grabbed some coffee. Some evil, evil person had left doughnuts. I took a chocolate one and headed toward my office, where the walls were encrusted with gold records and signed band photos.

"Are you just getting in?" Fat Red Rich had stepped out of some doorway and I turned to face him.

"Yeah, but . . . "

"You're forty minutes late."

"It's cool. I mean, we had the lineup nailed yesterday."

"What if there was breaking news?"

Like what? Another Kurt Cobain? If so, someone would have called my ass.

"Sorry, Rich," I said. Then, "Gotta go!"

Weird. We were always late, all of us. Why was Rich riding me now?

Didn't have time to think about it.

I took a deep breath and popped my head into my office just in time to hear the phone ring. The voice on the other end of the line said, "A low of sixty-four degrees, partly cloudy with gentle evening showers," and hung up.

By the time I said good-bye, Ari was gone.

Walked toward Makeup, waving at a flock of interns gossiping in the open kitchen. Smiled at them. They were shocked at first, since I was known as a sourpuss in the mornings, and then they smiled back.

I was getting too old for this. All of the other hosts were in their twenties, and I was thirty-two, and it wasn't that I looked my age (I didn't, and I probably never would) but I felt it. I got tired of listening to the shit that passed for new albums. I let the discs the labels sent pile up behind my desk and spent the days listening to my favorites from college, like Public Enemy, New Order, and The Cure. And then I went back further. Old Aretha and Marvin; Van Morrison, Miles and the Beatles; Billie Holiday, Cab Calloway, and Eubie Blake. The interns knew more about new music than I did, and they were slavering with anticipation of taking my job. I wanted them to go for it, honest, but not before I had something new, another bird in the hand. I couldn't be as poor and hungry as I'd been the last time the band broke up, I just couldn't. This job had saved me.

The makeup lady finished layering my face with color. Hair took her turn with the curling iron. I was who people saw, a perfect, empty visage. I wore my own black jeans under the froufrou top that Wardrobe had picked out for me, one of those things with extra curls of fabric that hide extra pounds.

I loved the studios. They were glass and chrome like the inside of a TV spaceship, with walls of video monitors and geometric carpet. All totally outdated of course. So 1992.

I high-fived the cameraman, sat behind the anchor desk, and put in my earpiece. Told the director good morning and yes, I could hear him fine. The new crop of interns gathered at the back of the studio. The CEO walked through, smiling as if the last profit/loss statement hadn't been "sub-optimal," and then the director cued me and opened my mic so we could make the magic of TV. And maybe it was the way they'd lit the studio, but I felt a sudden optimism. Maybe I'd be able to leave this place soon and for good. And then I had a burst of nostalgia, as if I'd already left, and I missed the place like a long-lost friend.

"This is Sky Lee," I said, my smile genuine for the first time in months. "And this is *Your Day in Music*."

Here's how you do TV.

Look into the flat black eye of the camera. This is your life. Act like it.

This is your mother, your father, your boyfriend, your girlfriend, anyone you've ever had to lie to.

Don't read the prompter. Blink.

Ask your guests the questions slowly, like you care. Then cut them off in twenty seconds. Move on.

Smile. Unless someone died.

Don't gossip during commercial breaks. The booth can hear you.

Keep reading, keep acting, keep smiling 'til it's over.

After the show, one of our camerapeople pulled me aside. I liked Kay. She was a heavyset, fiftysomething woman who couldn't care less about the videos we played but was damned proud of having a union job. Kay had a big mouth, so I tried to listen more than I talked. She was part of the Cabal, a not-quite-top-secret group of black female employees who met every month at the Pink Teacup. I was an honorary member. I would never commit to the meetings but I usually showed up anyway. A girl gotta know what a girl gotta know.

Kay leaned in, all obvious and whatnot, and whispered, "You better take care of your timing, Sis. They're looking at layoffs." Kay loved using the unspecified ofay, head-office "they." I had no idea who her sources were, but her proclamations were right about 60 percent of the time.

"We're at the Teacup next week. You coming?"

Why not? "See you there," I said.

On my way back to my office, I rounded the corner to find a human traffic jam. In the center was a caricature of a rapper, baggy black pants and shirt hanging down midthigh; platinum fronts (either that or tinfoil); and a piece of diamond-encrusted jewelry the size of a dessert plate hanging from a thick chain around his neck.

The twentysomething employees clustered around him, too cool to ask for autographs but not to bask in the glow. I remember when I used to feel that way about rappers. I'd go backstage after shows just to get a tingle and buzz from standing near them. I remember seeing the Fugees and Busta Rhymes in some basement venue for a Vibe event, and dancing next to Tupac at the Copa at the premiere of *Juice*.

I would never say to the kids in the office that those were the good old days. Too many people got shot. But musically and socially, they were the bomb.

I stood aside and watched the crowd until a woman from our marketing department dragged the musician toward me and launched into a fawning introduction. "Ill Meds, this is Sky Lee. Sky."

"Ill Meds. Unique handle. Nice to meet you," I said, offering my hand. He gave me the hard-thug look for a minute, then smiled, shook my hand, and shook his head, like, *Who this bitch think she is.* At least that's what I thought he was signifying. But then he said something I would never have expected.

"I am a big fan of the *Confess* album, no joke. I even sampled *Shadow* on my song "The White's Shadow.""

"Oh, that's where those little teeny royalty checks been coming from," I said. I wish it didn't come out sounding so harsh. I was flattered, honestly. I cashed the checks but had never bothered to listen to the song. I didn't want to be disappointed.

"Well, I gotta go. But if you ever wanna collaborate on some shit, let's hit it."

The kids hanging around him looked at me with newfound respect, or maybe it was straight-up shock.

"Really?" I said, my voice squeaking like an eager schoolgirl's. "I might be headed back into the studio. I'd be honored to take you up on that one."

"Cool, cool, cool," Ill Meds said. Probably his real name was something like Gary Moses Durant III, and he had grown up in a neighborhood like I had, right on that taut line between middle and working class. His parents were probably appalled that he had gone into hip hop until *his* royalty checks started rolling in. I imagined he had younger sisters and learned to braid their hair, and he even liked doing it until his boys got on his case. He'd definitely been one of those record store–haunting crate diggers who sampled everything from rock to electronica, old 78s, and new hip hop. And maybe this whole ridiculous getup was just that—a ridiculous getup, a comment on where the music had gone instead of a straightforward rehashing of the over-the-top gangsta archetype. Maybe he had a sense of humor. That would be cool.

So I imagined a whole history for MC Ill Meds based on our one brief conversation. Thought: maybe I should start listening to some of those CDs piled up in my office, including the ones Ill Meds cut. God, I wanted to leave work early but I needed to gather some intel on rumors about cutbacks at TV-C. That meant meeting with the Cabal, plus hanging out in the lunchroom instead of eating in my office the way I liked to. But before I went off on my recon mission, I stood and watched the MC as he pressed on through the throng. Was that even what I wanted, to go hop on the publicity go-round again, and sell myself like a product? Well, I guess I did that already on TV, but I'd never felt like this job was me. That meant I'd fall easy if someone hungrier was gunning for my gig. My job sucked, but I wanted the bird in the hand *and* the two in the bush—my nine to five and the chance to hit the stage again. So I had better find out ASAP what the hell was going on or I'd have no bird in the hand, none in the bushes, and no way to even keep a roof over my head.

The train was crowded. A woman with an enormous goiter on her neck cradled a small pigtailed child. Three men sat with their legs so wide they could have had elephantiasis of the balls. But no, like most of the people on the train, they were just rude. A pregnant woman got on. No one offered her a seat.

I was rocking this new electronica joint on the way home. The people flattened out and looked like cartoons to me, like a video game. I was just on the outside looking at the screen.

Got off at the next stop. It had started to rain. I wrapped my jacket over my head so my hair wouldn't 'fro and quickstepped back to the house. Just as I was fumbling for my keys, my cell rang. I checked the number. Mama.

I contemplated not picking up, but that would be counterproductive. She was like a stalker sometimes. I gave my hello and said, "Hold on, I'm just trying to get the door open." By the time I did, I was soaked . . . and she had the nerve to ask me what took me so long.

"Hold on, I'm just getting into the apartment," I shouted into the phone, sighed, and threw my wet jacket on the bench by the door. I probably shouldn't. It could warp the wood. That's the kind of thing my mother would say. After all these years, it didn't matter if she was near or far. She was inside my head.

She was also on the phone calling my name. Guess I'd zoned out.

"Sorry," I said. "How are you?"

I could hear the hesitation in her voice. It scared me for a second. Maybe Nana was sick, or my brother Matthew was acting up again. I know it wasn't about Erika, because Erika was the perfect daughter that Mama had always said she wanted. Maybe Mama should just focus on her and leave me alone.

"I'm fine," Mama said. "I was waiting to hear back from you about the travel plans."

Oh, right. I had made the mistake of telling her that I was getting an award at Harvard reunion next month, and then she had gone and assumed that she could come with me.

"You really don't have to come, Mama."

"I *want* to come."

Now that was the problem. "Okay," I said, "I'll book you a train ticket to come on Friday. The award is on Saturday. What time do you want to leave?"

Then I heard the old-school ring of my home phone.

"Hold on a second, Mama."

I picked up, "Hello?"

"Hey, girl." It was Red.

"I gotta go," I whispered, squeezing the cell receiver against my thigh. "I'm on the line with my mom. She is driving me crazy!"

"You always say that."

"Which means?"

"Which means the problem is your attitude, not hers. You choose your own reaction to stimuli."

"Don't get all metaphysical, new agey, chakra khan on me right now. I don't need it."

"Well, Mimi and I thought you might need a girls' night out."

"Bet. Where and when?"

"The Creamsicle at eight."

"It's on."

I hung up and went back to Mama on the cell.

"Sorry," I said.

"All you do is say 'sorry.'"

I let that one go. "So what time do you want to get back to Baltimore?"

"Well, I'm sure you want to see your friends *alone*," she said, as if that was a crime. "So why don't you put me back on the train after the ceremony."

"Okay," I said.

"And I can book my own ticket if you want," she said.

"No, Mama, it's fine," I said. If I booked the tickets, at least I would know that she really *was* going to leave, so I could have a little fun. "We'll have a good time together," I said, even though I was not sure of any such thing.

An hour later I was folding up my umbrella and pushing open the pearly white doors of the Creamsicle. It was a universe of rounded plastic retro-futuristic furniture, all white and orange, with matching orange walls, white floor, and swirly-striped ceiling.

The DJ was blasting some Lurch *thump bump* dance-tronica, even though nobody was dancing. Happy hour lasted until nine, and the fashion victim crowds were still squeezing in. One woman wore what looked like an oversize lampshade around her waist. A man wore red sneaker-boots that laced up to his mid-calf.

I spotted Red and Mimi in an all-white room off of the main bar area. You could actually make conversation there, if you were aggressive about it.

"Hi!" I yelled.

"Heeeyyyy," they yelled back.

I squeezed through the crowded room and collapsed onto a bench that made up the seating for the corner table. "I am too old for this shit," I said.

Mimi just laughed. I loved to complain about how old I was and then act like I was a twentysomething again.

Mimi was looking great tonight. Her jacket was the red of fresh blood, with a collar rounded like a little girl's shirt. Her hair was up in a sloppy wet bun.

"Let me guess, no umbrella."

A blond mop-top waiter slouched over with a notepad and pen. He looked like Kurt Cobain except, of course, alive.

"What can I get you?"

"The Creamsicle," said Mimi. Their signature drink was a teeth-curdlingly sweet mixture of Cointreau shaken with vanilla vodka.

The waiter flipped a lock of hair out of his face, and leaned close to her. "I'd recommend the Raven on the rocks. It's the color of your hair."

"What's that?"

"Black Russian made with black vodka. I just thought, you know," he bit his lip. "You look like someone who'd want to try something different."

This is the point at which another woman would flash her diamond ring in his face. Except, though Mimi had been married for a decade now, she never wanted a diamond, and her wedding ring was tarnished silver in the shape of a serpent swallowing its tail. I couldn't blame the poor boy for being confused.

Mimi actually blushed, her heart-shaped face filling with color. "I'll stick with the Creamsicle," she said.

The boy looked disappointed. He barely paid attention as I ordered the same thing. Red got a seltzer.

As soon as he was out of earshot, Red did a spot-on imitation. "You look like someone who wants something different."

"Was it that obvious?" said Mimi.

"Hon, are you kidding?" I imitated the way the boy flopped his hair forward as he bent toward her and then blew it out of his eyes.

Mimi laughed, then her jaw tightened. "You know, one of these days I should."

"Should what?" I said.

"Go for some cute young waiter, someone who reminds me of what it's like to just flirt and have a good time, you know. Nestor's just been acting so *stupid*. He came back the other day and he'd put a down payment on a helicopter . . ."

"What!" I said.

". . . so we can cut the commute to my dad's house. Like, what, we're going to put a helipad on the roof of our condo? The board would never approve it," she said, trying to joke. But she couldn't sustain it. "Maybe I need to put him back in."

"In" was in rehab, a resort-style clinic in the Wasatch mountains that Nestor went to every six months or so. Funny thing was that every time he went in, he came out with some new phone number in his little black book. Who knew that getting clean could be such a pickup scene? And Mimi not only put up with it, but she paid for that shit as well. Crazy.

"Mimi, you need to think about what you want from this relationship," Red said.

"I know what I want. He just doesn't give it to me!"

"If he doesn't give it to you, that means you are *hoping* he will act a certain way. And you need to deal with the *reality* of how he acts and see what you want from the real relationship."

Just then, our waiter came back. "Can I help you ladies . . . with anything?"

Shameless boy!

"I'll take another Creamsicle," Mimi said, knocking back the rest of her first one in one gulp.

"Are you sure that's what you need?" Red said.

"That's exactly what I need," Mimi said. "And give me a Raven, too. I just want to taste it."

"I'll try one, too," I said.

Once the waiter left, Red said, "You two should watch it."

"Thanks, Mom," Mimi said.

"My parents used to be able to stop. And then . . ."

"I know," Mimi said. "One day they couldn't. But I'm not your mom or your dad. Remember?"

When my Raven came, I sat it down for a couple minutes, just to demonstrate to Red that I wasn't in some big hurry, and then I took a gulp. It was damned good. But for the record, I preferred White Russians . . . they tasted like melted ice cream. The Raven did the job, though. All the backchatter in my brain slowed down, and I got warm, and I stopped caring. I mean, I stopped caring about everything: whether hitting the stage again was insane or Red was tripping about my drinking or I whether I should keep my job, no matter how much I felt it drained me.

"So what's our plan for the reunion?" said Red.

"Go, show, conquer," said Mimi, giving us the shooty fingers and blowing imaginary smoke off the barrel of the gun.

"Is Lin going?"

"No," said Red.

"I thought Lin wanted to go," said Mimi.

"We just can't afford it."

"I can pay for a babysitter."

"No, thank you."

Mimi could pay for an army. And though sometimes I was tempted to break our rule, we were strictly a pay-for-your-own-shit crew. I think it was one of the big reasons we were still together. No failed business deals, no financial exploitation. Just the usual girl-on-girl emotional blackmail.

"I have been looking forward to this for like *forever*," said Mimi. "Let's go dancing at DV8! Get a Scorpion Bowl at the Hong Kong. You know, just have a good time."

"I would be just delighted"—and her Creole came out, *de-LAH-ded*—"if I never saw most of those people again."

"We're not going for 'most of those people,'" I said.

"Hey," Mimi said. "You should play a show at the reunion. You and Ari. And maybe you can join in, Red."

"Oh, hell naw," said Red. "You must be thinking of someone else. I'm not trying to offend you, baby sister," she said to me. "I am just speaking my truth."

"Leo got us two more dates at the Orchid," I said, trying to change the subject. "And an offer to play this cool spot in Williamsburg."

Red leaned back and held my gaze. "So you have a thing for him. For Leo."

"I think it's mutual," I said.

"Well, is he a good manager?" asked Mimi.

"He's getting us bookings."

"Is he getting you money?" Red said.

"Not much. Not yet."

"I trust he will. He's hungry. He's smart. He knows how to work a room. But I know entirely too much about that Negro and if I knew he was going to play you like this, I would never have hooked you up."

"*Play* me?" I said.

"Look, I was there, remember? I was there, on the road. I know how easily you lose yourself. You get these crazy infatuations and then you get all stalkerish on a man and mad when he comes back at you with the same energy."

"Time out," Mimi said.

"I just don't want to go through this again."

I whipped up my left hand and started going through my fingers.

"One, what is *this*?

"Two, why do you think the mysterious *this* is happening *again*?"

"Three, what do you have to do with any of it? Stay out of my damned business. No one asked you for an intervention."

"Okay, guys, okay . . ." Mimi said.

"You're right," Red said. "So I don't want to hear any mess from you if this falls apart." She pushed back from the table. "I have to go home to my honey and my baby boy. Please do not call me hungover tomorrow because I will have *no* sympathy. Drink lots of water and take a vitamin B-12 before you go to bed, okay?"

"Okay," we said. We both waved her away from putting money on the table. Look, if things shook out the way they usually did, Red and I would be back in friend mode by the morning. Damn, I hadn't even talked to her about the intrigue at work. Well, that meant we'd have something to talk about tomorrow other than my bad behavior. Speaking of which, the waiter came over . . . and Mimi and I ordered another round. Just one for the road.

▷ 8 The Pretenders, "Back on the Chain Gang"

The next day, every time the train lurched, I nearly hurled. By the time I walked up out of the subway at Fiftieth and Eighth, I was actually keeping track of the curbside trash cans in case I needed to make a break for one.

Used my electronic key card to get into the building and got on an elevator filled with the late crowd. And while it was fine and good for the interns and the graphic designers to be twenty minutes late, that kind of time was killing me right now.

And yes, sure . . . I saw Fat Red Rich talking to my hair and makeup girls, and throwing up his hands and walking off. I was standing near the copier and peering out like some kid in trouble. As soon as he'd left, I ran in and told the ladies to get me in and out quickly. I couldn't pretend I had been there but at least I could show up early to the set as a sign of good faith.

"That man is not happy," said my hair girl, a Brighton Beach Russian who'd adopted a brightly American name. She did one last curl on my left side and started fluffing my hair. "You should try coming in earlier."

"You know how the trains are . . ."

"And *you* know how the trains are. That is not an excuse."

Okay, I guess it was "act like Sophie's mother" season.

"She's right," said Makeup. "Something's going on with that man. You need to come correct."

"Nobody else gets called out like that," I said.

"You are not nobody else," said Brighton Beach. And as usual, she was right.

Ari was sitting on a camel-colored couch between two people, a man and a woman.

The man looked French to me. Great ass (from what I could see when he turned), dark hair, sharp cheekbones. Sadness and self-confidence. Those French weren't bitter like the Brits. They just regretted that no one else in the world knew how to make a decent baguette.

The woman wasn't bad, either . . . a toasted-almond beauty with long dark hair that fell all the way to her waist. She used the hair as a veil when she leaned over to kiss Ari, and then swept it back dramatically as she leaned over Ari to kiss the Parisian. Then the Parisian would massage Ari's chest and send his hand creeping toward Ari's thigh. And when he'd gotten a good purchase there, he would send his other hand to Rapunzel's breast . . . all in the middle of a party filled with people.

Ari sat there enjoying the ministrations. I stared at him, and he nodded back at me. Frenchie and Rapunzel saw him looking and motioned me over to have a come sit. I flipped them the bird. They looked genuinely hurt.

The city was awash in E, chemical love that you paid for with headaches and malaise the next morning. You could get a pill for ten dollars—a pink one with a smiley face or a green one with an apple, or an ankh, or a U2. Another man joined the cuddle puddle. Ari didn't look for guys, but they looked for him; and he didn't mind a bit of recreational bisexuality.

For the past three years since the divorce, Ari and I had seen each other every couple of weeks. Rarely was it on purpose. It's not hard to run into your ex in a city of eight million people when most of those eight million people circulate among their own little clique.

Mimi turned to me and asked me if I was okay.

"I'm fucking tired of you asking me if I'm okay every time we see Ari," I said. Bitter, but honest. I usually said, "Of course."

"I should have stayed home to help Jack with his solar system," Mimi said.

"If you leave right now, he might still be awake."

Mimi ignored my acid tongue and went to the bar. I followed her, and my little black dog followed me. It had taken me years to recognize my mood swings as the outrage of depression.

Of all the metaphors for what I felt, Winston Churchill's suited me best. Maybe his black dog was a pit bull; maybe mine was just a pug. It was mean, though: the kind of dog who would bite a girl who fed it.

I poured a stiff gin gimlet—Bombay Sapphire and Rose's Lime over ice—and hoped that the poison I picked would wear well on me the next day. Then I saw Ari head for the bathroom and did all sorts of blocking and running moves to get in the door before it closed.

"What, are you desperate?"

"I need to talk to you."

"I need to pee," he said.

"I've seen you pee before. I've seen you do plenty of things."

We walked into the bathroom together. It was the size of most bedrooms. There was a bath and a separate steam shower; and against the far wall one of those old wooden toilets with the tank well above it, and the chain you had to pull.

I sat down on a low, wide chair with a round seat, crossed my legs, and tried to look nonchalant. It was difficult because his midsection was in my direct sight line.

Ari was pale as café au lait, but he had a black man's Johnson. Brown, not pink. I didn't have a big thing about dick color, but some of my girlfriends did. They said, with Afrocentric gravitas, that because of slavery they could never suck a pink cock. Me, I hated giving blow jobs, period. Not sure why I ever did it. Practice, maybe. Definitely felt inadequate when I couldn't make a man come, and come on my schedule. Blow jobs were such a good finishing move when you did them right.

You could fast-forward past all of that groaning and faking and get back to the cuddles.

Ari shook himself off, tucked, zipped, wiped his hands on his pants legs. "What do you want?"

"Aren't you going to wash your hands?"

"No."

"Might catch a cold."

"A cold?"

"Cold season is coming—well, in a couple months. The number-one way to prevent colds is by frequently washing your hands, so you don't rub the rhinovirus into your eyes."

"You came in the bathroom to lecture me on colds?"

"I came in the bathroom to see if we can make some music."

"Of course we can make music."

"On a schedule. We need to work out a schedule. And we need to be reliable. Leo says . . ."

"Leo is a cunt."

Why did men call each other cunts when cunts were the strongest things in the world. They could stretch to ten times their normal size, pop out a baby, and then shrink back.

"You know I hate when you use that language," I said.

"Leo is a turd, then. Leo is a piece of shit."

"Fine. Before we book some gigs, I need to know if you'll play. On a schedule. Like you mean it."

I had this fantasy that we lived out of time. But while I had gained weight and kept my unlined skin, I could see Ari starting to age around the eyes.

"I just want us to do this for us," I said. "For both of us."

"Why do you live in lies?" he said, moving up to me and sitting on his haunches so he was yelling right in my face. "You are living in lies. This is all about you. Don't try to pretend it's not about you."

Someone was knocking on the door, probably Mimi. I yelled that we'd be out in a second.

"I worry about you," I said. "Maybe not as much as I worry about me, but I still worry about you."

"Oh, don't worry about me. Now, Leo, that's the motherfucker you need to worry about."

"How can you say that? You're a fucking grifter. You still owe me four thousand dollars in rent and five hundred dollars running-around money, plus . . ."

Banging on the door.

"We are *coming out,"* I said. And to Ari, "Grifter."

"Takes one to know one. And Leo is definitely one."

"Fine. How's that trust fund coming?"

Ari looked at his feet. Any time I noticed he wasn't wearing new clothes, it was a good bet his dad had cut him off. Ari's dad, Richard, was in the music business, but the family money came from diamonds. They'd been rich for, what, four, five generations? Learned how to use money like a choke collar.

The banging on the door continued. A woman groaned, "I am going to fucking *pee* myself!"

It wasn't Mimi. And she sounded desperate.

"Do it for me," I said, switching effortlessly into beg mode. "Get your act together for the road."

"The only person I'll do it for is myself."

That stung. It hurt like fucking slap. But it was good. If I still knew Ari, those words meant he was already thinking about getting back together and making music for real.

Apparently there's nothing like fighting in a bathroom to rekindle a musical collaboration. Ari and I had done four shows since then. I'd been late to work after every show, and Fat Red Rich was lurking like a mugger around the corner from reception every time I came in. I clearly couldn't hold it down on four hours of sleep anymore.

Today was less of a chore. I ended up having an on-air flirt fest with this band called the <bleep>, three tiny but perfectly formed British guys who lived above a fish shop in Chinatown. (I can only imagine what it was like in August.)

After the show I went to Makeup and got them to scrub the spackle off my face. Rounded the corner toward my office and saw the last person I expected to see. Ari. Talking to Fat Red Rich.

I took a couple of deep breaths and walked slowly toward them.

"Oh, Sophie," Rich said. "I was just having a great time talking to Ari. Long time no see since . . ."

". . . The divorce," Ari said, drily. He was wearing an impeccable suit that a detective from a forties film would wear. All he was missing was a fedora.

"Right," Rich said. "Anyway, Ari tells me you're planning to go out on the road again."

I exploded into a supernova of invisible anger, imagined myself dancing around them with a sword and cutting off both of their heads, and stomping on their dead, cold bodies. I could go all the way *there* in my mind without so much batting an eyelash in real life.

"He did, did he?" I said to Rich. "You did?" I said to Ari. Daggers. Turned back to Rich. "That's wishful thinking for the moment."

"Well, you're such a talent," Rich said. "Both of you." He didn't even bother to spout one of his usual clichés, like, *You're such a valuable member of this team!* or *We can't imagine this place without you!* "We'll have to work out the vacation time for your tour," Rich said with a sly smile, and walked off.

I was truly not long for this world.

I quietly walked back to my office with Ari and shut the door behind us.

"You are *such* a fuckup, Ari, you know that? You don't think!"

And see, this was the thing with Ari. You could cuss him out to his face and he would act like he hadn't heard you. It was one of the best and worst parts of his personality.

"I don't?" he said, taking a seat across from my desk.

"Ari, do you get this? You talking to Rob about touring when I am about to get my ass laid off. This is not cool! I am not fucking around!"

"Oh."

"Oh, what? Oh, *sorry.* You could start there."

"I'm not sorry," he said, scratching his head. He'd let his hair grow out a bit since the show and I could see the deepening widow's peak his maternal uncles all had. "You can't keep sitting on the fence. We're in this, or we're not."

"Some of us don't have trust funds," I said, trying to keep my anger going. "I need this job."

"You don't need them," he said.

"So you're trying to get me fired."

"I'm just trying to make you think," he said. "And I have something to tell you."

"What?"

"Davide died this morning."

"Oh, God. I was going to see him. I was just about to call."

Ari didn't come over and hug me, or humor me in my lie. Instead he said, "It was for the best." Then he added, "Come by after work."

I did one better. Called my producer and said I was sick and needed to take off. Ari and I headed out together. Let the interns gossip all they wanted.

11 Handsome Boy Modeling School, "Rock 'n' Roll (Could Never Hip Hop Like This)"

The way that Ari smoked a joint seemed sacramental. First, he would crumble the weed with infinite patience until each broken bud was exactly the size he wanted it. Then, he would lay out two papers at once, stick them together, and let them dry. Next, he would sprinkle the weed in a thick line and roll the cigarette over his fingers. He'd twist one end shut and fold up part of another rolling paper to make a filter for the other. Then, he'd look at his work for a moment.

"This is the best one yet," he said every time.

Only then would he light it up, taking a little puff to burn off the end and then passing it to me for the first hit.

I lay back on his couch and took a pull as deep as my lungs could hold. I felt like choking, the burning air stuck somewhere between my lungs and my stomach.

I was such a straight arrow in high school (and even college) that basic drug use was still work for me. But I held the smoke down in my lungs, and by the time I exhaled, I was already in dream space.

I lay back on the vintage couch that centered Ari's living room and looked out at the rest of his apartment. He had this enormous, nearly subterranean space on the ground floor of a building in Spanish Harlem. Think of the light as gray. Think of the space as wood too dark and plaster too rough for the light. A back door led to what used to be a backyard but was now a rat-infested trash dump. People just threw things out of their windows, a constant toxic snow. Even his dog, Crisis, didn't like going back there anymore. I could hear her scratching at the back door with her paws.

Ari collected beautiful, spent electronics from the thirties, forties, and fifties. He'd topped the fireplace with a perfect row of old radios, stretching decade by decade from the turn of the century until the 1960s. He kept a tiny, ridiculously expensive stereo system from Tokyo inside an old ham-radio case. He opened the case and turned on . . . Vivaldi. *The Four Seasons.*

I just started laughing.

"What?" Ari said, coming and lying behind me, so we were both lengthwise on the couch, pressed together, spooning. He started massaging my side.

"Corny."

"No," he said. "We're just getting in the mood."

"To do what?"

"To do what? To write some music, that's what."

"Oh, is that all?" I said. I'll tell you this: Ari was a champion downtown man. Even though I hadn't let him so much as touch my punanny since the divorce, I still fantasized about the things he could do with his tongue.

Ari stroked my hair. My roots were a mess. Needed a touch-up.

"He's fine. Davide is fine. It's the rest of us who can't take this shit."

I listened to the dog whine and scratch at the back door, stared at the antiques, continue to smoke.

"You always think you know what I'm thinking."

"Is that so?" he said. I could imagine him thinking: *I know you better than I know myself, woman. I have sat and watched you sleep and breathe and fought and fucked and loved you. Of course I can tell.* But those were my words. Besides, a woman can never really know what a man thinks, or vice versa. What we had was like the ceiling of the Sistine Chapel. God reached out for the hand of Adam, both of them nearing touch but not making it. That space between us was what made us, and what broke us.

We lay there for a while, enjoying each other's scent, the warmth, the occasional brush of a hand on a thigh or chin or chest. But we'd never gone further than this since D-day, because that way lay monsters.

Ari was the one who sat up first, abruptly. "So let's start writing."

"I better head out."

"We're going to write a song before you leave."

"No," I said, reaching for my purse.

"You don't pick something to work on, I'm going to make you free-musicate."

"No!"

"Well, come up with something. One. Two. Three. . . ."

"Okay, fine," I said. There were basically three ways we worked together. One is that I would come to him with lyrics and the barest hint of a tune, and he would make music of it. That's what we did most of the time. Another, which only happened once in a blue moon, was that he'd come to me with the outlines of a song and I'd help him fill in the words. And finally, something we did more to keep ourselves sharp than to get great songs, was freemusication. I never liked it, but he made me do it (okay, I *let* him make me do it) whenever I didn't have a song we were trying to nail down.

He started strumming. It was a smooth, open, tuneless pattern that was more rhythm than melody . . . beautiful nonetheless. I started listening. And then I sat up and started rocking. Not "rocking" as in music but literally rocking back and forth, trying to drive the sound of that guitar into my soul.

This morning, I felt the lead in my gut and the dreams. . . . Last night's dream was that there was some kind of emergency and we were all out by the park, all meaning a bunch of people—white people—and then me and Mama. I was wearing a shirt and skirt and we were sitting on the ground because there were no chairs and my skirt and shirt kept riding up and Mama was riding me, yelling. I was angry and ashamed. More ashamed than angry, actually.

Yesterday I manifested as an eight-year-old boy and we were staying—me and his mama—in a creepy half-shut hotel. And there was a blizzard and (I) remember looking out and seeing snow and nothingness.

I am so angry. I don't know if I can tell the truth. But if I can't tell the truth when I'm singing, when can I tell the truth? No one wants to hear the truth. No one wants to hear the truth. No one wants to hear the truth. No one.

Everyone wants a lie. Everyone wants a story. Everyone wants a lie. Everyone wants a story.

Things were so great then. Things were so perfect then. Things were better than they'll ever be these days, these days.

Well, you know what: I love these days. Well, you know what: I love these days.

They're painful and they're hurting me but I know one thing: they're mine.

These days are my days. These days aren't her days. These days aren't his days. They're my days, they're mine.

This choice is my choice. This choice isn't her choice. This choice isn't his choice. It's my choice, it's mine.

So why am I so angry, still? So why am I holding this hot rock? So why can't I drop it or throw it.

I can't. I won't.

I can't. I won't.

How different is the difference between can't, and won't?

I broke off. "That is some hippie fucking crap comin' out of my mouth," I said. "I've been spending way too much time with Red."

"Just let it come."

"No, it's come as much as it's gonna," I said, standing up. "I should go."

"Sky . . ."

"It's not working. It's not working, okay!" Ari was always wanting to work on process. I wanted songs to be creatures that sprang out full-formed: no mess, no struggle.

Ari reached out to touch me. Just then my phone rang, a shiny, expensive new phone so small that sometimes I couldn't find it before it stopped ringing. I fumbled through my bag, dropped it on the floor, and picked it up.

"Hello?"

"Are you high?" said the voice on the other end. Leo.

"No," I said.

"Don't lie to me," he said.

"I'm not," I said. "I'm just not feeling great."

"Why?"

"Do I need a why?"

"Did you go out drinking?"

It was almost a relief to have a truth to tell him. "Yeah, I did. With the girls. There's some whack shit going on at work."

"I told you to stay away from the liquor. First of all, you're big. We need to get you back in shape. Second, you're bloated. Third, it's not good for your mind. Do you hear me?"

"I hear you," I said.

"One of my boys thought he saw you out last night. Some punk rock club."

"New wave," I said. "Bar."

"Was Ari there?"

I sneaked a look at Ari. "No, but why do you ask? I don't ask when you kick it with Kristal."

Leo laughed. "You mad at me?"

"Why would I be?"

"'Cause I would be flattered if you were."

"Hmmm," I said.

"Where are you now?"

"Home," I said.

"I was about to be down in that neighborhood. You want to chill?"

"Uh," *Damn!* "Sure. When?"

"Whenever I get there."

"I'm about to take a shower. Don't come by before—" I looked at my watch—"six. Okay?"

"Fine."

"We'll go out to dinner, grab something healthy, talk some business, and no liquor, right, baby?"

"Yes, sir!" I said.

I hung up the phone. Ari just looked at me with those cat eyes of his.

"*Home,*" he said, perfectly imitating my tone. "*Yes, sir!*"

"Well," I said, "it's been lovely but I must go."

"Yes, you must," he said. Instead of walking me to the front door, he walked to the back and let in Crisis. She started jumping all over him, and then she ran and gave me a quick lick on the hand. Then she ran right back to Ari. Boy, she loved that man. If I could love him that unconditionally, I thought, walking through the door, I'd be with him still.

▷ 12 The Rolling Stones, "Sympathy for the Devil"

I got home at quarter of six and hopped into the shower. I really wanted to wash my hair, because it probably smelled like weed, but being as I had to work tomorrow, and I was already making figure eights on thin ice, I better not show up with a nappy fuzzball on top of my head.

Threw on one outfit, all-red knit, that was a little too slutty. Put on jeans and a T-shirt. Made me feel fat. Then I put on jeans and a blouse—my favorite combination, always. Sprayed some perfume in the air and stood under the mist so it fell on my hair. Hoped that made a difference.

Then the buzzer rang. I used the intercom to let Leo in. Left my door open and continued fiddling with my hair and putting on some lotion. I liked the casual entrance. It played better.

Heard the creak of the door opening. Stepped out of the bedroom. "Oh, Leo, how are you?"

I went up and gave him a stilted hug, tilting my face up and away so he wouldn't be able to smell my hair, if it smelled like anything at all.

"You want something to drink?" I said, quickly adding, "Juice? Water?" I hope I had either.

"Nah, it's all good," he said, settling back into my overstuffed armchair.

"I'm going to get some water." I went to the kitchen and grabbed a glass, made a sound show of clinking the ice cubes into the glass, and filled it with New York City tap.

"So what's got you drinking?" he said, when I came back and sat opposite him.

I explained the work situation, and how it looked like Fat Red Rich was tightening the noose . . . for reasons I didn't completely understand.

I looked up at Leo and readied myself for the appropriate display of sympathy.

"That's not good," he said.

"No shit."

"Nah, I mean, I was counting on that cross promotion to carry us to gold or even platinum."

"Hello! I might not have a job!"

"Baby, either way we will make this happen, okay? Do you believe me?"

"Yeah."

"*Yeah.* What kind of an answer is *yeah*?"

"Yes, I believe you. We will make it happen."

"That's better," he said, easing back even farther in his chair. "We're going to need that confidence when we get ready to go to the record labels."

"Which will be when?"

"When you get a new band together."

Right. The new band we were going to get together with the mythical money we were making.

Then Leo fixed his eyes on me, dark as lava rock in the dim light. "So you said you were home earlier, right, babe?"

"Yeah," I said. "Left work early because I felt sick. I just hopped out of the shower."

"That's funny because I been here for the last twenty minutes, trying to get you some more bookings, and I just saw you come in."

I took a deep breath, started to say something. Then just closed my eyes and spoke with them shut. "So you were sitting downstairs stalking me like some dime store detective?"

"I told you, I was on the phone, handling my biz. . . ."

"And watching my door?"

"We did have an appointment . . ." I could see him start to get trapped in his own game.

"You know what, Leo. I don't need this kind of crap right now. Just make the bookings and stay out of my day-to-day, okay?"

"Whoa, what is the situation?"

"The situation is that you are on some power trip. You're bringing me down," I said, opening the door and showing him to it. Maybe I was touchy. But I'd had to take out a few restraining orders against so-called fans, and even if that made me too sensitive it was my choice how I lived my life.

"Damn, you are so touchy sometimes. Look, baby girl, don't even sweat it. I'm having a party Saturday after next at my crib in Harlem and . . ."

"Good night, Leo," I said, all but pushing him through the door.

Couldn't sleep. I grabbed a trio of aluminum take-out containers from the refrigerator and sat in front of the television. I watched teenagers flirt around a poolside, popping their pelvises in pale imitation of hip-hop moves. A man swinging from a building crashes through a window. A black girl with braces roller-skates through a house. Went back to the kitchen. Grabbed a half pint of New York Superfudge Chunk. Finished the ice cream and licked the spoon. Needed more. The windows began to glow with the first hints of sunrise. I ordered delivery: eggs, bacon, potatoes, and coffee.

In the morning light, my apartment looked all wrong. I had been meaning to redecorate for a while, but my credit-card debt put the brakes on that. Like so many New York apartments, only a couple of the rooms got any light to speak of. I needed to get rid of these dark, heavy fabrics and do something lighter and brighter.

The hallway, generously proportioned, was filled with bookshelves, mainly college stuff. *The Riverside Shakespeare. Beloved.* A book of sixteenth-century poetry. A collection of slave oral histories. And a whole bunch of Nero Wolfe, Agatha Christie, and science-fiction titles, everything from Ursula Le Guin to Samuel Delaney; Orson Scott Card and Octavia Butler. When people walked in they would flip out, as if I were a hermit.

Shoot, I thought, paying the delivery guy for my breakfast, I almost never reread any of these books, so why did I keep them? I needed to get rid of the past.

And that's when, just so the universe could remind me someone else held the ultimate remote, I turned to The Video Channel and saw "Confess." Red was seated at a drum kit, banging out a slow and steady rhythm to our goth-mope anthem. She was the heartbeat of our band. And you could trace back when things had gone wrong to when Ari and I got divorced. But they really stretched back even further, to when Red decided, three years before Ari and I called it quits, that she couldn't deal with our bullshit anymore.

She'd said: "I'm your drummer or your friend. Choose."

"Red . . ."

"Choose!" She'd found Ari's stash inside an album crate. It was enough to send him up the river on five different felony charges. "I have a lot of plans in my life," Red said. "And one of them is not to go to jail. Y'all are . . ." And here she unleashed her ultimate critique, "Y'all are forgetting you're black. In America. Along with forgetting your soul and your manners and your common sense. So I can stay in this band, and I can play with you. But I will take my own transportation, and if you go down, you go down alone, do you hear me?" Her whole body was tight and trembling. "Do you hear me!"

"Friend," Ari said, quietly.

And that was it.

I missed her so bad, the Red who could drive through three states in one day and then get onstage and bend time with the rhythm of her drumming. I missed the single Red who didn't have to worry about her girlfriend, their mortgage, and their boy child.

We'd burnt that woman out.

But the old Red still lived in that video. We'd shot "Confess" at one of the last shows we did together as a threesome. Started with a montage of black-and-white photos from different shows, going back in time to college. Then, sort of like that "Take on Me" video, we were inside the picture, playing to a crowd in the Adams House dining hall. One of Ari's friends had shot that video on Super 8.

At the college show, I had this asymmetrical haircut and a baby face. Ari was lean and wearing a pastor's collar and black jacket. And

Red, on a little riser at the back of our triangle, had an Afro bigger than a beach ball. Part of me wanted to laugh at us for looking so serious, and part of me wanted to warn those kids what lay ahead.

I came back into the present. Looked at the digital clock on the cable box. I had to be at work in two hours. I'd eaten leftovers and breakfast and I could barely move.

Being stretched tight with food was like being hugged from the inside. For a moment, I was complete, just like the days in college when I would binge until I was ready to burst. I stood in front of the toilet and flipped up the seat. Looked at the white rim. Almost walked away. I knew better. I had a choice. Hadn't done this in so long. I had a choice.

Then I leaned over the bowl. The place where the soft palate meets the back of the throat is smooth, almost sexual. My fingers traveled to that familiar place and I ran the tips of my nails over the soft flesh, listening for footsteps that couldn't come through a locked door.

Listen. Our bathroom door doesn't lock. I've braced the thick wood with a stack of magazines so my roommates won't come in. I read about this thing you do. I have to try. I am disgusting browned butterfat sickening, fingersful of flesh. I pinch myself when no one is looking, roll the fat between my fingers. And still.

The cafeteria serves cheese on the salad bar, grated. I melt it in the microwave in cereal bowls, eat it with pita bread, big slimy, gooey masses, white with a slick of yellow fat on top. That's what my insides must look like. Cut away the flesh and that is me.

It takes longer than you think. I pick up a magazine and . . .

Wiped my mouth. My nose. Looked at myself, eyes bright red in the mirror. I couldn't do this. I couldn't not.

Went back to watching TV. I still had half an hour before I had to leave for work. And in the kitchen, there was still a slice of cake.

⊳ 13 Cyndi Lauper, "Money Changes Everything"

I was late to work, of course. Fat Red Rich called me into his office. "We're going to have to put you on probation."

"What?!?"

"Two things." Rich leaned forward in his chair. "Sophie, you're not giving a hundred and ten percent. You're maybe giving sixty, seventy. Heard about that band of yours starting up again, and hobbies are great"—he spread his hands wide—"but you need to get yourself back up to speed so you can do what we pay you to. Besides, performances that are not related to *Your Day in Music* require prior approval, per your contract."

"You told me *years* ago that anything I did with the band was good publicity for The Video Channel."

"I don't recall that."

"I have notes from that meeting, dated and annotated."

"It's not in your contract."

"Is that where we are now? The contract? Because if so, there were some clauses that the company hasn't . . ."

"Okay, okay, Sophie." Rich quickly backed down. TV-C was known for breaking contracts early and often, and like most of the women I had plenty of dirt for a sexual harassment lawsuit. "Look a second, Sophie, you know I am doing you a favor here . . ."

Right.

"I like *big* girls." Could not believe he actually said that to my face. "But you're not keeping yourself up. Look at your eyes. You been taking a morning toke?" he said in that greasy you-can-tell-me voice.

"Actually," I said to Rich, "I was vomiting. Twenty-four-hour stomach bug." He eased back in his seat and then slid his seat back from the table, just a bit. This place was like a preschool and he knew that if I really did have something, he'd probably get it too.

"Well, we're watching you, Sophie. I really like you, you know. If I didn't, you wouldn't have lasted here this long. Go on, get to the show."

I sat there too long, part of me stunned and wanting to cry, another part ready to get up and kick his goddamned ass. And then I went and rocked *Your Day in Music*. And then I holed up in my office for the rest of the workday.

That night we had a gig at the Orchid. My throat was filled with gorge and I felt like I was sweating and chilled at the same time. I wasn't sick, I was angry. Angry at The Video Channel, angry at Ari, angry at myself.

See, before the show, we'd had a record company meeting. Our first. "We" was supposed to be me, Leo, and Ari. I made a point of showing up on time, beating Leo and the record company guys. And then Leo came, and the A&R reps. And then we ordered beverages and tapas. And we waited for Ari. Leo kept up a steady patter. Finally one of the A&R guys said, "You know, this is exactly the problem."

"We don't have problems here," Leo said, "only solutions."

"So what's the solution when you have this guy who's great on guitars and vocals, but he's got a track record of ODing or getting busted in every other city on the road? How's a label supposed to recoup? And where is Ari anyway?"

"I think he was under the weather," I said quickly.

"You think?" The guy who said that was the younger of the two, maybe even an intern, mouthy and trying to play the big dog for his boss. "Why don't you give him a call?"

I looked at Leo. Leo nodded. At this point we had nothing to lose. I dialed.

"Put him on speaker," said the junior rep. I looked at Leo again.

"I don't think that's necessary," said Leo.

"Oh, I do."

Ari picked up. His voice was distorted by the phone, and thick from sleep or drugs or both.

"Where are you?"

"Home. Chilling."

"We have a meeting right now," I said. "You remember?"

"Yeah, those guys fucked my friend Kevin over on his second album. Donwanna talk to 'em."

I'd hung up the phone before he could do any more damage. But it was too late. The men stood and left. Leo paid the bill. Then he chewed me out the whole drive to the Orchid. Great.

When I got to the Orchid, I decided to pretend I wasn't mad at Ari. He didn't notice a thing. Or more likely, he didn't care. As calm as I seemed on the outside, I was roiling on the inside. Until we took the stage.

Ari and I had settled into a groove where he stepped from the shadows with a sound burst, teasing his guitar into an instrument of deviously different timbres. I took the front of the stage, not standing stiffly the way I did the first night, but pacing and drawing energy from the crowd and giving it back full force times five. The die-hard fans were waiting for "Confess," and we gave it to them. But as an encore, I'd asked Ari to lay down an approach to a song I'd loved from the first time I'd heard it.

I looked out at the crowd, many of them the same music industry wags who would rip me to pieces if I were fired, and began with a warble that would have made Edith Piaf proud: "Non, je ne regrette rien."

And the demons had been chasing me all day, but at that moment I banished them, scared them off with a wall of sound. Ari pushed a couple of foot pedals and turned the sound of the guitar steely, brittle. No regrets.

The Cabal met once a month at the Pink Teacup for soul food and sedition. For once, I was early. Watched a long-haired dachshund and a corgi sniff each other's butts. The owners did their version of the same. It was one of those days of false promises, spring breezes, and strong sunshine that could turn chilly in an instant.

The Teacup was in the old West Village, with its neat brick buildings, curved cobblestone streets, and trees. A truck unloaded lights for a film shoot. The *Friends* exterior was on a near corner; a clip from *Sex and the City* shot a couple blocks down. I knew the terrain: two-thousand-dollars-a-month studios and million-dollar carriage houses. Good schools, better restaurants, no ads and billboards assaulting the eyes. People here bought teakettles that looked like architecture, floor rugs that looked like Mondrians, designer condoms, and French baby clothes.

I wanted this life so bad it made my teeth hurt. I wanted the life of the idle rich, people with a tenth of the intelligence of their house-cleaners. I wanted to study flower arranging, burn my pager, and pay off the relatives who asked for cash. I wanted my fuck-you money.

I stood just outside the door because the Teacup wouldn't seat incomplete parties. They were coming down the block, one after the other, all too caught in their own heads, it seemed, to notice each other. Sharon rocked a long weave. She had tight jeans, a gold chain with a cross, and a pink sweater tied around her waist. Kay, the main instigator of the Cabal, had hips two chairs wide, and this broken shuffle-walk from working on her feet as a camera operator for twenty years. And Robyn dressed like a grown-up Valley Girl, produced the late-night video show, shopped with a vengeance, and rarely got off her phone.

We all bitched about the soul-crushing combat of jobs we'd grown too dependent on to leave. At one Cabal meeting this Negress from marketing came in, stayed half a meeting, and walked out, calling it our "little victim club." And maybe she was right. I didn't want to stay in this club forever, but, Lord, give me a few more paychecks.

The Teacup hadn't changed in decades: pink menu, cramped tables, hard-fried chicken, strong black coffee. It looked like a little soul-food joint in Harlem. But given the neighborhood, the place was filled with a mix of black folk and white people, who overdressed to get their morning soy latte.

"How are you doing, Sis?" Kay said, giving me a hug. The waitress showed us our booth. Kay sat down heavy and I moved to give her more room.

"I'm hanging in there. How 'bout y'all?"

"Fine," Robyn and Sharon said.

"So they got your ass between a rock and a hard place," Sharon said, not wasting any time.

"Pretty much," I said.

"Do you want the job?" asked Robyn.

"No, I'm done . . . mentally. But Mama gotta pay the bills."

"Heard that," said Sharon. Our food came: a fried-chicken plate with cornbread for Kay; pancakes for Robyn; bacon, eggs, and cheese grits for me; and salad for Sharon. Sharon argued that if they got serious about letting me go, I should be able to get some walking-away money. If they were out to hire someone younger, cuter, and cheaper, the least they could do was give me a proper good-bye.

In my purse was a sheaf of flyers for my next show. I held them right there, in the purse, and debated putting them out. Thing was, I had never gotten together with these women outside of our bitch sessions, or the occasional dinner or cocktail party. At the end of the day, I didn't know how much we had in common except our pain.

"What you got?" Robyn said. "Turn it over."

I put the flyers on the table but spread my fingers over them. "I know you probably won't like our stuff. No pressure, really. But if you want to come by, let me know. I can even put you on the guest list."

"On the guest list, huh?" Kay pulled out one of the flyers and started reading.

"I wondered when you were going to tell us," said Robyn. "It's only like *five* friends of mine have told me to come see your show. But I was waiting for a personal invitation."

"But I don't know if you'll like it."

"That's okay. I won't ask for my money back."

"So this is where you've been spending your time," said Kay.

"Yeah."

"Well, your job is still your job. I don't remember that band ever giving you health benefits. So, if you want to go, go. But just don't mess up anymore," said Kay. "You know it reflects poorly on all of us."

"Kay!" said Robyn.

"No, really," said Kay. "All of you know that that's the truth."

15 The Smiths, "Shoplifters of the World Unite"

A five-minute stroll would get you from the Teacup to the West Village kiddie park. It was packed full of Range Rover yuppies, their kids, and their brown-skinned nannies. Every once in a damned while I saw a brown woman playing with her own child, and it gave me a flutter of pride and heartbreak all at once. I hated seeing all the Jamaicans and Beijans and Guyanese women caring for white children while their own were in some grubby, unlicensed day-care center . . . or so I imagined. Honestly, I just didn't want anybody to think I was a nanny. I hated the way the white folks looked right through me, and I hated myself for being so proud.

The phone rang: "Unseasonably warm, eighty-eight degrees, with clear skies and an evening low of sixty-nine."

Told Ari thanks, hung up the phone, and went over to Mimi, who was sitting with Levi in her arms, waving at me. "It's crazy how beautiful it is," she said, pointing at the sky with one arm while holding her one-year-old with the other. "You know Bernard and I used to play here." Bernard was her twin. He'd gone to Harvard with us, but lived in a different house and we barely saw him, which was too bad because I'd always thought he was hot. I could imagine them as toddlers, running through the sprinklers in saggy little suits, with their brown-skinned nanny (I'd seen pictures) keeping a watchful eye.

I said hi to Mathilde, who took care of Mimi's kids. She was a stoic Indian Trinidadian who probably had a good novel in her about the antics Chez Mimi. Four-year-old Jack pumped his legs hard on the swings, while Elizabeth, a little lady at the ripe age of nine, sat reading a book on a nearby bench.

"Sky? Hello!"

"Yeah, yeah, it's beautiful." I was itching to get out of this place, back somewhere where brown people weren't only servants. "Look, I had kind of a tough-love meeting with the Cabal. I gotta go."

"I thought you could stay for a while."

"I'm not good company right now," I said. Mimi began to cry.

Mathilde scooped up the baby, cuddled him, and stood him on his feet holding both of his chubby hands so she could guide him on a walk around the perimeter.

"It's Nestor," she said, her voice shuddering through sobs. "He's having an affair."

"Another one?" I wanted to say, but didn't. Now, this is what I didn't understand: *she* was the one with the money. She could dump Nestor's ass anytime she wanted to. It wasn't like she was a battered woman without a credit card to her name. You could find his name and picture under "fuckup" in the encyclopedia, know what I mean?

Instead of taking off, I walked Mimi to one of the many West Village cafés that claimed they'd served the first cappuccino in Manhattan. The space held the rich smell of old wood and new coffee. An Italian proprietor chatted up the customers while his Mexican barista pulled the espresso and foamed the milk.

"He was, like, 'I didn't make this call. Mathilde made this call,'" Mimi was saying. "And I was like, 'Mathilde is from Trinidad, not Brazil. And I'm damned sure she doesn't have a cousin at a *modeling agency*,' I mean." Mimi nearly doubled over with quiet sobs. "Does he think I'm stupid?"

Worse, babes: he thinks you're a paycheck.

"He hasn't had a job since the fucking *band*," she said, a thin trail of spittle leaping from her mouth to the table. "Sorry, that was gross." She took a deep breath. "Let me go get myself together."

As she staggered off to the bathroom, I flagged down the waiter and asked for a pile more napkins, plus an Irish Coffee, a carafe of water, and two pieces of chocolate cake. Emergency measures.

Yeah, the band. The three of us met at one of Nestor's shows. It was all ages so we left behind our fake IDs. Mimi was dressed out of a

Madonna video, crosses and black lace. We managed to get drinks any-how, giving a ten-spot to some guy who got to keep the change when he gave us our beers. We edged up toward the stage. Saw this beefy guy pounding a skinny one with braces in the mouth until blood ran down his chin.

As soon as the band came on, Mimi kept her eyes fixed on Nestor. Back then he had paper-white skin and dyed black hair. He waved to her as they ended their set.

After the show we went backstage. Nestor and Mimi went into the bathroom together. When they still hadn't come out after ten minutes, the drummer and his girlfriend made it their mission to keep me com-pany. She had dyed red hair. His was platinum. Davide. His name was Davide.

Mimi came back to the table, tasted the Irish Coffee, gulped it down even though it was hot, and dug into the cake.

"I was just thinking about the night all of us met," I said. "Crazy, huh? How everything worked out?"

"Or didn't."

We ate in silence for a bit. Mimi started a patter about the kids. Jack was getting into fights in preschool. Elizabeth's best friend got her period at nine. Wasn't that too soon? Mimi offered to pay for our little sugar binge. I snatched the check off the table instead. It just seemed like good form.

Mimi picked up the tab as many times as we girls would let her, which wasn't a whole lot. Mimi was seven-digit-trust-fund rich. I didn't want to take advantage of her, and I also didn't want to test my own limits. I thought if I started spending her money willy-nilly, the way Nestor did, that I simply wouldn't be able to stop. One day, she would stop to ask herself the last time I had picked up a tab, and it would be three years ago and what would we say to each other then?

What happened next was that I lifted a thin wafer of plastic from my purse, one embossed with little metallic numbers. I placed it on a silver tray containing a bill, and the server came and took it away. In between the time he took it away and came back to tell me, regretfully, that the card was declined, several things happened. All of the information on my card, starting with that string of little numbers, was encoded on a little magnetic strip. When the barista swiped the card through a reader, the information went across a telephone line, encoded as a series of tones, like the ones computers use to connect to the Internet. Those tones were relayed to a computer that authenticated my card, but denied that I had any credit left on it. The little paper slip that printed out of the card reader did not say thirteen dollars and thirty-two cents, plus a place for tip. Instead it said "Account Denied." And then I blushed and went fishing around in my purse for cash.

"I don't know what happened," I said, as I put my last twenty on the table. "It must be a mistake." But it wasn't any mistake. I was trying to live a trial lawyer's life on a paralegal's salary. TV-C wasn't exactly known for making its on-air talent rich . . . just, if you were lucky, famous.

"You sure?" Mimi asked. "I can get it."

"I'm sure," I said.

"Sophie?"

"Yeah?"

"Don't tell Red about this, okay?"

Red hated Nestor, who cheated on Mimi the way Red's dad had cheated on her mama: that is, with only the barest of pretense.

"What's said in the coffee shop stays in the coffee shop," I said, patting her head. But Mimi knew that I was lying to her. What were girlfriends for except telling your *other* girlfriends their business? It was twisted group therapy, where you had no secrets except the ones you truly kept to yourself.

Leo wanted to hear us with a richer sound, so he got the Orchid's house band to back us. Felt so decadent. The heartbeat of the bass carried me through the evening. The band had memorized our songs note for note, and improved on the instrumentation.

So afterward, Ari and I went out for a couple drinks with the Orchid's musicians. They were kids, really . . . talented kids. I made out with their bassist in the bathroom. Then he challenged me to go head-to-head in tequila shots. I think he was the one who made sure I got home to bed.

Picked up the phone in the morning. I'd drawn the blinds closed so I wasn't sure what time it was right away. But I knew I'd heard the phone ringing in my dreamspace. I just finally got it together enough to wake up and pick up.

Kay told me to turn on the television. I did. My show was on the air without me. An ambitious assistant producer with an *enormous* rack was fumbling her way through the show.

After a few more tries, I thought, she'd be fine.

Kay cussed me out for failing to uphold the race; then I saw there were seventeen messages on my cell phone; and then Rich called and told me I was fired.

So much for severance.

I turned off my cell phone. I disconnected my landline. I put an "on vacation" tag on my personal and work emails. And then I took a sleeping pill with a vodka chaser and spent the next six hours being nothing, nowhere.

That night I called Red. "You know you sabotaged yourself on purpose," she said.

"Isn't this the part where you tell me you feel sorry for what I'm going through?"

"I feel sorry for you. I feel sorry you didn't ask for help when you've clearly been out of control."

Leo called and told me I was stupid. Ari came through on call waiting. I hung up on Leo to take the call. Ari told me this was all meant to be, that I had to follow my path.

The next day I went to the TV-C studios and picked up my stuff. I looked good . . . full makeup, nice wardrobe. Hair was a little janky. Didn't have anyone to do it for me.

One of the girls from reception helped me carry out the boxes of gold records I'd gotten for doing fluffy interviews with up-and-coming bands. She even stood with me on the corner until I could flag down a cab and load them into the trunk.

And that was it. I was ghost.

17 DJ Krush, "Candle Chant" (A Tribute)

I told Leo to step it up on finding us a record label. I didn't have the luxury now of waiting until we'd put together a band.

Leo arranged a lunch in the French part of NoLita. The restaurant had blacked-out windows and no name on the door.

The storefront didn't have a restaurant permit yet, so the place was a sushi speakeasy, with a big bouncer who took your name and then, if it cleared, swept you through a purple crushed-velvet birth canal of curtains and into the room beyond. Now, Leo was on me hard to lose weight, so sushi seemed like a smart move. Except Ari had had nightmares about fish since he was a child, plus the smell made him want to puke.

Ari was wearing a Matrixy black suit and sunglasses. He sat covering his nose and drinking both a Kirin and a green tea. Translucent jewels of fish studded a lacquered platter on a lazy Susan in the middle of the table. I loved the carnelian-colored wafers of tuna; and pale yellowtail; and salmon marbled with fat.

Leo was wearing his best suit, and had his hair in simple cornrows. He introduced me to a couple of men dressed like Ari. These guys had the lizardlike composure of the comfortably rich. They told me their label was an indie spin-off of a major, and they were doing big things.

Ari snorted. He'd always said you could go with a major, and you could go with an indie, but never go with a new label, because they broke at least half a dozen artists before they got their shit together.

Ari began to quiz them on their plan for their label. He did this without lifting his fingers from under his nose, which made him look and sound extremely odd. Every question he asked, the label guys answered with, "We have our ways of dealing with that." Leo looked really annoyed. He was supposed to be the smart one, the in-control one. Maybe he'd forgotten that Ari grew up in this business, watching his dad cut these kinds of deals.

There was Indian music playing low in the background, and I was admiring the stitching in the clothes of the people who came to this joint, and then I was looking at the table next to us. The couple had ordered a whole live lobster, which the waiter strapped to a wood serving block. The lobster madly wiggled its antennae. Then, with the precision of a surgeon, the server whipped out a knife, sliced through the shell, splayed the lobster open, and began cutting the white flesh into chunks. The man with a Koizumi-like salt-and-pepper mane and the woman with unbelievably small hands picked up their chopsticks and began to devour the still-wiggling creature.

I turned just in time to see Ari run to the bathroom.

Leo and the two guys talked through the specifics of a development deal and what sounded like a pitifully small advance. When I sat up in my chair to ask more about the money, Leo waved me down as if I were a child. And as usual, I hesitated, then leaned back in my seat. At this point, my hunger to get back in the game was getting the better of my curiosity.

"So it's all settled then," the first guy said.

Leo looked at me and smiled, not that I had the faintest idea what we'd just agreed to. "It's all settled," he said.

I lay in bed, not sleeping, just breathing, as I watched my clock click past ten, ten-thirty. Kept coming back to the question: Was I going to Leo's or not?

Since I'd lost my job, Leo had kept us booked at a weekly slot at the Orchid. But that wasn't going to pay my credit-card bills, let alone my rent. I'd started taking credit-card cash advances to pay the utilities. Still hadn't told my mother I'd lost my job. She didn't watch TV-C, but she had radar. She'd find out soon enough.

There were really two options tonight: stay home, drink, eat, and puke; or go to Leo's and try to pretend everything was all right.

In five minutes I was in a taxi. In another ten, we'd gone uptown to Central Park South, skirting couples smooching in smelly horse carriages, and hit the long diagonal of Broadway. The meter ticked ten dollars, fifteen.

Tried to adjust myself in the seat but I was afraid I'd bust a seam on something. A red sleeveless slip dress put what Leo called The Twins on eye-popping display. I wondered if Kristal would be there. If I was up against that kind of competition, it was really no competition at all.

The driver talked about Pakistan. He'd left his wife and kids in some little house out in the sticks in his home country, and he lived in a brownstone full of men in Queens. The taxi company owned the brownstone, so they made money coming and going. Not this guy, though. "My wife, she want to come, but there is no money," he told me. "I miss my family so much I think sometimes I lose my mind."

I knew lonely. Slipped twenty-five dollars through the divider and stepped out in the middle of a row of brownstones. A long metal Dumpster held chunks of plaster and pieces of old furniture. Another house halfway down the block was just plain hollow, with plastic sheeting instead of windows. But this wasn't decay, it was renovation. Harlem was getting itself done up for company again.

Every weekend I flipped through the *Times* checking out the real-estate porn. These brownstones went for a hundred thousand dollars a decade ago. Now they were half a million and more. That was just for the ones like this, which came filled with housewarming gifts of rat poop and crumbling wallboard.

I walked up to the stoop and lifted a huge metal door knocker, like the one in that lovely old version of *A Christmas Carol*. It made a delicious resonant *thunk*. No one came to the door. I experimented with banging it down lightly, and then a little harder, and then . . .

My hand was still holding the knocker when Leo opened the door. He whispered, "Hello, still waters," in my ear, letting his thumb trace a curve down my back before pulling me in for a firm embrace. I got that dizzy, prickly feeling, same as when the plane hits an air pocket and drops midflight. I was falling. Before I could get too deep in my thoughts, Leo was off, leading me forward.

He pointed to his living room, where a few people mingled and drank. He pointed out the creamy marble fireplace he'd saved. He told me each floor was a thousand square feet, and each had a different layout. The main floor was open and grand; the hardwood floors were a deep cherrywood the color of Leo's skin.

"Now this ain't really a housewarming," Leo said for the benefit of anyone in earshot. "Just a preview for a few of y'all. Wait for the remix, folks be hanging out the windows."

He took me gently by the hand and led me upstairs. I could never figure out exactly what scent he wore, but I followed that rich smell as much as I followed his grasp.

"I lived here for the past month, baby," he said, pointing around the top floor. Some previous owner had carved three tiny SRO apartments with one bathroom into the space. The room on the left was covered in faded wallpaper, with a dented half stove pushed into the corner and a new mattress by the far wall.

"Check this out," Leo said. I stared at his shirt. He had truly gone hip-hop casual. . . . Thick boots, matching gold chain; and a shirt tight enough to show every muscle. Shameful. Delicious, too.

"Okay, the stove was here, right?" He pointed to a hole in the wall. "And the first night I wake up like I got cold-cocked. I was staggering, couldn't get no breath."

"You are so dramatic," I said.

He cut his eyes at me. "I was getting carbon-monoxide poisoning. Somebody didn't shut off the tap."

"That sucks."

"Look baby girl, I know things are rough, but just look around here and you will know all things are possible." He guided me down a flight of stairs to the middle floor, which was dark except for the streetlight through the windows. *Huge* master bedroom. Furniture sat underneath drop cloths and, in the dim light from the window, looked like big cats about to pounce.

"All I'm waiting for," he said, "is my king-size bed. These stairs . . . man, they caused me all kindsa problems. So we have to bring it in through the window."

He had floor-to-ceiling French doors that led out to a balcony. I had the urge to go and start singing "Don't Cry for Me, Argentina" to the 'hood.

Leo pushed me up against the wall, so close we were chest to chest. "I'm living the dream," he said. "And I want you to know I am looking out for your dreams, so if sometimes I seem a little . . ."

"Crazy and controlling?" I said.

He laughed, a low rich resonance I could feel in my own body. "You can choose to put it that way. Just know I am looking out for you, baby girl. Everything's gonna be all right."

Someone rapped the door knocker, waited a second, and then had the bright idea of doing a drum solo with the thing.

"Go get that," I said. My tongue felt thick in my mouth. His smell was intoxicating.

"I'm gonna get that," he said, slowing the phrase until it became loaded with desire. He stepped away and went downstairs.

I had to wait a moment before I followed him. I felt light-headed, for real. Was this, was *he*, what I wanted? Because if I wanted it, I could have it. But remember what Red said: *If I knew he was going to go for you like this, I would never have hooked you up.*

Heard Leo welcome his guests and waited to see if he would come back up to me. He didn't. I waited. So I went down. And then Leo ignored me. There was no other way to put it. I would walk toward him and his circle, and he would turn away and start introducing friends to other people. It made me feel, frankly, crazy. I mean, clinical.

I edged back against the mantel and nursed a gin and tonic. Two brothers staggered through the door with a grip of food. They unfolded a steam table and hauled out big pans of curry goat, roti, jerk chicken, and rice and peas. I wanted double portions of everything. Being ignored does that to me.

You can't eat at boy-girl parties. Not really *eat*. I took a tiny spoon of the musky goat curry and the beef patty with its flaky umber crust. Surveyed the room.

Robyn and Sharon were there from work. Robyn was still wearing her new wave miniskirt-with-tights look. I'd never seen Sharon like this before. She'd gone retro with a spaghetti-strap jumpsuit (but classy, not tacky), and her hair cascading down from a loose updo.

"Very Marilyn McCoo," I said.

She blinked. Probably didn't even know who that was.

"It's a compliment," I said.

"Oh, thank you. I saw this look in *Essence* last month. I'm man-hunting," she said.

"I can tell," I said. "You are going to bring home a trophy tonight."

"I better. I just broke up with my boyfriend."

"Ugh," I said. Go for yours, sister. As long as you don't go for Leo. *My* Leo. Or was that Kristal's Leo? Nobody's Leo, I guess.

Robyn did an exaggerated shimmy and raised her arms to the sky. "Sorry to interrupt your man talk but, did we forget . . . Your show at the Orchid was off the chain! It was fabulous."

"Fabulous," Sharon repeated as she surveyed the room for prey.

"What did Kay think?" I asked.

The two just smiled a polite smile.

"Thought so. It's all good. Has she forgiven me yet for disgracing the race?"

Robyn shook her head. "So, are you going to get any walking-away money?"

"Maybe. Not much. Anyway, let me go circulate."

"Why did you have to bring that up," Robyn hissed at Sharon as I turned away.

Leo and his crew had gathered between the bar and the tables. Judging by how hyped he was, he was probably still talking about his near-death experience. He gestured widely and kept his legs planted like tree trunks, with that delicious ass poked out.

I walked around to see who else was in the circle. Leo saw me and reached out and touched my arm. Suddenly I didn't smell the food. I smelled him—pickup basketball and shit-talking, slow jams and long kisses. Turns out he was explaining how fast food was a plot to kill the black man. "We need to get down with the organics. Everything on that table is organic," he said. Paused to introduce me as his "good friend." Continued his diatribe.

I started to wander away. "Let me help you find a place to sit, baby," Leo said. He steered me through the now crowded room to a table full of uptown moguls. I used to cover them back when I first started as a reporter at TV-C. They had a frozen look on their faces as I walked up that meant they were talking money, pussy, or both. I pulled a chair out just to scare them, then gave greetings and moved on. Passed by the table reserved for wives, girlfriends, and baby mammas a couple of paces away. These women were built like racehorses, lean and mostly light-skinned. They could walk miles in high heels and travel time zones without smudging their lipstick. Sitting next to them would make me feel like gum stuck to one of their Blahniks.

I perched on a low wooden stool against the far wall. Spilled my drink on my knee. Cursed everyone in the room for looking better and being richer than me. Leo had the place lit like an R&B video. The overheads were on superdim, and there were candles in all the corners. You know what? Everyone looks radiant by candlelight. We were back in Harlem! We glowed from underneath the skin.

"You look like you're as through with this mingling crap as I am." A man squatted next to me. The first thing I noticed was his old Chucks. Not exactly the designer footwear most of the crowd was wearing. I looked up and it was Bruce, who used to be my lunch mate at the commissary back in the early TV-C days.

"Bruce Xavier Yarrow!" I said, wobbling on my stool. "I don't think I've seen you since New Edition put out their comeback album."

"I was floating for a bit. Tokyo, London, Bahia, and East Saint Louis to name a few." He took another look at me on the stool with my knees practically up around my ears. "I would give you a hug, but you would tip over and go, 'I've fallen and I can't get up!'"

"Corny as ever. Now, Mr. Ha Ha, go get me some napkins. Please."

He returned and I dabbed at the liquid that had sunk into my outfit and took another bite of my beef patty. Bruce's hair was some ungainly mass halfway between an Afro and locks. He was wearing cargo pants and a black T-shirt with the sleeves cut off. It was a pretty rocking look for a freelance web designer, which is what he was doing last I heard. Big money working for some of these hip-hop websites.

"I was thinking about busting out of here. There's this great DJ . . ."

"I don't blame you. These things are always the same." I pointed to the diva table. "Tia's clothing label just bombed, thank God. Her shit was so tacky. And I heard Coco's man just had another child on the side . . ."

"Haters never win and winners never hate," Bruce said.

Was he talking to me? Was Bruce XY busting *me*? The best part of when we worked the urban entertainment beat together was racking up the stories we couldn't tell anyone. Between us we knew who was on crack or smack, which CEO liked to get peed on after sex, and who delivered beat-downs in the Presidential Suite at the Plaza. "What happened to the gossip whore that I knew and loved?" I said.

"Gave it up for Lent," he shrugged. "When I left New York. Never took it back."

Meanwhile, the table of fly girls was clowning Bruce right behind his back. Pointing, laughing behind their hands: just like junior high.

"That shit just holds you back," Bruce went on. "You know: worrying about other people's business and what they think of you."

I was about to ask him when he got so Gandhi, but the DJ turned the volume up loud. *Try to see it my way.* I know my music, and that was Stevie singing the Beatles. Hadn't heard that cut in a minute.

Bruce stood, held out his hand, and gestured to the empty dance floor. I hadn't finished eating. I had a wedgie I couldn't dislodge without reaching deep. And most important, once I started dancing with Bruce, the superbitches would start pointing at me. Yes, inside, I was still thirteen.

"No," I said.

"Come on!"

"Absolutely not." I waved him away with both hands.

"Come on, come on! What? You afraid of what these chuckleheads think of you? Because this is one chuckleheaded crowd and you are starting to make me think you are one of them." He stood up in the room and started chanting the zombielike refrain from the movie *Freaks*: "One of us! One of us!"

"Sit down, Bruce!"

"Not until you dance with me. '*One of us! One of us!*'"

"Fine!" I said. I took a moment to roll my eyes and brush the crumbs off my skirt. And then I reached for his hand and we hit the floor. "You remember that time Stevie played . . ."

"... At that soundstage in Chelsea ..."

"... Didn't even eat the food. I just shook his hand. And I felt ..."

"... Insane. Just that piano. Damn," Bruce finished. We were like that, the sentence-finishing kind of friends. Except, if I was being honest with myself, I had kinda dropped him. He was just too all over the place for the TV-C crowd.

But see, Bruce and I shared the same sound track to our lives. He was the only person I knew, besides me, who would put Mr. Wonder *and* The Clash in his all-time top-ten list.

When the DJ started pumping Fela, I fell into half-remembered African dance moves from a class I took right after college. Bruce surprised me by falling into step. The cascading riff of horns flowed around us and through us as we fell into the trance where music is everything.

"Do they know," Bruce said, having to raise his voice to make me hear him now, "what a genius this man is? Damn." Only a handful of people stepped out on the Afrofunk. And then, *bam*, the DJ switched things up. He was a thin brother with a high-top fade that screamed "1988," but he packed the floor. Biggie asked me to rub my titties if I loved hip hop. *Fight the Power*, said P.E. Naw, *Pop That Coochie*, countered Luke.

The floor was packed with all the tribes, from the patchouli head wraps to the players. Just before the DJ got on the mic and yelled, "I'm full up on requests, y'all," Latifah called for U.N.I.T.Y.

"Thank God he's going old school," I said to Bruce. I was actually beginning to sweat, I was dancing that hard. "Haven't bought a hip-hop record since, pffft, 'ninety-five."

"Hip hop is dead," said Bruce, looking genuinely sad. "We're just dancing on its grave."

We kept it moving for a couple more songs, but the DJ moved on to xtra, xtra whack mindless drivel from the top of the hip-hop charts.

So Bruce put his hand on my shoulder. "There's this party downtown, amazing DJ in from London." I nodded but I had just spotted Leo flowing through the dance floor like quicksilver, swaying by women just long enough to make them feel special.

"Sophie," Bruce said. I turned toward him, tried to focus. "It was great seeing you. I'm gonna head out now."

I looked at Bruce, so close to me, then Leo, doing his multiple seductions, and then at Bruce again. Bruce had that intense, almost autistic stare so many techies do, as if blinking wasn't part of his operating system. He focused on me completely, waiting. It was all too real, too honest, and too weird.

"Bruce, I've had a long day. I'm going to stay here," I said.

"Cool, cool. I was just asking, you know. Peace out." He gave me a quick squeeze and walked away. Later I'd feel guilty for dropping him, but I had business in this room. And I was willing to wait to finish it.

I hung by the corner while people paired off, passed numbers back and forth, got drunk, yelled, laughed, and headed off into the great good night. I hovered on the edge of a couple of bullshit conversations waiting for Leo.

The last people lined up to leave. I joined the queue by the closet and faked like I was getting my jacket.

First, I heard the door shut. Then Leo came up behind me and started breathing kisses onto my neck, holding my arms tight at my sides. He walked around to my front and stared at me, running his tongue over his full lips. Negro was always making love to himself.

I turned away a bit and he put one finger under my chin, guiding it back toward him. "Kiss me," he said. When I tried, he pulled away slightly so I had to stand on tiptoe to reach him. I watched as he walked the perimeter of the living room, blowing out the candles. All of a sudden it was like I was in a bad porn movie. But I couldn't help it. With each puff of smoke from the expiring candles, the anticipation, the wetness, the throbbing in my clit grew. *Now. Please,* I thought. Leo seemed ready to wander off alone, then came back and grabbed my hand.

He led me through the kitchen to a narrow wooden door. He inserted a skeleton key into the lock and led me downstairs.

The basement was only half finished. One exposed bulb threw a circle of harsh light on raw beams. Leo opened another door and took me to a cramped room. He flicked on another bare light. A clean, sheet-less double mattress covered the whole floor.

Leo knelt before me and took off my shoes, then his. His smile said *I knew you'd come.* He slid one hand under the skirt of my dress, pushing and rumpling it until he reached my nipples. His fingers were dry, rough, teasing.

"You look good, baby," he said, leaning me back against a wooden pillar. I jerked and pulled away. I slid my hand awkwardly behind my back, but Leo got to the splinter first, pulling it free and licking the boo-boo clean.

Then Leo shut the door. We were in a cramped cube. And then he pulled the chain to the bulb. We plunged into charcoal blackness, with light from the other room filtering around the sides of the door. I moonwalked on the springy mattresses, smelling him all around me.

Strong hands gripped my waist. I fell backward, twisting onto his body as he pulled me down onto the padded floor. Couldn't see, just feel. His chest, my hands on his shoulders. My hair in his mouth, his legs around mine. I scrambled to get astride him, pushing his arms down. Elbowed him in the mouth. By accident, I think.

"So it's like that," he said in the darkness.

"Yeah," I said. I heard him move, saw a blur of shadow. He pushed me, hard now. We backed into opposite corners. *Don't move until he moves. Don't move.* My whole body was a heartbeat, pulsing with red emotions I couldn't untangle—fear, lust, rage. *Now. No.* I loved the smell of his sweat. And then he was on me, one hand between my legs, another reaching for my face. Hard kisses, harder touch. *More. Don't think. Too fast.* I tried to get on top of him one last time. He flipped me facedown on the mattress, hard.

"Whose pussy is it?" he said, panting in my ear as he adjusted his hold. He took off his shirt, then gripped me with one arm as he took off his pants. Both of our bodies were slick now. "Whose pussy is it?" he said again, louder.

My face was stinging from the fall, and yet the only thing I could say, the only answer worth giving, was "Mine."

"Wrong answer," he breathed in my ear.

"You aren't the first person I've had this discussion with, you know."

"This is not a discussion! This is not up for discussion!"

I sighed.

"Come on, baby. It's all a matter of semantics . . . isn't that what you Harvard types would say? Some antics. You up for some antics? I need you to say it then. I need what *comes,*" he bore down, grinding his manhood against my buttocks, "out of your *mouth,*" he said, "to respect me. So . . . whose pussy is it?"

I hesitated for a second. I could argue, but I wanted him, right here and right now. "Your pussy," I said. "It's your pussy, Leo."

He breathed deep and entered me from behind, my face still pressed into the mattress. And you know what, he hit that spot, the one against the wall of my vagina, and while he straddled me, I quaked and trembled beneath him. It hit me all at once. I saw little sparks of red against a yellow background, starbursts like fireworks. Heard the rasp of the mattress scraping against the walls, and his moans. Felt his touch, a touch that took me completely into myself and made me feel like I was so small and could die right there. And since I'd turned as small as Alice in Wonderland, I walked through the looking glass and felt like I was him fucking me. I felt my life through someone else's breath. He was me and I was him and we were everything.

In the morning I let myself out. When I woke, there was enough light from a window to see Leo curled facing the back wall, naked as a jaybird except for socks. I hadn't noticed, last night, that he was still wearing socks. Ick.

I tried to buck myself up. I was a sexual adventurer, right? This was just another stripe on my pith helmet. But no matter what I told myself, the familiar self-loathing crept in from all sides. My dress was wrecked. I went upstairs and found one of Leo's track suits in the hall closet. Put it on and cuffed the pants, which kept slipping and dragging.

The morning was warm and bright. Still no cabs in Harlem. The jacket made me sweat like hell. A sprinkling of white couples passed the black folks, each in separate groups. Leo was made for this city, a city of perpetual strangers, which he probably loved more than he could ever love a woman.

I passed a wall covered in a bright graf. It proclaimed "Harlem Eternal" in looping spray paint. Hopped the number 3 and headed south.

Leo took me to the Palm. The maître d' led us to a table against a wall in the center of three dining rooms. The restaurant's walls are covered in portraits of their best customers, everyone from television celebrities to financiers and rappers, and I knew Leo wished he was up there. Getting his real estate would take a couple hundred more dinners, each of them several hundred dollars a pop. All I knew is that if he got his face on the wall, I wouldn't be paying for it.

"So I was thinking about a little promo tour," Leo said.

"I thought this was just a nice dinner between the two of us."

"It is."

"So please let's not talk business during dinner, just this once."

He slipped his hand into mine, "I'll make all the boring money talk up to you. Just come home with me tonight. That's a start."

I made a show of checking my watch. "How many women have been through your bedroom since I was last there?"

"No one, since I haven't had a bed in my bedroom."

"You know what I mean."

"I do. And I'll just tell you this: my king-size bed came today, special delivery through the balcony. Sophie." His voice ratcheted up in intensity. "We fit together, you and me. I have specific tastes. And you seem to share them."

I studied the menu as if my life depended on it. I was hoping the waitress would appear, and, before the silence grew too awkward, she did.

She was a sister with a short natural. The pantsuit uniform did nothing for her rounded figure. "Do you need a moment?"

"Yes," said Leo.

"No," I said. "I'd like the T-bone and the creamed spinach."

"Baby, you should think about . . . Lobster is lower in fat."

I shot him a glance. "Okay, I'll take the lobster . . . and the creamed spinach."

"How about the mixed vegetables?"

"I'd like the creamed spinach," I said, keeping my eyes fixed on our server. Thank God one of our people was making the big-tip money.

"You know that side is enough for two people," she said.

"I do. But I doubt he'll eat any."

"All that dairy will kill you," Leo said. The waitress took his order. He chose the vegetable plate, at the Palm! What a waste!

As promised, Leo didn't talk any more business during dinner. In fact, he barely spoke at all. At first I tried to fill the air with chatter. But then I let myself be silent, something I almost never did.

Silence scared me. Silence was a vacuum, a nothingness that made me feel like a nobody.

Leo barely said ten words as we finished dinner, paid the bill, and got the car from valet. He chose Miles's "Black Satin" for the drive uptown. He parked the car in a guarded lot two blocks away from his house, and guided me into his home.

The foyer and living room were dark. From the one light on in the kitchen, at the back of the living room, I could see the painters had finished the living room walls. They were the blue-gray of a winter sky. The oversize dark wood furniture with cream-colored cushions looked assured and imposing.

I started to go and take a closer look. Leo stopped me. He bent down and slid my shoes off my feet, kissing each one. And then he led me over to the grand, curtainless picture window that faced the street. He disrobed me right then and there. He worked from the bottom up. Skirt first, which he draped on an overstuffed armchair. Then my panties, which he removed by hooking his thumbs over the thin cords on my hips and pulling down, never touching my pudenda. Then my shirt. Then my bra. Anyone on the street could have seen, if they were looking closely enough. But since the window was shadowed and people were in their New York hurry, I don't believe anyone stopped to stare. I say "I don't believe" because for most of the time, I was facing the room, and Leo was facing me. Then he turned me around to the window, bare as the day I was born, and said, "You see that, baby."

"Yes."

"All that's yours. I will make sure that all of that is *yours*."

He led me upstairs and arranged me on his new king-size pillow-topped bed. The sheets were so soft they felt buttery. He splayed me out in an X formation, with my arms and legs spread wide, faceup.

"I'm going to ask you to do one thing for me."

"What is it?" I said, and my voice sounded startlingly loud after not speaking for so long. Leo put his hand across my lips. "Don't speak. Not a whisper. Not a sound. Not a moan, not a cry. Can you do that for me?"

I nodded.

He took a scented eye pillow, the kind you wear during massages, and put it on me. I couldn't see a thing. I heard the rustle of cloth, and then felt him creep on top of the bed.

I let him fuck me like I was dead. I didn't jump, jolt, or wriggle. I didn't let one sound escape my lips. I wonder if he was disappointed that it wasn't harder for me. But I was used to being quiet. I'd been quiet before.

There's a lot of things you can think about when a man has his dick inside you. Like birth control. I wasn't on any, and he definitely wasn't wearing a jimmy hat. That was dumb, right off the bat. Then there was money. Leo wasn't fronting any cash to make sure this band got off the ground. It would have to be me and Ari paying for the session time. And Ari didn't have any money, so really it was me.

Leo was going for a slow, deep, rhythmic groove, the kind Ice Cube said was "so deep, I put your ass to sleep." I didn't go to sleep, but I did go to twilight, that place where your dreams meet your waking. And I went back to the Man in the Moon dream. I'd been having it on and off since I was a kid, but it happened more as I got older.

I was in my bedroom, see, and I knew it was my bedroom even

though it was shaded black and gray like an old animated feature. I was in bed, and the moon was shining through the window into my bed. And then a man came in, and we made the shape of the moon together, with my head between his legs and both of us twisted into a circle.

As my mind slid between the past and present, I felt a piercing cold inside me. It was Leo's tongue, dipped in ice water. He'd done this before and it was my favorite from his repertoire. It turned and twisted like an eel. I still didn't make a sound, not even as I came.

Stood up. The room was shadowy but I could still see the door to the stairwell. I looked for my clothes. Dammit, they were downstairs.

"Baby, what?"

"I've got to go," I said.

Leo followed me, asking me if I didn't like it or what should he have done differently or what did I want.

"Nothing," I said, pulling on my clothes. "I've really got to go." And as I opened the door and walked through, I shouted over my shoulder, "It's not you."

I gypsy-cabbed it back to my apartment. Locked the door behind me, turned on the TV, and went straight into the kitchen. As usual, it was bare as a clear-cut forest. I couldn't trust myself around food, so I never kept more in the house than I was willing to eat at any one time. That meant that the refrigerator held an array of condiments: bright red sirachi chili paste; brown and yellow mustards; marmalade and mayonnaise; and, left over from who-knows-when, a few wilted leaves of mesclun.

I pulled out a sheaf of menus. In New York City, ordering in is just too easy to resist. First the sneaky delivery guys slip menus under your door, even if you post a sign saying not to. Everything is so damned cheap. Why cook a chicken when you can buy a barbecued one for less? Why bother washing dishes when you can get plastic flatware and paper plates? Every night's a picnic.

Right now I wanted buffalo wings. I could already feel the snap of the deep-fried meat between by teeth, and the burning at the sides of my mouth from the fiery sauce. It was the kind of food I could get lost in. The sheer mechanics of stripping each small bone completely clean could keep me occupied for fifteen minutes, twenty if I was lucky.

And that was what I wanted right now, to be so absorbed that I couldn't and wouldn't think. I didn't want to think about the Man in the Moon and the men in the house and the times back in elementary school when I was alone and when I was not.

I pick up the phone, dial the wings joint, give them my phone number. The delivery people already know where I live and what I want. They'll bring me food as I sit here alone.

Alone.

I'm back in my parents' house. It's the winter of second grade. I'm seven.

I get off the bus six blocks from my house. It's cold, but my mama has made sure I have gloves, a hat, scarf, sweater, *and* a coat. I walk past the candy store with the faded sign. I don't have a quarter. If I did, I'd buy Nowalaters or maybe the candy that looks like two eggs in the little frying pan. The sidewalks are empty. Grown-ups are still at work and most of the kids are already home. They walk to the school down the street. I take the yellow bus to the school where there are white kids, too.

All the houses on my block look different from each other. Some have siding; some are shingled; some are wide at the front, some are long from front to back. Our porch sags a little in the middle, but the paint's new. Next door, the porch doesn't sag but the paint is chipped, gray over brown. My friend Shantrelle lives there. She's in the same grade as me but goes to the school down the street instead of to Gifted and Talented. Her little brother's tricycle is lying sideways in the front yard. My mama says they don't know how to keep their place up.

My key is on a string of yellow yarn around my neck. I lean forward as I open the door with it still on, then pull my key out of the door and lock it behind me. Only then do I take the string off my neck and hang it on the nail by the door.

Sometimes I get scared. Our house makes noises. Sometimes it *huhhhhhh*'s like my Mama. And the floors crick and creak even when nobody's walking on them. I wish Mama still put me in After School. Miss Georgina has a swing set and a slide right in her backyard, and I'm not afraid of sliding down fast. But this year Mama said that After School was for babies, and I wasn't a baby, was I?

No.

So I follow the rules.

Don't drag home from school.

Don't talk to the men on the corner.

Don't open the blinds.

Don't eat before Mama gets back.

I'm standing in front of the refrigerator. It is round at the corners, huge and old. It rattles and huffs and puffs and then whines when it takes a break.

The light inside is bluish, like moonlight. I lift up bright Tupperware bowls filled with leftovers, shaking them to hear what's inside. The yellow one is a maraca of mixed vegetables. The heavy red one makes the sloshing sound of cold spaghetti.

I take it to the table my Nana gave us. It's red, too, with white speckles. A band of silver runs around the sides just like the diner in *Happy Days*.

I get a fork from the drawer by the sink and kneel on the soft vinyl chair with the rip in it. I love the sound the bowl makes when I take off the top. It croaks like a frog. I sit back on my heels and eat straight from the bowl. The sauce is sweet, just the way I like it. The noodles are squishy now, and the little bits of ground beef roll around my tongue.

I could eat the whole thing, but Mama would notice. I check my dress. It's a jigsaw of every color, so the tomato spots from slurping mostly blend in. I put down my fork and start to squeeze the top of the bowl on. I press too hard and it slides away, almost over the edge of the table.

I hold my breath and look around like there's someone there to look back. The only thing moving is the clock. It's right above the sink, on a wall painted robin's-egg blue like the cabinets. I close up the spaghetti, very, very carefully, and go back to the fridge.

Mama took us to the museum once and there was a painting of a table covered with food. It had to be important for someone to paint it. It had to make someone excited. I feel that way when I stare at the fridge. There are so many things to eat. I take them out one by one.

I slip one slice of yellow cheese from the stack and unwrap the plastic. The cheese doesn't really taste like anything but I eat it anyway.

I eat one olive out of the jar. Salty, vinegary.

I take one piece of bread out of the plastic. I want to toast it but Mama might smell. I put on butter and honey. It's like sunshine in my mouth.

I eat the smooth baloney in a circle, nibbling from the edges in.

I close the refrigerator. It's still two hours 'til Mama picks up Matthew and Erika and comes home.

I go and turn on the television. At three o'clock I either watch the *Stories* or *Speed Racer*. The people on the *Stories* have beautiful houses and fancy clothes. Mama likes it when I tell her what happened that day. But today I turn to *Speed Racer*. There's my favorite person, Racer X, in his black hood. I sit on the living room floor and turn the sound up. *Smash! Cra-bang! Oh, no, Speed!*

A hard thump. The television? No. The door. Now, Mama told Shantrelle she can't come over when Mama's not home, especially after she took the "P" out of our encyclopedia to do her homework and never brought it back.

I go to the mail slot and yell through it, "Shantrelle! Shantrelle! I'm watching *Speed Racer* and you can't come in! Na-aa!"

A finger pushes through the mail slot . . . a long finger. A face comes down and looks through: two big eyes and a moustache. I run to the other side of the living room.

"'Salright, little girl. Where's your Daddy?"

I sit on the floor with my back against the side of the sofa, hugging my knees.

"Answer me, girl! I asked you a question." His voice is sharp, angry. And then it gets sweet again. "Come on, Baby. You know I'm a friend of your Daddy's."

I haven't seen Daddy in a long time. If this man really is a friend of Daddy's, maybe he can tell me where Daddy is.

I get up slowly, go back to the door and peek under the bottom of the window blinds. The man is tall, much taller than Daddy. His lips curve in a smile but his eyes are mean. He's got his coat open and I can see his purple suit, my favorite color. His breath makes little white clouds.

Purple suit sees me peeking and bends down. I drop the blinds and back away. He opens the slot again. "You know me. I'm your Uncle Ray."

"I don't have an Uncle Ray," I say.

"You mean you don't remember me?" He sounds hurt.

I peek out again.

"No. Mama said—I'm not, I'm not supposed to open the door."

"That's real smart, honey. How old are you now? Six?"

Almost eight.

"So when is your Daddy going to be home?"

"He said he'd be home yesterday." I didn't mean to say this aloud. But the man in purple just says, "Okay, honey, I dig it." And then, as if he's talking to himself, "He cost us money. He cost us some money for sure. You can't just go and find a man in Hampton Roads with a standing bass at the drop of a hat, you knowwhumsayin? He cost us some money, and he's going to make good on that."

I don't know where Hampton Roads is, but it sounds important.

And then he's speaking to me again, "A week after you were born, I held you in my arms. We're blood you know, blood. Back a few generations, over a few cousins, and down again. We're blood. So when you see your Daddy, tell him Uncle Ray came. And give him this."

A plain envelope flops through the mail slot onto the carpet. It doesn't have anything on it, not even Daddy's name.

I hear the man turn and walk down the porch stairs. I sit and watch the envelope, listening for more footsteps, as if he's gonna reach his big hand through the little mail slot and grab me. The television goes from *Speed Racer* to commercial and back again. I pick up the envelope. It's shut tight. I find a pencil and write on it "Dady." Then I put it on the kitchen table.

Mama's gonna be mad.

I open the refrigerator again, and pull out the peanut butter.

My door buzzed: delivery. My hand trembled as I paid the short, red-brown man.

I alternated between bites of chicken and spoonsful of ice cream. It was a race. I was eating without tasting, trying to outrun my own mind. Then, as I had done since college, I walked to the bathroom to throw it all up, to purge myself and wipe myself clean from the inside out.

It was strange not having to go to work. I ordered in breakfast and lay around watching *Your Day in Music* before I left the house to see Red and Oscar. And then I couldn't decide what to wear. And then I decided to put on makeup.

The apartment was a shambles: takeout containers, bottles, and tissues strewn all over the place. So I had to clean up, just in case I didn't have a chance to do it before Leo came over. And then I was tired so I lay down to watch TV again. And fell asleep.

When I came out of my doze, I called Red but her cell didn't pick up, which meant she was probably still in the subway.

I decided to bust a move. Took the crosstown bus to the West Fourth Street station, and then I hopped an A train going south. I stood between a woman in a sharp mudcloth jacket and an androgynous teen in baggy jeans. I was almost on time for being late . . . meaning I would arrive within the fifteen-minute grace window that we gave each other. And then the train stopped in between stations because some other train in front of us was having maintenance problems.

I stepped off the train at 1:10 PM, seventy minutes late for my lunch/playdate, only to see Red and Oscar approaching as I stepped up the stairs.

"Kai Kai!" Oscar said, waving a toy truck in one fist and a beef patty in the other. I stooped in and gave his little Buddha belly a pat, kissed his forehead, rubbed his dark straight hair. Oscar was the color of wheat toast and, wearing a brown jumper, he looked like a strange little bear cub.

"Some people," Red said, one finger to her slender chin, "would call this a coincidence. Just as I'd given you up for dead, you appear! But I believe the universe has an inevitable logic, and your being *an hour and fifteen minutes late is part of that.*"

"An hour and ten minutes," I said. She gave me a long hard look. "I'm sorry."

"There are these things called cell phones. I know you have one."

"I know! But I thought I could make it, and then we got stuck by Borough Hall because of a mechanical in the train in front of us, and . . ."

"Never mind, girl. I gotta meet another mommy at my house at two. Let's have something warm before I have to go."

We went back to the Jamaican bakery where she'd been waiting and got two teas with milk and sugar and a slab of coco bread. I got a couple of chicken patties and callaloo patties to eat later. The sunny, clean storefront had Formica tables that were hardly used and a perpetually long takeout line snaking through the door. I unfastened Oscar from his stroller and he sat in my lap, dense and heavy as a cannonball, zooming a toy truck perilously close to my tea.

"Let me guess: the reason you haven't been calling me is because you're about to sign some fabulous record deal."

"We're working on it."

"You and Leo?"

"Yeah." I tucked my hair behind my ear.

"How's that going?" She looked at me, sucked her teeth. "You didn't. You didn't . . . Girl, I told you!"

"I know. I know."

"You said before it was going to be manager or horizontal mambo, but not both."

"I know what I said. But maybe that's just playing it safe. Maybe we can have it all."

Just then Oscar gave out a loud, wet, I'm-having-a-poopy fart. He just kept smiling. Red felt his diaper and said, "Maybe you can have it all, but you'll be the first person I know who found it. And Leo is not to be trifled with." Then, more to herself, "This was a bad move . . . ." She scooped Oscar out of my arms.

"Just let me live my life, Red, okay? And be happy for me. I have enough haters on tap already."

"Oh, girl, you know I got your back. Let me just go take care of this." She grabbed her diaper bag off the back of the stroller and stepped behind the counter to get to the back. The store didn't have a public bathroom but she came here so much that she was practically one of the family.

Kids were so great. They could be literally shitting their pants and they were still smiling. Us grown-ups, on the other hand, could turn just about anything into a tragedy.

"It's just that . . ." Red came back from the bathroom, buckled Oscar into his stroller, and launched into a monologue all at once. "I know you've been down this path before. You are an *amazing* talent, don't get me wrong. But this industry has never been kind to you, on a personal level."

"That's why I have Leo. He actually earns money, which is nice for a change. You've seen his house. And . . ." I saved the best for last, "I think he wants me to move in with him. Or maybe I'm tripping. But that's the way he makes it sound."

"Sophie, I'm going to say this one more time: Is Leo your boyfriend, or your manager?"

"I'm . . . I'm not sure yet. I mean, it's not like anybody else is asking me out and—no—before you jump in—we're not perfect. But we fit, sexually. And he tries to keep me on the straight and narrow with my diet and the drinking thing. He knows the music game. I really think he and I are meant to be together right now. Beyond that, I can't say."

"Watch your wallet and watch your heart."

"Thanks, Miss Buzzkill." I was loud enough that other people turned to look at us. Oscar just reached his little hand up and patted me on the side of my face, like a farmer saying to her horse, *There there, gal, settle down.*

Red finished off her paper cup of tea and sent it in a clean rim shot into a nearby trash can. "I know I'm overprotective of you, Soph. After all you've been through, give yourself a break. Take it slow. Don't spend all the money from The Video Channel. Keep track of what you spend *every day*—I mean, write it down in a notebook! You hear me! You did have money saved, right?"

"Well . . ."

"Oh, Jesus. Sophie, when are you going to grow up? Things aren't always cake and roses."

"I know."

"I just don't want to see you as sad as I've seen you, and I've seen you broken," she said.

"The only time I don't feel fake is when I'm making music. The only time I feel alive is when I'm making music. The only time I manage to finish songs I like is with Ari. So if we have to get to the finish line in some crazy three-legged race—or five-legged race with Leo, for that matter—I am *down*. I am back in the game. And if you're my friend, you won't try to get me out."

Red just put Oscar in the stroller and led us out of the restaurant.

By the time we got back to the subway it was raining, soft showers that wilted Red's Afro and made me put my jacket over my head. We walked down the stairs into the station, me carrying the front of Oscar's stroller, her carrying the back, him riding like a little prince on a litter.

Red was headed for her rapidly appreciating brownstone in Crown Heights; I was going back to primp for my night with Leo. We walked through the turnstiles together and hugged before going down our separate stairs.

"So are we still going to the reunion?" I asked.

"Of course," Red said. "Miss the chance to see all of our Harvard classmates and whether they have sticks up their asses? No way? I'm going to go solo, leave Lin and the baby at home, but it's too bad I can't wheel this around." She pointed to the back of her stroller. A bumper sticker on the kickstand read ASS, GRASS, OR CASH. NOBODY RIDES FOR FREE.

We hugged like we always did, so tight it was like we thought we'd never see each other again. And then I heard the grinding, moaning cry of an approaching express. Red and Oscar waved as I went down the stairs to get on the train. I got to my platform just in time to see her hustle her baby in and take off into the darkened tunnel.

⊳ 21 Tom Tom Club, "Genius of Love"

Leo arranged for us to start doing two gigs a week, one at the Orchid and one in Williamsburg. We were planning to start band auditions. And, of course, that's when Ari stopped calling me every day. We'd struck this agreement the last time he'd ODed. He'd call every day, read me the horoscope or the weather report, and then he could get off the phone and not worry about me calling 911.

We started doing our phone calls after a couple of rock-bottom moments.

Number one: imagine that you yourself are already high. And then you come home and find your husband (in name only, since you've filed divorce papers and he's moved out) sprawled out on your kitchen floor. You do the spoon trick they show on all the medical shows . . . hold it over his mouth; it fogs, that means he's breathing. You try to rouse him. He mumbles a few phrases that don't make any sense. You call the EMTs. And as soon as you call them, you panic: What if they find the drugs? I left him on the floor and started searching, cleaning, and flushing. I don't think the place had looked that good since I moved in.

Once the EMTs came, they just gave him a shot of epinephrine and he shot awake. He refused to go into the hospital and apparently, now that he was awake, they couldn't make him. Moreover, all hyped up, he punched through a layer of drywall. See, I'd told him I'd flushed his drugs down the toilet.

I'd never seen Ari that angry before or after. He was staying with a friend, but we still both had keys to the apartment. After he calmed down, we'd reached this agreement about him calling every day, even if we were mad at each other, even if we had nothing to say.

Incident number two: I was lying on a towel on top of the roof,

which was supposed to be locked except for emergencies except someone had hacked the lock long ago. I'd lain down a towel on the tar
beach, taken a Valium, and was listening to my Walkman. I'd had a
couple shots of vodka before coming upstairs. I might as well have been
on the moon.

So when I caught a bit of shade I was grateful. Not so much once
I discovered the person casting the shade was a tall girl with tattoo of a
bird's talon peeking from the hip of her jeans.

"Ari sent me," she said. Her voice was deep and gravelly, and her
knee-high black boots were well broken in. I stood to attention.

She was shorter than I'd thought. "Ari sent me to get the shit," she
said.

"The shit?"

"The shit.

"*What* shit?"

"*His* shit," she said. She puffed herself out the way pigeons do when
they're courting, or dogs do when they're bristling the hair on their
backs. I didn't need to think she was bigger than me to be scared of her.
It was five stories down and there was no railing around the roof's edge.
I walked toward the stairs, "Why don't we go in and talk about it."

She did a little shove-tap on my shoulder, "Why don't we not?"

"Well, if we're going to find the shit, we better go down into the
apartment, because it sure as hell ain't here."

The crazy girl stood still, so still I could see her eyeliner was tattooed on, not brushed across her lids. She contemplated for a moment.
"Okay," she said.

So I took her to my apartment. Our apartment. My apartment.
It was pretty cleaned out. In one corner Ari had left a pile of clothes
he couldn't sell at the secondhand store. I pointed and said, "That's all
that's left of him."

The girl grabbed a fancy organic chocolate bar that I'd spent my
last few dollars on and ate it in a few bites. Then she told me that Ari
had promised her some heroin, against which she'd advanced him some
cocaine, and she was here to collect.

I told her to feel free to look around. I really wish she hadn't eaten my chocolate.

Two hours and one takeout meal later (wings and mozzarella sticks, charged to my one good credit card), mean girl actually found the heroin inside a wasabi container in the refrigerator. "Your boyfriend was really holding out on us," she said.

And I said, "First of all, he's not my boyfriend, he's my husband. And he's gone. There is no 'us.'"

Before the girl walked off, her hips shaking like maracas she was moving so fast, she turned around and said, "I feel sorry for you."

And it's when you have junkies saying they pity you that you start thinking about this sanctity-of-marriage stuff, and remembering what the priest said about 'til death do us part, and how you'd never get divorced like your mama and daddy, and then thinking for the first time that the unthinkable was the inevitable.

A week after Ari's last call to give me the weather report, his number showed up on my cell phone. When I picked up, he was making these wordlike sounds but they didn't fit together. He couldn't answer me when I asked if he was okay.

I took a cab to his place in Spanish Harlem, watching the city change from low apartment buildings to glass office towers to designer boutiques and finally the bodegas and projects above One Hundredth street.

From the stoop of his building I could see the door to his ground-floor apartment half open, but I couldn't get through the front door. I called again and again, but he didn't answer the phone. This wasn't the first time he'd disappeared, but every time was a crucial one when I thought he might be killing himself.

I ran my hands down the entire roster of apartment buzzers, hoping that someone would break the first commandment of city life and let me in without knowing who I was. I waited and tried again, punching every single button one by one this time . . . and did it yet again.

Through the glass of the front door I could see a door open and a short, barrel-chested man appear. He was a caricature of a New York super, with a stained white undershirt and long shorts draped over hairy legs. He opened the door a crack. I spoke fast.

"My friend is sick," I said. "1-B. Can I come in?"

"Yeah," he said with a sour look. "Sick." He opened the door wide and the sound of television blared from his open door.

"You his girlfren'?" he asked. He was looking at my breasts, which meant I didn't have to tip him for my trouble because my body already had.

"No, I'm . . . ." And I wasn't sure why I told the truth, but I did. "I'm his ex-wife."

His eyebrows went up. "You loyal," he said. "I like that in a woman."

"Well," I said, reaching out to shake his hand, "thank you."

He took my hand, raised it to his lips, and gave the back a sticky kiss. I smiled. I wanted to punch him in the fucking face.

I yanked Ari's apartment door open and saw him lying on the couch, his head lolling on an armrest, a half-burned cigarette still smoking between his fingers. The big open loftlike space with mismatched antique furniture looked so gorgeous when it was clean. But now dirty clothes and old magazines covered the floor. Crisis was licking the edge of her master's hand and whining, her brown Rottweiler eyebrows seeming to arch with concern. I grabbed the dog by the collar and hugged her tight. "It's okay, honey," I said as much to myself as her. "It's okay. Let's get you some dinner."

Part of my brain was screaming, "Don't wait another instant, he could be dead already." It was a little fuck-you to feed the dog first. She probably needed to pee more than she needed food.

I scrubbed clean the crusty silver bowl and began to open a can of dog food. Crisis kept running back and forth between me and Ari, who occasionally let loose a mumbled fragment of a one-sided conversation, or moved his cigarette even closer to the couch. With the can half open, I ran over and took the cigarette from him, burning myself in the process.

"Ari?" I said. "*Ari?*" Jesus. When I met him, he was one of a posse of cool, rich punk-rock kids, taking out their daddy-anger through their music. I drank the Kool-Aid, thinking that his world-weary pose made him wise. By the time I started doubting his magic, I was in too deep to stop caring about him. But maybe I should. Maybe I should start right now.

And then he said, "Hey."

I said "Hey" back. I kissed him then, on the lips, telling myself it was a Sleeping Beauty moment, that every time I kissed him, no matter how gone he was, that worked. And he sort of sighed this time, but he didn't move, and I thought, *Fuck you for making me feel.*

"I'm feeding the dog," I said, walking back over to the kitchen. He said something that might have been "She likes that" or "My bike rack" or hell, who knows?

Crisis took the food in huge gulps, so quickly I feared she'd be sick. I went back to Ari.

"Let's walk," I said, hoisting him to his feet. His legs were rubbery but held. "Come on, baby, walk with me. Come on, baby. Come on."

He ran his fingers through my tears and smiled. "Pretty."

I hardened my voice. "We've gotta take the dog for a walk," I said. "Ari, let's take the dog for a walk." He only listened to me when I spoke like that—like his mother, or mine.

I let him lean against my shoulder as I grabbed the leash from the coffee table, hitched it to Crisis's collar, and headed for the door. No keys. I ripped the cover from a magazine and used it to keep the front door lock from catching, hoping no one came in and no one got robbed.

Crisis stopped immediately and took a long piss and huge runny shit on the sidewalk. I hadn't brought any bags and this couldn't easily be scooped, so I brought some supermarket flyers from a doorstep and put them over the mess.

Ari smelled. He smelled like stale sweat, but under that, he smelled like the man whose chest I used to rub against and hope I smelled a bit like him when I pulled away. He was starting to wake and walk straight. Then Crisis began to tug at the leash. God knows the last time she was allowed to run, and I struggled to keep the man leaning on me from toppling over as we lurched. Finally I tied Crisis to a lamppost and shook Ari, shook him and said, "You take the dog. *You* walk."

Instead, he leaned against the lamppost. He rubbed his forehead against the filthy metal like it was a cold glass of iced tea. He slowly untied Crisis's leash and turned back towards the house.

"You can't live like this. And you can't blame your father for trying to help you!"

He said, "I can."

"Don't call me, then."

"I didn't."

"You did."

"I did?" He was surprised but unrepentant.

"Yes," I said. "When was the last time you ate? When was the last time you fed the dog? I think she's sick," I said. But she was skipping along like a child at a carnival, happy to be back with her man at last. Her man.

"Let me take you to the hospital."

"No," he said. And I knew I couldn't have him committed against his will, not if he was sobering up and neither a danger to himself or others. If he didn't appear to be.

"Do you remember anything?" I said, as we got to his stoop.

"I remember I loved you," he said.

Loved.

The next weekend was our tenth Harvard reunion. I didn't expect Ari to come. But as I sat there in the Agassiz Theatre waiting to receive an award that I didn't deserve, who did I see walk in? Ari was arm in arm with an illustrated woman. Her tattoos were brightly colored, swirling Japanese figures of koi, geisha, demons. I didn't think she was class of '91, but it's not like you can memorize the faces of 1,600 people and then predict what they'll look like in a decade.

A voice reached through my cloud of brain clutter. "Miss Lee?"

Right. I was just part of a panel of Radcliffe alumnae, moderated by Mrs. Nancy Morton-Cuffee. She was the color of a paper bag and may have graduated with W.E.B. DuBois for all I knew. "Dear, how did you manage, at the age of twenty-five, to host a television show that speaks to your generation, and to become a role model for teens across America?"

The effusive praise was meant to center me, but it did quite the opposite. I told the people at Radcliffe that I'd left The Video Channel, but Ms. Morton-Cuffee didn't seem to have gotten the memo.

"I believe that all people have the potential to communicate. That's what my mother taught me. She's retired now, but for years she worked with emotionally disturbed patients at a group home down the street. The first thing I noticed"—and I paused here, not sure how it would go over—"was that most of them were white. There weren't a lot of people of that color in our neighborhood. But as I grew older, I came to understand they were different in other ways. Sometimes they were scared or angry or sad. Sometimes they were happy for no reason. My mama always managed to speak to each of them not just as if they were human beings, but as if they were family. So when I think of myself as a communicator, I know where I got it from—my mama."

The audience exploded into applause. They always do when I make that speech. Even my mother put her hands together, though she'd heard the same words a dozen times before.

"But there are many ways to communicate," I continued. "And so effective three weeks ago, I decided to leave The Video Channel, on amicable terms, and go back to my first love: songwriting."

The audience didn't know quite what to do with this one. Some clapped; some sat with their hands in the laps. My mother, to whom I'd broken the news, sat dour. Mrs. Morton-Cuffee smiled broadly, then brought the panel to final remarks and a close. Our host doled out awards, each in the shape of a golden coin with the Radcliffe insignia. Cue more applause.

I looked for Ari. He and his consort were already hustling out the door. I stepped over to the podium, thanked Mrs. Morton-Cuffee, and helped her down the stairs. My mother was already on her way over.

I made introductions.

"*Enchantée*," said my mother. We Lees liked to pretend we were partly Creole, even though there was no evidence whatsoever to support that belief.

"So you're staying on for the weekend?" Mrs. Morton-Cuffee asked my mother.

"No. I just came to Boston—excuse me, Cambridge—for the award. To support Sophie."

"You must be as proud of your mother as she is of you," Mrs. Morton-Cuffee said to me, adding, "You've made a wonderful success of yourself. What a well-deserved break to go back to your music. I heard you were quite respected in underground circles."

My mother cringed.

"Actually, we perform once a week and the rest of the time we're writing songs and cutting deals, so it's quite the full-time job. Mama," I said, "would you like some refreshments?"

"The train's leaving soon," Mama said.

"The train's leaving in two hours. It's a thirty-minute ride on the 'T,'" I said.

"Well, my dear, there's a taxi stand right outside the gates," said Mrs. Morton-Cuffee. "And then you wouldn't have to go up and down all those stairs."

"That would be profligate spending," said my mother.

"Well," Mrs. Morton-Cuffee said, while fondling her pearls, "you still have your legs."

We fell into one of those awkward silences that happen when people who've pretended to have the same class values suddenly have to 'fess up as to how different they are.

Finally, a group of older women approached and Mrs. Morton-Cuffee broke the silence. "I must be off. Congratulations."

"Thank you," my mother and I said at the same time.

Then it was my turn to face the posse. Red and Mimi had been waiting in the wings. I told them that if they saw me alone with my mother for more than fifteen minutes, they were to immediately come to my rescue. They did so just a little early.

"Mrs. Lee-ee!" That was Mimi the Loud. She was dressed impeccably, though in an outfit better suited to our college days than something a mother of three might be expected to wear. Red really was as Creole as they come, and I believe her ethnic authenticity made my mother nervous. Red stood on tiptoe to kiss Mama on both cheeks, and then murmured an extended greeting in Louisiana French. Mom murmured, "*Bien, merci.*"

"I'm just going to take Mama to the 'T,'" I said.

"Such a short trip!" Mimi said. "We're staying at my aunt's house. . . . would you like to spend the night?"

I made a stricken face and then reverted to my normal impassive gaze just before Mama turned back toward me.

"I think my daughter likes me better in small doses."

I laughed weakly.

"I guess we'll leave you alone, then," Mimi said, giving Mama a big bone-cracking hug. My mother was always startled when touched, and then she tried to hide it, which made it worse.

A few minutes later we were walking through the cobblestoned streets of Cambridge. On some level, this is where the idea of America had begun—the idea of meritocracy, and who could and couldn't compete. It wasn't a world built for black men, and black women were an absolute afterthought. But eventually we came, and so did people from across the world, all scrabbling to prove they were worthy of the same education the trust fund babies got. It made my mother so happy to see me in this place, as if I had validated not only the family name but the entire race.

Mama and I got to the T station. An acoustic guitarist played Dylan for change by the escalators. We went down into the bowels of the earth, pausing at a middle level to insert our tokens in the turnstiles, then riding another escalator to the bottom.

On the way down, I let my mind fill with facts and numbers instead of emotions. The Boston T has 272 miles of track, compared with 656 miles for New York. While the New York Subway has color-coded maps, the trains are given letters and numbers like the A, B, C, D, Q, 1, 2, 3, 4, 5, and 9. In Boston, the train lines are known by their colors. Harvard is on the Red Line. It's the second stop across the Charles River, the channel that separates Cambridge from Boston and where elegant crew teams row and race.

It was Friday of reunion weekend, and rush hour at that. The plan was for me to walk her into the station and then go back to my friends, but with every step I felt more guilty for not wanting my mother to stay. I had a vision of Mama riding on the crowded T, one arm up against a railing, one weighted down with her enormous handbag. Then she would get to the Amtrak station and wait, and look at the other people, and size them up the way she'd taught me to size other people up. Who had bright new clothes but shabby travel bags? Who checked the pay phones for quarters? Who had casual clothes but expensive shoes? And who, like my mother (and like me), looked surreptitiously at others, trying to figure them out?

Mama would sit on the train for hours, only slipping off her tight, hot shoes once they passed Philadelphia. And then, finally, she would debark, pick up her car from the lot across from Baltimore

Penn Station, and drive back to the clean white house where she now lived alone.

"Is Ari here for the reunion?" Mama said.

"Yeah."

"Well," Mama said, "don't do anything foolish."

"I think that ship sailed a long time ago."

Mama laughed, and in the kernel of her laugh was some old hurt she thought I couldn't begin to understand. She started with a hard, sarcastic chuckle, and then moved into a lower, quieter register.

"What?" I said.

"You always want to be different from me. But I guess we share something now."

And so we did. Failed marriages to men we still loved. Trite but true. And when was the last time she saw Daddy? Probably around the last time I saw Daddy, a good fifteen years ago.

We could hear the train begin to pull into the station. Passengers began to push their way to the edge of the platform. The train lights limned the tracks.

"You know I never liked him," Mommy said, adjusting my collar.

"I know," I said. I guess she thought that would make me feel better.

The train stopped, doors opened. "I love you," I said, giving her one more hug.

In return, she said good-bye.

The heels of my shoes sank deep into the damp grass. The stone-walled courtyard was gently lit by crisscrossing strands of small lights and the reflections from dorm room windows. Someone touched me on the shoulder. I jumped.

"Sophie?"

He was tall with thinning brown hair and the suit of a high-priced lawyer. Next to him stood a girl-next-door type in an Empire-waist dress, four or five months pregnant.

"Henry," he said. "From Chicago."

"I used to live in Chicago," I said.

"I know." His smile collapsed on itself. "We used to hang out there."

"Of course," I said to Henry. I turned to his wife. "Of course." I hesitated for a second, trying to think of some well-timed nicety. Instead, I turned and walked away.

As soon as I turned my back, I remembered him. I'd been in one of those flip-floppy phases, trying to decide if I was only dating black men, of if I was running the entire field. Henry and I had sex once while I was filming a segment for The Video Channel on new indie rock bands. He was just starting out at a big firm in Chicago; I was just finalizing my divorce. We made a date for rebound sex and pizza. The sex was cold. I remember that kissing him felt like making out with a rubber tire. Henry's dick (though these things are not supposed to matter to good girls, and I still thought of myself as one then) was the size of a baby carrot.

Now, the pizza I'd remembered without prompting. The crust was thick and soft like the inside of a pretzel. The sauce was not too sweet, the cheese pliant and gooey and heaped with every meat and vegetable in the kitchen.

Henry. *Henry.*

Why had I forgotten him? Memory like Swiss cheese.

I walked over to the bar and ordered another gin and tonic—very Cambridge—and overheard Red saying to a group of suburban-corporate black women, "If you want to fuck a black girl up, just send her to Harvard." Everyone laughed, including me. But I remember the days when the black clique (and there was one, and I wasn't part of it) used to talk behind my back. They didn't know what to do with a sister sporting a Mohawk and her off-white boyfriend.

A tall freckle-faced man, like RuPaul without the makeup, walked over and put his arms around one of the women in the circle.

"Sophie," the woman said, "this is my husband, Marvin."

"Marvin!" I said, forcing brightness. "How's business?"

He clearly remembered his parting gift to me right before graduation. Like some sixties revolutionary, he told me the community didn't need any more bourgeois artists. I guess that distinguished his own whack-but-black poetics from my music. Now look at him, all bankered up.

"Great suit," I said. And then, in case that seemed flirtatious: "Both of you. Great . . . outfits."

Red was looking at me like I was completely demented, and I deserved the look. Luckily, just then, one of the other women said, "Sophie has that TV show. I *love* that show."

"Actually, I just quit," I said.

"Oh," she said.

"I'm hoping to give back to the community," I said. "With my art. You know, something revolutionary."

Marvin winced.

Red came to life, saying some quick good-byes. "Well, I think I better get baby girl here home. It's been a long day."

"Don't treat me like a kid, Red," I said too loudly.

"Further evidence," Red said, grabbing my arm and pulling me away. She was not above completely humiliating me if she thought I was going to do worse to myself.

People were starting to leave the party in clusters. I noticed the lighting had shifted from a warm ambient glow to a harsh brightness, the universal signal for time to bounce.

"So what are we doing next?" Mimi said, sneaking up behind us.

"I have no idea." The whole conversation with Marvin had soured me on the idea of partying with my classmates. I thought about gathering a crew to go to one of the goth clubs by the Fenway like we used to do, but it seemed like too much trouble.

"I heard a bunch of people are going to the Hong Kong for Scorpion Bowls."

Red rolled her eyes. The sickly sweet cocktail was the kind of thing you drank when you were eighteen and sporting your fake ID, not when you were thirty.

"Come on, party pooper. Let's just go see who's there," Mimi said.

The night was deliciously mild, and clusters of people sat on the steps of the freshman dorms and the class buildings. A group of what looked like undergrads ran through the yard whooping and hollering. They'd probably just gotten off a shift as reunion bartenders or babysitters. There was a lot of money to be made this time of year if you wanted.

We came up on Widener Library. It was as grand and imposing as the Supreme Court building in D.C., with wide stone steps and columns. Then we wound around past the VES building, and saw a woman with bright tattoos and her consort heading toward one of the older folks' anniversary parties.

"That's not . . . ," I said.

"It is," Red said.

I didn't know what was going on, but it couldn't be good. "Ari!" I yelled. "Ari. *Ari!*"

He grudgingly stopped and turned toward me.

"Ari, where'd you disappear to? You missed the party."

His eyes were too wide and too bright, but his words came out slowly and clearly. "Oh, I'm going to the party."

I looked at the signboard by the door. HARVARD 40TH REUNION. His dad's year.

"You can't," I said, moving so I stood between him and the building.

"Why not?" he said. "Dad's not even returning my phone calls. So I guess I'd better come to him."

Ari's dad, a music mogul who made his early money off rap acts, had cut Ari off from his trust fund. I liked Richard Klein, despite the fact that he only dated black women (and kept 'em comin' and goin'). Richard still insisted I call him Dad, which was a little creepy considering his third wife was Ari's and my age.

I said to Ari, "I thought you said you were never taking his money again."

He looked embarrassed, then smiled. "I must have been high when I said that." He started to walk around me.

"Girls!" I turned to Mimi and Red. "Hey, you!"

The illustrated woman shrugged. "What do you want me to do, tackle him?"

Just then, in a spectacular bout of bad timing, Richard Klein came out of the VES building, his newest wife adoringly on his arm. I loved her pewter-silk cocktail dress, and for a second I almost went in with a compliment instead of a warning. Red hustled up and beat me to it.

"Your son is about to cuss you out for cutting off his trust fund," Red said, her southern drawl coming out, as it tended to, when she was under pressure. "I suggest you make a date with him to discuss this in a more civilized manner."

"Dad, look," Ari said, stepping forward, sounding more petulant than menacing.

"Ari Malcolm Klein." His stepmom still knew how to stop a bratty child dead in his tracks. "You will *not* ruin your father's night."

"Look . . ."

"Look *nothing,*" she said, moving closer to Ari. And I swear I heard her say under her breath that he should expect a cashier's check on Monday, so leave well enough alone. Maybe I imagined it. But wouldn't that just be the way to keep a wicked stepson out of your hair if you needed it? Just kick him a little something back.

"Do we have an understanding?" she said, for all to hear.

Ari didn't talk back.

"Okay," she said, and turned on her heel and went back to Ari's father's side.

Ari was already walking away, and the tattooed girl followed him. I was tempted to go give him a piece of my mind, but Red called me back.

"Oh, let him be. Baby." She looked me in the eye. "Give yourself a little time off from minding other people's business."

Red, Mimi, and I ended up postmorteming the whole thing over Scorpion Bowls at the Hong Kong. They thought I was right: stepmama *was* kicking him a stay-quiet bribe.

"She's younger than he is," I said. "Okay, she's younger than all of us."

"Yup," said Red. "I got the scoop. Stepmomma's still twenty-nine years old. And she had Ari by the balls. It doesn't matter that he hates her. You know, at this day and age I actually wish I could get married."

That totally came out of nowhere. I said, "I thought you said marriage was a bankrupt institution, even aside from the gay-folks-can't-get-married aspect of it all."

"It's different when you're a parent," said Red. "You know I could die tomorrow and in some states if my parents didn't want Lin to see my baby, she would never see Oscar again. Thank God Mama and Daddy are not that kind of people, although there is a reason they are not in the chain of command to take over if anything happens to us."

I thought Red was going to start cracking up at her own joke, but she started crying instead. I could count on one hand the number of times I'd seen her do that.

"It's my hormones. I just started bleeding again. Stopped breast-feeding, you know."

I had no idea but I didn't say that.

"Hey, I have an idea!" Mimi said. I thought she was going to suggest that we still go clubbing, but I was way too tired for that. "See, I've always wanted to plan a wedding."

That was, in fact, true. Every time Mimi talked about getting a job outside the home, she said she wanted to be an event planner. And then she'd volunteer to be on the committee of some huge, expensive, traumatic benefit. And then the trauma would wear off. Apparently now she'd found her new target. "Father's going to be away most of the summer."

Red dabbed her eyes. "It was just hormones."

"If you look me in the eye and tell me you don't want me to use Daddy's garden to throw you and Lin a wedding party, then I won't. But I need something to do or Nestor will die."

Red looked down at her lap. I guess that meant the party was on.

Exactly three weeks later, I woke up in Mimi's father's house, a couple of hours drive north from the city. It was a seven-bedroom estate bordering a nature preserve. It was done, like so many million-dollar homes around it, in a faux rustic style, as if the people who inhabited these mansions were farmers and not brokers.

The house had a prominent stone chimney that saluted from one side of the brown shingle building. Inside, the place was a technological marvel, with heated tile floors, whirlpool baths, and a home theater in the basement. The broad, manicured lawn could hold a Civil War reenactment. That's where Red and Lin would get hitched by an actual minister, though not within the bounds of civil law, this afternoon.

I went downstairs to see about putting something greasy in my system. Mimi and I had stayed up sampling vintages from her dad's private cellar last night. But you wouldn't know it looking at her. Mimi was up feeding the kids, looking like a dewy flower. The kids were doing what kids do, screaming at each other. With each yell I thought my head would explode.

"Inside voices, inside voices," Mimi said. But she didn't put any *umph* into it, and they didn't pay attention to her at all.

One of the family's maids asked me what I wanted to eat. I hesitated for a moment—it still made me uncomfortable to be catered to like that—but said bacon and eggs. The woman was Mexican, Latina at least, with deep red-brown skin and wavy black hair. She was a full head shorter than me and went about her business almost invisibly.

"So how are my favorite babies?" came a voice behind me.

"We're not babies," said Elizabeth, running to give her uncle a hug. Bernard had started to gray and it looked good on him. He gathered all three children in his arms at once and lifted them high. They screamed as if they were being squeezed to death, not smothered in pleasure. So he put them down and then they begged for him to do it again.

While Mimi was tall and willowy, Bernard was short and muscular like his father. He had the unplaceable accent of someone who'd lived in Europe half of his life. The last time I'd seen Mimi's brother his hair was longer, curly, and dark. We were in my house, and both of us were naked. I don't know what made me stop calling him back. Fear, I guess. Fear that I would screw this up the same way I did with every other man in my life. I owed it to him, and to Mimi, not to do that.

I said hello, the simple word almost catching in my throat.

"Sophie? You look younger than the last time I saw you."

I started to make some silly self-deprecating comment and stopped. "Thank you."

"So you're well."

"I'm well. And you?"

"Well."

We stood and looked at each other for a moment. I cuddled Elizabeth and started finger-combing her hair.

"Well . . . ," I said.

"Beautiful flowers," he said.

"Yes."

Rows and rows of centerpieces were waiting to be placed on the tables outside. They had huge, spiny red flowers sprouting from the middle of the arrangement.

He pointed to the center flowers, vivid and alien. "Ginger." And then he went around the arrangement. "Nasturtiums, roses . . . all edible."

"Roses aren't edible," I said.

"Oh?" he said.

We are in an Indian corner deli in Manhattan. Bhangra music fills the cramped store. We've come for cigarettes, because like all good Europeans, even ones who were born in America, Bernard smokes. He sees some of his favorite candies from England: rose jellies. He slips a dollar across the counter and tears the package open. He breaks a candy in half and lifts it high, the red jelly threatening to drip down on my face. I close my eyes and open my mouth.

"Yes," I said, just as Elizabeth bumped against my leg. "Well, I better get dressed."

"Aren't you going to eat your breakfast?"

The maid was standing discreetly by, holding a fresh plate of bacon and eggs.

I smiled at Bernard. I'd forgotten how he could make me forget.

Everything went swimmingly with the wedding except for the dull pain behind my eyes and the fact that my ass was too big for my dress. Red had offered to alter our gowns when we were fitted. That seemed like a high price for the bride to pay. And besides, I'd decided that that little five-pound gap between me and the dress fitting would be resolved by cutting out a drink here, a dessert there.

And yet, today the ass and the dress still did not get along. I'd gone to a department store and gotten one of those butt minimizers made out of über-strength elastic, the kind that could have been used as a tourniquet. It made my posterior smoother, but no less large.

Consequently, when I tried to put on my dress, I heard a distinct *errrippp*. The girls and I were all getting dressed together in the master bedroom. Red, Miss Cool Calm and Collected, started hyperventilating. Mimi left to find a seamstress and a shawl.

One of their maids had whipstitched the dress into the best form it would be. And maybe it was all a blessing. When I draped the bit of black lace just right, it covered not only my derriere but my big bologna arms. If only I had friends who were the same size as me, they wouldn't pick out these tiny scraps of cloth every time someone got married.

The ceremony was short, dry, and Northern WASPy, even though Mimi was Jewish, Red had grown up Catholic, and Red and Lin both were practicing Buddhists. Lin and the minister had once shared a group yurt at the Michigan Womyn's Music Festival. Red wore a long white slip dress; and her girl had on a white tunic and pants. They looked radiant. But the ceremony felt a little too cold and sterile and perfect, not like the kind of wedding I'd imagined Red would have wanted, with bright colors and screaming kids. Even the kiss was chaste. I guess there were too many scandalized relatives around to go in for a big show of tongue. Not that I'd recommend a tongue kiss at a wedding, just a little more of a show.

Afterward, I went and met Leo. "Beautiful, huh?" I said.

He *humphed.*

I ignored him. I would like to think my boyfriend was not a homophobe, so I had a strictly don't ask/don't tell policy on *his* attitudes.

"Your eyes look red. Were you drinking last night?"

And smoking weed, too. "Allergies," I said. Before he could tear into me again, an older lady who'd been sitting on the other side of us came up and started asking Leo about the business venture he'd been talking about.

"Oh, I'm being rude," she said to me.

"Not at all." I smiled to her and winked at Leo. Let her have him, for now.

I have to grant Leo this: he made a charming guest, talking with the old guys and getting admiring looks from the old ladies. I joked, as we later danced, that he should watch his step because he might end up kidnapped by one of the sexy over-seventy set.

I was pleasantly soused again, so much so that I was getting haphazard about the placement of the shawl. Our dinner plates were being cleared away and half of the head table had already gone by the wall to smoke. Mimi went after them. It was time for a toast.

I find that toasts are essentially comedy routines. Comedy routines tend to work best when you're completely honest but pretend you're only joking. I lifted my notes from my tiny little decorative purse, cleared my throat, and as Mimi rose to introduce me, felt the sweat began to bead on my palms.

I told everyone hello and good evening, thanked the Lemieuxes, Red's family; the Huangs, Lin's family; and Mimi's family, the Feldts. Then I lifted the paper and tried hard not to look like I was reading.

"Many people have met Red over the years and marveled at her beauty, her intelligence, her poise. Other people have wondered about something else: She went all the way to Harvard just to sew?"

Red's mother covered her mouth with her hand, laughing. She knew that one came from her.

"Yes, Red went all the way to Harvard just to sew because she has a gift. She believes that wearable art isn't just for rich people, it's for all people. That's why she's marrying . . . a librarian."

"I know the Huang family wanted you to be a lawyer, Lin. But I know when you saw Red walking through the stacks, looking for a book on medieval costumery, you felt compelled to *serve*. That's a lot better than meeting your boyfriend in the drunk tank when you're a public defender."

Some of the Huangs laughed; some didn't. It was a shitty joke. I just couldn't think of anything else.

"Lin," I said, "I look forward to getting to know you better. Know that you're the light of Red's life. Both of you know a good woman when you see her. Cheers."

Everyone saluted with their champagne glasses, or for those not drinking, whatever was full.

Red and Lin looked at me gratefully. I know they expected far worse.

I'd been surprised to see Red's last ex, this DJ named Shar, in the crowd. She was *hot*—hair dyed red and cropped nearly to the skull; dark skin; sardonic smile. She and Red fought all the time. But then again, every single one of Red's exes was in the crowd, even the hetero two-night stand who was Oscar's dad. It was a lesbian thing, I guess.

As the staff began clearing the dessert plates, everyone made those stretching motions you do when you're waiting to see what comes next.

"Would you care for a walk?" said Bernard.

I thought about begging off, but Bernard and I had to talk sometime. "Not until I change out of this dress," I said. I ran into the house, nearly upending a man carrying a huge platter of dirty plates. I took off the dress to find that the hole in the back had reappeared. I hoped no one had seen.

Two aspirins and a pair of jeans later, I came back downstairs to find Bernard talking to his father. It was easy to see what he would look like in thirty years, still handsome, still fit, hair more salt than pepper. They were talking money, long incomprehensible sentences about assets and risk, black boxes, and statistical models.

Bernard said good-bye to his father and we began to walk, in silence, along the grounds. There were miles of hiking trails that began just past the lawn. The leaves on the trees, mainly oak, were hearty and green, and the sunlight filtered through them to the shady paths below.

We talked about his father, who was probably going to get married again; and about his job, which I still didn't understand; and about how wonderful it was that Red and Lin had found each other.

"So what do you want to do?" he said suddenly.

"Now?" I said, sweat beading on my palms.

"With your life?" he said.

"My life? Wow. Make the album, of course. Make some money, buy an apartment, take long vacations. All of that."

"I don't just mean work," Bernard said. "Life."

I forced a smile, feeling that somehow I'd been critiqued. "I'm glad you have enough money to retire at thirty."

"I'll retire at thirty-five." He blushed. But he knew where I was heading. It was all fine and good for one of the highest-paid traders in Europe to retire, millions of dollars already in the bank. It was something else entirely for a wannabe television personality to give up her gig.

"Sophie."

"Yes," I said.

"Don't think me wrong to say this, but do you ever think . . ."

Elizabeth and Jack suddenly burst onto the trail, screaming and giggling. And then I noticed that Leo had was right behind them, pretending to watch the kids but watching me and Bernard. He motioned to me. I bit my lip, patted Bernard's hand, and walked toward Leo.

Leo lit into me like the sexual CIA. "Was he your boyfriend?" he said before I was even by his side.

"We never dated."

"But you slept together."

I started to say no, but Leo cut me off. "Don't lie to me, Sophie," he said. "You wouldn't like me when I've been lied to."

I loved the lichen on the exposed roots of the trees, and the smell of the mulch. I walked deeper into the woods. Leo hated nature. Maybe he would just turn around and disappear.

But he didn't. He kept pace with me along the trail. So I said, "Yeah. I slept with him. Once. But, what do you care anyway? Am I supposed to be a virgin?"

"No," Leo said. "But you're ashamed of it. You were ready to lie about it."

"Leo, sometimes you are pathologically jealous, you know that?"

"So I ask you a question, you lie, and I'm pathologically jealous. So that's what it is?"

"(A) I didn't lie. And (B), yeah, that's what it is." This wasn't working. I turned back to the party.

He was really digging into my arm now, trying to hold me back as I pulled away toward the end of the trail and the lawn with the reception.

"Is everything all right?"

Leo still had his hand on my arm, but softly now. "Yeah, Bernard," I said, pulling my hand free and straightening my hair. "It's fine."

"It didn't look fine," he said. He was looking not at me but at Leo.

"It's really fine, Bernard," I said, walking away. "God."

And a few feet away there was music and laughter and dancing. And after a while I got back into the mood myself. But a small, dark bruise was rising, the place where the tip of his thumb dug into my forearm, and I found myself turning my arm to hide it as I twirled and danced.

26 Ben Folds Five, "The Battle of Who Could Care Less"

Sometimes I wondered where all those days went, the ones that peaked and ebbed like a good piece of chamber music, with the highs and lows and drama of a quartet. Red had a small fashion show in Prospect Park, then took Oscar to visit the folks in hot sticky Looziana. Mimi asked me if I wanted to tag along with her tribe to the Azores, and I wanted to, but I had that nanny phobia and said no. It was just as well. Leo started riding Ari and me hard to get our studio and touring band together. And of course he had to run the auditions.

So, Leo pulled some strings to get us a cheap nine AM slot at Electric Lady Studios, the spot on Eighth Street that Jimi Hendrix used to record in. The street was all dodgy shoe and leather shops with a couple of pizzerias and a Gray's Papaya thrown in. Lady Studios didn't look like much from the outside but I was totally sprung on the history. Ari wandered in at nine thirty looking like chipped shit on toast. Leo told him he was wasting our money.

This was going to be fun.

So, we ran through a clusterfuck of drummer auditions in, like, two hours. Half white guys, half black. The last one was short and round, with a dyed Mohawk. He looked like a black bowling ball covered with a red cockscomb. He was so hungry to work I wanted to give him a sandwich.

"We're looking for a full sound, you know," Leo said. "But you gotta let Sophie's voice lead, you gotta let it flow, man. I heard you coming in a little too fast and heavy on the second verse, you gotta know when to step into the background and when to come up front. And add what you need to, man, you know, give it some flavor, nahmean? Niggas gotta relate."

The kid started talking fast and nervous. "I can give this a little punk rock edge, a little hip-hop swing. I'm versatile man. I'm ver-sa-tile."

"Hip-hop swing," said Leo. "I like that man, I like it."

Now, to make sense of this scene, you have to know Red's Theory of Leo. Her theory is that Leo was a washed-up hip-hop hack who decided to push a black rock band because he got frozen out of the big money game. The only part of Red's theory that I disagreed with was the hack part. (That Kristal track was tight.) But yeah, Leo hated rock music, and yeah, he wanted the money. But then again, I wanted the money, too. That's why I was here.

Leo reached out and gave the drummer a double-fisted bump, then ordered a third take on "Slavery and War."

"You don't know what the fuck you're talking about."

Ari had this way of speaking into the air, not looking at the person he was talking to, just letting the arrow hit the mark.

"Excuse me," said Leo.

"You don't know what the fuck you're talking about. Just 'cause we're two 'niggas,' as you put it, does not make us a hip-hop band . . ."

"I was saying that it needs to swing," Leo said. "Y'all are flatlining, flatlining."

Ari deigned to look over at Leo. "We're flatlining because you're pushing every Tom, Dick, and Harry on us. No offense, man," he turned to the hapless drummer. "You're fine. But we don't have any chemistry. There's no way this will work." Ari picked up his guitar case and started packing up.

The kid at the drum set started to stand, then Leo waved him to sit back down. He got stuck in this half crouch trying to read what was going on. Ari proceeded to walk out the door. Leo followed. I stayed inside. I heard shouting. The kid stood up and, head hanging low, walked out.

Ari passed me a freshly rolled joint. We were sitting on a rug near the fireplace. It had taken me half an hour to talk Leo down and another thirty minutes to get to Ari's.

"The label says we got to get our shit together or this deal is going to disappear," I told Ari. "I can't afford that. Literally. Look, your dad's got your rent. . . ."

Ari poked out his bottom lip and blew a long, theatrical sigh.

"No, really," I said. "Nobody's paying my fucking rent. I wouldn't have gone back to this if it wasn't for you. But you gotta play ball."

"Play ball," he said, stubbing the joint out against the corner of a wooden table. "So you're willing to settle for some eighteen-year-old mumblefuck as our drummer?"

"He wasn't that bad," I said. But I didn't believe it. Ari had been kind in his appraisal.

Ari looked up at me, with that dancing fire in his eyes, and a slow smile. "I got it covered."

"What do you mean?"

"Okay, we could have drums and bass," he said, "like everybody else." Our bassist auditions were just as tragic as the drummer ones. "But hey, I talked to Shar and Bruce . . ."

"Bruce who? Springsteen?"

"Bruce X.," he said, which is what he called Bruce Xavier Yarrow.

"He hasn't played with a band in years."

"But he practices every weekend. Has been since he quit the game." I didn't even know that. But it made perfect sense. Total, obsessive music geek behavior.

"And by Shar, you mean Red's ex-girlfriend Shar."

"Right."

"Isn't there anyone else who can play the bass?"

"She stays on turntables. Totally different texture than bass. Better."

"Oh, Jesus Christ, you're hurting my head. Why deliberately piss off Red?" I ran the scenario. Damn, we'd be tight. "Why didn't you tell me what you were thinking?"

"Because your business partner had to go through this little dance himself."

"You fucker," I said. But I knew he was right. Leo wouldn't do what Ari said unless he was desperate. And by now, he and I were both plenty desperate.

I sat silent for a while. "We'll all hate each other by the end of the tour," I said. "Like Red."

"It's a risk," he said.

I thought back to the way Red had made her ultimatum and stomped off the tour and the way Ari and I had fallen apart.

It's a risk.

Ari squeezed closer to me. "Come on, Sophie. Come on."

I didn't respond.

"Sophie . . . Soph . . ." He leaned around to my ear. "So-phee, So-phee, Sky, Sky . . . Sky. Come back, Sky," he said, so softly that the words were breath. "Come back."

I sniffled. Tears. Unexpected. Damn.

Ari tilted me down toward the floor and swung me around until he hovered over me. I let him. Then he started lifting my skirts.

"Don't," I said. "I didn't take a shower this morning."

"'Dear Josephine,'" he said, directly to my pussy, but loud enough my ears could pick it up. "'I will be arriving home in three days. Don't bathe.'"

"Stop it, Ari," I said, pushing him back. But not very hard.

I heard him breathing in my scent. He took his time, sniffing and smelling, then licking me through my panties, and finally pulling them off me.

"Relax," he said.

He really loved it. The first waves hit me and I tensed up.

Relax.

I hated giving blow jobs. I hated everything about them. I hated the smell of unwashed privates. I hated the gagging and the way it took so long. I hated covering my teeth with my lips. I hated the slimy texture of come. Leo loved it when I went down on him. Ari didn't care. Ari just wanted to please me.

Another hit. I arched my back. But I wouldn't give in.

Ari lifted his head above my skirts. "How many licks does it take to get to the center of a Tootsie Roll?" he said. And then he did this thing I loved. He took his cheek and his chin, and rubbed the stubble over my clit. And then, when I was almost raw, as if I could feel that soft thin skin opening space for my blood to rush in, he went back with his tongue. Soft as felt, cool as running water, soft as love.

Then the heat hit me, the warmth of sitting in a hot bath and then the feeling of the smooth muscle contracting and releasing. A lull, a tightness, a rhythm, a wave, the colors, the light inside my darkness and the darkness parting back to the heat.

When I was done and closed my legs and curled on my stomach, the way I liked to sleep, and feeling the aftershocks subside, he said, "How many licks was that?"

"Forty-two," I said, as the goodness gave way to fear. How was I was going to survive Ari and Leo and Bruce and Shar all at once?

We played our first gig as a full band in London, where we could fall on our faces without any New York music critics giving us hell.

The venue was in the same complex as the hotel. It looked like someone had built a bomb shelter and forgot they were supposed to tear it down. The backstage lounge was huge and impersonal, and when I saw what catering had brought for us to eat I rolled my eyes. Leo made sure all the food at the shows was inedibly healthy, brown rice tofu wraps, kimchi, and braised kale.

"I hate this job," I said.

"It's not a job," said Ari, tuning up. "I wouldn't do it if it was." Was I imagining things, or did he look a bit less strung out these days?

Leo walked up with a short, silver-haired man who looked like a highly paid accountant.

"Sophie, this is Charles Eck, head of the U.K. division of the label. I thought you'd like to thank him for bringing us here," Leo said. Oh, the fawning, the desperation. I hated Leo when he was feeling himself, acting like the cock of the roost.

"Thanks," I said.

Shar was trying to hype up Bruce, who looked like he was about to piss his pants. Tonight he was playing keyboards, not bass, and she had helped him program in some rough, rumbling ambients to layer under Ari's guitar. We were trying something new, versions of our songs that were a little less rock, a little more drum 'n' bass-y. The Brits had this way of making electronic music that could shake the marrow in your bones and still make you want to laugh and shout and cry. If we could get that rattle and hum and emotion right, we'd be golden.

Went onstage. The crowd was London über-multiculti, where everyone was a quarter Jamaican and a quarter Pakistani and a quarter Scottish and a quarter plain Dickensian white. If there were a movie version of *White Teeth*, these would be the extras.

There had been a band before us, a lovely spoken-word artist who chanted over a man playing the kora. They'd gathered contributions from the audience in a wide metal bowl that stood at the edge of the stage, some kind of permanent peace offering to underpaid bands. I found it hard to imagine the griot-and-kora combo being signed to any label, let alone one with worldwide distribution, but things were different here. People ate herring for breakfast, drove on the wrong side of the street, and said "Sorry" when they didn't mean it. So why not sign a band with a following of ten and hope they'd get remixed by some hot DJ and sell half a million records? It had happened before.

Leo introduced us. I could see how uncomfortable he was. This was his idea, but not his crowd. We started in safety, with "Confess," which was really a slow ballad, then went right into "Slavery and War," an ironic pop-punk paean with Ari wailing Bon Jovi–style on the electric guitar.

> *Oh, without slavery and without war*
> *There would be no America*
> *Oh oh oh! Oh oh oooooh!*

> *And, yeah! All the things that make us great*
> *Are the things we say we hate*
> *Oh oh oh! Oh yeaaaah . . .*

Ari and I sang the chorus together, then broke out into this kind of loungey patter.

> *Honey it don't make no kind of sense*
> *You walkin' round here so intense*
> *Just let the past be the past*

And Ari picked up:

Faulkner said the past ain't dead
And this all can't be in my head
I mean, motherfuck the American flag

Then both of us:

Knowin' your history is such a drag!

Usually the crowd loved self-flagellating Americans, but they were impassive. So we went back into the deep drum 'n' bass groove, with lots of synth and less guitar. Bruce was still getting his chops but Shar was right on time, bringing in these otherworldly snippets of sound, not just songs and loops but clips from newsreels and movies. It was good stuff. But it wasn't working.

I was just starting to thank the crowd and hustle off the stage when I heard the first bars of "Kind." Ari had moved back to his acoustic guitar and started with the spare melody that lured the audience into the song. Shar and Bruce stumbled into their parts, sloppy at first but gaining momentum as the song did. A cacophony of electronic instruments, a symphony of broken dolls playing for an audience of robots. And then my voice, purposely distorted by the electronic feedback.

Isn't it Kind of funny

It isn't hard to see

You don't hold back with your loving

You aren't Kind to me

I'm Kind of bruised by your love

I'm black and blue with your love

Nobody's fooled by your love

Nobody except me.

It was like a Gypsy song, built on layers of speed and repetition, circular, faster, spiraling, faster, faster. To hell with those blank British faces. Fuck 'em. Fuck us. Fuck this.

And the less I started to care, the more I started to let my voice go, moving away from what one critic called (and I would never forget this) my "color-inside-the-lines delivery" into funereal mourning. I pushed my voice to the limit until it cracked, letting out all the real, all the real I tried not to feel.

And then the crowd was with me, with me inside the music. Some of them yipped and yelled, but most stayed silent until they graced us with long, deep applause. Charles walked past Leo and came straight up to me. I looked up from Ari and into his eyes. "If you can get *that* on tape, that"—he searched for a word—"fire, then I think we can find the money to have you record here. Our studios are unbelievable. What do you think, Sophie? Do we have a deal?"

"We have a deal," I said.

Everything was gray. It was the color of the acoustic muffling and carpet in the studio, and the concrete building and the skies outside. Depressing, you'd think. But since Charles had given us a home, all of us started to relax a little. Last night Leo and I had a long night of playful sex, the kind where I danced around the room and did a striptease before falling into his arms. And in the morning, we walked hand in hand into the building, as if we were grade-school sweethearts.

Once we got inside, though, he was all business. It almost comforted me, to see him be himself again.

"Charles is *the* ticket, baby, *our* ticket. So when he comes in, give him your *full* attention, baby," said Leo. "I know how you space out sometimes."

"Hullo." Charles had crept in behind us.

"Hi!" I said, with a blinding smile. "How are you? Uh, do you want something to drink?"

"Do you have a Pellegrino?"

While Leo poured, Bruce started wiping his hands on his pants. . . . He might as well have made the sign of the cross. Shar sauntered over and introduced herself, cool and collected. Ari waved from across the room. In a very economically unstable and, of course, mean-spirited music world, this man could be our meal ticket.

We had a plan. Rework our songs. Create an undulating wall of sound, with Bruce laying down a heavy rhythm; then head-trippy sound clips from Shar, and rich, succulent guitar solos from Ari.

Charles watched us play, nodding slightly when he heard something he liked. He seemed to like it when I went wild, when I behaved in the studio the same way I could onstage. He liked it when I flipped my hair and rocked back and forth while I sang.

"You're ninety percent there," he said, and checked his watch, and left.

He came back the next day, only for fifteen minutes, but he came. And the next day. And the next.

I developed a repertoire of sighs and screams and moves Charles liked. Did them over and over again, a routine so complicated that it looked and sounded natural. Thinking of what to do with my body kept me busy enough that I never sank fully into the song. I liked it that way, floating just above the point when true feelings threatened to crest over me and wash me away.

But as the days wore on, Charles started nodding less, and then showing up less. We hadn't seen him for three days. We were working on "Kind," the umpteenth session, taking a break to talk through the instrumentation, and Charles walked in, came up to me, and said, "These rehearsals aren't for me. They're for you, you know? You . . . you were so close." And then he shook his head and walked away.

And after that I tried my best to get it right. I really tried. I tried not to sing, but to feel, to let myself be a vessel. And the energy charged through me, as surely as a lightning rod hit by pale blue fire. When it got too much I'd wave the band down. . . . *Stop, just stop*. I made these songs as a puzzle box, a place to keep the feelings safely from me. Because to feel the music, to really feel it, was to be born and die again and again. That's what Charles wanted. . . . He wanted me to hurt like this. And I did. Sometimes I'd come to, sweaty and doubled over, as a song was ending. As I was still singing. It was like waking from a trance and finding your hands around someone's throat. Around your own.

After each of those long days Leo walked me back to the apartment we'd rented nearby. The neighborhood was brick and cobblestone, row houses and warehouses, workingmen's pubs next to dot-coms. I learned to take comfort in the shelter of his arms again. We'd order vegetable curries for dinner and then he'd try to write songs for me. One of them had these lines:

Sun, moon, rain, stars;
life ain't complete with you behind bars.
But know I love you through and through
I'm gonna make life right for you.

Oh, man, that was bad. Leo was a great hustler but a shitty rock songwriter. Every now and then he'd write something perfect for Kristal or one of the other girls who sang the hooks while men with bullet scars and tattoos rhymed. But even though Leo never found my voice, didn't write anything we could use, I could hear him speaking to me as I sang his words back to him, trying to reach me from a place inside himself where he felt trapped and he wanted love. At least that's what I thought.

The sex stayed light in London. I didn't miss the rage and passion of our lovemaking at home, but I needed that then, and I knew I'd need it again, the way the boxer needs the ring. Here, though, he learned to hold me lightly instead of gripping, supporting me by my buttocks as I rode him, letting me be on top. Yeah, this way was good, too. He'd usually take about ten minutes to come, sometimes twenty. By then, to be honest, I was getting bored. When things went on too long, I'd find myself thinking about Ari, the way he used to worship my body even when I hated it. I'd always felt fat, even when I was much thinner. Leo, on the other hand, looked at me like a fixer-upper. Despite his tenderness, there were times and ways he looked at me like an old brownstone with good bones that needed a lot of work.

Charles took off for Tokyo without telling us. We stayed in London. The sessions dragged on and on until we had something we could stand to listen to without critiquing every breath and chord and phrase. Everything was so expensive, and we were set to roll as soon as we finished the final tracks. We had a party the night before we left, and all the sound engineers came. But the mood was off. Charles didn't so much as send an email saying congratulations or bye.

We came back to New York to more silence. We were Not a Priority for the label, and no one really explained why we'd gone a month and a half without getting any feedback on what we'd done. Red sucked her teeth when I told her about our limbo. She thought it was yet another sign that Leo had absolutely no game and no juice.

Finally, the album came back to us with a Post-it note from Charles. It read, "Do thirty percent better, please."

That night we gathered at my place, slouched into our chairs, relaxing into defeat like generals before a final siege. I took a risk on London. I'd gone from having a five-thousand-dollar credit-card bill to twenty thousand on three different cards. They wouldn't raise my limit any more. I kept dreaming that I was in an overturned boat with just a little air between the water and the hull. I'd breathe and suck in water. Most nights I woke up in my bed panting.

Two days later I got a package from London. Charles's letter was fifteen pages, single spaced. Not fan-mail-from-crazy-inmate, single spaced. It was in perfect outline format, alternating Roman and Arabic numerals, capital and lowercase letters. It was a blueprint, a schematic of everything from publicity and marketing to album cover design. It was like opening a Twix bar and finding an invitation to Willie Wonka's

Chocolate Factory. If you've ever followed a dream, you've probably wanted someone to play Yoda and teach you how to use the Force. I saw that in Charles, and clearly this schematic for success meant he saw it in me. Then I noticed that in the same packet, Charles included a termination-of-contract letter. He said time was running out and he couldn't wait around for us to get it right. His final line was "I'm doing you a favor."

A favor. Right. We were dead in the water.

There are times that days pass without meaning. I entered those days. The sunlight felt thinner to me than it should have, and my body was still off sync with New York time. I woke up at three in the morning, and paced through the darkness, then slept 'til two in the afternoon before I walked to Veselka for one of their all-day breakfasts. People with purpose came, got their burger or their kasha varnishkes, and left. Every day for a week I ordered runny eggs and kielbasa and challah toast and coffee, lingering over it until the yolks had turned to cold yellow latex.

Leo kept saying everything would be fine with a confidence I first found mysterious and now infuriating, especially since he'd chosen this precise moment to work on getting other clients.

Red made time to meet me at Veselka one day. "There is stupid," she said, picking at pierogies and drinking coffee, "and then there is stuck on stupid. You are officially stuck on stupid, and right now stupid's name is Leo."

"I thought he was your friend."

"He was. But remember a long time ago I decided not to mix friendship and business. And Leo and I were never tight like that. When are you going to cut him loose? When you go into bankruptcy?"

"He's not actually taking any money from me."

"No, he's just letting you pay the band's expenses while you get no money."

"You're right," I said. "I'm so dumb."

"Save the pity-partying. It wastes time. You need to look for a job and go into credit counseling."

"You are just being so Jamaican right now. Are you sure you're Creole?"

"Despite rumors to the contrary, my people are quite practical, thank you. Look, if you need to sublet your place for a while, that would get you a solid two grand a month and you could stay with me and Lin."

I actually thought about it for a second. Wow, that could be a nightmare. "Thank you, baby girl. I'm going to go back to the drawing board on this one and hit you up next week."

That night I called Leo up after drinking a bottle of mediocre chardonnay and cursed him out. He didn't stop me.

A couple days later Shar, Bruce, and I each got a letter. "Ken Earnest invites you to dine at his residence." The residence was on Sutton Place; not bad. Just as I was reading the invitation, Ari called. "Who the fuck," he said, "is Ken Earnest?"

Called Leo. He told me that Earnest was two levels *higher* on the label's food chain than Charles. But Leo wasn't invited to the dinner.

"It's nothing. You know how these folks are, just wanting to get a little amusement from their pet artists. If it was serious business I'd be in the room."

"Thanks. That's charming." I hung up the phone. God. But even though he was being a prick, I wished Leo was coming along. At this point, I had no idea what the label wanted.

The night of the dinner, the band and I gathered together at my place and cabbed it to the Upper East Side. The doormen looked at us like we might steal the chandeliers. A butler opened the apartment door and introduced us to Ken.

As it turns out, Ken was a tall man who spoke as if he was straining each word through his teeth. He decided to regale me with stories about listening to his father's blues records "and gaining a great appreciation for the African-American imagination."

"He knows we're a rock band, right?" said Shar, when he'd turned away for a second.

"I have no idea."

I'd worn a tight business skirt suit with thick semiprecious stone jewelry. Hoped it hit the right mix of sexy and give-me-money. "Leo sends his regards," I said as a servant doled out soup with a heavy silver ladle. "He's on business in Atlanta." Signing some strip-hop trio with gold fronts and a bad attitude, specifically.

"Oh, we've spoken," said Ken. "This meeting is for you. Well, I don't know how to say this, but there's been a bit of confusion on our end."

"Confusion?"

"Let me put it bluntly. We love your demo. It needs a few tweaks, but we love it. Such energy. And it's so nice to see African-Americans operating in the rock-and-roll space again." His white ass was going to wear out the phrase African-American, and "operating in the rock-and-roll space" was just too much. But Ken kept going, leaving his soup course untouched, waving it away and letting the servant dole out duck à l'orange. I used five-dollar words on a regular basis, but Ken whipped out a string of twenty-dollar phrases like "pernicious ingratitude" and "unfathomable willfulness." It took me a while to figure out he was talking about Charles. "We love the record," said Ken. "Would you forgive us?"

"Really? Uh, yeah, of course, I mean, there's nothing to forgive. You're keeping us under contract, right?"

"Would we be having dinner now if it weren't so?" Not with the price of this silverware. I looked at Shar, Bruce, and Ari and made what I hoped was a discreet *God-fuckin' damn, we're in like Flynn* face. And then Ken said, in summation, "Charles just didn't have the authority to make some of the choices he did."

"Well, you know, Charles always treated us well," I started.

Shar stomped on my foot with a stiletto. I yelped.

"Oh, I'm sorry. I must have stepped on your foot," Shar said. To Ken she said, "It's so nice to be appreciated. Charles always seemed a little off to me."

Ken smiled broadly. I didn't know that Shar was such a backstabber. She humored him through the dessert course. His butler showed us the door.

"We're a bunch of fair-fucking-weather friends," Ari said once we'd stepped outside. He glowered and lit up a cigarette.

"Um, I didn't hear you say anything," I said.

"It wouldn't have helped."

"Hmmm. Let's compare notes on loyalty. We just let this obnoxious self-important prick Ken talk shit about Charles. On the other hand, Charles just pulled a ninja move for us. Unless I'm reading things wrong, Charles told Ken he was killing our contract just so Ken would feel like he was getting the upper hand by keeping us."

"It makes my head hurt," Bruce said. We piled into a cab. "You know, maybe we should do something nice for Charles."

"What?" said Shar. "Send an assortment of truffles and a note that says, 'Sorry you lost your big important job, but thanks for saving our ass'?"

Bruce cringed. He was going to have to toughen up a bit to hang with us.

"That's not a bad plan," I said to Bruce, patting his knee. "A token gift and a thank-you note have soothed many an aching heart. We'll have to work on the language because Shar hasn't invested very much in her version."

"If any of you read the trades, you'd know that Charles got a seven-figure golden parachute."

"No way!" said Bruce.

"Well, in that case," I said, "I'll send a note, but I'm not paying for any chocolate."

31 Big Pun, "Still Not a Player"

Here's what I did until our album release date: ran up another ten thousand dollars in credit-card debt (once I begged Visa into expanding my limit); borrowed a thousand from Leo; took up doing band profiles for the downtown magazines again; did some on-camera wraparounds for a documentary; and, finally, in desperation and humiliation, sold some of my old designer clothes. They didn't fit me anyway, but I still felt I got pennies on the dollar.

Leo was being really tight with the money we'd gotten as an advance. If we spent it to live on, then we wouldn't have any money to tour, if we even got a tour. He was doing a good job with the prepublicity. Every little rock 'n' roll rag had a "second coming of Sky" story between its pages.

Finally the album dropped. I'd spent the night at Leo's; felt like I was straining out of my skin. All of a sudden I was tempted to try smoking a cigarette, the one vice that I'd never even tried. Five o'clock came. Then six. Leo wasn't picking up his phone. I went into the bedroom closet and got the secret stash of whisky hidden in my snow boot. Poured myself a ladylike drink. Then a less ladylike one. And finally a whopper.

I had some kind of supersonic hearing left over from my childhood, when I would press my ear against the common wall between my parents' bedroom and mine and try to decipher their shouts and murmurs. What I was hearing right now was Leo's key in the lock. I put the whiskey back in the boot, and did a course of mouthwash, followed by toothbrushing, more mouthwash, and gum; then arranged myself on our bed like a ballerina doll on a porcelain jewelry box, and began to strum a guitar I didn't really know how to play.

By the time Leo made it up to the third floor, I must have looked like the consummate craftsman-artist, hard at work. Or so I hoped.

I couldn't tell if he was happy or sad, so I couldn't tell if I was supposed to act happy or sad.

"How were first-day sales?" I said, putting my hand on his knee.

"Solid, baby, solid."

"What does 'solid' mean?"

"Top twenty. You get your tour."

I jumped up and down on the bed screaming. Label backing for the tour meant more money, more support, more free clothes from the stylists, more invitations to good parties, more more more more more more more. And that's what every good American wants, right? More of *everything*.

Leo let me jump and shout for a bit, and then he said, "It's just too bad."

"What?" I was laughing. I thought he was joking.

"Nah. For real. It's just too bad I won't be with you."

I asked him what he meant. He told me that Ken hadn't budgeted him into the trip. I felt a small thrill and tried not to show it. Goddamn it would be great to hit Amsterdam without Leo minding my business. "Well, I'll ask him about it," I said.

"And what makes you think you can change his mind?" said Leo.

"Nothing . . . but I can try." My tone of submission and sincerity was so spot-on that Leo gave me a second look.

"There is another way," Leo said. He told me how he could keep an eye on me, keep me on track. I would just need to break him off a little bit for travel so he could come see me. Plus his usual retainer as manager.

"But isn't the tour manager supposed to look after me on the road?"

"Yeah. Supposed to," Leo said. "If you trust him to." He put his hands on the small of his back and paced around a bit. "If that's what you want."

"*If that's what you want*" was a trap. On the one hand, I was a grown woman, and no matter whether we shared the same bed, shouldn't I get to make the decisions I wanted? Like telling Leo to stay at home and literally mind his business? On the other hand, let me just say that, and I'd have to sleep with one eye open. What the fuck, maybe this boyfriend-manager thing wasn't too bright. I could just end it now. But then again, he had twenty percent of my income for the next three years, no matter what, so I had better fucking stay with him. And if I was going to stay with him, I had to make sure he wasn't pissed off at me. So, in the end, I gave Leo permission to use my own money to mind me, paid for the privilege of being confined.

▷ 32 Rick James, "Give It to Me Baby"

The label gave us the money to tour and we started spending it.

Vocals, keyboards, percussion, drums.
Choreographer, dancers.
Director, designer, tour manager.
Makeup, hair.
Money,
   Money,
      More money.

"This looks okay, baby, right?" Leo said, holding the pen above a fat sheaf of contracts for me to sign. We were in his bedroom with some lackey from the label standing by. The renovations on Leo's place were done now. Photographers begged to shoot in the wood-and-marble palace that Leo had purchased and my record deal had paid for.

Shar, Leo, and Bruce had all booked tickets to see a resurrected early punk band from Detroit. I bought tix but then Leo scheduled a party, and he begged and whined until I caved and said I would stay with him. While my real friends were at the concert, the people that Leo told me were my friends circled on the floor below. I wasn't in the mood to be nice to them. I wasn't in the mood to sign documents I didn't understand. I knew enough about this industry to grok the meaning of a recoupable advance. We would go into personal debt if we spent the money the label gave us without bringing enough money back.

"I need a second to look this over," I said.

"Goddamn," said Leo under his breath. Label guy was sitting at the oval desk plopped near the French windows in our bedroom, an ugly reminder that our relationship was as much business as pleasure.

"Goddamn what?" I said. I'd finished drinking my secret preparty drink, and eating my preparty meal, so I could sip Perrier and nibble snacks like the real Manhattanites. I'd put on my makeup, layer upon layer of color as fluid and brilliant as a rainbow of oil on a misty street.

"Goddamn waste of time."

"Why don't I just step outside," said the lackey.

"Why don't you?" I said. Nastier than I meant.

Label guy left. Leo went off about why was I emasculating him, blah blah blah, heard it all before. "Because you're not doing your job," I said.

"My job is to protect you."

"I don't trust people who try to protect me from things I don't understand. I trust people who explain things to me."

"Look, baby." I could see him struggling how to play this. "It's like, when you have a baby, you don't say, 'The gas line runs to the stove. The pilot light sets the gas on fire. The fire cooks shit. Fire can burn you.' You just say, 'Fire hot, baby. *Hot*. Don't touch.' You also give him a little smack on his ass if you need to."

"So I'm a child now," I said.

"That's not what I meant."

"It's what you said."

All of sudden I wanted to just throw down with Leo, have things out on a physical level. But I wouldn't know why I was picking a fight, and I definitely wouldn't have been able to win.

As a kid, I was never good at fighting, unless the kids on the bus pushed me. And then I turned into a tornado of whirling arms, stomps, and kicks, the kind that brought blood and turned even the most avid members of the middle-school fight club silent. But every now and then they'd let some patsy, a kid new to the school, taunt me to the point where I felt myself filling with a deep purple rage. Right now, for reasons I couldn't fathom, I felt filled with anger and blood and sadness, with tears unshed.

Godddamn, when am I going to get my fucking period?

"When were you supposed to?"

So I'd said it aloud, not just thought it. I looked at Leo straight. "I don't know. A few days ago. I think."

"You don't even know your own cycle?"

"I'm stressed. My cycle, as you call it, is stressed, too."

"What will you do if we're pregnant?"

We. "I don't know."

He looked at me, disbelieving. "You don't know?"

"I. Don't. Know." I went to the closet and started pulling outfits to take on the road. Our first performance was in a week. I could pack and unpack for days with obsessive compulsivity. "I just, well, first of all, I don't think I'm pregnant. Second of all, I never wanted to have a kid without being married."

Leo gripped me by the shoulder. "What would you say if I told you I would marry you right now?"

This librarian told me that your mind works like a computer, or maybe an old card file. You're talking about one thing. And if someone changes the subject on you, your brain has to put away one file, like how much the damned tour costs, and pull out the other, the one that asks, "Am I pregnant? And do I want to marry this fool?"

I finally spat out, "I don't know."

"Well," Leo said, quiet. Vindicated. "One day maybe you'll meet somebody you don't have to think twice about. Maybe one day a good brother will propose to you and you'll hear him for real." He put on his jacket and walked out into the party. I could hear the doorbell ring, and the crowds of people. Someone asked, "Where is she?" And then the door shut and muffled the sound again.

Later I would think, Wasn't that sneaky? Asking me without asking me. Too punk to just take his chances. Wanted to know the answer beforehand. Didn't want to hear what I had to say, anyway.

And by the time I realized I still had to look the contract over, the words didn't make any sense to me. The numbers might as well have been kanji or hieroglyphics. Ugly little designs on paper. I could barely see through my tears. And why was I crying, anyway? Shit.

And you know, the thing was, I did enjoy the party. I got drunk and didn't care if Leo knew it. I don't think it bothered him one bit, though. I walked down the stairs and handed him the papers. I'd signed another contract and put it in his hand.

II.

Period didn't come the day after the party, or the day after that, or the next day either. Stopped drinking again. Without the alcohol laying down a suppressing fire, my dreams came back for a guerrilla sortie. See, since I was a kid my dreams had the power to wake me from my sleep. This time, I saw flashes of a short story called "The Rocking Horse Winner." Boy's mother and father fight about money. Dad bets the horses; Mom likes nice clothes. So the kid starts having visions. Sees the track when he's in his bedroom on his little wooden horse. He rocks faster and faster. The horse his Daddy's bet on wins.

All's well for a minute. Then Mom and Dad buy new clothes and trick out the house, and the money runs out, and they fight more. So the kid stays in his room, frantic, pumping his horse like a piston. Hears, *There must be more money, there must be money.* Like the walls are speaking to him. Like the house is breathing with him, rocking with him. He needs it, they need it, need it, it's needed (*more money*) and he's rocking, trying, faster. *More money.* And then he dies. Right there on the horse.

I think I was ten when I read that story. And I thought: Isn't that just the way it is?

I heard the same voices: *there must be more money.* My Daddy bet the horses, too. Mama worked herself hard. I learned to do what the Bible says don't: love money. *For the root of evil is the love of money.* But when you don't have something, you love it more. You imagine it's the most wonderfullest thing in the world simply because it's something you haven't defiled with your touch. And sometimes, still, the sound of the horses hooves would wake me, as they did this night.

Woke up next to Leo in the darkest part of dark, the quietest part of quiet. I could have been back home in Baltimore, where the night swept you up in a velvet-black curtain of muffled car sounds and cloud-covered stars. But I knew what dream had awakened me, even as the hoofbeats faded. I thought a shower would wash my mind clean.

Slivers of dawn light made it through the frosted window glass. Water ran cool, like spring raindrops. Lavender sugar scrub cupped in one palm. Other hand touching my stomach, same size as ever, waiting to feel if there was life inside. Heard my phone ring, a tinny version of *The Hustle*, and then heard it stop and Leo call my name. Goddamn I hated when he answered my phone, always snooping but claiming to help. Called my name again, and then three words: *It's your daddy*.

If I had any sense at all I would have called out to Leo, *I don't have a daddy*. A card nearly every birthday does not a daddy make. Nor does a phone call every few months, or a one-hundred-dollar bill tucked in an envelope come eighth-grade graduation. A daddy isn't someone who promises to visit but doesn't, or someone who comes once in a while, with a new girlfriend and a new suit, to take you and your brother and sister out to dinner.

But I washed the lavender scrub down the drain, turned off the water, slipped into a terry robe. Walked through the dressing room to find Leo talking like he would to one of his frat brothers. I gave him a long, dirty look and he handed me the phone.

"You got a good man there, baby, a good man." Daddy still sounded the same, like the taste of bourbon and honey. When I was a kid I thought he looked like Marvin Gaye: the eyes, the smile, the beard. Tight pants that flared out at the bottom; Afro pick in the back pocket. Always wore a jacket, even when it was hot. A jacket, he explained, was a black man's insulation against gettin' looked at like a street corner bum.

I imagined him in a jacket, a little worn around the collar and the elbows. Glass of Chivas beside him; or if he couldn't afford it that day, dark rum. So he happened to be awake at one in the morning and ready to talk, expecting I'd just be up and willing. It made me mad that I was.

"You there, baby?" he said.

"I'm here."

"How's my baby?"

"I'm fine, Daddy. I was in the shower."

"Well, don't let me interrupt you." Right.

"How are you?" I said.

"Fair to middling. You remember Charlene?"

"Uh . . . Uh huh."

"She passed away last week."

"I'm sorry." Truth be told, I barely remembered what she looked like.

"Funerals are so expensive these days."

"That's for sure."

"I was just hoping you could break me off a little something to deal with the expenses."

The money he begged was never for him. I asked why her family wasn't paying the bills.

"Things are so high these days," is all he would say.

"So give me the name of the funeral home and I'll send a donation in her name."

Daddy huffed. But if I thought I had him, I didn't. "This isn't for funeral parlor things. The extras. A big picture of her, all blown up, for the memorial. Flowers. Food for the wake. Just a couple, three hundred dollars. Not much for a big-time star like you. You know what killed her?"

I didn't.

"Cancer. God-damned cancer." And there was something in the quaver of his voice that made me remember he still had feelings, no matter how deeply buried. He wouldn't ask for the money again, but I would send it, Western Union or a money order, to the same P.O. box he'd kept all these years, no matter how many apartments he went through. "Charlene, she looked good 'til the end, though."

She who dies with her makeup on wins.

"How's your mother?"

Fine.

"There'll never be another woman like your mother. Never."

"Erika is fine, too," I said. "Matthew is about the same." I was done with this conversation. He won. The only victory I could keep was my own time. "I gotta go, Daddy."

"Well, tell your mother hello," he said. That quaver again. I almost felt sorry for him. Almost.

Before I could put on some lotion and get my ashy ass back into bed, Leo was on me to break him off something more to hire an outside publicity firm.

"Look, Leo, I am not about spending money I don't have on shit we don't need."

"Like what?" he said. "Like publicity? You mean to tell me you don't need publicity? Folks just going to be psychically drawn to your album? Or, wait," he said, pacing the room. "You gonna trust the label to handle your shit? When they got seventeen thousand million other albums to put out that year. Like yours is the only one they're working? You gonna trust them to return every call, make every pitch? I guess you don't need that because you're the shit."

"Leo. The album's doing fine. Better than fine."

"Let me tell you something, Sophie," he said. "I don't spend money on bullshit. 'Cause we a team. My money is your money, you hear me? All of it. This house. This home. Your money is my money, right? Right?"

"Yeah," I said.

"And our baby."

"We don't know if there's a baby."

"But you ain't got your period yet," he said.

"No."

"And what did the test say?"

"Didn't take it yet."

"Didn't take it yet? What you waiting for?"

"I just . . . I just think I'm late."

"Come on. We taking this test now."

"Leo, I just peed."

"You don't need but a drop."

"Leo, I'm tired."

"Now," he said, and grabbed me by the arm.

So we went into the bathroom, and took the test out of the box, and I peed on the little plastic stick. We waited. The bathtub dripped and every time the water hit the porcelain, it was like the ticking of a clock. When we looked at the strip again, there was a little plus sign, like you'd done well on a test.

My sobs drowned out the drip of the tap. Leo hugged me. "You happy, right?" he said. "Right?"

"Yeah," I said. "Just emotional, I guess." I didn't know what I was. Wasn't pure sad, certainly wasn't happy. Just overfull, overfull of every-thing.

"I will be here for you, baby. I will be here for *our* baby."

This was my cue to act reassured. All I wanted to do was say, Shit, why don't boys have the babies? I'd always been afraid of childbirth, the descriptions of blood and death in the Victorian novels we read for class. Didn't help that my ninth-grade teacher, Mrs. Keyes, spent a full class talking about the birth of her son. I can imagine it from her point of view, looking out at two fourteen-year-olds tumescent with life, try-ing to keep the rest of us from following. She said it felt like a man with a combat boot covered in nails had shoved his foot up her ass and kept kicking. One girl told her mom, who told the principal, that the teacher said "ass." Mrs. Keyes was suspended for a week.

Back to Leo. I said something smart-mouthed, like, does "being there" include time off for good behavior to kick it with Kristal? Huh?

"I am not your father. Don't lay that shit on me."

"I'm not your mother, either." His mother had favored her alcoholic husband over her children until the man died. My Mama had cut my Daddy off completely; Leo's never could.

I was going to have a child. With this *man.* Jesus. I sank into his arms, because there was no one else to hold me, no one else to comfort me. Jesus, though. Fuck.

I extended an olive branch, asked Leo to come home with me for my mom's big cookout. The Washington Family Fourth of July wasn't a picnic as much as an annual summit. Applicants to the club (suitors to the Washington men and women) were mercilessly vetted. Not to mention it was just a week after my birthday. Pouted. Leo still hadn't made any plans.

Leo looked irked. "Are we building? Are we building? We've got to prioritize. Are you seriously talking about taking off July Fourth weekend? I don't think we have the time."

Everything we did now was work, wasn't it? Even the parties, and the shopping. Dancing around the clubs, getting photographed by paparazzi who couldn't have cared less about us a few months ago. It was all part of the job. And only a lazy man would stop running, even if he knew he was ahead.

"I think I'll take off for Baltimore next Wednesday actually. Beat the weekend rush," I said.

"Well, fine," he said.

"Fine."

The women wore bodysuits and the men wore long shorts, both under their raffia skirts. The way the beat started. stopped. started, it seemed as if dancers and musicians alike had lost their place. Only instruments: three cowbells. Rhythm settled to place. Bellies rippled Middle Eastern style; shoulders and hips rotated with Polynesian speed; and then every now and then the men and women in a line would dip and sway, just like black folks do in the club. All of it African dance, ancient and modern at the same time.

Of course Shar and Red ended up in the same Congolese dance class. Red brought Shar when they were going out; and Shar loved it as much as her girlfriend; and then they'd broken up and each thought about dropping out. Instead, the love of the dance held them to their weekly commitment, and they made peace and became friends again.

Little brown children sat in a ring on the floor, swaying to the music, some in leotards and bright print wrap skirts or pants. Adults sat cross-legged behind them, and those like me who wanted an actual western-style chair sat further back. Behind me stood a screamer, an older man who yipped and clapped and shouted encouragement to the sweating, smiling dancers. Usually I wanted to throttle those people, but today I got caught up in *him* getting caught up in the dance, the pageantry of it, modern black women (and three men, all fine and possibly straight) dancing a dance hundreds of years old.

With one final trill of the cowbells, the dancers spun to a halt. Wild applause. Palo Mayombe's semiannual recital and fund-raiser: a complete success.

Bruce had been near the front of the room, snapping pictures like a proud papa. Mimi stood next to Bruce. She was about to take her shiftless husband, two nannies, and the kids to the Azores for the summer.

I couldn't believe it when Ari came from the back of the room. First, he hated these things. Second, he looked like hell. He walked like an old man with gout. Said to me once that junk pains felt like scarabs eating his bones. His skin felt clammy when I touched him. We walked to a corner with chairs so he could sit.

"You okay, baby? Let me get you some water." Shar had this way of getting real Southern right quick. In just five years in New York, she'd masked her Alabama accent except when she got emotional. I guess she'd never seen Ari like this, stripped of the fuck-it-all attitude that junk enabled, and fragile as tissue paper.

"I'm just cutting back," Ari said to me, his voice near a whisper. "It's always the same." He slumped forward. "It's always harder than I remember."

"I'm sure." My voice sounded cold to me. Since I'd found out I was pregnant, I was getting real practical about shit. I could only worry about so many people's problems, and Ari wasn't on the list anymore. But I had to tell the band my news. When? Anytime but now.

Shar came back with the water. Ari took a couple of sips.

I was happy that he was junk-sick. It meant that he was taking things seriously, trying to avoid another white-knuckle incident like the time we got pulled over for speeding in East Texas. He was trying way too hard to be nice to the cop. Usually he was veering right on the edge of fuck-you, but this time he was all yes-sir-no-sir-three-bags-full. Had a gram tucked under the backseat, which he didn't tell me until after the tour was over.

So: no junk on the tour bus. Which meant no reliable supply. Which meant cutting back was a necessity. And really, if I was being honest with myself, I did have to care. Because if he got caught, it was all of our asses, our whole contract on the line.

"You want to go get something to eat, baby?" Shar said. She'd shed her raffia for a miniskirt. She stood dark and thin and gleaming like Grace Jones in her early posters. She smelled like sweat and coconut oil. Delicious.

"I don't think I could stand the smell of food," said Ari.

"Well, then maybe we'll just hit the coffee shop."

"No. Go 'head without me." He smiled a wan smile.

"No, Ari!" Shar was still speaking Southern, her no extending to about three tones and syllables. "We care about you, don't we?" She looked to me and Bruce and we both quickly nodded.

"You ready?" Red was all freshened up, standing with Lin and Oscar, waiting to head to brunch. Through the plateglass window at the front of the studio, you could see the sun shining on Brooklyn's Smith Street, with its rows of trendy ethnic restaurants.

"Hold on a second. Ari?"

"I'm not going to a restaurant, Shar," he said. Tone of voice: final.

"Well, then, you go 'head without me," she said to me, Bruce, and Red. "I'll get baby boy home." She slung her arm around his waist and they walked slowly off together.

I got the hot tingles of jealousy. And for what? Lesbian bandmate nicey-nices with ex-husband? Hardly an etiquette crime. But that tingle never lied. I felt what I felt, even if it didn't make any sense.

▷ 35 Talvin Singh featuring Leone, "Distant God"

"Can you turn over? Ma'am, can you turn over?"

I hated being Ma'amed. Made me feel old. I'd fallen asleep on the massage table, soothed by the strains of new age music, the scent of lavender, and the strong, steady kneadings of my masseur. Told him I liked it hard, to break up the knots, especially in my right shoulder. The ache never left me, but it was a sweet soreness most of the time, the kind that felt good when I was stretching. But other times my fears and resentments coiled there like a nest of cobras, hissing their complaints as I moved.

I'd slipped into the shadow world as I napped. Could barely catch it now. I'd conjured up a blond woman with blood on her lips—that was Ari—lost with me in a house filled with stairs. I was good at spotting the doppelgängers in my dreams, but not so good at remembering the details.

Ordinarily, I couldn't sleep through a good, deep massage. But his fingers were agile enough, and I was tired enough. Hadn't slept through the night in what seemed like weeks. Now the shoulder felt fine as I turned, so fine that I wondered if this was my body, my creaky misused body, or someone else's limberness.

God, I loved massages. All of the best parts of sex, except the orgasm, with no obligation to please. *Just* be *pleased*, every stroke seemed to say. *Just be*. A new note of incense lay heavy in the air atop the lavender, and the music grew faster along with his strokes, the tops of my shoulders now, and the sides of the rib cage, and the legs, and finally the feet.

Chinese doctors say you can find every part of your body in your feet, and fix it with the right touch. The bodyworker put the pads of his thumbs into the tenderest parts of my soles, until at one point I yelled out.

"Sorry," he said. "Are you about to, ahhm, menstruate?" Oh, how it pained men to say the word. "That could explain. Unless you're pregnant."

"Whatever you say." I suddenly wanted this over. So much for the Zen.

Leo met me in the foyer, bundling up the credit card receipt for the massage, just the first, he'd promised, of my surprise birthday presents. The receptionist, a thin sister with marcelled hair, smiled at him a bit too widely. Maybe Leo was hitting on her. Or maybe she was just happy to see a spot of color in this white-on-white place.

"How was it?" he asked, giving me a peck on the cheek. Leo didn't believe in PDA anywhere near white folks, thought it conformed to stereotypes.

"Great. I'm just a little tired, though. Let's go home before dinner."

"Thought we could hit a couple of the shops first."

Leo had kicked his gear up a notch since we'd hit number one on the alternative rock charts, eschewing harder urban wear for buttery Italian leather and whisper-smooth silk ties. Today he was dressed down, in an egg-yolk shirt with French cuffs, a mocha leather blazer, and matching shoes. It was a bit warm for the whole ensemble, but Leo would rather wear the fall line in summer than have anyone beat him to the punch.

Leo opened the frosted-glass door. Flashbulbs flared; camera lights blinded me; shouts struck my ears.

"Sky. Sky! Over here, Sky."

"Here, Sky, here!"

"Is the tour in jeopardy?"

"Sky, is it true you're pregnant?" That was one of the young pups from The Video Channel. Guess he'd gotten my job. "It's Rob," he whispered, as if it made a difference.

I kept walking, steely posture, trying hard to soften my face. The camera was the camera. And in the tabloids, "Does she look happy?" would be the subhead after "Is she pregnant?"

"We have it on a good authority, Sky," said a man holding out a digital recorder. "Very good," he said, and I swore Leo winked at him.

I kept walking, talked to Leo from the side of my mouth. "You told them, didn't you? Jesus, you *told* them."

"It's just a rumor, baby, just a rumor." Leo looked into the cameras and smiled, "We have no statement at this point. But if you're lucky, your wedding invitation's in the mail." Put his arm around me. I whipped it off.

"What are you doing?" he said, his voice loud enough but his lips barely moving.

"Don't ask me what I'm doing," I said right in his face. "You. Are Fucking. Insane. I. Am leaving. Now."

"I don't advise that," he said. Same ventriloquist trick, as if his voice came from the air itself.

I ducked into a store, a midpriced Spanish boutique. The photogs massed outside, waiting for our exit.

Leo reached for me. I slapped his arm away.

"Fuck. You."

"Don't start nothing, won't be nothing," said Leo, all business now. "Remember where you are, and who you are. You have no private life. Everything you are and everything you do is owned by the public. And it goes through me first, you understand. Everything goes through me."

"Wedding invitation?"

"What? You gonna leave your child out of wedlock?" He knew underneath my post-punk exterior was a traditional streak the size of a six-lane highway. I realized suddenly and sharply that I didn't want to marry this man. But I also didn't want to birth a child into some kind of unmarried-mama drama, the kind all three of the girls I'd grown up next door to in Baltimore ended up in. And Leo knew that. And he had me trapped.

"We haven't even talked about it," I said, less firmly than I wanted to.

"No, we talked about it." That night of the party. "You just haven't wrapped your pretty little brain around the situation."

I wanted to say something eighth grade, like, "My brain isn't little *or* pretty." I wanted to pepper-spray him, kick him in the nuts, and leave him screaming. I wanted to call Red and cry. I wanted someone to rescue me from my life.

The soignée shop clerks stared. Leo glowered. I just looked back at him. A whisper of anger flared in me. It felt good. I hadn't really let myself feel in years, all that time I'd spent with Ari in our three-way marriage: me, Ari, and our substances. Years of numbness peeled away when I learned I was pregnant. Even I wasn't selfish enough to drown a baby in liquor. I wasn't selfless enough to be thrilled by my impending mamahood, either.

"So are we going out all smiles or what?" Leo said, cupping my chin in his hand. "Remember it's your day, baby girl, and you can play the cards any way you like. But everything's out in the open. Everything is on."

I stood, arms folded over my chest, silent. What a cunning man. Leo picked out some clothes, paid, and called our car to the curb. Until I reached the door I didn't know what I was going to do. But we stepped outside all smiles, arm in arm, with our bags, and we posed, and we left.

Inside, I was so hot I was molten.

▷ 36 Stevie Wonder, "Isn't She Lovely"

While Leo was out at a meeting, I bundled up every bit of my clothing and makeup I could find, called a sedan, and fled without leaving a note. But as I sped downtown, my stomach knotted, heart clenched. Earthquake in the belly, bile in the mouth. At a stoplight, I opened the door and vomited in the gutter; swilled from a bottle of water and spat. Some homecoming.

Didn't think it was just the pregnancy. I was heading back to *my* apartment, *my* East Village, *my* friends. My life. My loneliness. I could leave him anytime I wanted, right? Anytime.

A thin layer of dust covered everything in the apartment, from the takeout menus on the kitchen counter to the top of the television set. Twenty-five voice mails. And I hadn't turned on the celly since last night.

Home phone rang. Almost didn't pick it up. "I forgive you for not telling me," Red said as soon as I answered. "No guilt."

"Yeah." A catch in my throat.

"So I'm here."

"Where?"

"Your place. Well, downstairs at least. Just passing through."

"Right, I'm sure."

"Can I come up?"

"No. It's depressing in here. I'll come down."

There's a corner in the East Village where a stone church looks out over the low brick buildings like a beneficent matron surveying her brood, and the old Jews and Italians shuffle by the fast-moving hipsters and the hollow-eyed street dwellers—different worlds in the same time and space. The sun felt like a soft kiss, and I crossed the street to sit with Red on the steps of the church. A student was sketching the scene in broad charcoal strokes, and as I passed I saw he'd captured Red perfectly, wise and childlike in equal measures.

Told her yes, it was true. Yes, I was pregnant. Yes, I was still with Leo. Yes, I didn't know if I really wanted to be, either. All that said, yes, I was going to do this tour come hell or high water, and yes, I was going to have this baby.

Red grew up Catholic, like me. Not that Catholic girls didn't have abortions, oh, no. But if the religion hit you the right way, you could talk all the feminist game you wanted and still not feel free to excise what your body held, because you knew it was life. Men killed all the time, in peace and in war; grown people, not tiny little marble-size things. Red and I had talked once, way back in school, hesitantly confessing what we both believed. It was life. Not a baby. Not a person. But life. And you could kill it. But you had to admit to yourself what you were doing. You had to be strong enough to face the truth.

Red got Oscar's seed from a heterosexual rebound fuck after she broke up with Shar. I was there when she cried tears of joy and pain, knowing that she would have the baby, thinking that she would be alone. That was before she met Lin, who had what I thought was the unbelievable commitment to date a woman who was already pregnant. I never wanted to be a single mother, but I wondered if being with Leo was a blessing or a curse.

"I'll do whatever you need me to do for your baby."

"I know," I said.

"Move to Crown Heights; buy a brownstone near me. We'll take turns babysitting. I think they might sell the place next door."

Had to laugh. That was Red's fantasy from the jump, that we would all move not just to the same city, but to the same block, and raise our kids together, and grow old together, just like some sixties commune. Just like a dream.

"Why don't you come on the road with me?" I countered. "Just for the summer. You know, costume design. Whatever."

"And bring Oscar?"

"We can get you a nanny."

"And what about Lin?"

"She can come, too."

"And her job?"

"I know," I said. "I know. Stupid of me to ask." But that was *my* dream. There was something about being on the road with people you both liked and loved, people who could create a home wherever they went. Some musicians I knew brought their own candles and bedsheets to hotel rooms, hoping that would fend off the vertigo and loneliness of constant travel. Other people walked into a space and made it theirs, just by being. Like Red. "I'm jealous of you, Red. I really am. I just think your life is . . ." I teared up—God, I hated being the weepy preggo— "your life is beautiful. Full."

"I'm jealous of you, too," Red said. "You're a rock star. For real."

It still didn't feel that way. Seeing our CD in the New Releases rack didn't make me feel it. Having money in the bank and seeing our picture in the music magazines didn't make me believe it, either. The only thing, I suddenly realized, that made me feel like I was somebody was when that pack of reporters was chasing me and Leo down the street. I felt it. Hated it, but felt it. "Yeah. Crazy," I said.

"Life is, sometimes." Red checked her watch. "But you're not going to marry him, are you, Soph?"

"I don't want to, but I think I should."

She sat silent for a moment. Then: "I'm glad you're here." Adjusted her Pippi Longstocking–striped tights. "At your place, I mean. Not his." More shifting of garments. "I'm trying not to say anything I will regret."

"I can tell. Just bring it, Red."

"He's a petty tyrant, and I want to wring his neck for treating you like his bitch." Curse words always sounded false in Red's mouth. She was trying extra hard to change my mind.

"I just don't see what my options are."

"Leave him. Have your baby. We'll help you. All the girls, we'll help you. You should call Mimi. She's worried sick."

"Yeah."

"You don't need him," she said.

"My family would kill me if I had a baby without being married."

"So you're going to marry someone you don't love. You don't love him, do you?"

"I'm not sure."

"You love him, or you don't."

"I love Ari. Couldn't live with him. Couldn't change him."

There was nothing she could say to that. "I gotta go back to the store."

We wrapped our arms around each other, not so much hugging as resting in each other's arms.

"The offer to come on the tour stands, you know."

"And I'll let you know when the brownstone's up for sale. Market's rising. Rent is stupid."

"Don't start."

"Don't tell me don't start."

"I'll tell you whatever I want."

"I guess that's what makes us friends, huh?"

"Cue sitcom theme music."

Red stuck out her tongue. Then she saw the crosstown bus, and bolted into the crowd.

⊳ 37 Thievery Corporation featuring David Byrne (Louie Vega Remix), "The Heart Is a Lonely Hunter"

Could there be an uglier room in all of Manhattan? Looked like the visitors' hall in a minimum-security prison, gray, dank, and filled with a mix of broken-down folks and professionals. The guy at the front couldn't have been cleaner-cut: a former priest, he told us.

"I lost my parish to the drink. Oh, I'd spent so much time judging those in my congregation. By the time I made it here, you would think I'd gotten past the judging. But I showed up to my first meeting and said, I don't belong here. I don't belong with these people! Well, let me tell you, grace has led me to realize that every person here is my brother, every person here is my sister. We're in this fellowship together."

The lank-haired man in tattered jeans with faded tattoos nodded, as did the woman sitting between us, who looked like a teacher from a dusty one-room schoolhouse. The meeting was in Murray Hill, close to the East Village physically, but without all the flash and sizzle. I was praying I didn't run into anyone I knew.

"Some of us come in here every day in disguise, hat and sunglasses, hoping no one sees us coming in and no one here knows our face. And isn't that what got us to this point? Pretending how we looked to the outside world was more important than what we knew was crumbling on the inside?"

So the priest was psychic, too. Great.

All the lonely people, where do they all come from? Here, these meetings. Even the rocker couple near the front holding hands looked lonely together.

They got to the part where everybody started doing their personal shout-out to addiction. I felt like sinking under my chair. But once almost everyone in the room had spoken, I raised my hand. "My name is, uh, Clare"—I used my confirmation name, and hoped I wasn't recognizable—"and I'm an alcoholic. It's my first time."

Oohs and aahs from the gathered misfits.

They passed the collection plate. I pulled out a five, then changed my mind and put in a ten. People turned to congratulate me for coming. I didn't feel like congratulations.

The woman next to me handed me a scrap of paper with her name, Nancy, and phone number on it. "It can be hard, the first few days, you know . . . you might want to keep a lot of things around to drink; you know, fizzy water, orange juice, apple juice, just so you have a choice."

"Um, yeah. I, uh, well, I've been pretty much okay for a couple of weeks." A couple shots of tequila and one beer. A record low. I knew I was pregnant, not to mention the total bender the night of the big party, when my little lima bean probably got pickled.

Nancy smiled. Pretty much okay was clearly not okay enough if I was here. "Call me anytime," she said.

I walked past the court-appointeds getting their papers stamped, past the better-off volunteer soldiers; balled the yellow scrap with Nancy's name on it up, and stuffed it deep in the pocket of my black jeans.

⊳ 38 ABC, "How to Be a Millionaire"

The day I was supposed to head to Mama's house, the label called me in for a come-to-Jesus meeting about the pregnancy and the tour. I needn't bother to ask how they knew. All you had to do was pick up the nearest tabloid.

Ken Earnest was dressed more like a university president than a label exec. His vest was tweed. Silhouetted against the view from the forty-second floor, he smoked a blue-black pipe. In the corner of his office sat a tiny guitar and amplifier for his five-year-old son.

"Nothing like getting them started early," I said, trying to sound extra chipper.

"Yes. Soon you'll know."

The half-dozen others gathered in the room settled into an uncomfortable silence. Some I recognized; some I didn't.

"How far along?" That was Beatrice Weeks, their head of public relations. She was tall, creamy-skinned, dark-haired, and had the thick wrists and ankles of someone who'd starved herself far down below what a big-boned girl should weigh.

"About six weeks. I think."

"Well, she doesn't look any heavier than usual," she said to the others, as if I didn't exist. "How did they know?"

Leo, sitting beside me, tightened his grip on my knee.

Fuck it. "Leo told them."

He shot me a glare from the fiery depths of hell.

"Well, you did." I turned toward the others, shrugged. "He did."

"What were you thinking?" said Beatrice.

The only thing Leo liked worse than being cussed out in general was being cussed out by white people, and a woman at that. I wanted to break out into a laugh.

"No publicity is bad publicity. Remember who taught me that, Beatrice," Leo said through his teeth.

"And remember what else I told you: every rule is meant to be broken. *People* scheduled a feature. Now they're waffling. *New York Times:* we'd nailed an arts lead, now they're on the fence. I'm on your side, really," she said, turning to me, softening her voice. "But, honey, a black rock band is a hard sell to start. And some of those troglodytes at the *Times* think single pregnant black women belong on the op-ed page, not the arts page. Leo," she turned again, her voice tight, "what happened? I know you. You're careful. When you want to be."

Dayum. I took a second look at Beatrice. I could easily imagine her in the VIP section of some showcase, softening to Leo's ministrations. She'd know she was being played, but love it nonetheless. She'd dole out little treats to him—a freelance production contract here; a contact with some industry mogul there—always thinking she was in control. Maybe she felt that way until the moment she found out I was pregnant.

While I was busy imagining, Ken rebuked Beatrice. Took the tone of an elderly uncle with a trust fund who suddenly favored cutting his niece from the will. "But, dear," he turned to me, "you *are* getting married. When?"

"I don't know."

"Well, if you set a date, we can get the publicity department on it. There's nothing like a wedding to boost your Q rating."

Swallowed. "I don't know if we are."

Leo shrugged his shoulders, like, *See, she's crazy, I can't do anything with her.*

"Pardon?"

Louder. "I don't know if we are getting married. Leo just sprung it on me, and I need time to think."

Ken froze. I could imagine him mentally paging through everything he'd read in the Moynihan Report about the dissolution of black families: uppity black women and absent black men. But here was a well-dressed man who'd asked his negress to marry him . . . his pregnant negress . . . and she wouldn't go to the altar? Insane.

"What is it—money?" said Beatrice.

No, I thought, *it's not money, I've got more money than I've had in my entire life; it's just that I'm waking up out of a fog and I'm not sure I like the bed I'm lying in.*

"We can make things happen," said Beatrice.

"Absolutely," said the young man to her left, who'd imitated Ken's academic style to a T. "Free location; catering; photogs; I think we could get just about everything comped."

". . . Before you get so big you're showing," said Beatrice. "For heaven's sake."

"Where's her ring?" Ken said, all of a sudden.

Silence.

"Leo? Her ring?"

Of course there wasn't a ring, because Leo hadn't really asked me to marry him, just sprung it on me like a bear trap.

Leo said nothing.

Finally, Ken Jr. said, "We can get that comped, too."

They started reeling off the names of jewelers that might throw in a phat diamond for the right plugs—Harry Winston, De Beers—as if I wasn't even in the room. *I* was fucking pregnant. I was the one who was about to have go on tour while my feet swole to the size of melons, and not even a drop to drink. Man, I fantasized about having a good, long drunk, the kind that starts with Bloody Marys in the morning and rolls on until dawn. The less I drank, the less the songs came to me. And every time I couldn't write, I got panicked, like the last song I wrote was the last I'd ever write. The nerves started hitting me onstage; and it all went bad, fast.

Everyone in the room was staring at me, expecting me to fill a silence.

"No," I said. "This isn't right. I need time."

Silence. Again.

Beatrice turned to me. Uh oh.

"Do you remember your publicity photo?" she said.

Sure, the one they were supposed to put on the album cover. Me in front, eyes to the camera. Ari to my right, guitar balanced on the floor and his right arm on my waist. Shar and Bruce for accent on either side of the background.

"What does it imply?" Beatrice was hard, pedantic. I felt like I was back at Harvard.

"That your photographer had a lack of imagination?"

She ignored that. "A certain level of intimacy between you and Ari, don't you think?"

"Well, yeah."

"Well, yeah." She sighed. "You and Ari really are a tragic love story, you know that. And there are few things that teenage girls like better than tragic love stories. But this is not the fantasy, honey." If she called me honey one more time, I was going to leap across the room and strangle her. "You being pregnant is *not* on the script."

"Well, we're going to have to change the fucking script then, aren't we?" I said.

Ken yelled Beatrice's name, another warning. Beatrice said, "This is hopeless." I wondered how long it would take me to slam her face to the floor. Leo glared.

Ken looked at his watch, "I have a three o'clock. Which means all of you will be out of my room in two minutes. But remember this, Sophie," he said. "We've made a considerable investment in you. And we want you to succeed. But if you don't, you owe us." Damned recoupable advances. "And if you miss your chance, I daresay you won't get another."

I was nearly twice the age of the new names on the pop chart. Had I already gotten too used to this lifestyle, too used to all the freedom money could buy? It was too simple to think that freedom would come for free.

And how many people get a free wedding? It didn't have to last forever. (I of all people should know.) Our marriage just needed to last long enough to give my baby a name, which is all my Daddy gave to me.

I wish I could say that I turned to them again and said "No" with all the conviction of the first time. But I sat with my hands in my lap, and let the streams of words flow through my mind, pro and con, a Punch and Judy show inside my skull. Judy couldn't come up with any really good reasons not to do this, except that I didn't want to. And I'd done so many things already that I didn't want, what was one more thing?

"Okay," I said. "If you do the work."

"So it's settled, then," Ken said with a smile. "Beatrice, you'll personally be in charge of the nuptial campaign."

Beatrice clenched her hands. "Is that really necessary?"

"We don't have much time, Beatrice," said Ken.

"My department can handle this."

"Beatrice, this is settled. Done."

Beatrice looked pained. Leo looked relieved. I was confused: Who, exactly, had won?

Shar and the guys and I were camped out in our new office, a vast, bare plaster cube in SoHo. She'd sold me on the expense by saying having an office would give Ari someplace besides his house to hang out, and maybe give him an incentive to stay on the clean side. Bruce, who was still doing freelance art design just in case the band fell flat, was always happy for a new place to set up his computers. Shar brought her decks. She was putting the final edits on her latest mixed CD. She put out one a month, made a hundred copies, and passed them out for free. They were so hot, folks bootlegged her mixes, sometimes sold them on the street.

I'd been holed up in my East Village apartment on a steady diet of cable and takeout. All this camaraderie was a bit taxing. Bruce was karaokeing to Faith No More, and Ari was doing the chorus. It was like summer camp up in here.

I rubbed my temples, yawned, and put my head on my arms on the desk. Wanted to go home but didn't have the energy to move.

"Hey, Sophie, can I talk to you?" Shar said. I walked with her to one corner of the cube, away from the guys. "Thanks for telling us you're pregnant." Shar was trying to make it seem like a joke, but it came off how she really meant it: an accusation.

"And thanks for congratulating me." I wasn't about to apologize to Shar for not telling her as soon as I'd peed on the test strip. We weren't tight like that.

"What about the tour?

"What about it?"

"We're not going, are we?"

"Of course we're going!"

"Right. Silly." Shar skipped over to Bruce's desk and, under the guise of grabbing a fistful of paper clips, whispered in his ear. Bruce bounced on over to Ari's desk and whispered to him

"I'm so mad at you," he said.

"I really don't need this . . ."

". . . But I'll tell you this," he said. "If it comes down to the tour or the baby, take care of the baby. We'll figure it out."

"It's not like that. I just need more sleep."

He pulled me into a hug. We had our occasional dalliances, but he hadn't just *hugged* me in, well, years.

"Getting sentimental in your old age?"

"I feel old."

"So you're clean."

"Ish," he said.

"Ish is better than never."

"I really want this," he said.

"I know. So do I."

"Why don't you go home and get some sleep?"

"Good idea."

We walked over to the big loft double doors and he yanked them open.

"Thanks." I tried to rush out, but Ari put his arm across the door and looked in my eyes.

"It's going to be okay," Ari said.

"Isn't that my line?"

He brushed my cheek. And then Shar came up and put her arm around him. And I went and pushed the button on the elevator.

Instead of everybody worrying about Ari, now they were worried about me. Great.

Wouldn't it be crazy, I thought, walking up Broadway, if Ari went straight for real this time, totally off the drugs, and he could be the kind of boyfriend I always thought he could be. And wouldn't it be crazier if Shar went straight, too—a different straight—and they ended up together?

Ugh. Too much. I had to shut off my brain. And the way that I usually did that was with whiskey. And that way was no way right now.

⊳ 40 Blur,
"I'm Just a Killer for Your Love"

That night I dreamed about Ari. I was walking the bridge to try to reach him but the bridge kept going on and on and on. It was too much like the real past.

There was a time after Ari and I had split up, and before I had a job, that I thought the world had died. It was the center of summer, hot and still, and I'd walk from the East Village through Chinatown to the Brooklyn Bridge, and over to the tree-lined neighborhood where my lawyer lived. She was a friend of a friend of a friend, a woman who would take almost nothing to do nearly anything: divorces, adoptions, custody battles. Lived on the second floor of a brownstone she owned, with a gimpy gray-muzzled dog, and told me that my case was easy.

It didn't feel easy. Every step across the bridge felt like a betrayal, and I found myself drawn to the railings, looking down at the traffic just below and the wide-spaced beams that connected the pedestrian bridge to the edge. All you would need to do, I thought, was walk tightrope-style on a beam, and leap into the water. Why hadn't anybody thought of it? The Golden Gate Bridge was a jumper's paradise. The walkway was right by the edge. This would be more challenging, but not impossible.

Lost souls like me shared the bridge with tourists and Wall Street secretaries saving a few bucks by walking home, and a few lost souls like me. No one had figured out the jump yet, how easy it would be. No one had figured it out.

Every time I crossed the bridge, that was all I could think about, how drawn I felt to the edge, and how easy it would be for someone to jump. Not me, but someone.

Once an emptiness like that enters you, it's like demon possession.

You don't shake it easily. You don't shake it when, for example, your divorce becomes final; or you get a new job; or have sex for the first time with someone new. Sorrow lives in the marrow of your bones: the spirits gnaw you from the inside out. So that's what I was looking for when I met Leo: an exorcist. Or at least another demon to drive this desolate spirit out.

"Sometimes my arthritis is so bad I can't sleep. I just turn on the television and there you are. It makes me so proud."

My Great-Aunt Ophelia had trapped me between the potato salad and fried chicken. I contemplated evasive action but Aunt Noreen was to my right and Uncle Chet, whom Mom called Chatterin' Chet, was to my flank. I was thinking about the food. The potato salad had the perfect mix of eggs, mayonnaise, and a touch of mustard and vinegar. The chicken was neither breaded nor dry. The greens came from Aunt Martha's garden. Mama and I had spent all of yesterday cooking, even though I was tired from the trip down. I wanted my plate, and a place to sit down. No conversation. Fat chance.

Auntie Ophelia was still talking, more to herself than anyone else. Her grand pink hat shaded not only her face but that of anyone foolish enough to engage her in conversation. She believed that people who "carried themselves well" on TV could do no wrong. So far she hadn't mentioned the tabloid article, but I could see (or maybe I imagined) other family talking and shooting me looks.

It was bad enough that I was a musician; worse that I was a rock musician; and worst of all that I was already bringing shame to the family name. The Washingtons worked government jobs. We were teachers, city hall clerks, postmen, garbage men. We mistrusted anyone who did not draw a weekly paycheck. I kissed Aunt Ophelia's soft cheek, snared the last golden-fried breast before my cousin Kenny came back for seconds, and moved south through the three-picnic-table spread, hunting for Leslie's crab puffs.

The yard was packed. My kin made a noise I associated only with family reunions and funerals, which, come to think of it, are reunions themselves. All the cooing and oohing over babies grown, grown folks married, and married folks having babies made us sound like a flock of exotic birds.

Mom had pulled a blue-and-white apron over the designer suit she'd worn to church, and she was still tiptoeing around in those heels. She told Uncle Jay that he should buy in Southeast D.C. before the prices went through the roof. "Since Walmart opened, folks are dying to get in. Buying things that aren't even safe to live in. Now I," she leaned in for the kill, "happen to have a couple of listings left. Good blocks, too."

Mama's real-estate sideline filled all the hours between work, church, and minding other people's business. Carrying out huge aluminum platters of deviled eggs, creamy potato salad, and her famous oven-fried chicken kept her busy for the moment. But when she had a second, she would back you into a corner until you promised to buy a home you'd never seen.

No Washington in his or her right mind would miss the barbecue. At least four dozen of my aunts, uncles, and cousins, and probably some hungry folks that wandered off the street, squeezed into the tiny backyard and gathered around Nana and Grandpa. Mom moved faster than a hummingbird, hugging new arrivals and rearranging the food. Me and my cousins were privates in Momma's conscription army, getting plastic cups of Kool-Aid for our aunties and uncles, gathering garbage, and opening folding chairs.

"When do we get to get old?" said Trevor, my cute cousin. We all had family codes: the smart one, the fast one, the rich one, the evil one, the baby, poor thing he so slow, and so on. Trev had hair that looked like it was conked but wasn't. Back when folks still called him Little Trevor, he was my prom date. Couldn't get anybody else, and, come to think of it, he still had the most manners of anyone who ever took me out.

"We'll always be children," I said. Lugged a couple chairs to the corner of the yard. "And they'll always be the parents." I'd heard Trevor's wife carp about how she was pregnant again. Seems like she just delivered their fourth baby. They were smart upwardly mobile buppies, but they didn't seem to have any concept of birth control.

How Catholic.

"That's why we gotta start working on the young ones," Trev said. "Once we get old, we can roll up with the same deal, sit back and let them cater to us."

Nice to think. But Trevor's kids, like most of my cousins', were stone-cold brats. As we unfolded the chairs along the tall wooden fence, I saw Trevor the Third beating a Super Soaker over his sister's head.

"'Skuze me a second." Trev went over to his kids, held out his hand for the plastic weapon, and started preaching holy hell. Trevor's wife, Verna, was on the back porch, singing "Da Butt" in a cutsie little voice while wiping their eighteen-month-old's bottom.

I remember when my cousin Trevor jumped the broom with his pregnant bride, black Barbie with a bump, and I thought it was Ghet-Toe with a capital G. Everybody was in their business. But today his family looked straight-up Jack 'n' Jill: four kids, two cars, a house in Randallstown, Maryland.

I retreated to the shade side of the house. I'd worn black, which was exceptionally stupid. Thought it made me look thinner. But summer in the B-more was an endurance test, with day after day of 90 degrees and 100 percent humidity. You could lose five pounds walking from the house to the nearest grocery store.

I fanned my top to get a breeze, wondered what it would be like to walk around naked, wondered what my relatives would look like naked, and had a total mental shutdown. Auntie Ophelia sidled up next to me. "I didn't see you at Mass," she said.

And you won't anytime soon.

"It was lovely today. Father talked about the importance of giving."

I know. I'd been to the Vatican. That art takes a lot of upkeep.

Used to be every Sunday of July Fourth weekend we met at ten for Mass, then came back to Momma's and ate until we were ill. But the next generation of Washingtons had branched out. We had AME and Baptists, two Jewish in-laws, one plain white guy, and a Rastafarian. The believers felt sorry for anyone who wasn't Catholic to the core, as if we belonged to some great club you had to beg to enter.

I hadn't gone for more than Christmas and Easter in years. I could still smell the incense, though, and hear the prayers. *I believe in One Holy Catholic and Apostolic Church. I believe in the forgiveness of sins, and the life of the world to come.* Saw Little Trevor walking between the pews, swinging a sweet-smelling smoky censer. Father Michael behind him, ruddy-cheeked and gray-haired, dressed in white robes.

"You know your uncle Luke always asks about you," Auntie O said. That was well and good. I'd gotten married in the Church, but I knew the exact moment when I had stopped believing that spending time on my knees praying would do anything but give me bruises. I was nine. I prayed that my father would come back to us, and he hadn't. It was that fucking simple.

I snuck upstairs toward my old room, the walls covered with high school pompoms and a poster of Prince.

"Hey, Sis."

I jumped nearly a foot off the ground. Didn't know Matthew was home again.

We stood in the unlit hallway. His pecan-colored skin was covered all over with dark marks halfway between sores and scabs. His eyes were rimmed not so much with red but with rust, a tired-looking inflammation that I wasn't sure he was just coming down with or getting rid of. And he was skinny again. Matthew could fluctuate within a fifty-pound range at any point in time.

"Why don't you come downstairs?" I asked.

"I got food here."

He gestured to his room, and I saw he had a heaping plate that Mama must have fixed him before the guests came. There's nothing like having your junkie son pick over the chicken wings to put everyone off their feed.

Now I knew why my sister Erika wasn't here. She and Matthew repelled like magnets facing the wrong way.

"Well," I said. I was still clutching my plate. "Do you want to eat?"

He stopped scratching his wrists and gestured to his room. I hesitated, but it was clean only, surely, because Mama had cleaned it. Just give Matthew a few days, though.

Conversation came in fits and starts. Lost his apartment (again). Looking for a job (again). Was staying at the mission (again), until someone called Mama and she brought him home. It was hard to taste the food and look at my brother at the same time. It was hard to think that I was the same as he was, hardwired to love things that hurt me again and again.

With Matthew's window cracked, I could clearly hear the gossip below. "I've been going over to that house and watching them for five years now." That was Aunt Martha, named for Nana. "Don't know what to do when Pops runs off the way he does. I been called from work five times last month. Last time they caught him in slippers at the five-and-dime."

"So you want to put them in some home." Big Trev talked fast, all business. Ran the car dealership where Little Trevor worked. Gave money but not a drop of time to care for his parents.

"I didn't say that. But it's not just Papa. I have to take off work for the doctors' visits. They might have to take her other leg."

When I leaned a little out the window, I could see Nana smiling in her wheelchair. As she got sicker, she got more radiant. Smiled more, laughed more, prayed more. She'd tucked her long silver hair in a bun, covered her leg in a multicolored afghan she'd probably knitted herself. While Nana lost her body to diabetes, Grandpa was losing his mind. Medicare paid for a part-time home health aide. My aunts and uncles had been passing the burden of going over to their place at nights to try to keep them in their home.

What good was I? Momma raised me to better myself out of this place. Home was a country whose citizenship I'd renounced. I could visit, but I couldn't stay.

Then I heard a jolt of bass and a collective "Aww, yeah" from my cousins. "That's for all y'all from back in the day," said Trevor, triumphantly standing over the boom box that, until a moment ago, used to play a Quiet Storm station.

"You can't just come in your auntie's house and play whatever kind of foolishness you like!" Big Trev was walking over and calling his son out to the whole crowd.

"Dad. I am not a child. And this is not foolishness. This is *indigenous* African-American music, Pops."

"This is some bullshit," Big Trev said. "Ill-damned-literate street-corner hoods . . ."

"But no, Daddy, this is old school," said Big Trev's daughter, Lisa. He stared her down and she slid to the side.

Nana spoke, softly but firmly. "Let them play it." And so it was done. My generation had finally won the great hip-hop-versus-soul battle. I saw Big Trev sulking, and Trevor turning up the volume.

I'd have to sit down and tell Nana that it was true, that I was pregnant and getting married. But that would be hard. I knew she would ask me if I loved Leo. I didn't know what I would say.

Now wasn't the time for that conversation. I'd stay a couple more days, let someone else cook for me for a change. Let someone else make my bed, wash my laundry. Be a child again.

Yeah, stay for a few days more. That'd help make things all right.

Momma commanded everyone to gather for the picture. I grabbed a deviled egg off my plate and headed down. I didn't look back at Matthew.

Missed Leo in a physical way that I'd never missed anyone before, not even Ari. Since I was a kid, my fantasy and reality mixed and slid over each other. As I lay in my childhood room, I found myself spinning scenarios of Leo coming to woo me, an updated, hip-hop version of a Harlequin romance. He'd show up penitent and tired from the sleepless nights he'd spent without me; explain how his relationship with his harried mother had put him in a space where he couldn't fully open his heart to a woman; and finally confess that he'd taken the strides to change himself and commit to one woman: me, me, me.

Of course, by the time Leo finally made it to Baltimore, I had regressed to my childhood self, acquiescing to a schedule of church and library meetings along with my mother. I never doubted that any of the women I'd grown up with as elders loved me; I just wasn't sure they knew who I was. I spent half of a day sorting and cataloging donations to the library, most of them broken-spined books of dubious literary quality. My mother and my grandmother's best friend sat to either side of me. My grandmother would have been there, except she still felt too sick.

So, like some bold conquistador, in came Leo. He wore a brown suit with blue pinstripes, the gentler side of pimpish, with a brown suede hat held in his hand. I'd never seen him with a hat before. My guess was he reckoned B-more was the South, and in the South proper men wear hats. He greeted the ladies, squeezed my shoulder, then took my mother's hand in his. I could feel my mother stiffening at his touch, unwilling to be charmed. And so he loosened his grip, sat in between us, and gave Mama his full gleaming smile.

Like a nocturnal animal caught in bright light, Mama stared more than smiled back. Leo gave some rap about how glad he was to be there, dazzling the library ladies. *How long you gonna stay here?* he whispered in my ear.

How'd you find me? I whispered back.

Your grandmother said where you were.

And how'd you find her?

You left your address book at home. Dummy.

Didn't realize until Leo arrived that I'd been boycotting New York, putting my stay on extended play. Leo finally noticed everyone staring at him, excused himself, and asked me to step outside.

"I'm only halfway done," I said, going back to cataloging the donated books. A group of schoolchildren rushed in through the double doors. This library, our library, was pure fifties architecture, a variation on the one-room schoolhouse, with a sloped roof, high ceilings, and a mass of open space. Bookshelves divided the room, and the children, running through their teacher's *shh*ing, wound their way through the stacks.

Leo stepped outside. The church ladies shot me a look.

Five books later, Miz Rivers, who'd put her silver hair in French twists, said, "So that's your boyfriend."

"We live together," I said. Didn't know why, except it was the truth and I was too tired to lie.

We'd neared the end of the boxes of books. Found my palms sweating. Soon we wouldn't have the sorting and cataloging, and affixing the little bookplates and check-out stickers to occupy us. Soon we'd be left to our own devices.

"Seems like a nice young man," said another woman. She, too, was my grandmother's age, squat where Miz Rivers was lean. I knew I was supposed to say, "Yes, he is," but I didn't feel like telling a lie in a library. To me that was worse than telling a tale in church.

"He's very successful," I said.

"I can see from that suit," said my mother. She didn't approve of clothes that cost more than your car note. Funny, she didn't like Ari, either, with his threadbare corduroys and unpressed shirts, even when she found out his family had money.

Well, Leo and I had plenty of money in the bank now. I was free from the nine-to-five and he had six new clients. One of them just got a deal bigger than mine.

Leo was secretive, though. The more money we made, the less he wanted me to know about it. I began to piece together the language of percentage points and royalties the way an immigrant learns slang from watching TV. It was hard, fast, and dirty. I asked the label people questions when Leo wasn't in the room. When he was, he ripped me for asking stupid questions in public. When I asked him the same questions in private, he'd ask why I didn't understand what the other people said.

Focused on the library again. I noticed I'd run out of books to sort. "He's successful," I repeated, loading damaged books into a recycling bin. "And he loves me." The first I knew was true. The second I wasn't so sure. But as I took the recycling to the street corner outside the library, Leo walked toward me. His body language was humbler than when he'd entered. He put his arm around my shoulder and whispered in my ear, "I will be there for us, Sophie, swear to God, and for our child." I had a lot of choices then, including the choice to deny his words and walk away. Thirty-odd years ago, my mother had found herself knocked up with me, and my daddy professed his love. Like her, I chose to believe. So I took Leo's hand and we walked inside together, so that he could properly greet his new people: my people.

43 Eubie Blake, "If You've Never Been Vamped by a Brownskin, You've Never Been Vamped at All"

There's something different about making love when you're already pregnant. The quality of the touch is different, or maybe just the way you imagine you're being touched.

I remembered this one time I was in the desert with Ari, candy flipping. The drugs came on, and the baked earth that had felt like concrete before began to soften. Within a few minutes we were walking on a bed of soft talcum, or so I imagined it, every step sinking into powdery softness.

My body felt that way tonight. I'd never even dreamed of making love in my mother's house, in the small, short twin bed that I lay on reading books about dragons and princes. But she'd gone out to the store, feigning a huff to cover excitement, to buy us something special to eat for dinner. I took Leo up to my still-virginal bedroom, filled with band posters and novels I read for freshman lit. "So this," I said, spreading my fingers, "is where it all began."

"Damn, this place is a museum," Leo said, opening my closet.

"So what? I'm never here."

"You're here enough."

"Enough to what?"

"Enough to grow."

"I have no idea what you're talking about."

"I'm talking about you still acting like a little girl around your mother."

"I'd like to see what you're like around your mother."

"That ain't gonna happen," he said. Leo had put his entire family in the freezer, just shut them out of his life. He acted as if he had sprung fully formed into the world, as if I were strange for wanting to meet his kin.

I'd been massaging my shoulder, the one that gets all knotted up. He came over and put his thumb into the sore spot, brutal but effective, rotating it until he'd softened the tight flesh. And once that was done, he lay me back on my bed, and his touch felt warmer and gentler than it ever had. The touch wasn't soft, no; but yielding, unlike his usual master of the manse routine. I let him hook his finger through my panties, but when he started to pull them down I brushed aside his hand.

"This isn't right."

"Why?"

"Mama'll be back any second. I should go downstairs and get out some pots."

"Sophie," he said. "Stop listening for the sound of her car."

So I did. Felt my body sinking into the softness of my grandmother's quilt, and the lumps in the pillows I'd had since I was thirteen. My body opened in a way it never had before, a clenched flower bud yielding to the sun and rain.

I was so tired, really. I found it hard to sleep in this house. Too many ghosts of my old selves haunted the corners, tempting me to reminisce. But Leo's touch was hypnotic. I found myself half-asleep, half-awake, as he entered me.

I began to hear Mama banging around in the kitchen. I tried to figure out if it was normal-level banging, or a signal that she wanted me to come down and help out. I tried to pull away, but Leo kept me fixed.

We both came near silently, he with his hand over my lips. As soon as he was done, he said, "So you're going to marry me, right? No foolishness."

"Sure, why the hell not?" I said.

I hadn't known that was coming out of my mouth, but as soon as I said it, I felt better. I couldn't let my child grow up without a father, no matter how flawed Leo was. Not like I was perfect myself. Not like I was immune to the lures of marriage, either, especially the chance to plan a wedding and scoop up all the loot. All I know is that over the past decade, I'd shelled out thousands of dollars in wedding and shower gifts and I wanted some of that back.

The more I repeated the words to myself—*wed-ding, mare-ij*—the more that I liked them. I hugged Leo and he hugged me back, not in a stingy, stiff way, but all thickness and warmth.

I ran down the stairs and into the kitchen. Mama was rubbing herbed butter over big salmon filets. "Let me help you," I said, picking up a bowl of fresh green beans and beginning to snap off the ends.

"You seem happy," she said.

I worried that meant she could smell the sex on me, so I made some kind of nondescript comment. Before I could get totally embarrassed, Leo walked into the room, and I took his hand. "We have some news," I said. Mama put down the dish and wiped her hands on a towel. "Mama, we're getting married."

Mama looked at us for a second, her face a blend of pride and amusement. "I wouldn't expect anything different. You're a Washington."

"I was thinking about how we could dress up the church," I said, not letting her words sting, "We have money this time, not like last time when I couldn't care less about the dress or the hall or anything. I have some ideas now. And the label is going to help us pay for it. I think it's going to be really great."

There were six fillets: one for me, Leo, Mama, Erika, Matthew, and an extra in case someone wanted seconds. Mama carefully finished rubbing them, arranged them on a pan coated with tinfoil for easy cleanup, and put them in the oven.

"Well," she said, "I won't lie, I'd like you married in the Church, if only to show the bourgie biddies that you turned out well. Baby, you know it doesn't work that way. There's no repeat performance until you take care of that old marriage. You're still married in the eyes of God."

"Nobody really sweats that anymore."

"Sweats what?" said Leo, fidgeting and playing with his tie. This wasn't going according to script.

"It's one thing to get divorced," Mama said, turning to Leo. "But that's not enough in the Church. She has to take care of her old marriage."

"Are you saying you never got a divorce?" he turned to me.

"No, that's not it at all. It's just . . ."

"What?"

"You know how . . ."

"No, I don't know."

"Damn, stop cutting me off." I hated cursing in my mother's house. I took a deep breath, and explained, or tried to, that I was plenty divorced. But the Church didn't recognize divorce, only annulment. Annulment was an arcane process once reserved for kings and noblemen. Instead of breaking the bonds of a marriage, it erased the marriage outright. The rabbit disappeared from the hat; the clock ran backward. I thought annulment had disappeared into the veils of time.

"Nobody does it anymore," I said. "Right, Mama?"

"Talk to your Uncle Luke," was all Mama said. When I just stared at her, she said, "It's not up to me," and slid the salmon into the oven.

⊳ 44 Frank Sinatra, "Blue Skies"

You have to understand that Matthew and Erika showing up at the same time in the same place happened about as often as the Comet Hale-Bopp breezed by Earth. I have no idea what my mother told Erika, but she must have pushed every guilt button in the book.

My sister came alone, though she'd been dating the same man for five years. They lived three blocks away from each other, but refused to move in together or get married, which I know drove Mama mad. The way that she walked in the door—whispering on her cell phone, body language tense and tight—I knew she was on the phone with him, and he was trying to calm her down, and that was just making her more pissed off. She sighed a final sigh, said a grudging "I love you," and closed her phone.

"Hey, Sis," I said, moving in for a hug. Erika tensed up even more, and I watched her try to force herself to relax when our bodies met.

"So you're pregnant," she said.

"Yup."

"I know you probably weren't taking a daily multivitamin when you conceived, but it's not too late to make sure you're getting enough folate. The prenatal vitamins are key, but also be sure and eat cruciferous vegetables." She saw me looking blank and said, "Broccoli . . . and plenty of water. I don't care how much you pee, just keep drinking H_2O. If you want, we can go over a menu plan."

"Uh, right."

"Anyway, let me see what Mama needs." Further sigh.

Erika started to leave her purse on a table by the front door, then picked it back up and took it with her into the kitchen. It wasn't like Matthew stole all the time, especially not when Mama was coddling him so. But when he did, it was pretty spectacular. One time he went to the community clinic where Erika was a pharmacist. He'd not only stolen some Rx pads but forged a doctor's signature and convinced one of Erika's colleagues to give him narcotics. After that, it was on. Erika wouldn't come anywhere near Matthew unless there was a death in the family or her boyfriend was restraining her.

Ten minutes later, Mama, Erika, Matthew, Leo, and I were seated around the dining room table, looking at a lovely platter of grilled salmon and green beans amandine. Every now and then Mama liked to get fancy on us, so we had out the good porcelain, with a salad plate to the side already arranged and dressed. Mama asked Leo to say grace.

Leo no more believed in God than he did in the tooth fairy, or so he told me, but he liked a challenge. He reached to link hands, and we all did, even though we were the close-your-eyes-and-bow-your-heads types. I was seated at one end of the rectangular table, holding hands with Matthew and Erika. Matthew vibrated from a constant, hard, rapid tapping he kept up with one of his feet. After a long pause, Leo spouted off the most mellifluous dining invocation I had ever heard in my life. He sounded like Martin Luther King and Rakim mixed together. He said:

> Dear Lord, bless us and this bounteous table here tonight. Lord, thank you for bringing me into this fine family, a family whose potential is endless and hearts are open to a stranger like me. Bless Brother Matthew in his struggles. Bless Sister Erika in keeping our community healthy. And please bless Mrs. Lee [Yeah, Mama still went by Mrs. Lee, two decades after she split from Daddy.] for all her good works in this neighborhood. Please bless my dear Sophie and keep her and her blessed burden safe on her journeys. For you are He through whom all blessings come, and we accept your blessings with humility and gratitude.
>
> Amen.

Damn, he was good.

After grace, Mama was beaming like she'd won the lottery. Erika rolled her eyes. She looked on religion as urban legend, like alligators in the toilets. Our take on religion was very different. Although neither of us went to church, I believed in God, but feared Him. Or Her. Or It. Erika looked at those who believed as fools.

I can't remember what we talked about. As usual, the food was impeccable: fresh, high-quality ingredients, well seasoned and well cooked. In other words, dinner was boring. Anytime Mama was trying to impress, she ended up underselling food's sex appeal.

God, I hadn't cooked in ages, but when I did, I could burn. I was from the "I've never met a spice I didn't like" school. Every dish was a party, a riot of flavors. Mama could bust out with the superspice every once in a while, but her flavors were mainly garlic, pepper, onion, and salt, in various combinations, forever and ever, amen.

Everything was going great. Then the front door rang. Matthew rose. Mama rose. Leo waved her down. He answered the front door. A man. You know how in the movies bad men wear black? This man was dressed in all-white, including a pair of shoes I recognized as the primo baller athletic shoe, white-on-white, expensive, ultimately stupid-looking. The word white comes from a Norse word, *hwit*, that meant fearsome. That's how I felt: fearful, awed by this gleaming ebony figure in his white armaments. My brother, his suit puckering and gathering around his skin-and-bones frame, moved toward the man in white as if he was the risen God, as if he held the keys to salvation. Mama stood and went to the door to tell the man to leave. Erika ran to Mama to tell her to stand down, that this was a fight she could not win. Mama and Erika ended up scrambling by the door, fighting like schoolyard rivals while Matthew, a beatific smile on his face, walked slowly down the walkway to the man's truck idling on the street.

Leo didn't budge. Somewhere along the line I'm sure he'd learned Lesson Number One: never come between a dealer and his prey. I'd learned that the hard way with Ari. But, damn, it was Night of the

Living Dead out there. I saw three or so kids from the neighborhood lean into Mr. Hwit's SUV and make their hard bargains. Matthew and another one looked happy; the others, resigned. I went back to the table and continued eating. And after a while, the raised voices of Erika and Mama settled, and they came back to the table and ate as well.

Leo and I left B-more right after dinner. I didn't know until we walked outside that he'd called a sedan to drive us home. Should have been angry at him for spending our money this way, but it was just what I wanted, to float on a cloud of comfort. We didn't discuss whose home we were headed toward. I'd been away from Leo's long enough that it would feel foreign to me, but I didn't feel like sleeping alone.

We curled in the backseat like cats in a basket. Absence makes the heart grow fonder. Fondness makes the heart grow weak.

My mother would never have approved of spending money like this. While a lot of my friends' parents were coming to grips with the fact that their retirement money would never pay for their lifestyle, Mama had it on cruise control. After all those years of struggling, she had become so frugal that she couldn't break old habits if she wanted to.

Me, I was looking forward to getting into some of those new clothes I'd bought. I didn't dare bring them home to Mama's with me, because all I'd get was the yak yak yak about how much they cost and how I didn't need to be wasting my money like this. I got Red to design some new gear for me, and went out and bought a couple dozen pairs of shoes, plus bags. I was never a handbag type, but fuck it. I needed to look good. And now I could.

"What are you thinking about?" Leo said.

"Shopping."

He chuckled. That was a language we both spoke well.

"So we're going to Harlem, right, baby?"

"Yeah," I said. "We'll figure it out."

Somewhere on the New Jersey Turnpike, Red called.

"Hey, girl. I'm almost home."

"Where are you?"

"With Leo. Coming back to the city."

She paused so long that I called her name.

"Ari's in the hospital," she said. "Harlem Hospital."

"ODed? He's been clean."

"He ODed," she said with finality. "Shar found him this morning, but we don't know how long he'd been on the floor."

I told the driver we weren't going to Leo's house but the hospital, and Leo started to give me some lip and I just shut him down. I kept asking Red questions she couldn't answer. How bad was it? How long had he been using again? Why didn't someone call me earlier? (That, said Red, was up to Shar.)

When I got there, Shar was in the hallway of Ari's ward in a dingy plastic chair. She shot me a nasty look as I went into his room. I was still officially his next of kin; they'd told everyone else to back off.

It was a two-person room, and the family of the man in the other bed gathered around him. They were talking about getting revenge on whoever had shot the kid. Drainage tubes from the kid's midsection flowed a diluted red, like lymph and blood together, toward a bag. I didn't want to look but for a moment I couldn't pull myself away.

Underneath an oxygen mask, Ari's lips moved constantly. I wanted to lift it and hear what he was saying, even though it probably didn't make sense. His skin was the color of Sheetrock and there was a crust of dried blood around the tube into his arm. He kept trying to turn on his side but they had him strapped down.

My hands and feet started getting cold, the same as they always did when I was stressed out. I leaned down and whispered in his ear, but whatever I said to him was probably no more coherent than what he said to me.

A nurse came up and guided me away.

"Goddamnit," I said to him, and to myself. "Why can't you learn? Why do you have to keep doing this over and over again?"

There's one thing a hospital won't forget, and that's how to get their money. Shar had put down a credit-card deposit so Ari wouldn't end up in the charity ward. I called up the private rehab hospital he'd gone to in New York, told them what was happening, and gave them my credit-card info. They'd pick him up when Harlem said it was safe to transfer. Then I called his Dad, who should have been the next of kin after the divorce, except nobody ever gets paperwork right.

Richard Klein was out but his secretary was in. "Tell him his son ODed again. I'm going to give you all his info so you can make arrangements to pay for his care. And by the way: tell Richard to make sure he's listed as next of kin. I'm not putting up with this shit anymore."

I was meaner than I meant to be, but I thought the anger would set me free.

"I'm so through with this motherfucker." I was talking to myself but there was Shar, walking across the room, and she'd clearly heard me. And the look on her face was volcanic, ready to blow.

"Look, I know you've had your problems, and I know he has his problems, but it was cold for you to cut him off like that," she said in one big rush.

"What are you talking about?"

"Blocking his number from your phone."

"Uh." I cocked my head and looked at her like she'd lost her mind, which clearly she had. "What are you talking about?"

"You blocked Ari's number from your phone. He was trying to call you and give you—what is that little thing you do? The weather report? Well, obviously it's pretty important to him because he flipped when he couldn't reach you."

I kept staring at her. Ari had her wrapped up tight in his little conspiracy theories. "Look, if you're trying to blame his OD on me, think again."

"No, I'm not blaming you." Her face said different. "I'm just . . . Look, things have just been raggedy the last few days. He wasn't coming into the office so I knew something was wrong. So I went to his house. It was a mess. He said he was calling you to apologize, he said to, um, make amends. It was *important* to him, Sophie. When he said you'd blocked his number I thought you were tripping, but I tried it myself.

That was cold." She thought for a second, "I know he could have called you from another phone, but, you know, you sent a signal. Pretty fucking clear one." She slowed and backed off just a little bit. "We got it, Sophie. We got what it takes. Bruce and I aren't just along for the ride. We believe in this band. The only thing is, your boy is about to go one way or the other."

"He's been about to go one way or the other for fifteen years."

Shar sighed, put her hands on the small of her back, and massaged. Then she gave me a sharp look. "Who has access to your phone besides you?"

Only the man waiting outside in the sedan. Leo.

Once again Ari pulled the phoenix-from-the-ashes routine. In a couple of weeks he'd come back to rehearsal. His skin was the color of baked desert earth, so he'd clearly been out getting sun; and his hair seemed to have grown from a buzz cut to a short tight curl overnight. He was making quiet conversation. There was a look in his eyes I hadn't seen in a long time: calm. I walked up and squeezed his hand. Shar was perfectly polite to me, but she hadn't been truly friendly since Ari went into the hospital.

Because of Ari's little detour, the label assigned Beatrice to go on tour with us. During the meeting with the other execs, she looked flat-out panicked. She gave Ken all sorts of excuses about what projects she was working on, blah blah blah; but Ken wasn't the kind of man you could talk out of much. Beatrice was screwed.

First, we did club dates. My favorite part was meeting everyone's family. We played a small nightclub in Detroit, the block half-filled with empty warehouses, a strip club across the street. Bruce's cousins came all Prince-d out, with postfunk outfits and hair permed into a vertical crunch. Bruce programmed his keyboard to match the crowd, eighties electric funk style, and by the end of the night I felt like I was back at a club in college again.

In L.A., we got the ridiculous rich poseur kids from Harvard-Westlake and Beverly Hills High. Richard Klein and the Chocolate Stepmama took a booth in the VIP section. Just before the last song I saw them leave, smiling that "we're about to knock the boots" smile.

After our show in Atlanta, we drove to Birmingham to see Shar's family. We made a full field trip out of it, seeing the magnificent civil rights museum across from the Sixteenth Street Baptist Church, and then driving out to the country to see her aunts and uncles. They lived in houses out on the edge of fields which they still farmed, corn and tomatoes and greens. They might have been country, but they were also on it about the cash flow. Everything they grew was organic, and they were making good money selling to everything from co-ops to yuppie supermarkets.

On one edge of her extended family's fields was a small white country church. I wore a white dress with blue flowers. Shar wore a T-shirt and pants, and fluffed her Mohawk as high as she could, but she fit in better than I did. Sometime during the worship a few of the older women began chanting and humming, and one by one the others joined in, until it felt like I was inside God's chest. Ari skipped church, as usual, but Bruce came and smiled a deep, faraway smile. His lids fluttered a bit but his eyes stayed closed. I seemed to be the only one looking around.

In D.C., we played the 9:30 club. A bunch of the Washingtons, including Trev, came down from Maryland, and a few of the Lees came up from Virginia. My cousins on my dad's side were rougher and sexier, the kinds of girls with tattoos on their tits, guys with gold teeth or full grills. I don't think any of them really liked our music, except maybe my baby cousin James. Well, he wasn't quite a baby. He was twenty now, a junior at Georgetown. Mama always said the worst thing you could possibly say in the Washington family about James: that he hated being around his own people. I don't think that was it at all. He's not the one who'd made the family move out to Pikesville, where black folks were scarce and all the kids listened to pop, rock, or punk. That night I could see him from the stage, opening up, realizing that there were other black folks like him and they were gathered right here. I could see him whispering to a friend, a white friend, *That's my cousin,* and looking around at the black folks with hairdos and clothes their parents probably disapproved of, realizing that he wasn't just a freak and a misfit.

I was tired all the time. Man, this was a tougher nut than when we were twenty-two. But touring made us the real money. Album sales were nice and all that, but all that loot went to the label unless sales were off the charts. The more we toured, the more the checks came to our bank accounts. The money situation was fine, but the funny thing was this: the more we toured, the better reviews we got for our shows, the fewer albums we sold. Talk about a mixed blessing.

No matter what we did, I thought, everything was wrong. Everything was working in reverse.

We had toured before, just the two of us, Ari and I. We were six months out of college. We'd released a vinyl EP on one of those precious indie labels out of Washington State. Red had her come-to-Jesus moment with us and dropped off the bill only three or four dates in. Ari and I took a break and retooled for solo acoustic guitar. We drove around the country playing coffee bars and nightclub-taverns, the kind where one or two dozen shoe gazers grudgingly paid the five-dollar cover. Drove everywhere in his dad's old Pontiac Grand Prix. Despite the fact that the air conditioner was broken, Ari had spray-painted it black.

About a hundred miles out of Phoenix we hit a traffic jam that stretched for miles. The sun was setting over the mountains. They weren't the rolling mounds I knew from the east. These were all angles, sharp shoulder blades jutting from a thin skin of scrub and dry grass. Saguaros dotted the hillsides by the road. I didn't know they were saguaros until Ari told me. I just knew they looked like the cactuses (or was that the cacti) you saw in cartoons.

Needless to say, having the truck spray-painted black and being without AC, we were soaking the seats with our sweat. We were cranky and we smelled. Still, it was beautiful. Trucks lined the right lane of the highway, more than I'd ever seen together all at once. At first the mountains looked purple in the fading sunlight. Then they became themselves again, brown, against a deepening sky. The pattern of dark spots on the moon looked like a Pac-Man in midchomp.

I leaned over to kiss Ari and he slid the side of his hand along the sweat on my neck, lifted my hair, and blew. It might as well have been an ocean breeze, how good it felt, how cool it felt amid the heat. "I'm sorry I painted the car," he said, between kisses.

"Me, too."

There was this girl ahead of us in a Yugo. She watched us in the rearview mirror, her eyes flickering up to catch us kiss again and again.

I kissed Ari harder because she was looking. I'd never admit it out loud, but I loved having people watch. If I had any guts, I'd be one of those girls who has sex standing in the alleyway just to get the extra juice of feeling like I might be caught.

I wondered what this girl was like, if she lived in one of the one-light towns along the I-10 or if she was just passing through. If she was married or dating or single. If she'd ever seen black people kiss anywhere except the movies.

And when traffic started moving again, we didn't notice, and neither did she, until the guy behind us started honking and giving us the finger.

That was life on the road.

Oh, and one more thing I remember from that drive. After we got moving again, we saw this five-car pileup that had stopped us all. The shoulder was decorated with red hazard triangles that glowed in the headlights. The rest of that ride, I paid attention to the carcasses of automobiles from older crashes on the side of the road, plus the crosses and bouquets of faded plastic flowers that dotted the way.

Ari kept his right hand on my left knee and sang me French bedtime songs he'd learned when he lived in Montreal as a little kid.

Fell asleep. Dreamed I was in a club we'd played once, but it was a nursery school. The children sat in a circle on the stage. I sang them songs in French, or at least dream French, since I couldn't actually speak it in waking life. I could hear the pregnant sound of water gathering itself into droplets and hitting more water, as if an enormous faucet had been turned on in the heavens. When I finished the song I saw the water filling the floor below the stage, lapping at the barstools and the tables. I told the children to hold hands and instead they became dolphins. The water rose and carried us out to sea, a sea on the edge of the desert. That's all I remember because Ari woke me up.

The label put us on the summer festival circuit, doing those three-stage, thirty-band deals where all the audience and most of the artists were under twenty-five. The kids were wasted and sunburnt three, four bands into the bill. It was an absolute joy.

First stop: Wisconsin. I was wearing really tight violet sateen pants and feeling slutty and slightly uncertain. This wasn't my usual look, but I figured it would work with the crowd. I'd been feeling queasy, not like eating. I'd actually lost a few pounds. The doc said it was okay, as long as I ate the right things.

Wandered the maze of tents backstage that served as artists' dressing rooms and tried not to be so self-conscious. Somewhere in the background a Pearl Jam–esque five-piece slaughtered the slow drowse of this dairy-land farm town. I used to love all-ages shows, I swear, but these kids looked mean, a lot meaner than I'd looked the first time I'd put on black lipstick. Even at the height of my badassy badassyness, I was not even one tenth as badassed as these kids.

I met Ari in the commissary. Picked at a slice of pizza. Complained that all the songs I'd been writing lately were shit.

"But a lot of it is always shit. That is always the problem. So you throw those out and sharpen the good ones up."

"I don't know how."

"We'll do it together. Like we always have."

"The label wants to hear tracks for our second album in September. We're on the road eight out of the following ten weeks. So when exactly are we producing this thing?"

"We'll do it," he said, and looked at me with those luminous amber-green eyes, which seemed more heavenly than devilish these days.

I wanted a beer. Couldn't have it. Ari could have it, but he wasn't drinking. He was so lusciously calm these days. He wasn't caught in junkie slow motion or revved up to eleven. He just seemed himself, or his old self. His very old self. When he smiled, it was luminous and genuine.

A guy in long shorts and worn chucks walked by. He had a star on his naked belly like a star-bellied sneech, with a plume of dragon breath emerging from the star, and other red-and-black tattoos oozing across his chest.

Mama's number popped up on my cell. I usually let it ring until she disappeared back into the electronic ether, but I picked up.

Her "hello" sounded startled. I went into a preemptive rap, a full-on tongue massage about how busy I'd been and how I was sorry I didn't call and How was Matthew? And Erika? And Nana?

"Well," she paused. "Nana's not good."

"How not good?"

"She just got out of the hospital yesterday. They just can't control her sugar. Someone's got to stay with her but I've got to work so Little Trev is over there most nights."

I asked why she didn't tell me Nana was in the hospital. Nobody told me anything. Anybody who left Baltimore was on their fucking own, information-wise.

"I wanted to tell you on the phone, not on the answering machine," she said, her voice more tired than scolding.

"We have a gig near Denver next," I said. "But I'll try to come home."

Usually Mama would say no, no, but instead she said, "If you have time." That meant things were really bad.

Just then a stagehand came in and told us we were up after the next band. I saw Shar and Bruce already walking toward the stage, and vile Beatrice yelling into her cell phone.

"You ready?" Ari said.

"Enough."

Because of Ari's little detox detour, we'd barely spent any time practicing. But somehow we thought we could get onstage cold and bang out a few hits and misses and be just fine.

And you know what, we did. It's something, to leave the club scene and go to an arena filled with white teenagers and twentysomethings, people who don't have much more to do than learn to drive stick shift and then do doughnuts in the parking lot of the Dairy Queen. They're with you, they're really with you, at least for the first five beats, and then you're on your own. When it goes bad with a crowd like this, it goes real bad. Maybe not Altamont, but definitely Woodstock II.

We knew we only had twenty minutes, and we'd constructed a set of hits, plus one inside joke. Ari and I had come up with this little piece long ago, long before we thought we could ever split. We called it "The Breakup Song."

> *And I remember when the stars shone in my eyes*
> *And I felt sure you were my savior*
> *But all the chocolate and the roses in the world*
> *Can't excuse your bad behavior*

It was meant to be me channeling Robert Plant: vocal pyrotechnics and heavy guitar, very tongue-in-cheek. I had a surprise in store, though. Instead of a straight rock song, Bruce went for his electronic drum kit; Shar came in hard with the samples, and I found myself chasing the beat, and dizzying circles of sounds.

> *So now it's over (huh)*
> *No blood spilled in the street*
> *I can cut you quick and clean*
> *So now it's over (huh)*
> *No reminders of the days*
> *When you was my king; I was your queen*

This was one of our best songs for this kind of audience, usually. But this time the crowd was bored. They left; back to the beer and the funnel cake, back to macking the boys and the girls. By the end of it I was spent. We walked off to halfhearted applause.

"When," I asked Shar as we exited the stage, "were you going to tell me you'd redone the instrumentation?"

"That wasn't the problem. This bullshit festival tour is the problem."

"I didn't say your little unexpected riff was the problem, but clearly it didn't help."

"We sounded great," said Bruce. Oh, man, he was a classic middle child/peacemaker.

"We just didn't work," I said. Wondered when I'd lost control of this band. I used to think of them as an extension of my voice. Now they'd grown confident without me, and I was the one running behind. I stalked back to our tent well ahead of the others. It helped that my only instrument was my voice, while they had to pack up their gear.

When we got back to our tent, I threw a full can of soda across the space. It started spraying all over the place but I didn't move to sop it up.

"I hate them," I said. *"I hate them!"*

Turned around. There was Beatrice.

"Get it together," she said.

"Oh, screw you, Miss Labelista."

Ari, Bruce, and Shar walked in. I kicked the can and went to the bathroom. Going to the bathroom was all I did these days, except hate my world.

I soon found out that our gig in the Land of Cheese was one of our best dates that summer. Most places, everyone hated us. Everyone.

Hearing that I was a woman on the edge, Mimi came out for a couple dates. I could see her at the side of the stage as we played, looking aghast as the audience booed. At one date they even *threw* the funnel cake at us.

After that show, Mimi made me some tea. "Maybe they can take one black guy when he fronts a band, like Hootie. But not so much if you're all . . ."

"Black?" said Shar. "Melanin-enhanced rockers? Duh! Fucking redneck motherfuckers."

"But how do you really feel?" I said. "Ugh, you know what, let's go out and get some industrial-strength skin-lightening cream, just make things easier on ourselves."

Dead silence. "That was a joke," I said.

"Maybe we do suck," said Bruce, who now spent his time before and after shows sucking on Pepto-Bismol.

Shar was firm. "No. We sounded great. Remember: Prince got booed off the stage when he played with the Rolling Stones."

"That doesn't solve our problem," Ari said, rubbing his neck. "If we can't get out of the club and into the arena . . ."

"We'll never pay off our advance. We're screwed."

Nana still had her WAC uniform hanging in her closet, as if she would spring out of bed, grow back her missing leg, and be ready for the next war. I was paging through her clothes closet looking for a muumuu, her everyday housewear, something flowery and upbeat. She had a Medicare-paid home health aide now to do the heavy lifting, getting her out of bed, cleaning her bedsores, and all the other things I didn't want to think about. Aunt Martha had moved into Nana's house quick enough when it became clear Nana couldn't take care of herself, much less my grandfather. Since his Alzheimer's set in five years ago, the homebody grandpa I knew had developed a new habit of sneaking out the back door and wandering, sometimes for miles. Martha didn't like the chores that came with the free rent.

Couldn't blame her. Mama and my aunts and uncles told too many stories about what it meant to get old and get dying. I guess I'd been in the Ivy League too long. The WASPs pretended they were sheer and unbreakable, with bodily functions relegated to servants. I thought that was a good idea.

Nana, on the other hand, grew ill unabashedly. I don't mean a sloppy, don't-care-how-I-look, pity-seeking-missile illness. More a *yes, I'm human, I'm aging, I'm dying, and you will, too, one day* attitude. A beacon in the vast darkness.

Her dresser was covered with pictures: crisp black-and-whites of my mother, aunts, and uncles; grainy ones of Nana's brothers and sisters as kids; garish seventies color snapshots of me and my cousins; and one glorious full-color photo of Nana herself, singing at Ari's and my wedding.

The aide had come and gone, leaving her, to her annoyance, in a nightgown. "I told her I had two perfectly good housedresses in the closet." And I'm sure she did. But it was so crammed with items from every stage of her life except childhood that I couldn't find the right clothes. I rifled through the severe suits she wore as a principle, her crimped and crinkled dance dresses, and some wide-collared pantsuits of dubious fabrics and colors. Nana pretended to read the latest issue of *Guideposts* while I took a sartorial trip down memory lane.

"She may have put them aside," Nana said.

"Pardon?" Mama had taught me never to say "Huh" to an elder, or to anyone, for that matter, though I broke the rule all the time with my friends.

"Venice"—pronounced Vah-niece, not like the Italian city her mother named her after but couldn't pronounce—"may have put them aside." Pause. "She offered to do laundry. I don't usually, but I let her. I wonder," Nana said, trailing off. She put her bookmark in the inspirational magazine, just the size of *Reader's Digest* and twice as dull. "I wonder if she bleached them. And if they are faded."

"What makes you think that?'

"Venice asked me questions about how to wash them. *After* she did the wash."

I went down to the basement. In one corner was a pocket library, a crammed closet shelved top to bottom with books, most of them filled with silverfish. It used to be a luxury for Negroes to read, much less to own books. My grandparents collected, and collected, and collected so much they couldn't even keep their books aboveground.

The basement used to scare me. The space under the stairs. The back room with the boiler. The hard gray paint, industrial semigloss of the kind found in reform schools. I searched around the laundry area, then expanded my search randomly, then broke the basement into quadrants and searched each one with fierce intensity. Nana deserved to find her muumuus. I had a feeling she was right. Venice was well meaning, but no sharper than a crab mallet.

Finally saw a scrap of cloth underneath a folding table. There were two crumpled muumuus, badly faded, their tropical blooms looking like wallpaper left out in twenty years of sun. I took them upstairs and ironed them, though generally I would rather give a garment away than iron. The smell of the steaming cloth brought back too many memories of harried Sundays, running to church, only to find a hollow sermon and a subtle fashion show, which I always lost.

"They *are* faded." I'd brought the two dresses in, not folded but on hangers. For a nanosecond, my grandmother's eyes flashed anger. With an almost visible act of will, she put her emotion aside. "But then again, so am I."

"Never, Nana."

"There's nothing wrong with getting toward the end of your years. You're just getting closer to God."

"Yeah." I started to make some glib remark and held my tongue. "Should I, Nana, should I get you out of that gown so we can put on the dress?" Calling a muumuu a dress was like calling the things MC Hammer used to wear pants.

"No."

"No?"

"No. We can slip it over."

"Don't you want to take off your nightgown?"

"No, I'll be nice and cozy."

It was July, baking hot and still. Thunderclouds promised a spectacular light-and-sound show tonight.

I went over to Nana with the still-warm garment. First we collaborated in easing it over her head. Then we had a big wrinkle of cloth around her waist. Then I was at a loss.

She guided me. First she rolled over on the side of her short leg, the one that ended right above the knee. I slid the cloth down as far as I could on her left side, the one with the whole leg, but it caught under the small of her back. She rolled the opposite way and we edged down the cloth, edged it over her stump. But there was still a bulge on the back. So she rolled the other way again. And we got it down.

Then the phone rang. I was glad for the relief.

"No, honey, I can't do that."

Listened to her talk. A steady stream of denials and pushings-away. *Who-is-it?* I mouthed. *Matthew,* she mouthed back.

Fuck.

She covered the receiver with one hand. "He got into a spot of trouble downtown."

I still don't know exactly why my family's polite talk sounded more like what you'd hear in Leicester than in B-more, except that we watched too much Maryland Public Television, with its endless repetitions of British mysteries and sitcoms. My theory: we secretly thought it was better to watch television with no black people than with the caricatures you saw on American TV.

Nana listened to Matthew beg and rant (I could hear his voice bleed through the phone), never taking her eyes off me.

I said, silent, *How much?*

She said, silent, *Five hundred.*

I said, vocal, "Shit."

Nana gave me a look. Matthew was probably still prattling away in her ear.

She pointed toward a three-dimensional wooden cross that had lain diagonally against her dresser top for years. The simple golden-brown wood angled into trapezoidal dimensions off the cross shape. Nana took it in her arms, pulled and twisted, and suddenly a portal slid open.

Inside the cross lay hundred-dollar bills, coiled like rolled-up movie posters.

Nana took out about half, handed them to me. "Get your brother. Fifth precinct booking," she said.

Hesitated. Matthew could do with a good night in jail, actually.

"Sophie Maria Clare Lee!"

"Yes, ma'am."

"Take this and go get your brother."

"Let me, just, you know, we could . . ."—I started to say, "Leave him there," but Nana shot me a white-cold look. "I'll take care of it," I said. I had my own cash. I loved Matthew, but I felt our relationship worked best if we were at least two hundred miles apart.

"Take this."

"No, Nana."

"Sophie Maria Clare." She could still master a commanding manner. "Please."

"Nana, let me get it. It's no big deal."

"I pay my freight," she said. We went back and forth. And then she did something I'd never seen, not even at funerals. She began to cry. Not silent, fat tears and lip quivers. She cried like a child, full-on hard rain, hailing emotion.

I went to my cold, safe place. It was the first time I saw her scared, not of the process of death, but the diminishment of self. I was treating her like she couldn't make up her own mind. Like she couldn't pay for what she thought was worthy. Like she couldn't be she.

So I took her money and laid it as bail when it was even bets my brother wouldn't show up for court on time. After mumbling his thanks to me, he bolted out of the precinct, probably on his way to track down his dealer.

I didn't know why Nana still thought Matthew was worthy. I sure knew why I thought he wasn't worth saving.

Nana had faith in all of us. Take my wedding.

Ari and I married on the last Saturday of June, less than a month after our college graduation. I didn't even think about having a wedding that wasn't a Mass, and Ari didn't challenge me on it directly. But on our big day, as my relatives sat, kneeled, and stood, Ari's dad sat stock-still, as if shocked by the calisthenics of Catholic worship. His black relatives, Baptists, looked at us like we were crazy, but grudgingly went along with the priest's instructions. That priest was also my uncle Luke.

I was twenty-one and Ari was twenty-two (having repeated the fifth grade for bad behavior). Everyone, even my mother, told us we were too young to marry. Ari and I wanted to move in together once college was over, and my mother would never have let things rest if we'd lived together in sin. It was the first time I'd seen one of Mama's arguments about the way the world should work come back and boomerang her in the head.

I loved being a bride. I still had a waist then, and my dress hugged it tight and flared out like some Disney princess's. All of my counterculture leanings had disappeared when I looked at the shop windows full of white fluff, soft and seductive. Ari's tuxedo fit him just right, and he looked utterly comfortable as Father Luke took us through our paces.

Right before we took our vows, my grandmother rose and took the microphone near the foot of the altar. In slow, strong tones, she sang her favorite Mahalia Jackson song, her eyes on me the whole time. She'd grown up not Catholic but Baptist, and on Sundays after church she'd sing full-bodied spirituals, not the brittle Catholic hymns.

Nana was like a second parent to me, not a father-substitute but something completely different. She was the good cop to Mama's bad. She was my heart. When I told Nana that I wanted her blessing in marriage, she'd simply asked, "Do you love him?"

I could look her straight in the eye and honestly say, "Yes, I do." That was all that mattered to both of us at the time.

Uncle Luke was another story. We had to go to him for premarital counseling. Ari bragged through college that he was an agnostic black Jew; but he loved sitting around with my uncle Luke. Ari and Luke shared an incredible charisma and stage presence, even though Uncle Luke's stage was the altar. Looking in the rearview mirror, Ari also loved any chance to game the system. I didn't care if he took the counseling seriously, because I wasn't a big fan of the "Lord I am not worthy to receive you" school of faith. Yet deep inside I knew it was wrong to disrespect my family and my church, no matter what I believed.

Like one time, near the end of our sessions, my uncle said to Ari, "You understand: we're not asking you to convert. But we expect that you'll take this covenant seriously."

"Yes, sir."

That was the first time I'd ever heard him use "sir."

My uncle took a deep breath and plunged ahead. "Have you two had intercourse?"

"Uncle Luuuke!" I said.

Ari rolled his eyes.

"I'll take that as a yes. Sex is not separate from love, or at least it shouldn't be. It's a way of saying with your body what you're going to say at the altar: 'You are mine, and I am yours.'" He looked at Ari. "Forever. Do you understand? With your body you've made a promise. With your words, you keep it. Do you understand that?"

I nudged Ari.

"Do you understand that?"

He sat up, and nodded. "Yes," he said aloud.

"So we're clear. This is now, and forever."

"Yes, sir," Ari said again.

I just grinned. You have to understand that I was twenty-one, and I thought that I was old and sophisticated. I had lived outside my mother's house, had sex, gotten a credit card. Ari's yes this day meant a yes on our wedding day and a yes until we died. I didn't care if he didn't respect the religion; he loved me. I believed that to my core.

I dreamed that a girl who'd served me food at the festival found out she was pregnant by our sound guy. She decided to have it gone without telling him and convinced me to go to a small-town clinic with her, where I waited and looked at year-old copies of beauty magazines. The women in the clinic were comforted by men whose red-and-black tattoos pulsed in the light.

I'd been so careful, so careful for so long. Too long, maybe. I'd grown up around babies, and was all too happy to diaper and feed them. But I'd been on my own for a decade. And *now* I was pregnant? I was also unmarried and, maybe worse for my family, divorced. The Church (the One Holy Catholic and Apostolic Church) did not feel I was ready or able to get married again.

I'd picked up some papers in Baltimore about annulment. It was literally the disappearing of a marriage, a way to erase the past. Anytime I heard about annulment I made jokes about it, this medieval relic. Now I'd grabbed my old copies of all the pre-Cana guides the Church had given me and Ari, plus gotten new info on the annulment tribunal. Yes, they called it a tribunal. Jeez.

This was the deal: I had to write an accounting of why my marriage had gone so wrong that it never should have happened in the first place. I had to go back and reinvent the past in order to destroy it.

Too much, too much. Headed out from my East Village place to a nearby restaurant for an interview. It was practically across the street, but I took a circuitous route. Didn't want anyone knowing where I lived, since I didn't have a doorman. It was hardly top secret, though.

The reporter was this compact guy who I used to have a crush on, the kind of writer who seemed to have an endless stream of five-thousand-word *Vanity Fair* features and rattled off a yearly breezy best-seller. One Wednesday I'd gone to the Whitney to see the Biennial. It was three o'clock. The galleries were filled with art students and aging patrons. I saw him there, putting on the headphones to listen to a sound installation. I watched his back for minutes. Just his back: the way his hair peeked over his shirt collar, and the rumple of his jeans, and the way those jeans fell over the thick black boots that gave him an extra inch or two.

Everyone called him by his last name, Ortiz, and he'd recently moved into TV. His crew had cordoned off an alcove in the restaurant. Ari was already there. The alcove was broiling with the lights. Ortiz muffed the intro once, then again, and yet again. He wrung his hands, cleared his throat; sipped some water. The cameraman reassured him; the sound man rolled his eyes.

"It's cool," I said to him. "Happens to everyone." Certainly did to me the first few times I did remotes, and even once or twice on the air. Ortiz took a deep breath and started again.

Once he'd finished his intro about the second coming of our band, and our unusual dynamics—ex-husband and wife—he asked us the world's most boring questions. How did I like touring? (Fun, but exhausting.) Why had we cut a new album? (Me: Lost my job . . . I mean, I missed the game. Ari: it's what I do.) What was it like working with your ex? (Me: better than when we were married.)

This was all by-the-numbers stuff. Expose yourself too little and the reporter felt cheated and turned vindictive. Reveal too much and you felt used.

"And how did you get the nickname Sky, which, of course, is also the name of your band?"

My turn to pause, clear my throat, take a sip of water.

"My father gave it to me," I said finally. "Just about the only thing he did."

And then Ortiz surprised me. He asked Ari, "Would you marry her again?"

"No," he said.

"Nooooh?"

"I wouldn't put her through that."

And with that, his cameraman gave him the high sign—nice moment—and we quickly wrapped up. Ortiz invited me to a party I didn't want to go to, and I lied and said I would come.

"So you wouldn't marry me again," I said, walking out, to Ari, smiling to myself. I knew he was serious about what he said. He really meant the best for me. It was a long time since I'd felt that way.

"I wouldn't let you marry that idiot you're with, either," Ari said.

God, I loved him when he was grumpy. I loved him, period.

Leo was only the fifth man I'd had sex with, and the first without a
condom since Ari. Not like Ari and I had much sex without condoms.
I preferred the belt-and-suspenders approach, not only because I was
paranoid of getting pregnant but also because, as Ari did more and
more drugs, some vestigial common sense kicked in.

But anyway . . . sex.

It was better, *much* better, without a condom. I'd forgotten that
in the years between my breakup with Ari and my hookup with Leo.
Nobody wanted to admit it, but it was the truth. Didn't change the
facts, the risks.

One day in the shower Leo surprised me by soaping up my bottom.
I could feel him entering me and knew that if I told him no, he would
stop; but I was curious, and I wasn't disappointed. The tip of his penis
entered just the edge of my asshole (an ugly term, but let's be real).
Already I felt a rush of pleasure of a different kind than I had before: a
gentle, smooth teaser and an intense longing for more. He pushed, and
I tightened. He spent some time massaging my shoulders and back.

He could have asked, "Are you ready?" but in typical Leo fashion,
as soon as I relaxed just a little, he pushed straight into me. I filled with
a terrible light, saw colors, wanted to scream, *did* scream; heard myself
screaming from the outside. It felt so dirty and so clean.

Afterward, as we were getting dressed, I said, "Did you fuck me in
the ass because you're afraid of fucking me the other way? Because I'm
pregnant?"

He smiled. "You don't come unless I push you to the limits. I like to
watch you come."

If you've never seen two men fighting over fabric, you've never lived.

Bruce and Ari were busy inspecting a piece of blue-black velvet, not crushed but a short, thick nap that made it seem like a flat black from one angle and shimmering electric blue from another.

Shar, Ari, Bruce, and I were in Red's shop, which she'd shut down to do a special fitting for our European tour. We got to look over her stock of one-of-a-kind gear and then order custom sizes.

"That is *so* Lenny Kravitz," Shar said.

"Exactly," I said.

Bruce and Ari both put the fabric down, then they both reached for it again. I guess they couldn't figure out if that was an insult or a compliment.

Before I got pregnant, Red was fitting me for a black leather corset that gave me the figure of Bettie Page, plus deep purple bruises along my rib cage if it was too tight. Picked it up. Still loved it. Couldn't wear it. Threw it down in disgust. All the new clothes Red was making for me were loose in the middle, curved at the top, very Fleetwood Mac. It's not that I didn't love Stevie Nicks, but those dresses were better left in their time warp.

Asked Red if I could talk to her for a second. She picked the corset up, steered me to the far corner of the room. Since our dalliance *à la derrière*, we'd barely seen each other.

"Let me get this straight," Red said, picking the corset up and putting it away. "First, you say Leo is scheming and following you and taking your money. Then, when he gives you a little breathing space and actually gets his clients together, you automatically think he's cheating on you."

"So you're saying he's not cheating on me."

"No."

"So you're saying he *is* cheating on me."

"No," she shrugged. "It's just that if you're stuck with this hot and cold running bullshit, with nothing in between, that doesn't seem like any fun at all."

"Sometimes your talent for understatement astounds me."

"I've heard I've got a knack."

"But seriously," I said, "do you think he's, well, *over* me? I don't know, maybe I scared him away."

"Scared who away?" Leo was in the doorway with a fistful of roses and a smirk on his face. I knew he had heard the whole conversation, and I also knew that neither of us would admit that fact.

"Nothing," I said. "Sound guy. I can be a real bitch of a boss, you know."

"Yeah, I feel that." Leo came over and gave me a kiss.

"I thought you were . . ."

"I thought I was headed to Atlanta, too, until they canceled my flight. And I got some news."

I breathed a whisper of a "What?"

"Two new European dates," he said. Red squealed. I started to jump up and down. We'd been selling much more product in Europe and Asia than we were in the United States.

"That's our label's faith, baby. Like the faith you have in me, right?"

"Yeah," I said. When had it become *our* label? Last I checked, Leo wasn't in the band. Red turned and walked back to where Ari, Shar, and Bruce were fondling cottons, silks, and leather.

Leo had surprised me lately, exhibiting a thuggish sweetness and concern for my well-being that I'd never seen before. He pulled out a bag: my lunch. Grilled chicken. Greek salad. Loved it. Organic apple. Eh. Water. Double eh. He put his hands around my waist. For once he wasn't chiding me not to eat; since I'd started having morning sickness, he'd been begging me to. After losing a few pounds, I was just now getting back to my prepregnancy weight.

"How's the annulment shit going?" Leo asked.

"Haven't had time."

He looked annoyed and even a little bit sad.

"I'm sorry, I'll work on it." I *had* been slow writing up the annulment petition. Still didn't know quite what to do. Leo hadn't nagged me, though. We had a backup plan to rent this big, gaudy hall across from the community college and invite all my relatives and the press there. We'd play off the ridiculous castle theme of the place as kitsch.

One time, just once, Leo had mentioned inviting his mother to the wedding. Mama Masters was a lot younger than my Mama. MM, as I called her, had been just fifteen when she had Leo. These days she had a sometimey, drunk-assed boyfriend who I think, from overhearing Leo on the phone, beat her every now and then for good measure. Mama Masters called Leo all the time for extra money. See, she also had a kid by sometimey-drunkass, a six-year-old. Leo sent her two hundred dollars every month, just enough to theoretically keep the kid in tennis shoes and fresh shirts. Who knows where the money went.

I'd seen one picture of Leo and his mom. He was four years old, eyes much too sad for his age. His Mama looked hard. She was pregnant with his next youngest brother, hands on hips, belly sticking forward, skirt too short, top too tight.

Red walked back over to us, tossed her head toward the door. "Someone to see you."

"Me?" Leo and I said simultaneously.

"Sophie. Both of you, I guess."

Beatrice walked through the door wearing a plain but expensive suit that was built for someone with narrower shoulders. "How are my troops doing?"

"We're doing just fine, Beatrice," he said, shooting me a let-me-handle-her look. "Just working on the new gear for Europe."

"Homemade, huh?" she said, fingering a bolt of cloth. "That really destroys our product placement, doesn't it?"

Leo and I already had this talk. Some medium-cool sportswear label offered to send us a fresh box of clothes for every gig. All we had to do was wear onstage whatever they sent us, and nothing else. I mean: not our favorite T-shirt; not a skirt we found in a secondhand store. Nothing else but this one brand, like walking billboards. No fucking deal.

"You can't have just come here about the clothes," I said to Beatrice, taking a casual glance at my watch. "What else can we do for you?"

"Actually, I did come about the clothes; the wedding clothes. We have sponsors for the gown, the diamond ring, and the wedding band; you know, guitar and drums and covers of old hits' band, not the gold band, which is free, too."

"Got it."

"I want to review them with you and sign off on these contracts ASAP."

Leo looked at me nervously. I had shut him down on wedding talk until he apologized for blocking Ari's calls, which he still denied doing. Besides, I was never big into diamonds, and after Red lectured me about the Africans who worked in near-slavery to mine diamonds, I lost all taste. I thought an emerald, my birthstone, would make a perfect ring. But Beatrice pulled out a black velvet box, and opened it with fanfare. It was a simple square-cut diamond, bling with a lowercase b.

"Beatrice!" said Leo.

She must have mistaken his tone of voice, because she smiled as if to say, "Is this great, or what?"

Leo said, "Beatrice, that's motherfucking insulting. I could buy that myself."

"I like it," I said, adding, "Red is going to make my dress." So much for standing up for the enslaved Africans.

Beatrice looked me up and down. "I know you can't fit couture, but we totally worked Vera Wang to do something special in your size."

"Red. Is making. My dress."

Beatrice guided Leo out into the hall, spoke a few low words, and returned alone.

"I think we got off on the wrong foot," she said to me.

"Foot, leg, and torso. By the way, did you sleep with Leo?"

"Yes, I did. Circa 1997, in case you're wondering."

That bold-assed bitch. I didn't like her any better, but I admired her.

Red had been hovering nearby. She stared at Beatrice and said, "So what exactly is it you do?"

"I make things happen at the label. And right now what I'm making happen is Sky, specifically our *urgent* deadline with the wedding."

I could tell Red wanted to pull me aside and give me the same old speech on not going through with it. I shooed her away.

"Beatrice, what do you want from this wedding?"

"Publicity and sales."

"You don't give a fuck if Leo and I are happy."

"That's not my business. Business is my business. Babes, this is good P.R. The best. Easy to pitch. Has legs. The planning, the big day, the honeymoon. Slightly scandalous. Pages and pages of press. Morning shows; entertainment rags; evening interviews. I might get Larry King if I work things right."

"If you're so on top of things, why aren't our records selling better in the States?"

I thought she'd say, "Because you're an all-black band," but she surprised me. "Because you sound better live. You sound so much better live that it's your fans"—she emphasized, one hand slapping into the other—"that have stopped buying your records, not the fad-of-the-weeksters. Your fans. You know, I didn't want to work with you."

"I know."

"But I like a challenge. And you guys are a *challenge*."

I stretched and looked around the room. Somewhere in the middle of our conversation, Leo, Bruce, Ari, and Shar had walked out. The entire space was filled with a fine rag dust, powdery bits of cloth that floated in the air, stuck to surfaces, and made you want to sneeze. What would it be like to live like Red did? She acted like some eighteenth-century seamstress, alone in a room, poring over threads and fabrics. She was limited only by her own imagination and the size of her clients' waists. Red loved making the clothes; hated selling them. She used to be open to the public at least part of every weekday, and then, as her private clients grew, cut the hours back to just Fridays and Saturdays.

Most people would have hired an assistant; kept the shop open more hours; made more money; thrived. But Red would rather create and be left alone.

I couldn't be more different. Wanted to create and get instant feedback, instant adulation (which I then didn't believe); and instant criticism (which I believed and feared). I always wanted to know what everyone thought of me. Wanted to be judged. Needed to be judged.

I needed and needed and needed.

Needed Beatrice, perhaps.

"So what else do you want from the wedding?"

"I want everything recorded for TV and radio, or in print. I want you everywhere. I want total access to your life, 365, 24–7."

She'd probably picked up that lingo from the hip-hop game, or from Leo. So far, Leo had done a better job selling the band than we would've on our own. The question was, Could Beatrice do better still?

54 The Black Crowes, "Wiser Time"

The week before our European tour, Mama called to say that Nana was in and out of the hospital.

Took the train, then a cab, straight to the house Nana, Grandpa, and Aunt Martha shared. My aunt greeted me at the door and started giving me a full-on account of what was going wrong inside Nana's body, but aside from the words "diabetes" and "sugar," I just spent time feeling my own panic. Nana's bedroom had been transformed into a hospital ward, with pills and tubes and an adjustable bed with rails along the side. I wondered what happened to her old bed, the one so thick and high it seemed like heaven. When I was a kid, Nana's bed was magic to lie and dream on.

Nana was sleeping. I held her hand and it was the softest pillow in the world. I wanted to hold her the way she must have held me as a baby, with all the love and care in the cosmos. I let my breaths slip into the same rhythm as hers, and tried not to cry, and tried to remember good things. But it wasn't working. Until Nana woke up.

She didn't move, just lay still on the pads and pillows. Her eyes were bright and sharp.

"I'll be here tomorrow," she said in a low voice. "You go have dinner with your mama."

I wanted to say, *"You promise?"* I couldn't make her comfort me at a time like this, though. I simply said, "I love you, Nana." I saved my tears for a private moment on the porch.

Aunt Martha dropped me at Mama's house. We were both silent the whole way, rolling past houses that people kept up and ones that had gone to rot or drug gangs. Mama's block was still neat and untarnished, an oasis of kempt homes in an otherwise touch-and-go neighborhood.

Erika opened the door for us. Matthew was there, too, plus a surprise guest.

I didn't recognize him at first. He'd toned down his pimped-out gear; shaved his sideburns; tempered the way he used to sprawl out over a chair as if it were a throne.

"Remember me, baby!" he said, standing. "It's your uncle Ray."

"Yes, Uncle Ray, I remember."

"Well, give me a hug, now."

As I hugged Uncle Ray I gave Mama a look, like—*what is this Negro doing in our house?* I felt like I had to leave a space between his body and mine. With my real uncles, the tighter the hug the better. But Uncle Ray had a way of looking at me and Erika, when we were girls, and even now, that made me feel clammy. I don't understand how Mama didn't see it.

When Erika and I were about eleven and thirteen, both of us with tight little tits under our chaste clothes, the men on the corner started whistling at us and giving us their little ratter-patter. Mama would admonish us to straighten up, walk fast, and turn our eyes. That was bad enough. But when I was a kid, just eight years old, Uncle Ray would try to dance with me, grown-up dances, and Mama didn't seem to mind. Or maybe she didn't notice. She was out of the house so much, working two or three jobs, that maybe she was too tired to see the man I saw.

I sat on the far end of the table from Uncle Ray. He and Mama fought about local politics, which was a blood sport in my family. The white guy had beat out two marginal black candidates for mayor. Uncle Ray was arguing it was a shame that a 60 percent black city couldn't get it together enough to support a Brother or a Sister. Mama said if there was a black man worth his salt running, then things would be different. Ray went low: Wasn't it a damned shame that Mama still was trying to undermine the community?

"How?" Mama said. "By cutting my grass and paying my taxes on time?" She'd been beefing with this guy named Fred who lived across the alley. "Places looking like vacant lots," she muttered.

I served myself a helping of fried fish and greens. Mama wasn't cooking carbohydrates anymore because carbohydrates were evil (though not, I guessed, the spicy cornmeal mix dusting the fish). For Ray's sake she'd put out a basket of bread, white bread at that. In Mama's mind, white bread was the ultimate attempt to kill black men and women, a nutrition-free spongy parasite that clogged up your intestinal tract. Of course, I loved it. I didn't go for any at the table; didn't need a speech. But I was already planning to sneak downstairs later at night and toast up a couple of those bad boys with honey and butter.

I was squeezing out of my clothes again, the first trimester nausea abating. I found solace from the impending tour and from Nana's illness in Korean barbecue, char siu bao, mushroom knishes, and chocolate bread pudding from the bakery down the street.

"So how you keepin' yourself, Brother Matthew?" asked Uncle Ray, reaching for another piece of bread.

"Good. Fine. I'm staying with Erika," he mumbled into his plate.

What? That was a recipe for a murder-suicide (Erika doing the killing, of course). Without me having to ask any questions, Erika made a point of saying it was only temporary, that things were looking good to get him into a group home in a decent neighborhood, not the kind of place he'd gotten beaten up in and broken his nose.

"That's a damned shame," said Ray. "Matthew's a good man. Just needs some course correction, am I right?"

"Right," said Matthew. When would that man at our table stop acting like he was real family? I was trying my best to keep quiet and eat my food.

When dinner was finally finished, Uncle Ray demanded, and grudgingly received, another hug from me. Erika complied as well, holding him as far away as a cobra. Mama gave him a long, strong clench and walked him to the door.

"What was 'Uncle' Ray doing here?" I said as soon as Mama'd shut the door.

"I don't think I like your tone."

"Well, excuse me. What was he doing here?"

"He had some information about your father."

"And?"

"Your Daddy has been feeling poorly and he thought I'd want to know."

"Do you care?"

"Of course I care. He brought me you three beautiful children. Ray went over his house and says he might have a heart condition or something."

Erika sniggered. "Ray wouldn't know a pimple from psoriasis, so why would he know what a heart condition looked like?"

"Maybe he saw your father fall ill."

I chimed in. "Daddy's suffering from psychosomatic cash-flow disease. He thinks everybody owes him money."

"Sophie!"

"Sorry, Mama," I said. "But Daddy just came and visited my ATM. The way Uncle Ray used to visit Daddy's." See, Uncle Ray had made loans to Daddy after Daddy lost his job, and collected at a loan shark's scale. Somehow Mama never blamed Uncle Ray for the usury, only Daddy for the stupidity. The money let Uncle Ray into our home. In lieu of getting paid on time, he'd sit down and have some of Mama's cooking, and he'd sit around me and Erika . . . and wait.

"Well, that was a long time ago," Mama said, taking the twist-tie off the white bread and dumping the slices into the trash. Damn. "Time for bed." She always said "time for bed" as an imperative, as if the whole world woke and slept when she did.

I let Mama go on ahead, touched Erika's arm to signal her to stay. As soon as she got upstairs, I said to Erika, "Uncle Ray skeeves me out."

"Duh."

"What do you mean, *duh*?"

"I mean, remember he stayed with us for a while?"

"Yeah." I remember a little bit. Not so much. Didn't want to remember the days when everything was falling down, and Daddy had left, and Uncle Ray moved in to "help my favorite family out."

"Remember how he used to babysit me when you were at Girl Scouts?"

"Yeah, I guess." I didn't really, but Erika had a memory like an elephant. She never forgot, and she never forgave either.

"He'd be reading *Playboys*."

"While he babysat you?"

She nodded.

"He is one nasty old man," I said. "Why did Mama even like him?"

Erika rolled her eyes. "Hello!"

"No!" I said.

"For being my older sister, you are so naïve sometimes."

"Are you for real?"

She shot me a look.

"Mama wouldn't."

"Mama did. Not 'til Daddy left, but, yeah: I'm pretty sure she did."

I froze silent with my eyes wide open. Goddamn: I'm really always the last person to know.

My uncle Luke used to be the kind of man who could make women cross the street so they could get a closer look.

I squeezed through the church doors just as he was finishing his daily seven AM Mass. People came from all over the city because there weren't that many parishes with daily services anymore. I'd always felt like it was enough of a trial to go to Mass once a week, let alone every day. Yet here and there you saw young folks scattered in with the senior citizens, getting their dose of the Father, the Son, and the Holy Spirit before heading off to work.

Two elderly women brought up the bread and wine for communion. One wore a skirt and pumps and a blue lace mantilla on her head. The other one dressed in slacks, with short hair and simple earrings. I remember when women simply didn't wear slacks to Mass. It made me feel both old and happy that the world wasn't standing still.

Father Luke consecrated the bread and wine. As people queued for communion, he saw me and motioned.

I hesitated for a moment and joined the line. What did it mean that I didn't believe, and I still took communion? Did it damn me to hell double time, save me, or leave me in the same purgatory I'd been in for years? When I got to the front of the line, I cupped my hands in front of me, one over the other, and closed my eyes and opened my mouth. Father Luke placed the tasteless round wafer of bread on my lips. I hesitated but walked past the wine station, and sat at a pew in the back.

After Mass, Father Luke walked into a back room. I stood outside. When he came out, he was wearing a plain black shirt with a white collar. He was still a priest, but he was also my Uncle Luke again.

"This is an unexpected pleasure." His hair was thinner and grayer, but he still gave backbreaking hugs, wide warm smiles.

I told him I was visiting Nana. He said he'd stopped by at six in the morning, and Nana was awake, looking stronger.

I'd told him, in one of the postcards we still sent each other, about the record deal, the tour, and how much I was looking forward to seeing Europe again. I'd stay home longer, I said, ashamed, but I had to catch a flight to Paris.

Uncle Luke went to Europe all the time. He was a hot ticket on the Catholic circuit, a good preacher who spoke French, Latin, and Italian; a great fund-raiser and administrator. When he'd left the military after Vietnam and joined the priesthood my Mom and her brothers and sister were shocked. Made sense to me. The priesthood and the military both took priority over everything else in your life, demanded absolute loyalty, and gave you a chance to explore the world and, if you wanted to, your own soul. Imagine the comfort of coming to a place where you didn't have to hustle to pay the rent and you didn't have to kill and you didn't, at least for the first few years, have to think for yourself. Uncle Luke still sent me postcards from his travels, the way he did from ports of call on his Navy ship. He was one of those people who made me want to believe.

I kept making small talk about Nana, but Uncle Luke knew that wasn't why I was there. "How can I help you?" he said. Waited a minute, then two. "Sophie Maria Clare! If you are going to sit here like a girl in a silent movie, I have books to balance."

"Uncle Luke, I need an annulment."

He sat silent.

"I need one"—I patted my belly—"relatively quickly."

"God doesn't run on your time."

"Uncle Luke . . ."

"You made a fool of me. That's fine. You made a fool of the Church. That's unforgivable."

"Uncle Luke!" I'd never seen his jaw set this tight.

"I didn't mean to," I said.

"You can get a civil marriage."

"I want to have it here."

"You can have it in plenty of churches."

"I want to have it here."

"Why? Because you're family? I love you, my daughter, but I'm not here as your uncle. I'm here as your priest."

I started crying, silently. Uncle Luke didn't seem moved. We sat there for a few minutes, me looking at the marble sconce holding the holy water, and the little closet for the robes and accoutrements the priests wore during Mass.

Finally, he spoke. "The only reason I'll help you with this is because I believe you have a valid appeal. It's my fault." He got up and paced the room. "I never should have let you two commit to marriage. He wasn't ready."

"Neither was I," I said.

"Well," he said, sitting back down. "Sophie, are you in love? With this man? Now?"

"I'm working on it," I said.

He *hrumphed*. He didn't want the Washington family having an out-of-wedlock child. "Write your story for the tribunal. Then we'll talk."

"Where do I begin?"

"At the beginning, of course." He gave me a small smile, but his eyes were still serious. Then he showed me the door.

Beatrice insisted on coaching me on how to be a proper rock star. She chose a boulangerie off Canal Street for our first meeting, or "lesson," as she called it. Leo insisted on coming, though Beatrice said she'd prefer to see me alone.

"You're not going to get in my way, are you?" she said to Leo.

"I want what's best for Sophie."

"And you're not going to get in my way."

"That's what I said."

"Look," she said, turning toward me, "every band is disposable and most are forgettable. The label's invested just enough money in you to send me to try to get their stake back."

"Well, is the label trying to, uh, alter our contract?" I was getting used to the monthly checks coming in, fat hot sweet nuggets of money, like the rib tips you get at those no-shoot-me, Plexiglas-fronted-ghetto Chinese food shops.

"No." Beatrice pulled out a portfolio and spread it out on the table. "I've sold the media rights to your wedding. Multiple platforms, including television and the web. . . ."

"Excuse me?"

She spoke with exaggerated slowness. "I. Sold. The. Rights. To. Your. Wedding."

"I thought we were just talking about a couple of pictures in magazines. When did all this come up?"

She gave a quick sideways head nod toward Leo. "He helped."

I got up and walked out. Wanted to punch a light post.

Leo ran after me. "You don't think they just give us all this stuff for free, do you? Do you?" The look in his eyes was almost pleading. "Just come back and hear her out."

I brushed his hands off me, stood still for a moment, and walked back inside.

Beatrice detailed an entire plan to pimp my wedding from start to end, beginning with a series on the making of the wedding. Every stop on the European tour would become an opportunity to seize some special, rare, or expensive item. The product placement would get us a final multipage spread in a celeb-friendly lifestyle magazine, scores of freebies, and a promise of extra tour support from the label.

The last one sold me. I'd heard the label was lukewarm on giving us enough money to do the European tour in style, i.e., posh hotels and exec-class flights. I was tired of trains, vans, and dives. And it wasn't just about me, was it? It was about all of us, the band. We all liked sleeping on king-size pillow-top mattresses, except the band didn't have to show its ass in public. I did.

"Here's the thing," Beatrice said. "You're a good singer, a great performer, and a shitty celebrity. You know that? You have no *feel* for this business."

"And I guess you do."

"That business is *my* business. Like, what are you wearing today?"

"Red made this." I admit, it wasn't one of the best choices. The purple suede skirt looked better on me when I didn't have a potbelly, and ditto for the ripped black T-shirt.

"Do you ever wear anything your friend doesn't make?"

"Sometimes."

"We'll work on that. And, God, your gaze."

"My gaze?"

She imitated a suspicious stare, a fairly good imitation of me in a bad mood, which, frankly, was most of the time these days. "Celebrities don't stare. They smile. Or they look mysterious. Can you look mysterious?"

"Can you get the fuck off my metaphorical dick?"

"Whoa, whoa, baby," Leo grabbed my shoulders with both hands. "She's just trying to help."

"Well, tell her," I said, speaking directly to him, "to chill the fuck out with that attitude."

I swear Leo mouthed something to her, maybe *hormones*. To me, he said, "This is free consulting, baby. Like charm school."

Sometimes he surprised me with the shit that came out of his mouth. "Charm school?"

He shrugged. "You know."

I turned back to Beatrice. "A'ight, Charm School. Do you have anything more to say or are you on your way out?"

"I think we need to sync."

"Sync what?"

"Our calendars. I'll be traveling with you for most of the European tour. I sincerely look forward to it." She turned to leave. She had an ass as wide and flat as the Great Plains, despite whatever pills she took to keep down her weight.

"I still have no idea what you're talking about, Charm School."

"That's okay. *N'importe quoi*. See you in Paris."

▷ 57 The Clash, "Should I Stay or Should I Go"

Leo slept on the flight to London. He'd wanted First, just for show, but I made us shave a little bit off the already spendy tix by sitting in Business. I took the window, unfolded my tray table, and grabbed my Moleskine notebook, pen, and a glass of mineral water. I'd taken a sleeping pill but, obvi, no liquor. Drowsiness wasn't progressing to sleep. The cabin filled with flickering colors of a mediocre movie. I fiddled with the pen and waited. Just as sleep waxed, I lifted the pen to the page. I couldn't keep procrastinating in writing to the Tribunal.

Begin at the beginning, said Uncle Luke, but everything in my life had a false bottom; nothing seemed like the start.

I could start when I met Red, who introduced me to Ari. She helped me go from a high school girl who lived in my mind to a college girl who tried to live in the world.

Red and I met in a fiction class freshman year. Our teacher was tall, wore all black, and had blond hair sweeping his chin. It was strange how easily I could speak to him, when most of the students made me crazy. He let us call him by his first name and brought us Cadbury bars every other week.

I fantasized that Clark grew up in New York City and had parents who were artists. Then I found out he'd grown up in a small Midwestern town with a father who ran a five-and-dime. When he was ten, his mother had a nervous breakdown (she had eight kids, and Clark was the oldest). Clark knew what it was like to take care of people, and he knew what it was like to worry about making ends meet. Plus, like me, he loved Depeche Mode. I had my first and total gay-man crush.

I couldn't relate to most of the undergrads. They seemed like the characters on TV, sophisticated in their manners, but just so helpless when it came to practical things. People who could fix things, like my family, didn't go to Harvard. People who could eat from the land, or farm it, were not there. Or people who could call the bill collectors, and talk them into waiting another month for their fee; or people who could take a second job, and live on no sleep. Instead, Harvard College was filled with people who named things. The men who'd built universities like these created the world of language, a shadow world where what you called something was more important than what it actually was. You had to be precise. You had to weave the spell. Words misspoken were worse than words unspoken.

Or so I learned in critiques. These two prep-school boys would snicker behind their hands at the work I submitted, stories that still smelled of high school fantasies about love and magic and fame. Red would say kind things, even if they were small. On the other hand, Clark was warm after our work together was done, but he didn't worry about being kind in critiques. He let me know what my words were missing: my self. Don't try to be like everyone, he said; don't worry about the snide remarks. He'd also come from a place where people did things and built things, not one where people named things. Making the journey from that place to this was what I should write about.

As my writing got better, his critiques got more specific. Clark knew exactly what I could and couldn't take. I'd lost touch with him over the years, but I'd never forget him.

Anyway, back to school. Back in '88 Red had this huge party and Clark came for five minutes just to say hello. I thought that was so cool. And so was Red's party. Like words, parties are alchemy, cauldrons full of sound and emotion. A group of kids were arguing about The Clash v. The Cure, a Beatles versus Rolling Stones argument for the goth-punk eighties crowd. The Cure was taking a beating. I loved both the bands, typical Sophie equivocation, and I had the temerity to stand up for the Brit boys who wore smeared lipstick instead of combat boots.

"What do you know?" Ari said. Most of the people in the cluster were arguing just for argument's face, but his face was a snarl. He yelled, "I hate goddamn fucking poseurs." A few people glanced our way.

For some reason, instead of folding in on myself, I looked him straight in the eye. "I know how to double-Dutch and how to throw a punch. And I know your middle name, Ari. It's Malcolm. For X." By now everyone in the room was looking at us. The DJ had even forgotten to play the next record. "We did Academic Decathlon last year," I said, my voice softer. "Not that you remember."

"Oh, fuck!" he said, his face turning to delight. "No way. I was just there for shits and giggles. Weren't you? "

I didn't dare admit that it was a huge honor (and stress) to me and my family to go and try to win medals at the national competition. We had to raise money for our airfare to L.A., too. I got the highest single score on my team, but this other girl won the overall medal for our team. We didn't embarrass ourselves but we didn't win any national medals, either. Ari's team, on the other hand, swept about five.

I bet he never noticed me, but I noticed him. Same lithe grace, hair in an unkempt semi-Afro, body a little lankier and less muscular. He was always at the pool, not studying. I spent a lot of time going through flash cards while sitting in a deck chair. My hair was permed and blow-dried, and even though the competition was only a week, by the end my hair had turned into a barbed-wire nest. I wore lipstick that didn't remotely match my skin color, these awful peaches and pinks; and shorts that were too short, and shirts that were too tight. And on the last day, just before the bus came to take us back to the city, I kissed Ari's best friend, who was handsomer in an LL Cool J kind of way but not nearly so magnetic. Ari was the one I'd wanted.

"My name's Sophie," I said. "Or you can call me Sky." It was an old nickname, one I hadn't used in years.

Ari stood there for a second, "Sky. Definitely."

I said something brilliant like, "Okay," and Ari got another drink and the DJ put on The Clash and we both started pogoing like maniacs and the next thing I knew he grabbed my wrists and was spinning me around so fast I think I knocked a couple of people off the dance floor and I know I started to see stars. Then the DJ put on "Love Cats" and Ari surprised me by letting go of the tough-guy thing and doing this tap-swing-dance routine. For a minute I forgot how ugly and stupid I felt around Ari, whom I'd considered my dream boyfriend for months. It was magic, and it was happening to *me*.

Reporters waited for us when we got off the plane. Nothing Beatlesesque, no mad mob scene, but a handful of rumpled music journalists hoping for a quick word or two. One of them was a baby-faced black girl with tragic mulatta hair and a Cramps T-shirt that came down to her knees. I shook their hands, gave a few sound bites, took their names, and made Leo promise to put them on the guest list for our first London show.

Leo was still groggy from the flight, having refused to take a sleeping pill. He bossed the roadies who'd flown coach (not bad, actually, because it was Air France) into claiming our personal bags as well as the gear. As soon as we cleared customs and walked into the lobby, I saw an enormous black stretch limo idling by the curb. In addition to wondering whether it could actually make the turns on some of London's tight cobbled streets, I just thought the limo was in bad taste.

"I want to take a taxi," I said to Leo.

"What?"

"I want to take a taxi."

"Baby, we already paid for the limo."

"*You* already paid for the limo," I said. *I* already paid for the limo, really. "But I want to take a cab."

To me, London taxis were the epitome of style. The drivers knew the streets the way a neurosurgeon knows the lobes of the brain. The cabs themselves were lovely scarab-shaped pods, with room enough in the backseat for three people, and cute fold-down seats for two more.

"Come with me," I said to Leo.

"You're wasting money."

"It's my money," I said. Whatever. "See you there." Ari, Bruce, Shar, and I had barely been communicating. I think they'd bonded over how much they hated Leo, Beatrice, and the whole idea of pimping the wedding. It was time for all of us to get on the good foot. "Cab?" I said. "You all ready to go?"

Shar looked surprised. "Sure!"

"I'll see you there," I said to Leo. The four of us left him behind and hopped into the cab. Bruce took the jump seat. Shar sat between me and Ari.

"Jailbreak, huh?" Ari said.

"I'm sick of him."

Shar said, "You're still doing it."

"We are," I said. Going out. Getting married. Having a baby. Not necessarily in that order. "For now."

"Well, anytime you want to talk about it, let me know," said Bruce. I was beginning to think the poor boy had a crush on me. Or maybe a dead psychotherapist had taken over his body.

"I don't. Want to talk about it, that is. Who's up for a little fun?"

"Me," said Ari. He flashed me a smile and a set of rock 'n' roll devil horns. I told the driver to speed up. All of a sudden we were flying down the wrong side of the street (wrong for America, that is), whooping and hollering. Just like old times.

After two days of club hopping and record shopping, it was time for business. I was chatting up the lead singer for KPS (Kilometres Per Second), the band we were opening for in the U.K. He had one of those broad foreheads that must have busted his mom's pelvis, and blond hair with dark eyes. He just kept hanging around me, asking me questions. Stupid, stupid questions.

"So, love, you grow up in the, ah, urban areas?" Obviously that was his polite slang for *ghetto*.

"In the city," I said. "A-frame houses, big front and back yards, very few shootings. Especially during the daytime."

"You like Blind Willie Johnson?"

"I've got one song of his on this tape a friend made me."

"What about Leadbelly?"

"I guess."

"Oh," he said. "I've got one. What about Hendrix?"

"Of course I love Hendrix. *Everybody* loves Hendrix. Look, Tommy . . ."

"It's Thomas, love" he said.

"Sorry, our rep told us it was Tommy."

He shrugged. "I just changed it last week."

"Thomas, if we're going to be friends—and I'd like us to be friends—you have to stop asking me about old blues artists. It's insulting."

"Insulting? It's the most marvelous music."

I gave him the hand. "I'm not asking about the evolution of skiffle, okay? Blues is great but you're giving me the ethnic twenty questions and I'm over it."

Thomas just looked at me. I know he was trying to be friendly but I wasn't in the mood to humor him. Frankly, I worried I wouldn't be able to keep my eyes open for the show. Felt this heaviness in my abdomen, and every now and then a sharp twinge. Ate this dodgy falafel for lunch, must be. And, Jesus, needed more sleep.

"I'm going to walk the crowd," I said and headed for the door from backstage into the venue.

The fans weren't London multiculti like before; mainly white kids this time with a few chocolate sprinkles. The crowd was large, loud, and raucous. From the street, the Victorian music hall looked battered, but inside it was in perfect working condition. I almost expected the lamps to be gaslight and not electric.

Wandered around the crowd a bit before the opening act took the stage. After them there would probably be a few dead minutes to sell lager, and then us, and then the round-headed boy's chart-topping trio. A couple people took second looks as I passed, but I'd donned a trashy blond wig and sunglasses so I could walk freely. I was a pop princess now and I got into my role. So good to be among the people, I thought; to smell them and see them whisper and laugh. It had always felt as if there were an invisible barrier between me and the audience. In some ways, singing was just a way of getting as close as I could to the glass.

This little Cocoa Puffs couple, a South Asian guy and black girl, recognized me as I passed and went absolutely bonkers. I put my finger to my lips, *shhh*, and handed them a pair of backstage passes. That was my favorite part of all: playing the fairy godmother. They squealed and I turned quickly and walked to the security guard, flashed the laminate I'd stuffed down my shirt, and went backstage. Ugh, that feeling again. I rubbed my belly.

"You okay?" Ari walked up and put his arm around my shoulder.

"Yeah. Just . . . I don't know. Tired and kind of, stomachachey or something."

"We can cancel."

"What are you talking about?" Jesus. Did everyone think I was made of glass?

Funny how things were between me and Ari now. He acted like he was my brother. My sober brother. Something was definitely going on with Shar, judging by the way they looked at each other, took long lunch breaks together, and went together for tea. While they were off having deep convo, I was either with Leo or sleeping my pregnancy torpor off. Bruce looked lost, like a kindergartner left solo at the back of a line of classmates holding hands. Things weren't exactly perfect, but we still had the chemistry onstage.

Ari stepped away for a second and came back with a bottle of water. Then Leo came back my way and Ari split. They couldn't stand being within five feet of each other unless absolutely necessary.

Leo took the wig off of my head, stroked my hair, and said, "You're beautiful." He smelled the way he did when I first met him, spice and danger, but the more I lay my head against his chest I sensed something else: sweeter, softer, mellower. Can you smell love? If so, I didn't smell it, but Leo was being kind and I liked it.

When he buried his face in my hair, what did he smell? Success? Evidently nothing too critical. Leo walked off again.

"So that's your man?" said Tommy—I mean, Thomas.

"My *man*? Just stop with the Afro slang, Thomas. You can't carry that water. Leo is my fiancé, and our manager."

"Sorry, love, no offense. I just came over"—and he leaned in for a conspiratorial whisper—"to tell you I talked to my mates and it's okay if you use the big screen. You can play vids, go live to cameras on the band, all that. We were s'posed to be saving it for our set but we've got that plus something else up our sleeve."

I'd seen it tested during rehearsals and it set my eyes and mind on fire.

"How much you gonna charge?" I asked. Thomas looked offended.

I motioned our stage manager over. This was going to be good.

We were in the middle of "Slavery and War" when I called for the effect. Suddenly a huge blast of light came from *behind* me. The crow roared. I peeked over my shoulder and saw scenes of each of us in the band. It wasn't real-time, but vids of each of us walking around the stadium before the show. I was wearing the blond wig, and giving the tickets to the young couple. Ari was standing by the side of the stage, holding hands with Shar. I didn't even know we were being taped. That Thomas was sneaky and definitely generous with his toys.

I was mesmerized by how hyped the crowd was. When it came for a song change to "Kind," I hesitated a bit too long. Nobody seemed to mind.

In the middle of "Kind," the crowd roared. I looked back and saw myself looking back in real time, my face the size of a VW bus. The crowd yelled again. I waved. They waved back. All of them waved back, a huge, undulating force.

We went offstage to wild applause.

"I think I had an orgasm," I whispered to Shar. "I'm serious."

She smiled. "It's good, huh?"

"It's really, really good."

When KPS came offstage, I looked for Thomas and kissed him on both cheeks. "For that, you can ask me anything you want about blues, my baby daddy, or the 'hood. By the way, your set was amazing." KPS had three drummers or percussionists, plus keyboards, guitar, all that. For visual spice they flashed images on the screen plus shot off huge jets of flame at the side of the sage, dropped clear balloons, and handed out glowsticks. The crowd was a mass of bobbing rainbows, and I stood just off the stage taking it in. It was mad love all around, and very tongue-in-cheek, post-Manchester fab.

Thomas murmured thanks and looked me in the eyes a bit too long. He knew I was pregnant and partnered, so on the one hand it squicked me, but on the other I felt flattered.

I'd always had a thing for British guys. The rich ones were pretty limp, but the working-class boys had the anger. I liked the resentment. I liked the fire. They'd been stepped on by their own people even as their people were stepping on the world. Okay, I was a sucker for accents, too.

"So you're going to perform with us again?" Thomas said.

"We're headed for a couple other gigs in Europe, but if you want us back we're totally game. Well, I have to ask the guys but I can't imagine they wouldn't be down."

Just then, Leo and Ari and Bruce and Shar came up in a cheering, chattering mob, swept me up, and carried me out with them. I waved back at Thomas. It was the first time I had seen Leo act as part of a group. Aces and flowers all around.

I was happy in Paris for fifteen minutes. I strolled to the tip of the Île St-Louis, past the gay men sunbathing near the Seine and then around to the thatch of shops on the slim island. Tucked on one of the small streets was the most perfect ice cream in the world: Berthillon. I took a seat at a table outside and had the *glace fraise*. It tasted like summer raindrops and sugared kisses. And strawberries, of course.

A model was posing for a shoot on the street corner. She lay on the cobblestones the way I would on a chaise longue. The front of the dress must have looked fine, but in the back there was a rip that showed two very pale butt cheeks. I burst out laughing. The man sitting next to me, fortysomething and *fort,* raised an eyebrow.

"I was really laughing at myself," I said.

He shrugged.

"I guess the French don't do that. Laugh at themselves."

Now he laughed. "What brings you to Paris?" he said in nearly unaccented English.

"Je suis chanteuse," I said. I looked at him a bit too long. He was an olive-skinned, straight-haired white man, but still there was something in his body language that reminded me of Leo.

"Vous parlez français?"

"Non, sauf quelques phrases."

"You're modest."

"I wish."

He leaned in close. "I'd like you to come over for dinner."

"What? Oh, no, no, no. Thank you," I said, standing. "I've got to go."

He stood as well. *"S'il vous plaît, un moment . . ."*

"Non, merci," I said, and walked toward the hotel, quickly and a bit

regretfully. Even when I'd been single, I didn't have the moxie to pick up guys in other countries. I just liked to flirt and stare.

By the time I got back to the hotel, Beatrice and Leo were sitting in the lobby looking highly annoyed. The photographer, chic and soignée, practically had cartoon smoke rising from her ears. Apparently we were late for our first photo safari for the wedding piece. Had to get photographed shopping for French products to feature in the wedding, and just happen to stop by Chanel to buy watches for the bridal party.

I hadn't forgotten our appointment as much as I'd willed myself free, levitating above the demands of my schedule. I told them about Berthillon. Leo was unimpressed; Beatrice mildly interested.

The Chanel shoot was all work. Endless shots with shiny baubles, gifts for the bridal party. Had to pretend to look amazed and surprised by every item the shop clerk presented on their velvet pillows. God, I made myself sick.

Afterward, I whined until we set a course back to Berthillon, making all these ridiculous turns through the narrow streets. I purchased small cones of the perfect strawberry ice cream. The look on Beatrice's face was blissful, childlike. The photog bought new cones so Leo and I could pose together, cuddling against a lamppost, fresh ice cream in our hands. Beatrice beamed from a safe distance.

Beatrice, Leo, and I had set a date in mid-September for the wedding. It would be warm enough to be outdoors, in tents if rain threatened. We were going to do the wedding at Mimi's father's house. If it ain't broke, don't fix it.

After the shoot Leo indulged me and said we could go wherever I want. Didn't tell him, just took him, on the Metro, to the catacombs. A teen with beautiful dark eyes was playing the accordion on the train, and I snuggled against Leo and watched the other passengers. Walked to the entrance, paid the fare, and took him down.

He didn't stiffen when we went into the hall of bones. Under the city streets lay centuries of the dead, bones piled neatly skull upon skull, thighbone upon thighbone. The artistry of the skulls on skulls and the pyramids of long, cool beige limbs was amazing. In the late 1700s Paris had emptied out its cemeteries to build more real estate. Wasn't that just the way.

My fascination with death had always confused Leo. He walked politely through the halls. A droplet of moisture fell on my shoulder; a shiver of delight. And then the faintest cramps again—unmistakably my womb, and not my stomach. I told Leo and he insisted we go to the hospital.

The doctor, after three hours' wait and two cartons of juice, told me that some cramping was normal, but I needed more liquids and more rest. Yeah, I was really going to get that with our schedule. At least, *merci, France,* the doctor was free.

That night we played a Gothic hall where the sight lines seemed to go on forever. The stage went part of the way down an aisle. The production designers had lit hundreds of candles.

Without asking Shar and Bruce, I started singing "Confess," alone, slow, breathy, and almost off-key. Definitely off the rhythm. And the space answered me with a sound that was fainter than an echo, but stronger than imagination.

Bruce hadn't mixed it up much since our disastrous festival show. He started beating his hands together under the mic, varying the intensity and speed. Shar and Ari added their rhythm, not always the same but always on time. And the audience joined.

The hall spoke back to us with its wood and marble. We were divine. We weren't alone.

If you're anything like me, you look back at your life and think that most of it is nothing. You did enough nothing, worked enough nothing jobs, talked enough nothing on the phone, watched enough nothing on TV that now you forget what moves your soul.

Then there are times when you remember everything. Instead of being compressed, time expands and fills each corner of memory.

As I walked through London and Paris I began to remember more of the trip Ari and I took right after college.

On our first European tour, I'd stopped in Venice on the way to Rome. The golden cathedral was mobbed with people except for a room filled with relics, little boxes filled with the knucklebones of saints and such. After I had trouble with the little electronic audio guide, one of the docents approached me. He was blond-haired and blue-eyed. Not very *italiano,* I thought, but playful and handsome. It took him about sixty seconds to go from fixing my gadget to asking me out to dinner. I imagined as he lay me down he would stroke me as gently as someone polishing a chalice. Of course, the next day he'd give his boys at the cathedral the blow by blow about his encounter with the *negra bellissima* the next morning. I gave him a kiss on the cheek and left.

Ari and I had arrived in Rome too late to order room service. While he slept, I'd woken early and walked down the Spanish Steps toward the Vatican. I preferred navigating the streets to trying to figure out taxis or buses. By the time I arrived, clusters of the faithful and curious were converging on the city's gates.

I remember the gold, gold, and more gold; glass cases filled up with handcrafted pieces of history. Ah, the paintings! All those unsmiling men clad in cardinals' red and papal white; the brushstrokes of the wings of the angels.

Finally, I had gotten my money's worth out of Catholicism. All of my tithing was the most expensive museum admission in the world.

Scaffolds surrounded the Sistine Chapel, but the hallmark image of God and Adam nearly touching fingers was already cleaned and ready for viewing. We are so near and so far from God, it said to all the faithful, except that back then I didn't believe in God. For me, it was just an image: not sacred, just beautiful. Perhaps that should have been enough.

I was tired, the kind of fatigue that comes from working to have fun for too long. It was stupid of me to go on this flight, stupid of me to keep pushing myself, stupid to keep doing the tour. Erika had said that, and Red. I just wasn't ready to listen.

When I finally told Leo that I was ready to do what the French doctor suggested—that is, rest—he got cagey on me. The wedding series was a smashing success with the weekly magazines. Our domestic album sales were way up. The rest of the band got to take a few days off, but Leo and I had to keep up a steady schedule of photo shoots. Next stop: Switzerland. Diamond country.

We went to downtown Zurich, to a modern building in a historic neighborhood. The man who ran the shop was jovial, muscular, ruddy. His pampered wife and daughter ran the front desk. The owner took us "backstage," to a walkway overlooking a warren of glassed-off rooms where men peered through eye loupes at the precious rocks. He showed us a place where lasers could alter the color of the stones. He said the only way to know what was real was to come to a man like him.

It was easy to come up with a nickname for him: Mr. Diamond.

"You'd like white?" he said, hand resting on my shoulder, a hint of double entendre in his voice.

"I'd prefer an emerald, actually, but that doesn't fit our publicity plan."

Mr. Diamond toned down his smirk and led us to a private show-room where his wife and daughter had rearranged themselves in front of a display case. The stones were three or four times as large as the first ring Beatrice had showed us, the one Leo referred to as "the crumb." I'm sure Mr. Diamond had gems here as big as dinner plates, but promotional generosity only goes so far.

Turns out Mr. Diamond was a big-time partyer. He dragged me and Leo to a late-night dinner at a private guild that dated back to the sixteenth century. It was cylindrical, like the turret of a castle stuck down on a city street, and only opened its doors to women every once in a blue moon. In the basement were the guild's treasures: heavy jeweled goblets, swords, and mysterious aged leather masks. The main floor had twenty-foot ceilings and a spiral staircase that led up to a dining hall. The hall had painted beams and long wooden tables. The main dish was the ubiquitous Swiss veal, the one meat I didn't eat.

I certainly didn't go hungry. The chef made me a special portion of roast duck and spaetzle. I tried to act the way Beatrice had coached me, to sit still with a mysterious half smile, Mona Lisa–style. I watched Leo fumble through the assortment of cutlery, even though I told him it was simple: just start from the outside in, and save the setting at the top for coffee and dessert. Mr. Diamond switched effortlessly between English, French and German, all in a booming voice. He had an animated multidirectional swivel that allowed him to be in several conversations at once. It made me dizzy.

During the middle of the dinner I got up, went outside, and made a call from my cell phone. We'd gotten new chips that worked in Europe, all very high tech and exciting.

When the line connected, I heard what sounded like a sports match on the television, in German, and loud; then Shar's rapid-fire laugh, and Bruce's, too.

"Football party?" I said to Ari.

"Room service and Manchester United."

"Cool." My favorite British team was Arsenal, just based on the name. I had no idea if they were any good.

"What are you doing?" Ari said. He yipped into the phone, which meant Manchester had scored.

"Diamond shopping."

"Are you okay?"

Of course not, you fucking idiot. How long have you known me?

How long has it been since I called just to talk? Much less in monosyllabic words. *God just read my mind.*

"I just needed to step off the merry-go-round for a second," I said. "Okay, talk to you later."

"Sophie . . ."

I hung up.

I was ready to go home.

Just give me my free diamond and a little sleep and I'd figure it out from here.

The band met us for a charity concert in Zurich. We simply and plainly rocked the house. The night before the show Leo and I had a huge, screaming fight. I. Wanted. Home. Even for a week. That was how long we had between the charity gig and our next one, in Rome. Leo said absolutely not. Claimed that he was looking out for the baby, the fewer flights the better. Honestly, he was fascinated with the private bankers who held some of the world's dirtiest cash. Wherever there was a dictator, there was a Swiss bank account. Just think if hip hop got in on the game.

I was mollified when I saw the hotel Mr. Diamond had suggested we switch to. The spa in Bad Ragaz was filled with acres of marble. The staff struck a note neither obsequious nor too intimate, but efficient, available, and slightly standoffish. Leo seemed bored, but Ari, Shar, Bruce, and I spent the day deciding between hot jets and cold, steam or dry heat, in an endless array of pools, baths, and saunas.

The day after we checked in I got a surprise. Red and Oscar appeared, both blinky and tired, at the front desk as I was headed for the spa.

"It was supposed to be a surprise," Red said.

"I *am* surprised," I said. I was more so when Lin rounded the corner, pushing a jog stroller filled with a diaper bag.

"It's not even my birthday," I said.

"Leo thought you could use some company. I guess he's not all bad." Lin's voice was husky and low, and she was never one to mask her opinion. She looked unruffled by what must have been an overnight flight from New York. She handed her passport to the front-desk clerk to complete the check-in.

"Where's the party?" she said.

"Party?"

Turns out that one of the label execs had a home here, and we were invited as his guests. As usual, I was the last to know. For heaven's sake.

The next day I primped in Lin and Red's room. Even some of Red's handcrafted dresses were starting to stretch tight over my baby bump.

"You look good," she said, but I could see she was worried about how faded I looked.

To get to the party, we rode an antique train through the Emmental, wending our way through the valley. The mountainsides were dotted with compact wooden cabins and black cows that produced the milk for the famous Swiss cheese. The label had sent a man to fetch us, another Swiss, and he sat with me and made small talk and watched the scenery. He'd grown up in the Emmental, he said, and the life was hard. Everyone he knew had moved to the city. He also whispered that CDs were toxic to the environment, that the very things he made were eating away at another part of the earth he'd once worked.

For days, Leo had put me on the phone for interviews with American radio DJs just as I wanted to sleep. I felt my body begin to break down slowly but surely. Got night sweats and a tingling in my throat, then stomach upsets and chills. Leo didn't notice any of it. Honestly, I could have stayed at the hotel this night had I insisted. I wanted to meet Karl Renggli, the manufacturing giant who'd just bought our label, plus a huge bundle of other media companies. He was an honest-to-God billionaire. I'd never met one before, let alone been invited to dinner.

We got off the train and a luxe minicoach took us up a mountain to his home. I wasn't impressed. It was pretty enough, a white minimansion in the mountains, almost Southern in style. Then the Emmentaler told me that in a shed at the side of the house, there was a wide, gleaming, stainless steel elevator that went down into the high-tech vintner's den. Behind the hedges of yellow roses surrounding the house were vineyards, acres of grapes, which Renggli turned into his own private label of wine. Every bottle was gifted, never sold.

Went up to one of the three staffed bars and ordered a thimbleful of one of the reds—I couldn't resist. The waiter did precisely what I ordered, giving me a few sipsful in the bottom of a glass. Quality was B+, a little acidic, not bad for a rich man's hobby. I handed the glass back and got mineral water.

"Where the fuck is he?" I whispered to Ari, who had a mineral water as well.

"Ah, Miss Sophie Lee . . . Sky Lee. Which do you prefer?" said a man who'd suddenly appeared by my side. He had chestnut-brown hair falling in an unfortunate arc across his broad forehead. His chin tapered to nearly a point. He stood far too close, as if he were tragically near-sighted or socially tone-deaf.

"Uh, depends on who you are. My *friends* call me Sky."

"You must excuse me, I'm Karl Renggli."

"Oh. Hi!"

I felt Ari brush against me, convulsed with silent laughter.

"The show in Zurich was magnificent," he said. It was, of all things, a benefit for injured survivors of the African civil wars fueled by conflict diamonds. Most of the crowd came not for the cause but the music, and that was fine with me.

"You weren't in the VIP section," I said. I would have noticed a forehead like that.

"No. I like to hear what the people hear."

The people. Who were "the people"? Would he know "the people" if he saw them? Aloud, I said, "Yeah, I understand."

I'd been tired and cranky. My voice took on a hoarse edge that the impeccably dressed crowd adored. I screamed "Confess" until the pit of hell threatened to open beneath us. I'd been pushing myself for the whole tour, really. Ari had told me to ease up, it was going to be a long ride. I'd wanted to say to him, since when have you eased up on anything?

Renggli gave us a tour of his subterranean wine factory. I'd been on vineyard tours in France, and seen oaken barrels in catacomb-style warrens. This was more like the subterranean nuclear shelters of some fifties movie: white walls and stainless steel tanks, pressure gauges and mysterious dials.

"Winemaking is like the music industry: so much waste to produce so little. Yet when you get the right vintage, it is magnificent. Did you taste any of the wines?"

"Just a tiny sip," I said.

"What did you think?"

"It was . . . wonderful."

"Too tannic this year. I wouldn't drink it if it weren't mine." He wasn't just brutally honest with his own product, but ours. "Your album lacks life," he said. "We can't trace your river to its source."

"We need to do a live album. You going to pay for it?"

"I am just a simple businessman," he said, spreading his fingers. He smiled and led us back upstairs to the party, patting my arm in farewell.

"Okay, whip out the decoder ring," I said to Ari.

"What did what mean?"

"The speech. That pat. Was that a 'good job' pat? Or a 'you can do better' pat? Or, wait." I froze. "Maybe it was a 'I'm going to cut you from the label' pat."

"Why would he invite us to his house and then cut us from the label?"

"People are mean."

"I think you need a few days off."

True. My eyes felt like sandpaper. All the furniture in Renggli's house was severe and angled, and there was nothing I wanted more than to curl up in an overstuffed armchair and let myself drift to sleep.

Red and Lin, on the other hand, were in heaven. They'd left Oscar in the care of a nanny employed by the hotel. They perched on the edges of facing chairs, fingertips brushing each other's, sipping wine and smiling. They were so cute. On the other hand, Leo had barely touched me since we'd gotten to Europe. He was so busy cutting God-knows-what deals with Beatrice that he could barely focus on me.

I remember what it was like the first time I came to Europe, the shock that everything we thought was old in the United States was new here, and that all the countries we thought were so stodgy and settled were roiling with age-old rivalries. I understood how intoxicating that could be. Or maybe he was fucking Beatrice again. Either way, I missed his touch.

I laughed to myself.

"What?" said Ari.

"Can you get tired of living the life of your dreams?"

"You can get tired of anything."

After a few days at the spa we had a gig in Rome. We took a small private jet with deep leather seats, a gift from Renggli. Guess we weren't getting cut.

Beatrice, who'd reappeared out of nowhere after a weeklong absence, took the seat next to Leo and pulled out page proofs for the next magazine layout. I sat between Ari and the window, and folded a pillow so my cheek could rest on the cool glass. I dreamed I was performing for the seniors' group at my church. I was dressed like the eighties Madonna, in some outrageous mix of crucifixes and tulle. All the people I knew from my childhood smiled and waved as if it were an Easter pageant, but there was someone still and silent in the back of the room, a dark smudged form I could barely make out.

The show went fine as far as I know. My voice was hoarse, but it broke in all the right places, like those eighties rock stars from the Midwest who pushed every note to the limit.

Fell asleep on the plane ride home. Slipped back into the Man in the Moon dream, trying to float out of the moonlit room and getting stuck on the ceiling. I'd wake up just enough to hear the hum of the engines, look around at my friends lounging in the plane's polished wood and leather seats. Then I slept and dreamed the dream over again.

At some point Ari must have touched my shoulder. I shrugged it off and heard him whisper something low and urgent to Red. I felt a series of hands touch my back and my cheek; more whispering; then motion.

"Can you get up, honey?" said Red. "We're here."

I was usually on my feet as soon as the plane pulled into the gate. This time the plane was empty, except for Red, who sat beside me, and a flight attendant near the door. I rubbed my face and eyes and tried to say something reassuring but only let out a barking cough. I let Red lead me to the door. The air, to me, had a liquid quality, hard to move through and breathe, and the light seemed to bend around this imaginary water so the world seemed soft and fluid.

I heard people arguing over me as I retched into the airsick bag Red had thought to take from the plane. We were in a small, cozy waiting area for the private jets, a place not unlike the first-class departures lounge for international flights. Ari said to Leo, "You can't just run her like a locomotive." And I thought of the metaphor, of myself as a train filled with passengers, Ari and Red and Shar and Bruce, clipping along some mountain pass with Leo as a mad engineer.

I woke up back in the hotel, but in a different room. German news was playing at low volume from the television. Red squeezed my hand and lifted a glass of water to my lips. I tried to swallow but tears came to my eyes. A woman I guessed was a nurse, though she wore no uniform, had me open my mouth and sprayed something in. I swallowed and my throat went numb. I drank the glass of water and lay back on the pillows. *If she doesn't keep her fluids down,* said the nurse in barely accented English, *we'll take her to hospital.*

I didn't go to the hospital. I lay in bed in a fugue state, with the muffled voices of Leo and Ari and Red blending with the television. At some point I dreamed that there was a tadpole trying to swim through my belly button. It was brown and speckled, and had just reached the stage where it had tiny arm and leg buds. It swam inside me, and banged around my insides, dark and scared and lost. Then it turned into a star, a bright, white hot ball, and tried to squeeze its way through my hips. The star got bigger and bigger, and the passage got smaller and smaller, and I cried out. Finally, sometime during the night the star burst through, and left me wet and sobbing.

I remember hands and being washed with warm soapy water, then accusing voices, shouts and countershouts of people each claiming the other had made the wrong choice.

"Please shut up," I think I said, as clearly as I could, and all the voices went silent.

Slept a deep, flat sleep, no dreams, just the vague sense of time passing. Eyes snapped open. Saw Red.

"Honey," she said, her eyes puffy and nose dripping, "I have something to tell you."

"I know what happened," I said. And suddenly, all in a rush, I did. "The baby's gone."

The next two days I stayed in bed, watching German news, not understanding the language but needing the curtain of sound. Red and the nurse brought trays filled with pills and droppers of liquids, like the cold medicine children get; and bowls of broth. The walk to the bathroom seemed like miles. I was in a ground-floor room designed for people in wheelchairs, and as soon as I was well enough, Red sat me on the little fold-down shelf in the shower and helped me clean myself and wash and dry my hair. I smelled rank and wondered how long I had been out. "Three days," said Red.

"Did I miss a show?"

"Just one," she said. "But I'm not sure that's what you should be worried about."

"What should I be worried about?" I said. My voice was flat enough to scare me.

"You should be worried about yourself. Do you . . . does it . . . do you hurt?"

"No," I said. And I didn't. They'd given me something to dull the pain of the cramps, and it had the complimentary effect of dulling my mind. Nothing hurt. Nothing at all.

We canceled the last two dates in the European tour. Shar, Bruce, and Ari flew home. So did Lin and Oscar. Red slept in a cot by the foot of my bed, and Leo slept in a room connected by a suite door. I could hear him talking on the phone.

I slept again. Red was always there when I woke up; Leo, never.

I told Leo to go home. I didn't know whether to be insulted when he didn't argue. Red stayed with me as one week stretched into two, then three. Red cajoled me into leaving aside the room service and taking my meals in the dining room; and then adding a daily walk around the gardens; and finally spending my afternoons reading in the parlor instead of sitting motionless by the TV.

Finally, I told Red to book us our tickets home. On our last day in Bad Ragaz, she and I went to the spa. The entire first floor was a complex of marble and gold fixtures, acres of ways to torture and tone the body. I went into one pool with a course of jets that ran from foot level to neck level as you walked along. The pool was empty and I flinched when I passed the jet that hit me right below the pubis.

The morning of our departure, I went for one last tour around the spa. I had gone most places except the specially scented spas. One was called the Lemon Spa, and it was filled with a grotto of artfully fake trees, scented like the real version of the plastic fruit. I took a deep, sharp-scented, cleansing breath and let it out as a sob. A day or two earlier I would have choked on the torrent of my own tears. Today my breath came easily, but I didn't want to be better. I didn't want to leave.

III.

When I was a kid, I always wanted to be free *to:* free to do something, like go see Prince in concert, to dress in short skirts and high boots, or to spend the night away from home. Then at some point, longer ago than I'd realized, I started wanting to be free *from*: free from drinking a lot to block out the world, then waking up ashamed and replaying everything I could remember in my head; free from my attraction to bad men; free from the need for approval from my fans, my mother, my sister, Leo, Ari, even the girls. Free *from.* I wanted to be free from myself. Until I could figure out how, I was still free *to: to* drink, in this case.

Mimi had to remind me that I had a birthday coming. Saw no need to celebrate, but she disagreed. At the last minute she invited people to dinner without me even knowing. Location: Windows on the World.

Mimi picked me up at my East Village apartment in a sedan that night. The night was crisp and clear, and I rolled down the window and watched us enter the strange, bland terrain of the Financial District. We found ourselves miraculously alone for the hundred-plus-stories elevator ride up to the top of the World Trade Center. After the first few seconds, you felt weightless.

"So, do you want to talk about things?" Mimi asked me as the elevator rushed upward.

"No friggin' desire whatsoever."

"You always know you can try again."

"I don't want to talk about it." My voice had taken a hard edge. This ride, with its headrush and the subtle *clack clack* as we passed each story, had lasted too long.

Elevator doors finally opened. Mimi and I strolled out, heads held high. The restaurant was awash in miniskirts, fishnets, combat boots, and the occasional, ironic, necktie. The handful of normal couples cowered at their tables. When they called for reservations months in advance, they obviously hadn't asked if a bunch of self-satisfied It Kids would be wreaking havoc. One older woman actually covered her ears with her hands. Then again, she was right by the speakers for the five-man band doing live karaoke.

The maître d' led Mimi and me to a huge horseshoe-shaped banquette. Mimi had booked my birthday dinner for rock 'n' roll karaoke night at the Top of the World.

I grabbed a cocktail and checked who'd come. Not Red, not Leo (not sure Mimi had invited him and besides, I wasn't even returning his phone calls), not Ari, Bruce, or Shar. (They'd gone to UCLA to give a lecture on the evolution of sampling in rock music.) These were Mimi's friends.

I settled myself between a starlet named Martine and a banker couple who'd gone to high school with Mimi. Across from me sat a seventeen-year-old model making out with Ned. I knew Ned, in the biblical sense and otherwise. The publicist tried, and failed, to look two decades younger than his forty-odd years. Don't get me wrong: he was so massaged, trained, and spritzed with products that he had a better body and skin than most men half his age. It was precisely his over-grooming that gave his age away.

We made fun of the fashion victims who'd come for their big dinner on their big New York vacation: you know, the hammertoed, three-chinned, Walmart-wearing troglodytes who had spent a week's salary to take the family to the highest viewpoint in New York. They were people like many of our families, really, but we made fun of them now, as they wandered by our party looking confused or angry that we were ruining their ambiance. It didn't matter whether we'd grown up rich, like Mimi; proud strivers, like me; or self-proclaimed "trailer trash," like one performance artist at the table. We were all masters of irony, and irony was the last reason the normal people had spent half a week's salary on a steak, a bottle of bubbly, and a view.

As I looked out from above, the city that had always seemed so welcoming to me now left me cold. Angles, glass, metal: this part of New York held nothing warm, nothing curved, nothing soft.

Ned took an Altoids tin from his breast pocket. "Vicodin?"

Thank God. I slipped two in my purse for later and passed the tin around. "Lovely spot, eh?" said Ned, pouring more Dom.

"I hate the city right now."

He stopped kissing the model long enough to look me in the eyes.

"You don't look like you hate the city. I think you think it hates you."

I looked down at the Statue of Liberty as a DJ gave way to a band and waiters passed more champagne around. I was squeezed hip to cheek at the table, and I couldn't stand the touch of the people on either side.

"Look at that sick fuck," said Ned. His business partner humped the stage as he wailed "Can't Buy Me Love." "He's got it all wrong," Ned said. "Money can buy you love. It can buy you anything you want." Ned looked down at the model.

The model had blond hair, a heart-shaped face, and Asian eyes. She looked quizzical but indulgent.

"Take me, an old fart like me," said Ned.

"You're not old," the model said. She was a bad liar.

"I should not be dating a child like you."

"I am not a child." Of this, she was convinced.

"You shouldn't be dating her because she's your client," said the woman next to me, part of the banker couple. She was several drinks louder than when I'd met her once before, and wore a severe, stylish suit. Mimi reminded me before we arrived that she was also a lawyer.

"That's another conversation for another time," Ned said, trying to hush her.

"Like when you get sued?"

"Sued for what? For love? She loves me, don't you? You'd go out with me if I was poor, right?"

The model looked momentarily stumped. It was hard to reconcile Ned's wardrobe and maintenance with an image of him having to buff his own nails. "I've gone out with poor people before," she said. "Like, when I went to high school. Before I started getting jobs."

I couldn't help myself. "Does anyone else notice that when folks in fashion talk about taking jobs, it sounds just like the way prostitutes talk about their work?"

"Sky!" Mimi said.

"I was just noticing."

Ned chimed in. "Curtis," he said, looking at the husband in the banking power couple. "What's the going rate for a whore these days? A good one?"

Curtis, spinning the ring on his left hand, blushed. "I wouldn't know."

"Right."

Banker babe said, "I was once offered five thousand dollars for a 'date' with a businessman."

Curtis jumped in his seat.

"Oh, honey, it was before we met. And I didn't go, of course." She took a beat. "Price was too low."

Ned and the rest of the table howled. Curtis looked mortified.

I slipped out of the conversation and focused on the scenery and the champagne. I made small talk. Then I just stood up, told everyone thanks, and started walking. The sky was clear and the views through the windows stretched on forever. Loops of lights on the bridges pierced the night's velvety blackness. The Statue of Liberty looked exactly the size of a postcard. From this height, the city was stripped of grime and people. It looked pure.

"Sky!" Mimi came up behind me and grabbed my arm. "What are you doing? We haven't sung 'Happy birthday'!"

"I know that. I hate 'Happy Birthday.' I always have."

"But you have to stay."

"No, I don't," I said. "This was your idea. I'm your pet project. I get it. I appreciate it. I just don't like it. Liking it stops here."

To the sound of "Happy Birthday" done Hendrix style, I headed for the elevators.

God, when did I become such a bitch?

My place was empty and dusty, and the refrigerator held a few wizened apples with a flowering of mold on top. There was only one thing I feared more than Leo's temper, and that was the kind of vengeance I'd wreak on myself if I spent another night here alone. I could spend a few days eating, drinking, and throwing up, then brushing my teeth and wearing shades to hide the bulimic's red-eye. I could score some weed and take more sleeping pills: anything to fill time or *stop* time.

Or I could cowboy up and go see Leo, whom I'd been avoiding for the week since I got back from Switzerland. He left the country ahead of me when I needed him most. I hadn't forgiven him for that. When I got back to the States I blew off a couple of his calls. Instead of pursuing me harder, he'd stopped calling. Radio silence. It was time to break the impasse.

In the morning, I took the train uptown, unshowered but wearing clean clothes. I could smell my emotions before I felt them. Fear was vinegary; comfort a faint musk. Smell is the first sense you hone as a baby. Today, I smelled overripe flowers. Passion, death, and rebirth.

Got off the train and walked to his house. Was surprised to see Leo's front door open a crack. He didn't think much of his neighbors, whether they were young and bourgie or Harlem's old guard. Maybe he'd had a change of heart and planned an open house. Or, more likely, he'd called up my friends for a let's-save-Sophie summit, and Red and Lin were inside manning the phones.

Instead, as I mounted the steps, I heard a woman's laughter. "Don't be such a stranger, then . . ." I knew that voice. But who?

I found out as soon as I pushed the door open a crack. Kristal and

Leo were nose to nose, hands clenched, the back of her high heel holding the door open. Leo saw me first, but didn't move, and said to her first, not me, "Okay, baby."

"What?" Kristal turned. I stared that bitch down for a good sixty seconds until her gaze dropped to her feet.

"I was just leaving," she said. Then, "You look great."

"Thanks," I said, never taking my eyes from her face. "You, too. Now leave."

She did. I walked in, closed the door, and turned on Leo.

"So I guess we've called it off."

"What?"

"The wedding."

"What are you talking about?"

"That bitch up in your space."

"That *bitch* is my client. If you had come home, you would have known we had scheduled a meeting."

"I'm leaving. Just to confirm: the wedding is off." I didn't need a baby daddy no more.

"Off? The wedding is going to be a *cover story*. Do you know what that's going to do for your album sales?"

"I'm not talking about a fucking cover story," I said. "I'm talking about a marriage." And all of a sudden it hit me: I was in this for the baby, and for the wedding, and for the free gifts. I had never been convinced Leo would be a good husband. Now I could take a step back and make a decent choice.

Leo's tone turned conciliatory. He moved to touch me and I moved away. "All right," he said. "I came down and got you when you were all messed up in Baltimore, didn't I? I was there for you, wasn't I? If that's not love, what is?"

"Doing all the same shit you did, but not throwing it in somebody's face, for starters."

"I. Love. You." The tone of his voice said different. "I am just, very, very angry at you right now. Angry at you for letting go of our child."

"Let go? I didn't *let go*. And wait, hold on one minute. Who was pushing me? Huh? Who was pushing *me* to keep going when I felt sick?" I felt the air tingle with static electricity, the anger of the fight.

"Were you drinking with the baby inside you?"

"No." Mostly no.

"Tell me you never had a drink the whole time you were pregnant."

"You know I did!" He looked victorious. "The night of the party."

"And? When else?"

"I can't talk to you right now. You are *insane*."

With that, he stepped forward and slapped me. Sound ricocheted off of the walls; cheek stung like fire; eyes watered.

You know, my dad had done this once. It'd come out of nowhere, the slap, the argument. Or maybe it had been brewing for a long time. I was about ten. Mama and Daddy had gotten back together, but he still didn't have a job, and she still reminded him of it every day. This day, after school, it was just me, Daddy, Uncle Ray, and a couple of their boys in the house, drinking beer and watching TV. Matthew and Erika were at day care; Mama was working second shift. Uncle Ray had asked me for a beer. I'd parroted back some shit my Mama had said about how it wasn't right for folks who did their duty all day to come home and take care of grown men who didn't do shit. I can't remember if I used the word "shit," but that was the essence of it. Daddy pulled me aside and slapped me hard on the face in front of his crew, and told me to stop saying my mama's nonsense in front of his friends, in his home. I knew he was right *and* he was wrong. He was right I was just saying what Mama was saying. But it wasn't nonsense.

Leo said, "I'm sorry," but my mind wasn't on Leo. I didn't do anything for a moment, just stood stock-still. Leo started panicking.

"Sophie? Honey, I'm sorry."

"This ain't even about you, Leo," I said. "But, yeah, you are *sorry*." I grabbed my purse, rubbed my still-stinging cheek, and left.

Tonight, the Chinese food arrived the same time as the drugs. I waved the long-haired bike messenger into my apartment, told him to hold on a sec, and handed a couple of twenties to the guy from the noodle shop. Once the noodle guy turned toward the elevator, I locked the door and went through protocol.

"Hi," I said. "I want to buy some pot." I wanted to forget, but heroin was too lethal for my tastes.

He slid his bag over his shoulder and let it drop on the carpet. "Nice place."

"Thanks," I said, leaning into the corner. I was tired. It was hard work, blocking Leo's calls and weathering the storm of competing tabloids that said I was either partying and pregnant or partying and lost the baby. "Whatcha got?" I said.

The drug delivery guy squatted and rifled through small square plastic containers for the bags, fifty dollars each. "Well, here's our basic store brand," he said, waving large packets of seeds and stems. "And then we have Jinx." I held the smaller sealed bag close to my eyes. No seeds, no stems, all green. Then he smiled and passed me a packet no bigger than my thumb. "Rocket to Mars. Hydro, Oregon." Streaks of purple and brown ran through the fat buds, little Buddhas sitting in contemplation.

These guys delivered to everyone: the fashion studios, the networks, the bankers, the brokers. I'd never seen the same man or the same brand twice. And they were all so cheerful. I imagined a skyscraper office, central dispatch, women with headphones scrolling through the names of clients from the mayor's office to the barrio. *"May I help you?"*

This guy reminded me of someone I'd slept with once. I enjoyed watching his wind-chapped face, the smile lines around his mouth. "Whaddya think?" I said.

The buzzer: Mimi.

He told me Rocket to Mars was the best they'd had in months. They always said that about their top of the line. I ordered five Baggies anyway. Pot was like sugar. Someone was always borrowing.

The door buzzed again. I hit Enter, slipped him a thick wad of twenties, and he was gone before Mimi's crew came up the steps.

Mimi spoke into her cell phone. "Okay," she smiled into air. "Ciao."

"Nestor?"

"Yeah. For once I'm the one catting around."

Far be it from me to give anyone morality lessons. Sometimes I felt an emptiness inside me, a space where I missed the baby; or maybe I just missed *wanting* to miss the baby. I made sure my house stayed stocked with whisky and Hydro, and the emptiness got filled.

"Ooooh!"

The woman who'd "oohed" was tall, ebony-skinned, and drop-dead glamorous. She was pawing a faux rabbit-fur pillow. I'd gone on a shopping binge and redecorated the apartment. It was very L.A., very retro chrome and leather, white shag carpet, seventies movie posters on the wall.

"Sophie, you remember Jimmy and Paul. Paul, Jimmy: Sophie. And this"—she pointed to the woman plumping the pillow—"is Tracy Valentine." God knows she wasn't born with that name, but with her figure and that slinky red dress (with matching heels), the name suited her to a T.

It was hot enough outside that everyone's favorite fashion theme was "naked." Mimi's long-ago ex, Jimmy, was junkie skinny and wore a studded belt and a sleeveless "Jesus Is My Homeboy" T-shirt. Paul, her ex from high school, lived in Hollywood and had a snarl of black death-rock hair. Tracy was Paul's new girlfriend. She worked in the music industry and lived at home with her parents in New Rochelle. Yeah, she was black, but it struck me she lived like that clique of young Japanese women who work, live at home, and spend all their money on designer gear. Mimi once told me that every day in winter, Tracy wore a floor-length mink on the train to work from New Rochelle. Tonight, since it was too hot for fur, she carried a purse that even I couldn't afford.

I saw Paul while clicking channels late one night. He was playing the mutant leader of killer extraterrestrials. He had jagged fake teeth, his own rocker hair, and his big line was "Yeearrrghhh!" In between the horror flicks, he'd played a hit man in some two-million-dollar hip-hop video. In that same video, Tracy was rocking a G-string and pouring champagne over a lyrically chunky rapper. Over a plate of lukewarm enchiladas dished up by craft services, love was born between the mutant and the beauty.

Never knew what Mimi saw in Paul. Jimmy was another matter. He had a perfect chameleon face that could go from boyish to macho in a second. Think: a messy brush of thick black hair over perfectly even olive skin, with eyes so dark they looked black from a distance. He was a little gawky, like one of the Beasties or Thurston Moore. In the fickle world of fame and fashion, Jimmy was It: a white boy who DJed hip hop that other white people liked. And honestly, he wasn't half bad. What bothered me about our nightlife situation is that I used to take Mimi and her friends to parties because they amused me. I was the social rainmaker. Now I'd been out of the scene so long, I was these guys' fifth wheel.

"Come on, Miss Mopey-pants," Mimi said, clutching me by the arm. "You ready to party?"

I shrugged. "I'll give it my best."

The boys walked around the room doing a coked-up shuffle. The girls settled on my leather chaise and started smoking my weed. Nobody wanted to eat. I grabbed an egg roll and put the rest in the fridge, dragging my bare feet through the white shag. I grabbed a handful of nuts from a tray, came back. Tracy smoothed back her bone-straightened hair, rolled up the cuffs of the man's shirt she'd thrown over her red dress, and worked at crumbling the weed. "'Sup?" she said.

"'Sup? Let's see: my fiancé wants to see me, but I don't want to see him. I want to see my ex-husband, but he's off on vacation with my lesbian bandmate. And the other guy in the band is reportedly *auditioning* because we're not paying him enough attention. You know. Like that."

"Raw," said Tracy.

"Raw," I said.

"Man, have you seen the new shit rolling out of Sean John?" Jimmy said, leafing through a magazine. "I mean, for real, it's, like, tight." I realized he probably wasn't on coke; maybe speedy E. He was working on the high you get at home before you go to the preparty, where you get high; and then the club, where you get high; and then, if you're lucky, the afterparty.

Jimmy's real job was going from magazine to magazine, appearing on their covers. I heard a copy of one of them in the bathroom saying he'd reinvented the medium. DJing had been around for decades; should have its own hall of fame in the South Bronx, with walls and walls of Puerto Ricans and Jamaicans and black folks like Roc Raida making the silly slapstick smiles folks do in old school pictures. Put up some plaques for the white turntablists like Cut Chemist, too. But Jimmy wasn't in their league. He was good but not great, a label exec's son with connections. I went from lusting after him to hating him in an instant; and then I went back again.

"Shit's tight. For real," said Jimmy. Paul said, "Word."

This was the zeroes. White boys trying on blackness like it was a new clothing label. Video 'ho as an entry-level job. Me as a spectator.

I said, "Let's go."

I was instantly, shudderingly tired. Fell asleep in the cab, that half sleep that makes me cranky when I wake. Mimi nudged me. We were at Kent's. A dented metal door stood next to a glossy Chinatown dressmaker's shop. Cabs dislodged a steady stream of hipster *gweilos* who hit buzzer number three.

The hallway smelled of sweat and cigarettes. The Ivy entertainment mafia was on the prowl. We were backed up down the staircase. Turned to Mimi. "We stay half an hour. Tops."

When we reached the apartment level, Tracy scanned the room, unimpressed, and took a joint out of a silver case with her thin bitter-chocolate fingers. She waited in vain for one of the boys to light it and got a real man to do the honors. We didn't see her for the rest of the night. Turns out they left together shortly after.

Kent turned the entry fiasco into a receiving line. *How good to see you. Yes, it* has *been a long time.* The main room was open, with a kitchen on the left, windows on the right, and *Young Frankenstein* projected simultaneously against three walls. The black-and-white comedy cast shadows like moonlight on water.

Earth, Wind & Fire came on. The room went dark, then light. Kent was one of those men who'd gotten handsome since he'd married. We talked about business, indie films he'd produced with money he made by selling his ISP. "Kimmy," his remarkably tall, plain wife, who graduated a class under us, "is upstairs with the kids. I don't think they're screaming yet."

This was my cue to say how fabulously my album was selling; or that I was pregnant, which he'd probably heard, and which of course was no longer true.

Instead, I pointed left and said, "You remember Mimi. Just squint and imagine her in a vinyl miniskirt." Kent did just that; flashed back to one night when they'd had a drunken roll in the hay. "Oh, right, Mimi, um, great to see you!"

I buzzed through the room so fast that anyone who asked about the tour got a wave and a nod. The space was bare except for a few silk curtains and pricey, clear-molded plastic chairs. Too bright for dancing and too loud for talking.

The nook near the stereo smelled like weed. It was filled with the famous, the would-be, and those who fed on them. A wild-eyed former child star was talking into a reporter's minicassette. "Celebrity," she said, enunciating each syllable into a reporter's minirecorder, "is a pathology. I'm sick."

Bright red fireballs lit up the walls, rocked the room with energy that spread from the sides inward. We let out a collective "whoa" and turned to watch. The video looped. It was Keanu, skating on a plank of bus floor with Sandra Bullock. They spun away and the bus arced toward an airplane. The plane exploded in the most beautiful clear burst of red a painter could ever wish. And then it started all over again.

Kent came over with a couple of hedge-fund managers who had heard the album and loved it, and I switched on my charisma, and I made pretend I was thrilled by it all. Underneath the pretend was the real: I loved this stuff. I lived for this. I was cheap, I was shallow, I was a miserable mess.

I kept my eye on the cabbie as we passed the drugs around. Jimmy handed me a small vial of white powder and a Baggie of E. I stuffed them between my breasts. Sometimes I wondered why Mimi rolled with this crew, but that would be like asking why I still felt the need to drink myself to sleep every night. Some things you do *become* you, and stopping means killing the person you've become.

We slipped out onto the street, the waiting room of clubland. Everything vibrated bass, the kind of beats that rock your internal organs. Piss-yellow light from the street lamps showed grim warehouses flanked by a line of gossiping club kids. The asphalt had buckled to show the cobblestones underneath.

We walked toward the sonic boom. Big brown men with arms crossed and legs splayed blocked black metal doors. Mimi pranced up, gave them little kisses on the cheek, and they waved us through. We made a joke of the search: everything but body cavities. For us, frequent fliers, a light touch. I spread-eagled for the security girl. She had platinum hair and walked like an army private. Patted me down gently, making the wide loop of my underwire bra, gave an approving smile, and let me pass on.

The cover was forty dollars, but Jimmy got us comped, led us through a red lit corridor into the main hall. So loud we spoke in exaggerated mouthings and sign language. *Meet back here. Bathrooms.*

It was only midnight, and someone was already puking. One stall, two sets of feet. Another stall, two sets of feet. I went into a stall with Mimi. She and I opened a little pillbox and each popped an E.

Against my better judgment, I took a chaser of water from a leaking tap. We went back to the dance floor to pass the goods to the boys and let them have their turn.

We got our first round of drinks. I wanted water, too, but didn't want to pay five dollars. I didn't want to pay even though the E would rip through my body and make me heat up like I had a fever raging inside. I knew what these chemicals did to my body, and I chose to take them anyway. The kids didn't seem to have a clue how drugs worked. Drugs were chemicals, and these chemicals had rules, and one of the rules of Ecstasy was "Drink lots of water."

Now, if you were a club owner, you might want to charge five dollars for a bottle of water. If you did, though, a lot of people wouldn't drink any water at all. That led to dehydration, fainting, convulsions. Cops. Ambulances. Drug tests on prone, clammy flesh, the kind that stays stiff when pinched between fingers. No free water was a cheap and stupid rule. No free water turned the music off.

That was just my soapbox, and it was early enough in the night that everyone's brain and liver were functioning just fine, thank you. After a couple minutes the E started to kick in, like a smile in my belly, a sunrise spreading from my deepest parts.

"You feeling it?" said Jimmy. And suddenly he didn't look so gawky. I didn't even mind the fact that his father was worth fifteen million and he dressed like a street punk and used words like "Word." If I was being honest with myself, he wasn't so much a caricature of hip hop but a caricature of Ari, another rich boy gone bad boy.

I answered him with a "Yeah." A long yeah. Extended like the beat that shivered around the sides of the room. The bass became physical. Concussive. Ballistic. Faster now. The DJ played with the beats and arms jumped in the air like people throwing gunshots.

"Wanna dance?" said Jimmy.

The only clear spot on the floor was near the speakers and we moved there but it was unbearable, not just deafening but crippling, our skins and organs pounded by the sound waves. We danced our way into the crowd and Jimmy had some rhythm or maybe I was imagining. He had hips like a girl's (okay, a white girl's), flat and thin. Whipped them around like Mick Jagger. I laughed out loud, a silent *ha ha ha* in the middle of *thdunk thdunk thdunk*. He laughed with me, pulled me close, and we synced up, like the beat of two tracks overlapping.

The crowd was very Friday night, a rainbow of colors, ages from fake ID to should know better, pretty boys and party girls and goombas. Everything New York.

I threw my arm up like a gunshot.

Like a gunshot.

Red leaned back and yelled in my ear, It is straight-up Africa in here*! This was our spot in New York. Ours. Brothers on the edge of the floor did moves they didn't even know went back across the Middle Passage. Homes came up to Red and said, "You Puerto Rican?" Red just smiled. The brother with me bobbed and weaved like a boxer. Without missing a beat we threw back our heads and answered the call.* Ah Ah Ah Ah Ah. *So close in the middle the only way you could tell who you were with was whose hands were wrapped around you, who was whispering in your air.* Ah Ah Ah Ah Ah Ah Ah. *R and I didn't even drink then, just came to get our freak on.* Ah! *I could feel him, hard through his pants, and I turned and gave him some of that ass right up in it.* Ha! *Bent over and showed him what I got.* Hah! *I didn't even hear it pop off. Just a rustle in the crowd and Red running up to me with a look of cold hard panic. A brother next to her saying,* "Nigga shot a girl in the face. 'Cause she wouldn't dance."

Freeze.

"Where were you?" Jimmy said.

I was stock-still on the dance floor. "One of my past lives."

Jimmy put one finger on the side of my chin, looked me in the eyes. He had sad clown eyes in a sleek boy's face. He breathed out through his mouth and I caught the hot moist air in mine as I leaned in. Our fingertips met and danced before he clasped my hands and placed them behind me. The panicked, rigid part of me made to-do lists. *Call Mama. Call Daddy. Call Leo.* The wet, hot part of my brain locked the worker bee in a closet. *Fuck that.* I touched the hairs on Jimmy's neck, downy, slick with sweat. He cupped his hands around my ass and lifted me off the floor just enough to put his face in my chest. I felt weightless and small. "You're so juicy," he said, when he finally let me down. "That's corny," I said, but I was smiling like a fiend. He was a beautiful, sweet consolation prize for everything I'd lost.

When the lights came up, we headed for the bathrooms, the handicapped stall. I came out first and met Mimi, whose expression could have curdled milk. She said, "He's not good enough for you." My body still vibrated with the ghost of the beat and his tongue. I was about to tell her to keep her damned opinions to herself when she said, "I should know. And he has a girlfriend. One in every city."

"We were only dancing," I said to Mimi.

Jimmy and I went back on the floor, but the rhythm wasn't there. I kissed him good night, a flat, dry kiss. I went home alone.

Beatrice came running in with my outfit as I sat in the makeup chair. "We don't have time for this shit." We were back at the Orchid to record our live album. The audience was filled not with fans (who would have been reliably enthusiastic) but tastemakers, and tastemakers didn't like to wait.

Beatrice texted a message, talking fast without looking up. "Listen, I might be out of a job tomorrow. You need to sing your *ass* off tonight. You need to look sexy as *hell*. You make love to one person in the audience and that's Ken. We are dropping contracts right and left. You're lucky Ken likes you. I'm lucky I still have a job. Sophie, what did you do to your hair?"

I let my hair go, that's what. Nappy roots were topped with the usual perm, making me look like I'd stuck my finger in a socket. The hair stylist soaked my hair in a mess of gel, began pinning it back tight, and put a long glossy wig over it.

"It's a little Chaka Khan, don't you think?" I said.

"Chaka is sexy," said Beatrice. "That girl knows how to work her fat."

Since vile Beatrice had decided that I was good for her career, she had been dropping words like "girl" and "honey" and "sista" into our conversations far too frequently.

Beatrice turned back to her two-way, started punching furiously. I lay back and let the makeup woman go at it. Beatrice handed me a protein shake, the flavor of McDonald's vanilla. I squinted as the eyeliner went on, thanked Beatrice, and took a big slurp.

In another part of the backstage area, Ari, Bruce, and Shar were lounging. Their outfits didn't have to pass maximum muster; their faces didn't need to be powdered. But in order to get a great live album, we needed a great live crowd. Part of getting our crowd hot and wet was me looking good enough to eat.

"You're ready," said Makeup. And so I was. I looked strange to my own eyes, the portrait of drama and desire. Thought of Leo and got fiery angry again. I would sing to him tonight. I would sing *through* him tonight, piercing him with my voice, even if he wasn't there. I didn't know if he planned to come or not, but every singer needs someone to sing to, and he was still the one for me.

When I went to meet the band, they all feigned checking their watches. (Only Bruce wore one.) "So we ready to do this thing?" I said.

"'*We*' been ready for an hour," said Shar.

"Sorry."

"It's fine," said Ari. He came over and kissed my cheek, then crossed his fingers, put them over his heart. "Let's do this."

After my worries that the crowd would be snooty, the gig was almost too easy. Play a mix of all your top songs, throw in a bit of banter, and watch the music-industry sycophants clap and smile. The band was on their game. Sometimes I just wanted to sit back in the cut and listen. Bruce, on electronic drums or keyboards or both, made musical love to Shar's turntablism. Ari held it all together, his guitar winding catlike between the other sounds. I vamped it up every now and then for Ken, who was seated at the right hand of Renggli. Underneath that patrician mask and the Swiss reserve, these two moguls were just men, no more and no less; easily moved by a smile, a swivel of the hips, and a song. Maybe I was selling myself too short.

Ari kicked into the first bars of "Kind" as our encore. Then a man entered the back of the room with a wide-brimmed hat covering most of his face. He couldn't be hidden, not from me.

"Sorry. Stop." I waved my arm. "Stop."

Shar, Bruce, and Ari ground gracelessly to a halt. Ari looked particularly pissed, but maybe it's because he'd seen the same man in the crowd that I had.

"I want to go off road for a minute," I said to the audience, grabbing the mic from its stand. "I think a lot of you know, thanks to the tabloids, that I been going through some rough times. I'm not much of a one for Southern sentimentality, but I make a few exceptions. At my Nana's house we used to listen together to old Mahalia Jackson records. One of those songs just came to me today."

I leaned back to tell Ari, Shar, and Bruce to give me a little space. "But you can join in if you want," I whispered. "If you know the song."

The board op had dimmed the lights and hit me with a spot so bright I couldn't see anyone in the audience. I stood perhaps a moment too long, then reached back to channel a voice from my past.

> *How I got over*
> *How did I make it over?*
> *You know my soul looks back in wonder*
> *How I made it over*

After a while, I could hear a few feet tapping and a few hands clapping, or people humming along with the song. Somewhere in the middle of the song Bruce had walked over to his keyboards, punched it into the key of an old church organ, and given me a little backup.

> *Tell me how I made it over*
> *I had a mighty hard time, coming on over*
> *But now my soul looks back in wonder*
> *How did I make it over?*

If there was a God, that God lived in the space between the notes of my voice. That God nestled in the emptiness of the song of the sinner. Even saying that I was a sinner implied that I believed in something: But what? Perhaps it wasn't the right time to puzzle over how or what

I believed. Maybe it was time to try, just try to shout my troubles over. With my last note—a perfect, sustained burst that almost hurt my own ears—I tried my hardest to do just that.

Then the whole crowd was applauding, all of them. All of them except the one I wanted to hear my cry. That man, Leo, was walking out the door.

Right after the show, we all went our separate ways. Ari and Shar walked off together; Bruce hopped into a cab with his friends. After I joined Beatrice, Ken, and Renggli for a drink at the bar and a bunch of much-needed ego-stroking, a woman I hadn't seen in years sidled over and invited us to a party at her SoHo penthouse. The labelites declined; I said yes.

Talia was Spanish but raised in Tangiers, in the mélange of cultures, laws, and attitudes that inspired *Naked Lunch*. Sometimes she took her mission of bringing the psychedelic old Tangiers to New York a little too seriously. After we air-kissed, Talia put something in my mouth; something that crumbled and tasted bitter and reminded me that I swore I would not do this again.

I could have spat it out. Instead, I washed it down with a glass of sweet red wine and we took a cab to her house, where the party was already in full swing.

A woman was street-corner preaching, preaching in the middle of the party. She hardly looked the part of a prophet; more like a gallery dealer. Kept saying how God was a computer. Cascades of binary decisions rule the world. Garbage in, garbage out. God a victim of bad data? Perhaps God needs a more efficient microprocessor. An OS upgrade. A better way of sorting wheat from chaff. Sins are parasitic screen savers, transferring viruses and spyware. Things gum up.

As whatever substance took me away, I leaned against a wall by the bar and watched the crowd. They were exactly the kind of people I'd always wanted to hang out with, beautiful and many hued and smiling mysterious smiles. But I didn't feel a part of them. I didn't care enough about them to dislike them, either. I felt nothing for them. They were nothing to me.

As I put my hand to my head, I saw contrails of color, so my hand seemed to shudder up at me through space and I anticipated it reaching my head before it actually had.

As much as I tried to stay in the moment, I was lost.

I dreamed we were three, walking down a cobblestone street lit only by the moon's shine. It could have been the North End of Boston, or a town outside London. It could have been any land of brick townhouses in that light.

I was myself, but the two that flanked me were lions who shape-shifted into and out of human form. One lion was tawnier and leaner, with a smaller ruff; the other was more vividly gold, almost more like an illuminated manuscript than a lion itself. I walked between them knowing in dreamspace that the best way for me to stay alive was not to look left, not to look right, and not to touch, but to let them remain glimpses in the corner of my eye. I walked carefully, one foot in front of the other, hands folded across my chest so I did not accidentally brush them and make them aware I was not a lion.

That's why I didn't see the lioness amid streets that had become catacombs. She pounced and sunk her teeth into the back of my neck. I tried to shake her but every time I did my back got stickier and wetter. The smaller male lion disappeared; and the other simply watched me bleed.

I woke, not knowing where I was, tried to pull a ratty T-shirt tighter around me. I was in a room of the house I hadn't seen and Talia was looking at me.

"You fell asleep at the party. I suppose I can't throw them like I used to."

"Oh, I'm so embarrassed," I said, looking at my bare wrist and then around for my watch.

"It's two," she said.

"Oh, Jesus."

She cocked an eyebrow.

"I was supposed to meet Red. You know Red."

She shrugged, noncommittal.

"Your things are downstairs," she said. And it was only then that I noticed I was wearing a long, man's T-shirt and not much else. I knew there was a story there, but I didn't have time to discover it. I went downstairs, found my things in a neat pile, and other guests sleeping in the alcoves of her apartment. Talia kissed me on the cheek and I left.

When I turned on my phone—still in my pocket—and checked my messages, I had one, angry, from Red. She'd been waiting at our little Jamaican bakery for an hour, with Oscar, and I could hear him crying in the background. They were going home, she said. She'd told him I was coming and he got excited. And I could play with her time, and her friendship, she said in a colder voice than I'd ever heard her use with me, but not with her child's.

I didn't call her back, and I didn't delete the message. I just turned the telephone off, and got into my clothes, and got into my grief and shame. I knew I shouldn't, but I wanted to stop at a liquor store on the way home. 'Cause then I could really beat myself up good, better than anyone else could.

The doctors finally took Nana's other leg. Mama had this slow, quiet way of grieving, even when she first called me on the phone. She told me about her real-estate business; and how well Matthew was cleaning up; and she said last, and almost in passing, about the surgery.

"I'll be down."

"She'll be okay." I think Mama really meant, *Nana doesn't need you here. But we do.*

Mama and I lived in the practical world. No copious "I love you's," just an understanding that she would be there for me and I would be there for her, to the best of our abilities. My devil side decided to take her literally and say, "Okay, call me when you need me." And don't call anytime soon.

To make myself feel better about basically turning off the emotional switch of fear and love and guilt about my family, I got on the E train. I knew enough about neurochemistry to be warned that Ecstasy could burn out the serotonin in my brain. If I did a lot back to back, every high would be followed by a deeper crash. But it felt *soooo* good—it was all love, love, like living in a world made of chocolate and melted honey. I called Leo out to dinner and told him how much I appreciated him as a person. I was wearing a luscious blue terry cloth dress with dragon embroidery and matching platform sandals, very ghetto bananas fabulous. And I had water instead of wine and stroked Leo's hand as I told him all of our problems were as incidental as the tiniest crater on the moon.

"What are you on, Sophie?" he said.

"Why I gotta be on something every time I treat you nice?" I said.

"I don't know. Why do you?"

"Well, if you don't want to be here, then just go."

"I got too much respect for you to just walk out on you in a restaurant. But the food don't taste good to me right now. Let's get the check." So we did, got our entrées in doggy bags. He gave me both of them, then drove me home. I turned on the radio and slid like liquid against the interior of his car seat, not even bothered that he wasn't trying to touch me or hold me. Maybe I'd call Jimmy. Maybe he'd be in town.

But Jimmy wasn't. And I was out of the little smiley-faced pills that I'd gotten from Paul. Fell into the pit. Woke up so mournful low I could barely get of bed. I'd stop and stare just anyplace. I could be squeezing bread at the store or buying a pair of stockings. Stopped talking in the middle of conversations. Mind kept slipping back to other days and times. Surely this was madness.

I bought plenty of food and stayed locked in my apartment. Sounds bothered me the most: doors that clicked like insects, the voices of people talking just below hearing reach. I knew they were talking about me. I knew they wondered when I'd be okay.

I tried so hard in those long, flat days to see the good in anything. But I had no appetite for joy.

Began to hate the sound of my own voice, the look of my own face, the smell of my own skin. Smelled musty with undertones of acrid. Failed to bathe so I could smell it more deeply. I liked the smell of my own rot because it allowed me to hate myself more completely.

Sometime in the middle of all this I saw my own face in a corner of the tabloids. "Sky Falls" was the headline, and they'd caught me when I looked like hell, coming back in slippers from a grocery run.

The alcohol and the sleeping pills were only taking me deeper into the pit. The only thing I had left was a bag of shriveled magic mushrooms, tucked into the butter slot in the fridge. Most organic poisons are bitter—nature's early warning sign to us and the rest of the animals. Mushrooms are just as rank, chewy, and foul as an uncured animal hide left in the sun. I washed the dried caps and stems down with the last of the limoncello I'd gotten in Rome. Ten minutes later I was walking south on Broadway.

It was, to anyone who wasn't both clinically depressed and hallucinating, a beautiful springlike day, plopped in the middle of a long hot summer. The NYU students walked as if they owned the earth, slouching around in hundred-dollar jeans and sneakers that were semaphores of wealth and class.

The shrooms started hitting as I approached Chinatown. I was on Broadway near Houston when space began to bend. A policeman was standing at the corner talking to a guy in a car. The guy in the car was holding a bloody rag against his head. That policeman's partner was nonchalant, observing the crowd. I asked the idle cop about directions to an underground club. At the same exact moment so did a gay white guy. The cop had the info and the gay guy and I walked off together. What were the chances of that? (Especially the cop being helpful.)

I can't remember his name, but let's call the gay guy Adam. Adam was just about as generic (cute but not handsome; fit but not ripped) as you could make a downtown club boy. He'd just moved back to New York after living at home in the Midwest for a couple of years. He'd returned to conquer New York and be the photographer he'd always wanted to be. I wondered what made him so sure he could do it this time, since it was clear he'd walked this path before and gone home with a fistful of nothing.

We got to the club and it was empty. It was like a rec room with a killer sound system, scuffed but clean wood floors and white walls, a coat check, and a nonalcoholic bar. The men who took our money and then our coats were black and gay and maybe alcoholics or drug addicts. After all, as Adam later told me, this place was founded by men in AA who had no place to go and dance and feel the spirit without the demon rum or demon gin chasing them through the halls.

It was, like I said, mainly empty. A few men were dancing in ways that would have made the ancestors proud, dipping and twirling and using their muscles like slingshots to catapult their bodies higher and higher; and the music was ecstatic, house music, a praise song loud enough to reach a God with deaf ears.

The place began to fill up with more men and a few women. The men who jumped and twirled and moved began to constrict themselves in tighter arcs to make room for lesser dancers. It must be like Tetris, I thought, to do all *that* among all *this*.

One man out of all of them was lost to the revels, flattened from being so drug-high. He looked so stupid, walking around like a zombie amid men who could jump and leap and spin. Their movements left dizzying stripes like the zigzag of a flashlight whipped 'round in the dark. The music swelled and ebbed and flowed; the men were jumping and the praise song flowed endless from the speakers. And it was the beginning of the feeling that one day I might know God.

Adam and I danced a bit and talked about his dreams for the future until he made eye contact with a taller, broad-chested man and I drifted away to let him pursue. I usually hated people who left me alone to face the swelling crowds at a party. This man, whom I would probably never see again, had connected to me just when I needed it. But still, I was once again alone. Didn't want to dance. Couldn't drink. It was time to go.

On my walk home I felt my heart constricting to a red dwarf, which threatened to become a black hole and consume not just me but the entire known world. When I got inside I called Bruce, choking on my words as I kept trying to explain why I was crying. Bruce rang my buzzer in record time. "It was the mushrooms . . . I took so many . . . but they were old, and I thought they weren't that strong . . . and I was out of E. I was just trying to be happy . . . but I was just so sad!" And I laughed a little because it all sounded so jumbled and predictable and self-centered and stupid at once.

I couldn't stop talking. I just kept talking and talking and talking to Bruce about my night and what was going on in my life and I could tell from the way he looked at me that some made sense to him and some didn't.

As I lay sobbing in Bruce's arms he said, "It had to happen. You just needed to let go and let it happen. It's not the lie; it's the cover-up. Trying to pretend you're happy is such damned hard work."

The next day Bruce walked me five blocks from his house to his shrink's office. On the way he told me about his blues, the kind that kept him locked in his house, in bed, with only the radio for company; and the other times he'd thought he'd snap and punch someone in the face. I had a hard time imagining Bruce getting vicious. He had the kind of even temperament that bored women like me.

His doctor, Amy Krause, had an office next to the Au Bon Pain on Eighth Street. She had a broad Long Island accent and a way of staring through you. Her office was utterly boring, blank, cream-colored, with a couple pictures of beaches and children. I instantly wanted to leave.

Dr. Krause said, "I don't usually get tandems. Couples."

"We're not," Bruce said, "a couple." The way he said it made me realize, if only for a moment, that he wished that were the case.

I was mainly spacing out, though, looking at all the prescription samples lined up on a shelf along the wall. Celexa, Prozac, Wellbutrin, Effexor. All these made-up names, all these shots at being happy. I'd tried half of them, and given them up. Some made me feel dull and stupid; other ones made me feel jittery and hyper.

Dr. Krause dismissed Bruce to her waiting room.

"So what drugs do you take?"

"What?"

"What *drugs* do you *take*?"

"None."

"None?" She looked at me, twirling a pencil in her fingers. "None like, no prescriptions, or none, like no coke, no weed, no alcohol."

"Oh. Even alcohol?"

"Is a drug," the doctor said.

"Well, I mean, I . . ." She was still staring at me. "I drink. Sometimes." Exhaled. "A lot. And weed sometimes. But not so much now. I've been hitting the E a bit. And once . . ."

"Yes."

"I got into downers: sleeping pills, Vicodin, Valium."

"Okay," she said. Looked at me for a moment. "I want you to break it down for me, in five-year increments, from when you were ten."

"Ten! I wasn't using anything when I was ten."

She nodded, not skeptically, just thoughtfully. And I remembered. The time I got into Mama's wine stash, just after she and Daddy broke up for final and good, and I started sipping a little from the bottle here and a little from the bottle there, until she caught me and chewed me out, and even then I went back for more.

"Look," Dr. Krause said after I'd talked for a while. "It's a simple circle. You feel bad; you respond to the drink and the drugs. Then the drink and the drugs bind with or block some of the neurochemicals flowing to your brain. Plus, not everyone is born the same. Your dad, for one, sounds like he has a biological predisposition to depression, maybe paranoia too. What I'm saying is: you can keep doing what you've been doing, and getting what you've been getting, or you can try something different. Maybe we can't fix it, but we can fill the gap with something similar enough that your mind is, if not fooled, at least satisfied. Okay? Try legal drugs for a change." She smiled, as if that were an inside joke.

She went on a riff about side effects: tapering on, tapering off, the dangers of stopping cold, the false euphoria I could experience. By the end of the session, she'd sold me on a Wellbutrin shot with a Klonopin chaser, if I needed it.

"Let's get one thing straight," she said.

"What?"

"I can be your psychopharmacologist, but I can't see you every week. I don't do talk. Look, I only agreed to this because Bruce said you needed help now. So before I give you a prescription for this medication, you *have* to promise me you'll find a therapist."

"I promise," I said.

She looked hard at me.

Thought she wasn't going to give me the scrips. She did. Whatever. The first thing I did—no, second, after filling the prescriptions—was put the names of the therapists she'd given me in a drawer I rarely opened.

Bruce became my spirit-guard. He talked to me, and listened. Cooked for me: lemon pasta with chicken; and grilled vegetables; and strawberries with fresh-whipped cream. On a date out to the movies, I noticed how much cuter he'd be if he just took care of his skin. Boy had a patina of ash on him like some kid who'd been adopted into a white family and got stuck using their lotion. So I introduced him to the cheap wonders of petroleum jelly.

As I rubbed the Vaseline on his body, I felt like that woman in the poem "My Man Bovanne," stroking away the dullness of his skin and bringing back an ebony glow. I told him to turn over so I could do his chest.

"Naw," he mumbled.

"What, you hard?"

He was. So I gave his Johnson a little polish, too. And then when he was good and ready, I put a condom on, decided to ride him for a little pity fuck, except it felt good, it felt good to be with someone. So maybe he was just pity-fucking me.

Afterward, I told him, "I think this was the first time I've ever had sex sober."

"How did it feel?"

"Good. Weird. Very weird. But good."

That night we fell asleep side by side on my bed, the television providing a cover of chatter. I woke up through the night, saw him sleeping next to me, and thought how he was the kind of good man my aunts and uncles hoped I'd marry. I wondered if he woke up and looked at me and what he thought.

And I felt better. Really. Brighter. Calmer. Then Bruce told me he'd made plans to go visit his family in Houston. I was panicked but tried not to show it. I took a cab to the airport with him, and kissed him good-bye.

That same night, I'd invited Red and Lin over to my house for dinner, so I wouldn't be alone. They walked in with wary looks and guarded smiles. When they saw that I'd cooked for them, they stopped standing like soldiers at attention. When they saw I wasn't serving them wine just as an excuse to drink it myself, they settled in.

We were three glasses of mint tea into the meal—a Moroccan theme—when they started talking about themselves. I'd made a vegetarian tagine, with roasted chicken on the side for me and Lin. When Lin turned down the meat I was surprised. She smiled and patted Red's hand and said she was giving this vegetarian thing a year. The carrots and yams and squash and onions tasted like summer and fall dancing. The sauce flashed with cumin and left you wondering about the other spices. I'd put out finger bowls and we ate with our hands the taste and the smells, the smells and the texture, the texture and the touch.

The house filled with a comfortable silence, the soft nothing you hear in an expensive car going down a highway.

"It's not like voices, like some other people," I said unprompted. "It's just yourself and yourself and yourself, nagging nagging nagging."

They looked at each other then, and I couldn't be sure what their eyes were saying. "See I told you, she was crazy . . . ," or "It's not as bad as we thought."

"We were worried about you," Red said, finally.

I said, "I was worried about me, too."

I sat on the fire escape of my apartment, looking down at the street, listening to Red babble into my headset and try to convince me that I should go to some meditation class.

"And after, I found this great place where we can go and get veggie frittatas. Or they have this really good tofu scramble."

"When in my life have I ever eaten a tofu scramble?"

"You could try it."

"Not today. If they can hook me up with some bacon and eggs, I'm even willing to try this, what did you call it?"

"Zazen. Sitting meditation. Eleven o'clock, Smith Street. Consider it's this week's session," she said. We called our weekly get-togethers "sessions," since I only half-jokingly called her "my personal shrink." Between her and Bruce, I had a fighting chance to making it.

Thought for a second. "Cool. I got mad parties Thursday night. Sunday sounds fine."

"Sophie!"

"I'll be good."

"It's not about being good for anyone but yourself. Or *to* anyone but yourself."

"I know, I know."

"Fine, then. I'll see you at ten thirty."

"Didn't you say eleven?"

"We're meeting at ten thirty," she said, her voice tight.

At five of eleven, I rushed into a karate studio on a street filled with overpriced vintage clothing stores and half a dozen restaurants. A few folks, all black, were taking off their shoes and jackets. Through the front room was a room they must have practiced in, except today it was filled with large, square pillows in a geometric grid.

"Always cutting it close," Red said, looking annoyed *and* relieved.

"That's just what my mama says."

"And she's right." Red helped me get seated on the cushion. Tried to turn me into one of those human pretzels you see at carnivals.

"Try these." She put bolsters under my knees. My belly stuck out too far for my liking, and my knees hurt.

"I feel like a Weeble," I said.

Red choked back a laugh, provoking the woman seated at the head of the room to turn her head. She was black, and bald, and dressed in black robes. A metal bowl sat in front of her.

Red explained what was going to happen. The teacher will clang the gong, and then you will sit. Let yourself be empty. Try not to think. "That's like trying not to breathe," I said. Red just squeezed my hand and smiled, "No, you can breathe." Then she went to settle herself on her own cushion.

"Breathe," the teacher said. She had a Mona Lisa smile, kind and mysterious. She lifted a thick pestle and ran it around the inside of the bowl until it sang, guttural and high and metal and human at once.

We sat.

Five minutes later, maybe less, a chant had taken up residence in my mind.

I can't do this, I can't do this, I can't do this, I can't do this, I can't do this.
Knees hurt, knees hurt, knees hurt.
I can't do this . . .

It was like a locomotive, chugging slowly, whistling, moving, faster faster faster faster.

"Stop thinking," the teacher said to me. She'd materialized behind me, whispering in my ear, but it felt as if her voice was resonating in my head, resonating like the sound of the singing bowl.

"Breathe."

For one moment, I was nowhere and no one, just an empty space of self. And by the time I got back to *I can't do this,* it wasn't long before the teacher sounded the singing bowl again.

"So what do you think?" Red said as I limped over to retrieve my shoes.

"I think that my butt hurts, my back hurts, and my knees hurt."

"And your mind?"

"It doesn't hurt." I took a deep breath. "Wow, I actually feel good."

Red gave me her beatific, gap-toothed smile.

"All right," I clapped my hands. "Let's get some bacon and eggs."

"Must you get bacon?"

"Yes, I must. Bacon is an international human right in fifty-three countries."

"'Zat so?" she said, linking arms with me.

"'Zat's so."

Three weeks later, Red wasn't in town but I came. I opened the door slowly and peered around it as the others nodded at me and smiled and removed their shoes.

After zazen, we pulled our numb legs out from under us, massaging them. Our teacher asked us to share challenges in her life.

This beautiful woman, round as a partridge with flawless skin, started talking in a babygirl voice about how she had roaches underneath her bathroom sink. As a Buddhist, she didn't want to kill them. So she was meditating on what to do.

I thought, hit the spray, fool.

Then, the next morning, I opened the door and a roach dropped in. Literally. Probably on its way up from getting its grub on in the garbage bin right outside the front door.

I *never* had roaches in my house.

Without any regrets, I lifted my foot and let my sole say good-bye.

With my newfound Zenergy, I decided I could talk to Leo about money without wanting to commit homicide or suicide. We chose an Italian-style café in a newly renovated building on Malcolm X Boulevard. It was black-on-black gentrification.

I'd thought about bringing Ari or Red with me, but then I thought that might only make things hostile. I came alone and let him buy me a cappuccino. He was more fit than ever, and dressed better than ever, but there was something defeatist in the set of his shoulders and the arc of his full, beautiful lips. After all his beef with his own family, I realized I never really imagined him wanting one of his own; just a publicity stunt. Maybe I was wrong. I wasn't in his mind, though, and unlike Ari, I realized: I never quite understood this charming, ruthless man.

"I know you're double-dipping, maybe triple-dipping on us," I said after we got settled. "You're manager; tour manager; God knows what else. I want to see all the balance statements of what we made, and I want to see them now."

"You couldn't understand them."

"I know people who could explain them to me," I said. "And don't try keeping two sets of books. I'll just ask the label for theirs."

He laughed then, slow and bitter. "So it's like that, huh?"

"It's been like that for a long time. We just haven't talked about it."

He gave me his version of the finances. According to him, the cut he took was more than I'd hoped, but less than I'd feared. Maybe he was even telling me the truth. He even whipped out a couple of spreadsheets and ledgers. I leaned in next to him to see the figures, I smelled it again: his spice. I'd forgotten how important scent was to me, how it moved me on a purely animal level.

Out of the blue he said, "Come home with me." His eyes were pools of sorrow and regret, or maybe I imagined that. Maybe I saw what I wanted.

"First, that's not my home. It never was. If it becomes my home one day, a lot of things will have to change," I said.

"You know I love you," he said.

"I'm not sure I even know what love is. I know it *isn't* what you did the other day."

"That was an accident."

"An accident." Now it was my turn to laugh. I pushed back from the table and sat back in my chair. "I have a great story for you. My Nana's Nana had a husband that was a lot like you. One day in the kitchen he raised his hand to her. She raised up a hot kettle. She didn't hit him with it; she just put it up last minute in the path of his hand. When he struck it, he burned his palm so bad he could never ball a fist with that hand again.

"Leo, you know me. I don't make threats, and I don't keep them. I just fade out. I'm ghost."

"Don't. I'm sorry."

"For what?" I didn't break eye contact.

"For . . ." He balled his knuckles. "For slapping you. For saying it was your fault."

"Keep going."

"For making you feel less-than."

And that was it, right? Always someone making me feel less-than. Leo was just the latest in a long line. Mama when I didn't make the honor roll or keep the house clean; Daddy when he left; Uncle Ray when he sized up my body; Erika judging my drinking (well, everyone judging my drinking); and Leo shaking my money tree.

"Come home with me," he said. "Please."

And you know what? Fool that I am, I did. No accounting for taste, or loneliness.

The brownstone looked unlived-in neat and clean, as if it was on the market to be sold. Cold. We went upstairs to the bedroom, both of us silent. He sat me on the bed and knelt to slip off my shoes, then massaged my feet.

He wanted it raw; I insisted on a condom, even though I'd gone back on the pill. It wasn't our usual athletic sex, or angry sex, or anything we'd done before. He asked permission for everything, as if we were Antioch students. And I gave him permission to touch me and stroke me and sweet-talk me until finally I was ready for more. He was slow and gentle, and I was silent, except for the tears. What if I had taken better care of myself? Would I still be pregnant today? Did I even want the baby? Or was this a blessing in disguise?

"Don't think," he said, as if he could hear my thoughts. Just like my meditation teacher. Don't think. Don't think. Don't.

Afterward, he got down on one knee and said, "Will you . . . still . . . marry me?"

It was the last thing I expected.

"I don't know. We can't go back," I said.

"But we can go forward."

"We'll see," I said, picking my clothes off the floor. "Let's just wait a while and see."

Beatrice called us all in for a meeting. "So, there's this concert in South Africa. Big international bill, big international stars."

"How much are we gonna clear?" said Leo.

"It's free. It's for charity. We can get the travel comped."

"No money, no way," said Leo.

"Nelson Mandela will be there." Collective inhalation of breath from those of us in the band. "Probably."

"He'll be there, or he'll probably be there?" said Shar.

"Look, he's old. I can't guarantee he'll be there. The organizers said he would, and that's the best I can do, okay? God! Gift horse, mouth?"

Three days later we were on an American/South Africa Airways code-share to Johannesburg. The organizers were too cheap to fly us business class and I was too cheap to spend my money on a five-thousand-dollar ticket, so we resigned ourselves to the cheap seats for a fifteen-hour flight. I wanted a window seat. Ended up next to a pair of big-game hunters. They were Americans imitating British explorers, with fancy khaki bush wear and endless stories (as I was trying to drift to sleep) of shooting animals I dreamed of seeing alive in the wild. They'd killed lions, more than one. I thought they were beasts, but I hoped that my occasional "mmms" and "mm hmms" would suffice until the sleeping pill took effect. Then Ari, who was seated in front of me, jumped in.

"Fucking assholes," he said. He said it to no one in particular, but loudly enough that I feared everyone on the plane could hear.

"Ari!" I said, leaning between the seats. "Keep your voice down." Sometimes that worked. Sometimes if I just acknowledged him it kept him from spiraling off into a chain of crazy mutters and shouts.

"No. These fucking *colonial imperialists* still think they own the land of the people."

"Who died and made you Fidel?" I whispered.

"The worst part," he said, even louder, "is that you are *humoring* them. You are making these safari rednecks think that they're fucking Robert Redford and Meryl Streep."

I looked at the couple next to me.

They had turned stony, staring straight ahead.

At least they were quiet.

I slept.

By the time we arrived in Durban we looked like we'd been locked in the trunk of a car for two days. Our guide, Chester Patel, met us at the gate.

Chester loaded us into a luxury van and began his smooth tour-guide patter as the driver wound through the seaside city. He stopped talking when he saw us all drowsing off.

When Chester announced we'd arrived, I reached for my purse, assuming that once again Leo would forget the basic courtesy of a tip. Instead Leo pulled out a band of bills, made an ostentatious show of peeling off a few, and pressed them into Chester's flesh.

The hotel could have passed for any slightly sub-luxury accommodation in any city in the world. It had ornate, gilded chandeliers and a curved desk of concierges, who were all white or South Asian, and an army of bellmen, who were all black. Leo and I had a corner suite with a living room overlooking the boardwalk. I could see children in faded T-shirts and raffia skirts dancing for tourists' change, and stands selling food and handicrafts. The hotel didn't have twenty-four-hour room service, and it didn't have a spa. After Switzerland, I'd gotten spoiled.

There was a Victorian fainting couch near the window. I lay on it and tried not to think. Trying not to think is harder than you think.

"Why don't you get ready?" Leo said.

"For what?"

"For the party."

"Whose party?"

Leo explained that a few wealthy expats—black expats—were throwing a shindig.

"Oh, I don't know," I said.

"It's good business," he said.

"It's good business for me to get some sleep."

Nonetheless, I went. We all did, tired but showered and freshly dressed, to see how those enterprising Americans lived in the new African land of opportunity. And when we'd been let off by the fountain at the drive and personally led in by a smiling servant; and greeted by a silver-haired entrepreneur with a watch that cost as much as a small house, and his younger wife, in a flowing batik-print gown; and given glasses of champagne (except Ari, who declined), we got a sense of just how much money Americans here were making.

Leo and the American hosts and guests hobnobbed with the new South African elite, who were indistinguishable except for their accents. Same flossy suits, same expensive accoutrements, same focus on buying, selling, keeping what you made, and making sure no one else got what you had.

The band and I pulled back and hung out in a corner of the garden. Our hosts had lit the space by torches and thin strings of white Christmas lights. Even from our retreat, the servants made sure to come by and see if we needed anything. Bruce greeted each server with *"Sawubona,"* and said *"Ngiyabonga"* every time they brought him a new appetizer or drink.

"Go 'head, international player," I said.

"I make it my business to know 'Hello,' 'Thank you,' and 'May I take off your panties,' in every possible language."

"Sometimes you are so stupid," I said, laughing.

"So are you."

"So are we." I felt like a "we" tonight. It had been a long time.

"Look, can I talk to you for a second?" Bruce asked.

"Sure."

"Um, can we . . . ?" he motioned to take a stroll.

The gardens were English-manicured along the walkway, and luscious and dense by the fences.

"I don't know where you are with this whole Leo thing, but you know how I feel about you."

I was afraid of this, afraid but prepared.

"This is quite possibly the worst time for us to have this discussion, and I won't," I said. "There's no 'there' there when it comes to us. And if you have a problem with that, we all have a problem."

"Okay," he said. "Okay. I'm just going to . . . I'm going to hit the . . ." He didn't even finish his sentence before he took off, walking fast and then practically running toward the comfort of the brightly lit house.

My words came out even harsher than I'd intended, and I'd intended them harsh. I loved Bruce in a gawky, younger-brother way, but he was the kind of hardhead who would not hear anything I'd told him unless I made it explicit. People think women were the only ones who confused sex with love, but I had hard proof in the form of Bruce Xavier Yarrow that that wasn't true.

I strolled back to Shar and Ari. "So what are we going to play?" I said.

The concert took place over two nights in conjunction with the U.N.'s World Conference against Racism. I'd eavesdropped on a couple of conversations about the conference tonight. Apparently the official event was a cauldron of resentment: Indian Dalits and European Romany and Africans and Asians all competing for the title of Most Oppressed. The Europeans didn't want to admit slavery was a crime against humanity, because it would open them up to legal claims; some Africans said black Americans didn't deserve reparations, because we'd *benefited* from being taken to America. The U.S. and Israel had walked out. So much for working together.

Off-campus, so to speak, there was the usual conference mischief: expense-account dinners, cocktail parties, and plenty of conference sex. The zipless fuck lived on.

"We have a twenty-minute set," said Ari. "We should do whatever we want, because it'll go by"—he snapped his fingers—"like that."

Leo came back, flushed with the excitement of hobnobbing with moneymakers. "Black is beautiful," he said.

"If black is so great," I said, putting my empty champagne glass on a servant's tray, and waiting until he'd left, "then why are the help acting like they just stepped off the plantation?"

"Somebody's always got to be the nigger," said Leo. Damn. Just when I was beginning to not hate him.

The night before our show, I asked Chester to take us to where the real people lived. We ended up at a long table at a tiny curry house in Durban. There was a Castle Lager clock on the wall, above plates of very hot prawns and curry goat and roti. On my right, a bear of a man told jokes in crisp Afrikaner cadences. On my left sat someone I called Mr. Hands, who had one of his on the small of my back. Leo wouldn't motivate from the hotel, but Ari, Shar, and Bruce all came. Chester had arranged a meet-and-greet with his friends, a mix of Asian Indians, Xhosas, Zulus, and coloreds, a deluxe Crayola box of flesh tones. The older men and women reeled off tales of going to prison freeing their country from tyranny, or seeing their fathers get killed for fighting back.

Two of Chester's relatives debated the Future of Blackness. Seeing yourself as black (which they all pronounced "blek," like the villains in antiapartheid films) was apparently out of fashion among young Asians.

"So it's demeaning, now, to be blek?" said Uncle Kumar, spoiling for a fight with his nephew. He'd called himself proudly black, black to the core, and had spent years on Robbin Island to prove it.

"That's not what I said, Uncle," said a sheepish young man. "It's just, we're not, you know, blek. We are what we are."

"That's the white man in you talking."

"Uncle . . ."

"Oh, shut up and have another round," said Chester.

"Another?" the owner asked me. The answer should've been no. Since I got here I'd been staggering through my jet lag, aided and abetted by whiskey and Castle. And I'd been nice. Listening to Mr. Hands tell stories about Robbin Island. Watching him feel up every girl in the room in front of his wife. Get drunk. Act the fool. That's what being a political prisoner will do to you. Or maybe he was always like this and apartheid was just an excuse.

I turned to his wife, whose jet-black hair and cinnamon skin matched her husband's. "Can't you see what's going on here? Are you fucking blind?" She passed me a basket of bread and said, "Given all my husband suffered for this country, the least you can do is service him."

Of course, that didn't *actually* happen. Instead:

Everyone ordered another round. They'd started to tuck into their food. The proprietor had his pad out and was looking at me. "And you, love?" he said. I leaned forward in my chair and scratched my back. "Yes. Another."

When the owner came back, he didn't have any drinks, just a slip of paper. "Sophie? Sophie Lee?" I waved my hand. He swung his head sideways to indicate I should get up. I was smack in the middle of the table and had to displace half the room to get by.

Call me right now. It's about your Daddy. Leo.

I'd rented a South African cell phone with two-dollar-a-minute international calls. Didn't leave it on, but no doubt Leo had left a message there as well. I turned on the phone but had no idea how to dial the hotel number.

"Can I help you?" the proprietor said.

"It's a local call."

He pushed away my cell and dialed the number on a sturdy black phone propped against the bar. Leo picked up on the first ring.

"Baby, you should come back to the hotel."

"Why?"

"I'll tell you why when I see you."

"Just tell me."

He hesitated for a moment, knew I was hardheaded enough not to come when called. "Look, baby, your daddy died."

"How?" I said.

"Cancer." God-damned cancer.

The room grew cold.

"You coming back to the hotel?"

"Okay."

"Good. I've booked a flight out first thing tomorrow morning."

"What about the show?"

"What about it? I'll cancel."

"No, we're doing it."

"With your daddy dead?"

I regretted it almost as soon as I said it. "He'll still be dead when I get back after the show. Leo"—I slowed down—"I made a promise to do this, and I'm keeping it."

"What about your promise to your family?"

"What about his promise to me?"

"What about all your Zen shit?"

"What *about* it? Fuck." Slammed down the phone. Everyone in the bar looked at me.

Went over to the table and explained I had to go. Ari, Bruce, and Shar wanted to go with me but I told them to stand down, that we'd talk tomorrow. Made my good-byes, stepped into a cab, and headed back to the hotel. The city that had looked so welcoming a couple days ago now looked dead to me, spare and soulless. My stomach hurt. And I really did want to go home, not just back to a hotel, but home. I just didn't know where that was.

▷ 79 Miriam Makeba, "Pata Pata"

The concert was magnificent, except that I wasn't really there. The stadium wasn't filled, maybe not even half-filled. Concert tickets were real money for most people in South Africa. Harry Belafonte was in the VIP box next to ours, with a common area set up with food-and-beverage service, and we peered over at him and smiled. Before we went on, we'd seen a fantastic Mozambican hip-hop trio; and after we went on, the magnificent Miriam Makeba. But during our performance, I'd walked onstage and immediately gone back in time.

I am eighteen years old. My mother has just finished frosting a seven-layer chocolate cake with the words "Happy Graduation" across the top in pale yellow icing. The house is done up for company, with new plastic tablecloths across every surface my little cousins could possibly get their hands on.

"Don't let me catch them in my china cabinet like I did last time," my mother says, fussing over a bowl of potato salad. "And don't let me catch you standing in the corner eating before you've greeted everyone."

I mmm-hmmm her and sneak a fish cake off a plate. I hold it behind my back so I can sneak out of the room and pop it in my mouth.

"I saw that," she says. Eyes in the back of her head.

I toss it in my mouth anyway. Can't go back on the plate.

Graduation was a-ight. Standing out in the sun in B-more in June is nobody's idea of a good time. I think I turned three shades darker, out there in the center of the football field with all the guests up in the stands. My Nana fanned herself all the way through and still felt so faint at the end that my uncles had to help her to the car.

"Damned shame," my mother said, cursing for once, "that there's no shade."

I'll work at the library for three months and then head for college. The house seems suddenly smaller, as if it has closed up around me. I look at all of my childhood photographs on the wall with a sense of distance. My old selves are just that: old.

Finally the family starts arriving. My uncle Trevor comes with Nana, helping her up the stairs. We were going to have the party outside, barbecue, but after yesterday's heat no one would have been able to take it.

The men open the cooler of beers on the porch and twist-top bottles of wine. Uncle Trevor offers me a glass. I take it and gulp the sweet drink, too fast. Momma frowns when she sees.

"Come on, sister, your girl's grown now. Your girl done grown."

"I don't see it that way," said my mother, ladling green beans onto a platter and sprinkling them with almonds. "As long as she's in my house, there are still rules."

I want another glass of the stuff, and another. But no one offers it to me again and I don't have the nerve to ask.

"So little girl is going off to Harvard," my uncle said.

"Yes." I looked at my feet.

"Baby girl, we're so proud of you," says my Great-Aunt Ophelia.

On it goes, an endearing, embarrassing litany of praises that starts during arrivals and continues during supper. I spend a lot of time thanking people for their gifts and gazing at my toes. Mama keeps telling me to stand up straight and look people in the eye, but she looks proud of me, satisfied for once.

Someone puts on some music, the O'Jays. My little cousins and my older cousins' children start to dance. The rest of us stand around the room stomping and clapping, urging them on. Uncle Trev, always the show-off, even takes to the floor and does an exaggerated shimmy, pretending he's still a child, sending the little ones into quivers of laughter. I don't even hear the doorbell.

My mother comes up and taps me on the shoulder. "Sophie," she says, an odd quaver in her voice, "it's your Daddy."

I come out to see a man I barely recognize. His hair, once a luxuriant Afro, has been cropped short. He is thinner now, so thin that his tight-cut jeans hang loose on his hips. Over the jeans he wears a clean shirt cut in an out-of-date wide-collared style, and a jacket, which, if not new, is at least in a fashionable style. He has a wide, seeking smile.

"What are you waiting for?" he says. "Come and give your Daddy a hug."

All eyes are on me as I walk across the room and embrace him. He smells like sweat and cologne, as if he hasn't showered or he walked a long way before he came.

"I have a present for you," he says.

"Thank you."

". . . But I just haven't picked it up yet from the store."

"That's okay," I say. And then, even though I'm not sure it's true, "I'm glad you're here."

"Can I get some of that wine, brother," my father says to Uncle Trevor. My uncle has a strange look on his face, a look of contempt and regret masked by basic civility. He comes back in a twinkling with a glass.

"A toast to such a fine woman, raised by such a fine woman," my father says. When he raises his arm I can see a bald patch on the elbow of his jacket.

Reluctantly, my family lift their glasses.

"And you are still a fine woman," my father says, moving closer to my mother.

"Get out of here," she says in a sharp, low bark. I can see that some part of her still wants to reach toward him.

My father turns for the door.

"Wait," I tell him. But it's too late. He's gone.

And I remember at the end of the set, Ari having to nudge me; and, suddenly hearing the clapping, I bowed and said, "Thank you very much."

⏵ 80   Luther Vandross, "Dance with My Father"

I got a bereavement rate on the flight back, and booked business class. Leo tried to snuggle. I didn't know what the hell was up with that. Thank God the seats had immovable armrests.

Twenty-four hours, three cognacs, and two sleeping pills later the flight attendant asked me to stow my footrest. We were making one of those looping arcs around the city in preparation for landing. The forest of steel spikes in Midtown thinned out over the Village. The towers stood guard over the bottom of the city. I'd seen them from the air dozens of times and maybe I've willed them into this memory, like a close-up spliced into a film. I was in the window seat. When the plane tilted, I lay almost against the glass. I worshipped the city in those moments. It was my lover and we were palms to the sheets, regarding each other as the beloved.

We landed. The old terminals are ugly, like parking structures. Brown men from many countries whisper "Taxi, taxi," under signs telling you not to accept their rides. The baggage was late. Leo had called a sedan to drive us all the way to the funeral in Maryland, near the D.C. line. That wasn't where Daddy was living, just where someone from his side of the family found a free plot to bury him in.

We'd arrived at seven-thirty in the morning. The burial was at noon. When Leo told the driver this, he made it his personal mission to get us to Maryland before my Daddy was laid in the ground. We hit ninety and stayed there the whole way.

Pulled into the cemetery just behind the funeral procession, actually passed them on a straightaway, and were at the grave site before anyone else. I recognized my Aunt Vy, and, of course, Missy. Missy was the half sister whose existence most rudely awakened me to the reality that my Daddy would not be coming home. I didn't like to think about my own mother and father having sex, but the idea of Daddy sleeping with someone else was just too much. He hadn't stayed with Missy's mother, either.

I hadn't known anyone to wear opaque hose—the kind that make a black woman look ashy—since I left Baltimore. Missy did. She was a decade younger than me, and country as a buttermilk biscuit. Her mother was a severe Southern-born Baptist, and to this day, though Missy was in her third year at Howard, she wore below-the-knee skirts and pumps at all times. Hadn't seen her since she was fourteen. Leo and I stood a respectful distance back from the grave. Missy caught my eye and motioned me over.

No. Shook my head.

She motioned again.

No.

"Come on over, sister," she said, and I did. And I put my arm around her waist, and she put hers around my shoulder, and we watched our father laid in the cold, cold ground.

Later, I called Mama. I told her about the burial. And then I asked, "Did you love him?"

"As best as I could," she said.

81 DJ Spooky, "It's Nice Not to Lose Your Mind"

After Daddy's funeral, I decided to tell Ari that I was erasing our marriage. I'd kept the secret about the annulment and the tribunal for months, and I was tired of carrying all this weight.

I wanted to let go of the past, including what Ari and I once had, whether or not I married Leo. I got some papers back from the Tribunal that I had Uncle Luke decipher. He said that I was close, and I didn't need Ari's permission to finish the process. At least I wanted him to understand.

I made a date for us to have breakfast at a French café across from Tompkins Square Park. It was such a glorious day, the purest part of autumn, warm but not stifling; sunny and clear. I'd worn a tank top, which wasn't quite warm enough. Ari took off his jacket and wrapped it around me. He'd cut his hair off again until nothing but a short fuzz stood straight up from his scalp. Monkish. I snuggled in his cloth jacket. It was the color of roasted corn.

I explained the whole idea of an annulment, and that I just wanted to be washed clean.

"So we were never married?" he said, when I finished.

"We were but, yeah, God, I guess, we were never *really* married."

"How is *really* married different from married?"

"It's about intent. And understanding. I know this sounds self-help corny, but I wanted to be with a 'you' that didn't exist."

"You don't even believe in this shit."

I was silent for a moment. Looked up at him. "Ari, I do. I do believe. It's the first thing I've believed in for a while. I need to let us go. Ari!"

He got up, paced out of the restaurant's iron grillwork fence onto the sidewalk. The fence was one of those airy but remarkably effective psychological barriers that New Yorkers put between their semiprivate space and the bustle of the streets.

"Are you angry?" I said. I hadn't seen Ari angry in years. Drug-addled flare-ups, yes, but not honest-to-God, I-have-been-wronged angry.

"Yeah, I'm fucking angry. What the fuck do you think? Fuck!"

"Look, Ari, I'm proud of you. You've become the man I should have married."

"Thanks for the consolation prize." He was still standing, leaning against the grillwork and staring down at me.

"Ari? I just want your blessing in this. It's not about Leo. I just want to be clean. I just want to be done with all of this. Give me your blessing to let *us* go."

"I can't give a blessing. I'm an atheist. Or have you forgotten?"

"You know what I mean."

"No, I'm not really sure I do."

After a moment, he walked back through the gate to the restaurant patio and took his seat. We sat without speaking for a moment. Still hadn't ordered food. The waiter was getting antsy. "Two coffees, for now," I said.

"Let's pretend we have no history," Ari said out of the blue.

"What?"

"Let's pretend we haven't done things to each other. That we didn't fuck up so bad."

"If we didn't do what we did, we wouldn't be who we are." I signaled the waiter to refill my coffee, and I ordered a bacon, mushroom, and cheese omelette. Dietary salvation could wait. Ari ordered buckwheat pancakes, no syrup, no butter.

"Look, Ari, if we weren't who we are, I wouldn't be sitting with you. I don't talk to strange men."

"Is that so?"

"That," I said with a smile, "is so."

The waiter came with the coffee. And then Ari, who was facing downtown, stood. So did all the people facing downtown. The waiter nearly spilled the pot of coffee on me. I was used to, say, the trannygirl who rode the huge tricycle or some other hoo-ha passing by and stirring folks up, but this wasn't that kind of reaction. So I stood, too, and looked where everyone else was looking.

We couldn't see where it came from, but a long dark plume of smoke was coming from the south, toward the tip of this crowded urban island.

Like most restaurants in the East Village, the place we were brunching was on the bottom of an apartment building. A man at the next table went around the gate, expertly leaped up, grabbed the bottom rung of the retracted fire escape ladder, and pulled it down. He started climbing. Then Ari, despite my calls for him to come back, did, too. Bits of rust from the fire escape fell on the mosaic tile of our table.

When Ari clambered back down, just a minute or two later, he looked more shattered than I'd ever seen him. He looked worse than he had when he was using; and worse, even, than when he first went clean.

"I don't know where to go," Ari said. People from the restaurant were running in all directions, like ants stepped on by a malicious child. Some didn't move at all but waited to hear what was going on, and then they began to move with purpose or simply in shock. A group of people headed toward the open apartment building door.

"Ari. Ari! What is going on?" I asked.

Instead of telling me, Ari took me by the hand, led me into the building, and we started walking up the stairs.

Four flights and one ladder later, we emerged on the rooftop. By now the downtown vista was clotted with smoke.

I could see one of the Twin Towers on fire.

"Jesus, that's some electrical fire," one guy said.

"Didn't you see it?" said a girl with shower-wet hair and a slip dress on.

"What?"

"The plane!"

Just then, we saw the second strike; that is, the second plane hitting the second tower. One man started to cry, but most of us were silent except for a sharp intake of breath or a whispered "Jesus."

Two things filled my mind at once. First: We made this movie already. This bloom of death wasn't any stranger than all the Armageddons that hit movie screens every weekend. Second (and I tried to stop myself from thinking this, I swear): It was beautiful. The smoke filled the New York skyline; the flames burned like hell. If you've ever watched an action movie without hating yourself for sucking up all that well-faked death, all the anger-fueled pyrotechnics, you know what I mean. *Die Hard. Fight Club.* Why do we watch that shit? It's beautiful, that's why.

But this time it was real.

I tried not to let it feel real to me. This was just an aesthetic event, like the pyrotechnics at the KPS concert we opened for. I let the world go flat and two dimensional and I was just watching the screen.

Around me, everyone who wasn't sobbing was asking where to go. Some left the roof as soon as they snapped out of their stupor. The rest of us, a dozen or so, watched the world burn. We sat on rooftop machinery or the grubby tar beach and saw the flames shoot up the buildings and the smoke blow toward us. From the roof, we could see a steady stream of people walking north, toward Midtown and Harlem.

"They already shut down the subways," said one weather-beaten guy as he emerged on the roof with a hand-cranked emergency radio.

"You got it together, huh?" Ari said to him.

The man with the radio had a lean body and the skin of someone who lived for years in the sun but thought sunscreen was for pussies.

He said, "I lived through Northridge *and* the L.A. riots. Holed up at my place in Echo Park with a shotgun, some Dexedrine, and a whole bunch of supplies. Stayed awake three days, fired warning shots at the looters, and lucky for them didn't have to kill anyone." He leaned in. "I'm not telling a lot of people, but I've got fifty gallons of water and a bunch of MREs in my place. You seem like nice people. If you need something . . ." He nodded his head downward.

When Mr. Survivalist turned away, I yanked Ari's arm and moved a few feet away.

"Don't even think about it. I'd rather take my chances with whoever ... whatever ... than a nutjob like him."

"You say that now."

We stood in silence.

This was just a movie.

Just a movie.

When the first tower fell, there was the sound of hysterical panic coming from the reporter on the radio, mixed with a quieter but more frightening gasp from those gathered around us.

"Now we have to go," said Ari.

"Where?" I asked.

"Now," he said, answering a question I *hadn't* asked. He took my hand and walked me downstairs and tugged me onto the sidewalk.

New Yorkers were great at calm. In addition to the people trudging uptown, I saw a woman walking her dog, one of those Boston terriers. The locals carried walking bags of food from the corner stores. There were long, long lines at the ATM machines. A few lucky people had bikes and backpacks and pedaled their way through the clog of cars. Ari and I walked slowly past the Tenth Street Baths. We held hands.

There was nothing to say.

82 Bob Dylan, "It's Alright, Ma (I'm Only Bleeding)"

We went back to my apartment. My building was full of writers and web designers and people who didn't leave for work until quarter 'til ten. A gaggle of neighbors, some still in their pajamas, stood in the lobby debating what to do.

A thick-bodied white guy from my floor was trying to take charge. "Run your bathtubs full of water, and be prepared to drink it if you have to. I think the deli is cleaned out by now, but you know, whatever you can get your hands on to eat is good. Enough for three days. That's what I'm hearing. Hold on for three days."

"I'm not staying here for three days!" said a woman in black heels, black skirt, white shirt, azure sweater, and pearls. I'd seen her only once in a while and my guess was that she was making for-shit money in publishing, sharing a rent-stabilized apartment, and living mainly with some rich boyfriend uptown. Clearly this had interrupted her morning commute.

"What are you going to do, walk to the Bronx and cross the bridge into Westchester?" said some smart-assed punk chick.

Several of my neighbors paused. They hadn't thought of that.

To hell with them. The last thing I wanted to do was take a poll on how to save my own fucking life.

I walked upstairs and went in my own frigging apartment. For some reason Ari stayed behind. I scoped the scene inside. Electricity on: check. Water on: check. I was focused enough to start filling pots with water. I hadn't cleaned the bathtub in ages and there was no way I was drinking from that.

By the time Ari knocked, I'd poured myself my second stiff whiskey, neat with just a touch of water.

"Now's not the time," he said, trying to grab my glass.

"Now's the *perfect* time."

"Dammit, Sophie."

I laughed.

"What?"

"It's just so perfect. We've come full circle, haven't we?" I took a gulp of the brown liquid, coughed, and took another. "Go ahead, get out of here. I'll only depress you."

He didn't leave. I called Leo on the landline and reassured him I was okay . . . and my Mom . . . and Erika, Red, Mimi, Bruce, Shar. Everyone was holed up, for now, but we talked about making a break for Mimi's dad's house if the roads cleared up a bit. Shar lived down by Chrystie Street, much closer to the towers than I did, and she said that tanks had rolled into her neighborhood and soldiers were setting up roadblocks.

Ari and I curled up on the couch, watching endless variants on the explosions on television. The cable was crisp and clear as it was on any other day. The news channels looped the footage over and over again into an extended remix. When I saw the people jumping to their deaths to escape the fire—small, desperate, broken birds falling and falling with their clothes flapping; falling for the cameras until the video cut away right before they hit pavement—I finally turned the television off.

We ate what was in the refrigerator. Watched darkness fall. Watched the television in small bursts just to see if anything more was happening. At some point I slept. Dreamed I was a puppet, a character in animation. It was black and white, hand-drawn, and I was crawling up a hill. The hill was made of bonemeal. It was loose and cream-colored. On the top was a mansion, lit from within.

Saw trees in the nighttime, black shadows on the hillside, a light from the window, a person inside.

I crawled through the window, found myself in a living room. I opened a wall safe. Ari's father walked in from another room. He, too, was a puppet, with sharp teeth and white skin. There was blood on the safe walls. Somehow it was a portal. He motioned me toward it, so I could go to the other side.

And I said, "No, you go." So he did, disjointing his shoulders and his hips to fit through a space barely wide enough for a poodle.

And I couldn't leave. And I couldn't wake. Bounced from dream to dream, always coming back to the bonemeal hill.

Then it was morning. Ari still slept. I saw people on the street, acting relatively normal, with cups of coffee and newspapers. I took care dressing. I wore blue shoes I'd bought at the thrift store down the block. There was a watermark on the powder-blue silk on the left on the front, and that was why I bought them: because they were imperfect.

I flipped to The Video Channel. It showed the same footage as all the others, rubble still smoking, downtown streets filled with tanks.

Walked outside. It was like stepping onto a movie set. I had a scarf on, and a kimono, and a little black dress. The kimono was short, hardly dramatic, but it was black, and if there was ever a day to wear black, well, there it was. My sunglasses matched, black wraparounds, and I'd pushed them hard onto my nose. I thought I looked like a sort of pan-ethnic Jackie O.

I listened to people's conversations. The ATMs were all out of money; the delis had all run out of water and anything except the nastiest canned goods; but there was this restaurant on Eighth Street that was serving free food all day until it ran out; and by the way, Sammy's brother was missing and his picture was on the wall at Union Square. I didn't know who Sammy or his brother was, and I didn't know until that moment that there were pictures of the missing posted in Union Square. I just let all the new information wash over me.

Turned up First Avenue, toward the Filipino breakfast place. The Ukrainians were closed, and the kosher place was closed, and the fancy boulangerie was closed.

On the next corner, there was a crowd. It was a drab storefront mosque, blended in with the aging storefronts, and now besieged by screaming people.

This wasn't how people in *my* neighborhood acted, or at least that's what I thought. Drifted toward the melee and accidentally got shoved in the middle, between the people shouting on the curbside and those shouting back who flanked the mosque wall. A couple of cabs passed, and people ran after them to try to get in, but they had their off-duty lights on and ran the red lights.

Back to the protest, if that's what it was. One group of people shouted, "Go home, Arabs!" Another group screamed at the first, "No, *you* go home!" The people who actually went to the mosque, men in kufis and women wearing the hijab, stood silently by the doors and let the others duke it out. Mind you, the folks screaming "Go home" were not dolled-up like racist skinheads or wearing Klan robes. Everybody looked like what passed for East Village Normal to me.

I stood in the center of the screaming, just looking around. A woman in blue jeans and a trendy top said, "Go home, Arabs!" "You go home," said a different woman, who wore a vintage tennis dress.

It was hard to tell the good guys from the bad guys. They all looked the same.

▷ 83 Peter Gabriel, "Don't Give Up"

Like dogs, like rats we ran for the hills and put aside our fears and lives to reach the other side.

I didn't want to hear these words, but they came to me unbidden. It was too soon to slip into songwriting mode when everything was still happening in real time. Couldn't help it: I drowsed and the words fell into a rhythm with the jumping of the car.

> *Like dogs*
> *Like rats*
> *We ran for the hills*
> *And put aside*
> *Our fears and lives*
> *To reach the other side.*

I woke, and slept, and woke again. I'd forgotten how beautiful the countryside was, what it meant to see trees that weren't the stunted, runty little things alongside Manhattan streets but full-fledged and defiant of urbanization.

"They're taking over," Bruce said to Shar.

"What?"

"The trees."

His laugh was tired and almost hysterical. Bruce and I had taken one of the Klonopins Ari's shrink gave him. I slept part of the way, my head on Bruce's shoulder, Ari snoring slightly to my other side. Shar's dog, Master, took up the front seat. The pit bull–Rottie mix was strapped into a safety harness and looked out like a sentinel on the road ahead.

The trees were magnificent, though, huge green canopies overhanging the roadside. Sheba, Shar's cat, growled by our feet.

"How long . . . ?" I asked Shar.

". . . Is it going to take us to get there? I don't know." Shar was snappish. Traffic had gotten worse, not better, on the other side of the bridge.

"No, how long do we think we'll stay?"

"Oh. I don't know," she said, slowing to go around an old-fashioned traffic roundabout and patting Master on the head. "As long as it takes."

"As long as it takes to what?"

"As long as it takes to want to go back."

Finally, we pulled into the mile-long private drive. The motion of the car, moving slowly but unchecked by traffic now, lulled me the way that trains used to. The scenery moved by in a seamless blur.

"We're here." Bruce gave me a little wake-shake. Mimi's father's house looked even larger than it had at the wedding. Mimi and Nestor and the kids were here, and much to the band's dismay, Leo was headed this way as well. Plus Red, Lin, and Oscar.

Suddenly Mimi's son Jack ran out of the house. His face was wet and reddened from crying. "Mmmmommmmy . . . !" He choked on his own tears.

"What?" I said, grabbing him in a hug. Ari didn't wait. He ran in through the open door, toward God knows what.

"Jack." I squatted next to him. "Jack—are you hurt?" He shook his head no. "What happened?"

"Mmmmommy . . . Mommmy and Daddy are getting divorced!"

I felt relief: that wasn't so bad. Maybe for the best. Then thought of how I felt when it happened to me, the worst betrayal of my young life.

"I'm sorry, Jack," I said, hugging him tight. "How about we go inside?"

He nodded and let me pick him up, which he hadn't allowed me to do in years, since he declared himself a "big boy" at three. I held Jack close to me and walked up the stairs into the foyer.

The voices were louder in the dining room, but coming from the kitchen. I peered in and saw Ari standing, like a traffic cop, arms extended between Mimi and Nestor. Nestor looked like he'd slept in his clothes, black leather jeans and a T-shirt. Smashed porcelain coated the floor. I knew from my own wedding shopping that that pattern cost two hundred a setting.

"Now hold on," Ari said.

"No! Today was the last fucking straw. I catch him on the phone with his *girlfriend*, comforting his *girlfriend*, while his children sit here scared out of their minds."

"Right now," I said, "you're scaring them, too."

Mimi turned. Her eyes were bright red, one hand still clutching a dessert plate. "Fuck you, Sophie."

"Okay." I threw up my hands. "Fine." Jack was still in my arms, and he curled tighter around my neck. I turned and walked away to take him upstairs to bed.

"This should be a nice, restful few days," I muttered to Shar as I passed her. On second thought, I turned around. "Come with me. I'll find you a bedroom." She grabbed her cat carrier and her suitcase and we went upstairs.

Sometime around four PM, things settled into a routine. Everyone had had a snack, or a nap, or both. The house was quiet. People had withdrawn with their books into corners. A couple had gone to the home theater to watch the news.

I was still muttering under my breath: *Like dogs, like rats we ran for the hills / and put aside our fears and lives / to reach the other side.*

It had the rhythm of a tongue twister, without the twisted tongue. No matter what I did, the steady drumbeat of the words stayed in my head.

Life took on new rhythms. Jack was allergic to cats, so he went from eyes red from crying to eyes swollen shut from histamines. Then there was the fact that Master and one of Mimi's tiny little yappy dogs got into a fight. Well, it wasn't really a fight. Yappy nipped Master and Master just took one massive paw and smacked that little fool across the room. As a result, Master was banished to the backyard. I thought the big girl doggie had shown restraint.

At least Mimi had settled down. Nestor had taken his things and gone to stay in the pool house, while Mimi stayed in the master suite near the kids. The house had three master suites, each with Jacuzzi tubs and steam showers, and four other bedrooms with twin beds and shared bathrooms. I got a master suite because Leo would be staying with me. So did Lin, Red, and Oscar. The three kids took up two of the bedrooms. Shar was in another; and finally Ari and Bruce. I lay in bed for a while. The cell phone service was still spotty. Leo had called me from a pay phone to say he was on his way, but I wasn't sure how long he'd be.

The sunlight filtered in through a crack in the curtains, and I tried, and failed, to will myself to sleep. The air was too heavy. Time stretched too long. I did one of the few things I could do that would calm me. I decided to cook.

Went downstairs to the kitchen. It was bigger than most studio apartments, a gleaming palace of brushed chrome and pale blond wood. A housekeeper walked into the room, her dark hair pulled back in a bun.

"Uh, *hola, como estás?*"

She gave me an amused smile, and said, in only slightly accented English, "I'm doing great, and you?"

Obviously this wasn't the same woman I'd met at the wedding. Suddenly I had a panic attack: What if she was a family friend and I'd insulted her?

"Sorry, uh, um . . . Do you work here?"

"Yes."

"Can you show me around the kitchen? I mean, I wanted to cook dinner, but I'm not sure what we've got."

She led me back into a pantry, if you could call it that, stocked with enough food for a grocery store. And then she opened two double-wide freezers, filled with wild salmon and porterhouse steaks, pans of home-made lasagna and vegetables.

"Damn," I said. "This is no joke."

"No," she said. I chose salmon and a rack of lamb. Went over to the refrigerator and found a stunning array of fresh fruits and vegetables. Rosarita—that was her name—must have gone out as soon as the planes hit the towers and stocked up.

Took out the basics: garlic and onions. Then chose Chinese long beans and shiitake mushrooms. Grabbed some fresh basil and tomatoes. I'd make pasta and a light sauce. The sun was beginning to mellow, less glare on the windows, and I pulled up the shades. Outside, Shar was playing fetch with Master, both of them leaping and teasing each other. Jack watched warily from the porch. I could see Nestor far in the dis-tance, smoking a cigarette and looking at his feet. I put the vegetables in a colander and began to wash them.

Rosarita showed me the pans. Oh, the ecstasies! Copper-bottomed and restaurant-sized, these pans were ones I could only fantasize about. They wouldn't even fit on my stove, but on the eight-burner professional model they had here, no problem.

Made a charmoulla for the lamb, pureeing garlic, cumin, lemon juice, cilantro, oil, and salt and pepper. Smeared it over the meat, popped that in the oven. The salmon I decided to cook stovetop. I'd read a way to cook the fish frozen, which actually seared the outside and kept the inside moist. Added garlic to the salmon, too. So sue me, I loved it. Placed the fish in a single layer on a huge frying pan, with olive oil and thin garlic slices that would melt in the pan, and then ground a bit of mixed grill spice on before closing the top. Next to the long beans. Rosarita helped me snap the ends, cut them in the middle, and layer them in a casserole with slices of shiitake. For them, I drizzled olive oil, and added a dash of five-spice seasoning and soy.

People started walking by, pausing, asking questions.

"When's the food going to be ready?" said Bruce.

"When it's ready," I said. I gave the same answer to everyone. If you'd cooked long enough, you learned to smell the readiness in the food, the smells of browning and caramelizing; and when you lifted the pans, you could take the tip of a knife and test the doneness. I turned the salmon. Was beginning to gather a crowd.

"Go away," I said, but with a smile. Had started to boil the water and dice the tomatoes for the pasta and sauce, a simple mix of diced tomatoes, yet more garlic, olive oil, and basil.

At least the vampires wouldn't get us tonight.

Served dinner at eight. Rosarita started to set the table, and Shar and Bruce pitched in.

Nestor came to the dining room door and peered in. Mimi looked up, annoyed. "Come on in, man," Ari said, and Nestor pulled a chair between his two youngest children.

"Let's bow our heads," said Shar. "Dear Lord, we thank you . . ."

Lin broke right in. "We don't do that in *our* house."

"Do what?"

"Coerce other people into buying into our religion, or lack thereof in my case."

"Not now, Lin," Red said softly.

"You're the one who taught me how to say what I meant."

"You don't have to say 'Amen,'" said Shar. "You don't even have to listen. I just wanna say some grace. All I want to do, now"—and her tone implied the unspoken word "Bitch"—"is say some grace."

"Let's make a toast," said Red, standing. "To life."

"Which is empty and meaningless," said Ari, leaning back in his chair with his hands folded across his chest. "Right, Zen girl?"

"Look, the phrase 'empty and meaningless' has a totally different meaning in philosophy . . ."

"You mean new-agey self-help," said Ari.

". . . in philosophy than what you are implying."

Nestor was enjoying it all. "Your friends are a bunch of brats!" he said to Mimi. Then he turned to his son. "Can you see those brats, Jack? Brats!"

Jack didn't know whether to laugh or not, so he bit his thumb. Nervous habit.

Mimi screamed out, "Nestor!" She whispered to me, "It's an ADHD thing. I'm trying to decide whether to put him on meds."

"I think Jack just needs some peace and quiet," I said. As did we all.

There was a completely different conversation going on across the table. Ari was saying to Red, "If not now, when can we speak our minds? When can we tell the truth?"

"After dinner!" I said, standing. "You can tell the truth after dinner. Right now, fill your plates."

We ate in silence. I took it as praise. Wondered if my Mama was cooking salmon tonight. I'd called her again. She was fine, and doing much the same thing that we were. Matthew, Erika, and Erika's boyfriend were all staying at her house.

After Mimi had put the children to bed, or abandoned them to computer games; and Lin and Red had put Oscar down, too; and after Nestor had slunk back to the guesthouse; the philosophizing began again. Lin grumbled about "those Harvard people who have to over-intellectualize everything." Red gave her a look. Lin turned to Shar. "Look, I'm sorry about interrupting the prayer. I didn't know you were such a Holy Roller."

"That's not an apology, Lin!" said Red. "Geez!"

It was funny to see tiny Red flanked by her leading ladies past and present, both happy to joust for the princess.

"If you want to know the truth," said Shar, "God snuck up on me again. I was trying to leave Him alone. But I missed it too much, praying. Believing. Singing in church. Letting go of the poison. I missed Him. And I know that doesn't make me too popular around here, but I missed Him."

Most of us nodded.

"And you believe it's a *Him*?" said Lin.

"I call God Him. That's how I was raised, but it's just words, you know. It's just words."

"I'm sticking with empty and meaningless," said Ari. "Can we get a vote on this? Seriously." He got up on his feet. "How many of you believe in God? Really? Even after that show in Wisconsin?"

Shar raised her hand; and Bruce; and Mimi; and, slowly, me.

"You, too?" Ari said.

"Yeah, God snuck up on me, too," I said, vocalizing it for the first time. "What was it that Descartes said? If you don't believe, you're stupid, because if God doesn't believe in you it's one thing, but if you don't believe in God you're just screwed."

"That was Pascal's dilemma," said Mimi. "And you got it totally mixed up."

"Whatever."

We had five empty bottles between us, and Ari wasn't drinking. We retired to the parlor. Mimi made a fire, Ari turned on the stereo. Started out with Billie Holiday. Then we lay down on the thick rug in front of the fire. I went and lay beside Ari, and Bruce beside me, and then Shar on the other side of Ari. "I love you guys," I said.

"I love you, too," said Shar.

"And you guys." I turned toward Red and Mimi.

I blame Mimi for starting the crying jag. First she opened the faucet, then I started, Red, and Bruce. I heard the others sniffle, I swear. Even Ari.

The mournful music may not have been the best choice for some, but for me it was like lancing a wound. Needed to get it out, not just the events of the past days, but everything. Everything.

Drifted into a drowse and thought about the way music was my whole life.

My great-grandfather sold Billie Holiday reefers, back when she was a bad little girl and he was a dirty old man. A withered-up, little yellow man. Always looking at the girls of school age. A sailor, in and out of port. In town just long enough every time to get Great-Grandma pregnant. And wasn't it just like me to love Billie, all of her, even her vices.

Then there was my first musical love, Michael Jackson. I was six, and to my child's eyes he seemed just enough older to know a lot of things I wanted to learn. He was pure music, shimmering, shimmying, shaking, grooving, moving, liquid hipbones, and fluid bell-bottomed pants legs, denim, slouchy caps, a sexy choirboy backed up by his older brothers; plus television, dancing lions and tin-men, a too-old Diana as Dorothy. But wait, that last part was later.

Still, the Michael from *The Wiz* was always linked to my six-year-old mind. When I was six, my daddy and I went to see *The Wiz,* way before the movie with Michael and Diana, before the nose jobs and the skin lighteners and the hair straighteners and out-of-court settlements. Strange third-person memory: I see myself and my father walk toward the exit, along a half-lit aisle, with the play unfolding (bright reds and golds) behind us.

But: Michael. His was the music of longing, in a man-child's voice that a little girl could understand before she truly knew desire. I liked Michael the same time Daddy liked to play the Isley Brothers. I didn't understand their lyrics (thank God), but their guitar licks and keyboards made it hard for me not to dance; their whispers tickled my ears.

Older still: When my Girl Scout troop had a party I brought Stevie Wonder and my friend Ronnice brought Michael Jackson's "Off the Wall," which was everything you needed to know about the difference between uncool and cool. Stevie was uplifting and parent-approved; the teenage Michael was your best friend's cool older brother, a boy whom you had a crush on so bad you thought you might melt every time you saw him. Ronnice was in fifth grade and I was in third, which might have been part of my problem, but not all of it. She was what my mother called "fast," fast and loose with the boys, hard and unforgiving with the girls.

I loved Michael, don't get me wrong. How could I not? He was my first. But I mounted a defense of Stevie, which all the girls took as a weak-assed move.

When I was in eighth grade, Ronnice had an abortion. Like most of my fast girlfriends, she loved house music, the kind you heard in the clubs she'd sneak into. She was underage but built like a brick shithouse and nobody checked her ID. When she got into LL Cool J, I was loving Prince.

Later, I worked my way through alternative rock, romantic R&B, gay dance disco, Public Enemy, Madonna, and Grace Jones. Music ecstatic and anthemic, smoke drifting through laser lights, trannyboys in platform heels and lip liner, parties on the subway platform, lots of drugs but not down my throat or up my nose, the music simply lifting me, carrying me like the wind under the cape of a superhero or a pigeon caught in an updraft from a subway grate.

The music, just the music, used to be enough for me. Everything else came later.

I wanted to get back to those days again.

When I woke again, almost everyone had gone to bed and the fire was dim. Someone had put a blanket over me. Someone was still in the room.

Turned to see Ari on the couch, watching me. He got up and walked toward me, motioning me to stand. Without speaking, he led me to the backyard. It was crisp but not quite cold. We crossed the lawn toward the pool house. He slid back the cover of the hot tub.

"As long as the Church says we're still married," he said.

"I don't know."

"Comfort me."

When had he gotten so blunt?

"Just sit in the water with me," he said. "For old times' sake."

We took off our clothes. I was surprisingly bashful, turning my body away as I undressed. It was a different body than the one he had lain in bed with, larger and, perhaps, more damaged by life.

The water felt like heaven, just hot enough that I had to ease myself in slowly. A cricket hopped on my shoulder and then leaped, I hoped, to safety, not to a watery death. I submerged my head, surfaced again, to find Ari on my side of the six-person tub. I don't think we'd made love sober during our entire marriage. Either one or the other of us was always fucked up. Tonight was no exception. The wine had made me dream-filled and drowsy. Not that we'd make love. But when Ari began nibbling the tip of my earlobe, I didn't tell him to stop.

Even in the moonlight, he was golden, this tawny-skinned man with mesmeric eyes. Maybe if we'd met later, things would have been different. Maybe not.

He kissed me, gently and then with vigor.

"I can taste the alcohol on your lips," he said.

"Do you want me to brush my teeth?"

"No," he laughed.

Ari's technique was impeccable, a gradual increase in pressure and depth and the breadth of the swirl of his tongue, and then a withdrawing, and a moment for breath, before he began again.

"How did you stop?" I said.

He paused. "I kept trying. The whole time I was with you I kept trying. I wonder if you knew I was trying."

"It was worse you going on and off than being high all the time. Because I never knew what to expect."

"I know . . ."

"No, you don't know. You know what you know from inside. I know what I saw. I know what I felt."

"I'm sorry, Sky."

I swirled my hands through the water, back and forth, smoothing it all away.

"What did you ever see in me, Ari?" I asked.

I know what I saw in him. Beauty and the anger I couldn't let out. I loved his anger. It was strange to see him so still inside.

"I think I fucked you up real bad," Ari said. "When I tell you how beautiful you are, how brilliant, how innocent, you won't believe anything I say."

"People I loved lied to me well before you ever came along. Don't take credit."

He laughed.

We let the water soothe our bodies for a bit. Ari let his fingers play along my arms and shoulders. "Do you love Leo?"

"Not the way I loved you." Loved.

"One last time then," he said.

I ran my hand over his washboard stomach, and his nipples, and his throat. Paused. "I can't," I said. "I can't." I was just starting to know my mind, speak my mind, and do what I wanted instead of what someone else did. Going back to Ari, even for one night, would still be going back.

"I think I should go to bed," I said, beginning to get up.

"I still love you," he said, resting his palm on my thigh.

"I still love you, too," I said. "It's just not the same."

Got out, slung on my clothes, and started walking toward the house. Shar was outside, gazing up at the stars.

"Leo's here."

"He's here? Where?"

"Well, he'd been watching you for ten minutes, but when you started kissing Ari he walked away."

"Why didn't you tell me?" I said.

"You're grown," Shar said, looking down at her feet, then back up with a steely mix of anger and regret. "We're grown. We do what we like."

Leo wasn't in the parlor, living room, dining room, or kitchen. I walked upstairs slowly, wanting to turn back with each step. I tiptoed to my bedroom, the only open one, and stepped inside.

The room was dark, except for moonlight through the windows with curtains pulled back. Leo sat on the bed, his back toward me, he face toward the window.

"So this is how you repay me," he said without turning.

"Leo . . ."

He unfurled his anger and tented down the stakes of his rage. "So *this*," he said, "is how you *repay* me!"

"Leo!"

"Do you need some help here?" Lin stood at the door rubbing her eyes, her tattoos gleaming in the moonlight. I was hoping this night would end without her putting his blood on her kneecaps.

"No," I said. "Thanks, but no. Sorry."

Closed the door. Turned back to Leo.

"Keep it down. There are kids here," I said. "Plus Lin. Lin will kick all of our asses if we wake Oscar." I paced a bit. "Leo, I'm sorry."

"I'm sorry, too."

Then Leo did something I'd never seen him do before. He cried. He sobbed full-on like a child. He moved to face a corner and sat down heavy on an ottoman. I think he was holding his breath for this moment: betrayal by a woman he loved, a woman who didn't always straighten up and fly right, a woman like his mother. Did we always seek out the same flavors of remorse and repentance and romance that reminded us of the past? Know this: I didn't mean to hurt him. I was just too damned selfish not to.

Went to comfort him. Leo pushed my hands away. "God knows what diseases you and your junkie boyfriend gave me."

Leo flipped from teary to threatening. He walked slowly toward me. I backed all the way to the door, and stood holding the handle. Leo leaned over me and whispered his next words.

"Did you sleep with him?"

"No, Leo."

". . . On the tour . . ."

"*No*, Leo."

"So what was that about out there?"

"That was closure. So is this."

"What do you mean?"

"Leo, when I met you, I was looking for a man who would never leave me. And I found you. You won't ever leave me. You'll just stay with me and keep treating me like shit. Sometimes I feel like I'm only worth that. But not tonight, Leo. Not tonight. Hopefully not tomorrow, either. It's done. We're done. Done."

Leo lifted his hand. This time I stepped back.

"Been there, done that. If you try again, I will hit you back and scream. Then all my friends will open this door and take their turn on your sorry ass. With all that's been going on, I can't promise how fast the ambulance will come."

He stepped back, set his lips, and gave me another scornful look. "I thought you were somebody."

"I am."

"I thought you wanted to get somewhere."

"I have. Maybe not where I wanted to get, but I got. You got, too, Leo. You've been milking me like a prize cow, so don't even fuck with me. Go," I said. "Just go."

He did.

I cried so hard I wondered if it was burning calories.

I'd have to untangle our finances and pay Leo enough to step away from the band. Stayed in the room. Red and Mimi took turns bringing me food.

Sometime in the afternoon, I heard a knock at the door.

"Who is it?"

A little voice said, "Jack."

"Come in," I said, sitting up in bed and wiping my eyes.

"I wanted to play, but Mommy says you're sad."

"Just a little," I said. "How are you?"

"Fair to middling," he said.

"Who taught you that?"

"Grandpa," he said. "He's with Uncle Bernard in Paris. They both say hi."

"Thanks," I said. He snuggled a little closer to me. I tousled his chestnut hair and held him tight. "Life doesn't always turn out the way you want, does it?"

"Nope."

"Well, anytime you're feeling sad, you can give me a call; and when I'm feeling sad, I'll call you."

"Okay," he said, and sat with me another couple of minutes before saying bye and scampering away.

That night, most of us went outside and lay on blankets and watched the stars. Out here, there was no light, no pollution, no traffic noise, no interruption to staring at the blue-black curtain of night. A shooting star flashed across the velvet darkness.

I told myself just breathe.

I can't, I can't, I can't . . .

Breathe.

I can't . . .

Suddenly, I was alone, but not lonely.

I was filled with stars.

I chose my meaning. The meaning of life is just *life*. It's the ache behind your eyes when you've been up too late and worked too much, or cried too hard, or eaten too little. The color between day and dawn; torn trash bags ornamenting trees whose roots burst through sidewalks. Sex, drugs, and rock 'n' roll. And, maybe, God. A line from a Shakespeare play I'd acted in in college popped into my head: "Lord, can you hear a good man groan, and not relent and not compassion him?" Maybe God wasn't forgiving. I didn't know. Whatever I thought about the divine was still inchoate, unformed. But I did know that we here on Earth had to do our best to compassion each other. Life was just too damned hard otherwise.

Jack played with Oscar. It was beautiful to see a preschooler who will still play with a baby, having so recently outgrown baby things. Then Jack got up and walked over to my blanket and lay down beside me.

"To what do I owe this pleasure?" I asked.

He shrugged. "I got the feeling you were feeling sad."

"I was," I said. "But I think I'll be okay."

The best place to sit in the world, if not the cleanest, is Astor Place, by the cube, in the fall, in the afternoon. The entire world passes by and if you don't want them to notice you, they won't. When you're trying to pick out a song on a new guitar that you don't really know how to play, then people do tend to pay attention, at least for a New York minute.

I strummed a series of cords, a couple of them the ones I actually meant to play, and started to sing.

> *When you burn your life to the ground*
> *All you need is a fire*
> *First you rip your heart out*
> *Then you build a pyre*
> > *and you burn*
> > *and you burn*
> > *and you burn*

I didn't mind that most folks stopped for just a moment and then moved on. I just wanted to know that I had the guts to try this: to play and sing and risk.

> *You'd think the memories would be the first to go*
> *But then you find they're indestructible*
> *What do you know?*

One of the passersby did stop for the whole song, this tall white guy in a knit cap. He even clapped when I finished. Then he asked, "Didn't you use to be in that band?"

"I still am," I said.

"Why are you playing on the street?"

"I'm just trying to work some stuff out. The song's not finished."

"It's good," he said. Then he pulled out a dollar and gave it to me. "You need a basket. Don't ever turn down money. You might need it."

He walked away.

Sometimes that's all you need, one person to get you through the day, one person to listen, one person to help you create. One person to believe in you. Just one.

▷ 90 John Coltrane, "A Love Supreme"

"So you're my competition now," Ari said, pointing at my guitar.

"I wish."

I'd called him over to my house to give him the letter, the one saying our marriage was annulled. I handed it to him. "You're free."

"I don't want to be free."

"Do you want some coffee or something? Oh—this is so cool—Ill Meds just finished the remix of the new songs." Ill Meds was the rapper-producer I'd met back at The Video Channel. He was serious when he'd said he was a fan. I'd been spending my nights in his studio, watching him work magic with boards and boards of electronics, turning our songs into something that twentysomethings would dance to. Sky, the band, was old now in music years. Just plain old.

Ari put his hand on my shoulder. "Don't try to fill the space, Soph."

He meant the silence. Sometimes the silence between words said more than the words themselves. I always tried to fill those silences so I didn't have to hear them or think about what they meant.

"They were right, you know," I said. "The Tribunal. We weren't spiritually ready, or healthy."

"Like the majority of people in America?"

"You can be mad if you want."

"Thanks so much."

"I guess that was patronizing."

"You think?" He got up and paced the room. "You're not even getting married anymore."

"All the more reason to take care of this now."

Ari came over and put his hands on my shoulders, gave me one of those ridiculous impish smiles. "One for the road, then?"

I could feel the heat of his body as he leaned in for a kiss. He'd put on a little weight, about fifteen pounds of pure muscle from substituting the gym for substances. Touching him I felt the new contours of his body and remembered the old ones at the same time.

I sidestepped him and said no. It was getting easier to say, if not always to stick with.

"Are you sleeping with Bruce?"

"No! Are you sleeping with Shar?" I asked, then added, "Not that I care."

"Yeah, on and off," he said. My stomach tightened. My body wanted what it wanted, even if it wasn't good for my heart, soul, or mind.

Ari kept going. "All that time and energy I put into drugs I can now devote to fucking. It's less expensive."

"And it burns calories."

I expected Ari to edge toward the door, but he just stared at me. I just started running my mouth again to fill the acoustic space. "The drinking's pretty good, or the nondrinking," I said. "Every now and then I go for it, like, a two-bottles-of-wine day. Then, nothing for weeks. It's like Morse code, but the dots are getting shorter and the dashes are getting longer, you know?"

I moved over to the couch. Ari came and sat next to me and turned sideways on the couch so his leg brushed mine. He didn't say anything. I kept on talking.

"I don't even like it. I just don't know what to do with myself sometimes."

Ari put one hand between my legs and another behind my head, and started kissing me on the neck, up the hairline, and across the ear.

"This isn't fair," I said.

"All's fair in love and war."

"Which is this?"

He had these soft lips and a five o'clock shadow that tickled when he brushed his face against mine. "Both, maybe." He didn't say the words as much as exhale them. And then he started to work his hand under my skirt.

"No. That is a no." I stood up. "Besides, you wouldn't have much fun with me these days. The sex was always better when I hated myself."

"It was pretty good wasn't it?" he said, smiling and looking me straight in the eyes, the light catching their color. Damn, I would miss him. I would miss this.

I stood. "Okay, get out of my house," I said, but in a harsh-but-friendly tone, the way New Yorkers say "Fuck you" when they mean hello.

Ari got up, slowly. "I'll see you in a couple hours." That band that we'd played with in London, KPS, was in town. They'd kicked us the opening slot on their local arena dates. I could use the money. Especially since my apartment was going condo. Especially since our albums still weren't selling that well in the States. And particularly since my ex-fiancé was still holding out on us financially. Mess. I deserved a consolation prize.

I could hear them in front of me, to the sides and to the back, talking, laughing. They weren't mean or anything. They just weren't paying attention to us. There were twenty thousand KPS fans in this arena, and they weren't paying attention to us, not even after three songs. It was a short set. We were ending with my song. Mine.

I started solo acoustic. My voice cracked on the first note.

> *When you burn your life to the ground*
> *All you need is a fire*
> *First you spit your heart out*
> *Then you build a pyre*
> > *and you burn*
> > *and you burn*
> > *and you burn*

There wasn't some crazy movie moment where everyone pulled out a lighter, but at least the crowd got quieter. I kept singing, looked back at the band. They nodded. I was going to play my instrument for the first time in public. I hoped this worked.

I picked up my guitar. Ari had switched to bass. Bruce was on drums, Shar on rhythm guitar.

I tried listen to myself instead of the buzz of the crowd.

> *You can try to leave behind the ones who hurt you*
> *You can hope they write you off as dead*
> *But the salt and sweet of human life are lies and courage*
> *And the ones*

That you left behind
Live on in your head

The band came in hard, just like we'd practiced. I stood up tall and straight. My voice was a mountain and I was the sky.

And the ones you loved who lied and hurt you
Will always get their sweet revenge
Until you learn that what you're burning
Is already dead
It's all in your head

I filled my lungs and got all anthemic.

Like your mama said
Or the rabbit said
Or your doctor said
Or your teacher said
Or the Bible said
Or the Buddha said
Or your daddy said
They're already dead
It's all in your head

As I sang, I saw a lighter in the crowd. Then more. Maybe they were the lights of cell phones. Whatever it was, I'd take it. I'd take it all.

We brought the energy back down, let Bruce and Shar riff a bit. Then I took a huge breath and started the chorus again.

When you burn your life to the ground
All you need is a fire
First you cut your heart out
Then you build a pyre

For a moment I looked out at the darkness filled with people and hoped they really heard me. You never knew, but all it took was one person to make this worth the work and the pain. I felt that now, truly.

I ended by slowing the pace and letting my voice go soft and low. We'd practiced this, and Ari, Shar, and Bruce followed my lead exactly.

> *You'd think the memories would be the first to go*
> *But you find they're indestructible*
> *What do you know?*

We trailed off into silence. End of set; lights rose slightly for the set change. The crowd clapped for us, a decent patter. I even heard a few yips and yowls.

Walked back to the band. Smiled. We walked off shoulder to shoulder. We were a *we*.

As for me, I didn't know how many times I'd have to start down the right path again.

But I would. I would.

Acknowledgments

To my friends, my family, and all those who have taught and loved me . . .

My editor, Malaika.

My agent, Richard.

Tanya Selvaratnam and all those who read early drafts.

And most of all, the amazing, wonderful, glowing, fabulous, loving, and extraordinary women of The Finish Party. Your sisterhood made this happen.

Kiss the Sky—The Playlist

(Songs written for the book are marked by an asterisk.)

I.

1. The Smiths, "Unlovable"
2. *Sky, "Confess"
3. Tony Touch, "P.R. All-Stars"
4. N.E.R.D., "Provider"
5. The Main Ingredient, "Everybody Plays the Fool"
6. Craig Mack, "Flava in Ya Ear"
7. Air, "Sexy Boy"
8. The Pretenders, "Back on the Chain Gang"
9. Nine Inch Nails, "Closer"
10. The Buggles, "Video Killed the Radio Star"
11. Handsome Boy Modeling School, "Rock 'n' Roll (Could Never Hip Hop Like This)"
12. The Rolling Stones, "Sympathy for the Devil"
13. Cyndi Lauper, "Money Changes Everything"
14. "The Negro National Anthem"
15. The Smiths, "Shoplifters of the World Unite"
16. Musafir, "Ninderli"
17. DJ Krush, "Candle Chant (A Tribute)"
18. Praga Khan, "Remove the Armour"
19. Miles Davis, "Black Satin"
20. Beenie Man, "Romie"
21. Tom Tom Club, "Genius of Love"

22. Talking Heads, "This Must Be the Place"
23. Bryan Adams, "Summer of '69"
24. The Cure, "Close to Me"
25. Jill Scott, "Slowly Surely"
26. Ben Folds Five, "The Battle of Who Could Care Less"
27. Emergency Broadcast Network, "378"
28. Sade, "By Your Side"
29. Elvis Costello, "Radio Radio"
30. Orbital, "The Box"
31. Big Pun, "Still Not a Player"
32. Rick James, "Give It to Me Baby"

II.

33. Dilated Peoples, "Trade Money"
34. Malonga, "Ngongui [Cowbell]"
35. Talvin Singh featuring Leone, "Distant God"
36. Stevie Wonder, "Isn't She Lovely"
37. Thievery Corporation featuring David Byrne [Louie Vega Remix],
    "The Heart Is a Lonely Hunter"
38. ABC, "How to Be a Millionaire"
39. Faith No More, "We Care a Lot"
40. Blur, "I'm Just a Killer for Your Love"
41. Sugarhill Gang, "Rapper's Delight"
42. The Isley Brothers, "Footsteps in the Dark"
43. Eubie Blake, "If You've Never Been Vamped by a Brownskin,
    You've Never Been Vamped at All"
44. Frank Sinatra, "Blue Skies"
45. Orbital, "Sad but True"
46. The Chemical Brothers, "Elektrobank"
47. Ella Fitzgerald, "How High the Moon"
48. Beck, "E-Pro"
49. Ella Fitzgerald, "Starlit Hour"
50. Mahalia Jackson, "You'll Never Walk Alone"

51. Stereolab, "Transona Five"
52. Ol' Dirty Bastard, "Baby I Like It Raw"
53. Carl Hancock Rux, "No Black Male Show"
54. The Black Crowes, "Wiser Time"
55. Prince and the Revolution, "The Beautiful Ones"
56. Sarah Vaughan, "Peter Gunn [Max Sedgley Remix]"
57. The Clash, "Should I Stay or Should I Go"
58. David Bowie, "Heroes"
59. The Clash, "Sean Flynn"
60. Benjamin Biolay, "Les roses et les promesses"
61. Jeff Buckley, "Eternal Life (Live)"
62. Glenn Gould, "Variation 1"
63. Roni Size/Reprazent, "Brown Paper Bag"
64. Cpt. Kirk &., "Puscher"

III.

65. Soundgarden, "Black Hole Sun"
66. Sarah McLachlan, "Possession"
67. Stevie Wonder, "Higher Ground"
68. Jamiroquai, "The Kids"
69. Chemical Brothers, "Song to the Siren"
70. Mahalia Jackson, "How I Got Over (Live)"
71. Dirty Vegas, "Days Go By"
72. Bob Marley and the Wailers, "Redemption Song"
73. 16 Horsepower, "Sac of Religion"
74. New Order, "True Faith"
75. The Average White Band, "I'm the One"
76. Ladysmith Black Mambazo, "Homeless"
77. Juliani, Johny-Boy, K-Swiss, & Agano, "Fanya Tena"
78. Everlast, "Black Jesus"
79. Miriam Makeba, "Pata Pata"
80. Luther Vandross, "Dance with My Father"
81. DJ Spooky, "It's Nice Not to Lose Your Mind"

82. Bob Dylan, "It's Alright, Ma (I'm Only Bleeding)"
83. Peter Gabriel, "Don't Give Up"
84. Cab Calloway, "Everybody Eats When They Come to My House"
85. Oliver Mtukudzi, "Mutserendende"
86. Marcy Playground, "Sex and Candy"
87. Duran Duran, "Come Undone"
88. U2, "I Still Haven't Found What I'm Looking For"
89. Nina Simone, "Rich Girl"
90. John Coltrane, "A Love Supreme"
91. *Sky, "Burn"